Viola Sends Her Regrets

Silversmith
PUBLISHING

Across Time & Space series

The Eternity Stone
Mountain of Glass
Desert of Fire
Desert of Ice
The Hidden Door
Whiter Than Snow

Fairytale Memoirs series
The Mostly Forgotten Memoirs of Rose Red
Viola Sends Her Regrets
Gifted

Standalone books
Breaking the Glass Slipper
Unshakeable
Tyger

For information on new and upcoming books,
go to **mmarinanbooks.com**

Viola Sends Her Regrets

A Fairytale Memoirs Novel

M. MARINAN

First published in New Zealand in 2018
by Silversmith Publishing

A catalogue record for this book is available from the National Library of New Zealand

ISBN 978-0-9951108-6-1

Inspired by Charles Perrault's 'The Glass Slipper'
and every other Cinderella story.

With thanks to Kate, Anne-Marie and Bryanna
for your support and feedback.

Key:
COUNTRY
(Novel)
NORDANTE
(Gifted)
Veestlun
ENORIA
(Gifted)
THE
WINTER
SEA
Hunting Lodge
The Aileron
DANVIA
(Rose Red)
BRESA
GENTRAVIA
DELMANY
(Viola Sends
Her Regrets)
Leewhey
OSTRAIME
THE
SUMMER
SEA
Fortrente
Novas
Strenley
The
Fairytale
Memoirs
Map
CRISTONIA
(Viola Sends Her Regrets;
The Hundred-Layer Quilt)
CRISTON
BRELFNE
(Bluebeard's
Last Wife)
LANCASTRE
SUDANTE
The Red Desert

Contents

1
An Invitation to the Ball

The village of Fortrente, Delmany,
1672 FTE (fairytale era)

"Viola!"

The voice called from a distance away, but I ignored it. Nellie would shout for me, and I'd come, and half the time she'd have forgotten what she wanted anyway.

"*VIOLA!* I've got news!"

She'd bothered to come right into the room I was working in, so it must have been more important than just a scratched finger or a handsome man smiling at her. I carefully stood from where I'd been scrubbing at the mouldy patch at the top of the back stairs, turning towards my stepsister. "What is it, Nellie?"

She was pink-cheeked and breathless with exertion, but somehow that just made her look even prettier. Genetics had been kind to her; making her petite, golden-haired and curvy, and 'as lovely as an angel', to quote an enthralled admirer. Today she wore a plain red and white day dress, but on her it may as well have been a ball gown. Speaking of which…

"There's to be a royal ball," she announced with glee, her bright blue eyes wide and guileless. "The prince is to choose a bride, and they say that any eligible girl can come. *Anyone!*"

Ah, so that's what the excitement was about. This wouldn't be the first time that my stepsister had become so enthusiastic over some marital prospect. None of them had panned out, mostly because she chose men out of her reach. But it was certainly the first time she'd aspired to marry a *prince*. "Define eligible."

"Well…between sixteen and twenty-five, never been married…"

So far, so good.

"Delmany-born…"

Of course that made Nellie eligible, since she'd been born in this kingdom. As for my family and I, we'd come from neighbouring Cristonia to the south, and that would shut us out even if I had considering trying. Ha. Only if the prince was blind, or else had a strong penchant for tall, skinny girls with bland colouring…

"And a landowner who can procure a gown suitable for a royal ball," Nellie finished in a rush.

And here it was. "Nellie, you're not a landowner," I said patiently. "You might technically own half of the Bluebell inn-"

"I do, even if your mother runs it!"

"…but it doesn't count as being a landowner. You own this building along with our brother, and you have a hundred-year lease from the landlord, and that's Squire Jonathon, remember? So even if you could somehow magically find a gown that would get you into the ball, you'd fail on that count." I finished gently, but she had already got that angry, mulish expression she so often wore.

"You just don't want me to be happy," she accused, and her expression changed into the one that had got her everything she wanted from her father (until he'd died, that was). She looked at me beseechingly. "Oh come on, Viola, can't you see that this is meant to be? I'm beautiful enough to be a princess, everyone says so! The prince just needs to set eyes on me…"

It sounded arrogant, and it was, but it was also true. Nellie AKA Petronella *was* beautiful. Very beautiful, in fact, and she'd been told it every day since she was an infant. Males did tend to fall at her feet, even though her looks were yet to produce her an acceptable marriage proposal. And by acceptable I meant rich – her standards, not mine.

Chances were that if the prince set eyes on her he *would* be infatuated…and it would probably last long enough for her to become his mistress. Prince Royce didn't have a good reputation, at least not here in Fortrente. He was cut from the same cloth as his father, who while not exactly wicked, was hardly a model of Christian charity. Funny to think that the king before him had been so horrible that when he'd been eaten by a dragon, everyone had celebrated at the change of leadership.

But all I said was, "Even if he did fall for you, I don't trust him to follow through with marrying a commoner, Nellie."

"I'm not a commoner! Mother's grandfather was a count."

A count who'd had his title taken away by the same king who'd been eaten by a dragon. "It doesn't matter. It's all hypothetical. You aren't a landowner, and we can't afford to buy you a gown that nice." Not at all. The inn that Nellie was so reluctant to do housework for scraped by, barely keeping us fed and clothed. We would need a good injection of cash to clean it up enough to get the wealthy customers coming through. Speaking of which...

"Nellie, have you considered the squire's offer? He'd keep you well; far better than you live now."

"I'm not marrying the squire," Nellie stated flatly. "He's old and ugly, and you need to stop trying to make me!" Her face crumpled, and tears sparkled in her eyes, somehow making her look even prettier. Completely unfair, because whenever *I* cried, I just got snotty. But I'd long ago accepted that with my stepsister, life wasn't fair.

But her tears didn't soften me. "I'm not trying to make you marry-"

"Yes you are!" she sobbed. "And if you won't help me to better myself, then I'll find someone who will!" Tears streaming down her face, she lifted her chin and stalked off back down the stairs.

I sighed, then crouched down again to scrub at the mould patch that seemed embedded in the old wood. See, it was dramas like that, acted out in public no less, that made me and my mother out to be villains. I'd never known anyone who could act as well as Nellie, but that was probably because she believed every word that spouted out of her mouth.

She'd been terribly spoiled by her father, my late stepfather. Even when she was older and he began to see that he should have been a bit stricter, all she had to do was pout and beg prettily... or perhaps turn on the tears. As for me, I'd tried it once and been told to stop whining.

Oh, well.

I thought again of how she'd called Squire Jonathon old and ugly, and felt offended on his behalf. He was a widower of around thirty (alright, twice our age, but hardly *ancient*) and while he wasn't precisely handsome, he was also one of the kindest people I knew.

Three years ago when my stepfather had died in the carriage accident that had ruined my mother's legs, and we hadn't been able to pay our rent, he had waived it for a full two months while we got ourselves back on track. While I didn't love him – at all – I'd have been perfectly happy to marry him if only he'd looked my way.

Unfortunately, standing next to Nellie any other girl looked like a hag, and me more so. I was tall and thin with strong facial features and pale colouring that took after *my* late father, and the comparison with my stepsister wasn't kind. When my mother had brought my younger sister and I here to Delmany to begin our new life, the then seven-year-old Nellie had taken one look at us and said, "I don't like my stepsisters, Papa, they're *ugly*."

That was the first time anyone had ever suggested that I was less than acceptable, and even though my new stepfather had hastily told her off and Nellie had never again said it (she had been only seven, after all) that sort of thing wasn't easily forgotten. While by now I had concluded that I wasn't actually ugly, but I wasn't pretty either, my younger sister Edwina still struggled with that nickname.

You see, while Nellie might not have meant it, she'd said it in public – loudly – and some of the neighbourhood children had picked it up. We still got called the 'ugly stepsisters' on occasion, and even though Edwina was no Nellie (but then who was?) she always seemed pretty to me. She was only fifteen now, but I could see how it still hurt her. King's crown, it still hurt me, even though I'd decided long ago that I wouldn't let it bother me. People could be such fools.

Half an hour later the mould patch looked less like a pit to hell and more like an old brown stain, and I called it done. Walking back into the inn's entry where my mother sat doing the bookkeeping, I said, "I've cleaned the stain as well as I can, although I still think that we won't get rid of it without either replacing the boards or getting a rug. Or perhaps some sort of potion might help."

"I'll put those on the genie list," my mother replied placidly, making a note on a separate piece of paper. It was a very long list, and 'genie' meant 'there's no way this will ever happen without a miracle or a very good marriage' because as far as we knew, genies had been long extinct and weren't going to be granting anyone wishes any time soon. "There are still the hens to be cleaned out tonight. I've put James onto that, and then when Edwina's done in the kitchen we can all work together on the spare beds."

And by 'all' she meant the rest of us, Edwina and I and our ten-year-old half-brother James, since she had trouble walking ever since the accident, and had to rule benevolently from this chair. "Where's Nellie? I sent her out to get flour, but that was two hours ago."

I shrugged. "She was all excited over some ball in the capital, and then got mad when I told her she wasn't eligible." I quickly explained the terms of the ball, and Mother reacted much the same way I had.

"Huh. I shall have to warn the Squire not to listen to any offers to borrow against the value of the inn," she said briskly.

"Do you think she'll try that again?" The last time had been a year earlier, and Nellie had wanted a new wardrobe to try to catch the eye of a passing nobleman. We'd had to do some fast talking to make sure that she didn't go off with the man, new wardrobe or not, because it had been obvious to everyone except her that his intentions hadn't been honourable.

"Probably not," Mother replied. "She's not stupid, no matter how she might act sometimes."

No, Nellie wasn't stupid, but she also hadn't developed what I would call common sense. She seemed to go through life thinking that no matter what happened, it would turn out well for her because she was special and beautiful. Generally it did, but I figured that she just hadn't made any truly terrible mistakes yet. One day she would, and then…

…then I could say 'I told you so' and go about cleaning up the mess, likely getting blamed for it along the way.

I sighed heavily at the thought. No matter how annoyed I got with Nellie at times (and trust me, I got annoyed) I still cared for her. She wasn't at all malicious, just careless and spoiled, and underneath all of it she had a kind heart that would show itself at the most unexpected times. So if I'm sounding like I really disliked her, or that we all did, it wasn't true.

We'd lived together for ten years as sisters, and it was the small difficulties of everyday life that wore on us as a whole. Nellie refusing to pull her weight, or acting like she was overworked every time she was asked to do a chore; well, that was just the straw that broke the camel's back. And if we were to be honest, it had become a running joke with the rest of us, a little light relief perhaps.

Just then the door to the kitchen swung open, and Edwina poked her head out. She was of medium height, soft-featured like Mother, and her light brown hair was pinned in neat curls in spite of the heat of the ovens. She'd responded to the 'ugly' taunts by dressing as well as she could on our limited budget, and in my opinion she'd done well, even if it seemed like a poor use of energy. "Dinner's done. Shall I serve up?"

"The sisters from Brelfne are at the table," Mother replied, referring to two of our newer guests: young women from the religious nation to our south-west, passing through on their way to visit family. "And John Tailor said that he'd be eating out tonight." He was a regular customer who stayed with us once a week as he travelled, our primary appeal being that we were cheap.

"I'll serve them then come help with the beds," Edwina said. "Then we can eat."

Later young James came in from cleaning the henhouse, smelling a little of the dirty straw that was used there. Nellie followed him in, smiling as if the earlier incident with me had been forgotten, and perhaps it had. Then I saw the reason why: one of the boys from the market had carried the flour all the way here, no doubt for the reward of a smile. He set it down where she pointed, then received the aforementioned smile. "Thank you, Clemence. That will be all."

"Um, it's Clarence," the boy corrected, but he didn't seem upset. "Do you need anything else?"

"That will be all for now," Nellie replied with another dazzling smile, and off Clarence went, seemingly unaware that he'd been used as a servant to do a job that she could have done herself. Then to us she burst out, "Did you hear about the ball? Not you, Viola, I mean the others."

After Nellie went into detail Edwina seemed interested, although disappointed she was too young *and* not the right nationality, but James was the one who spoke the truth. He was only ten, with the white-blond hair I'd had as a child and dark eyes from his and Nellie's father, and a big mouth. Metaphorically, not literally. "But we've got no money, Nellie. How would you get to the ball?"

"If we could spare just a few silvers, I know someone who'll sell me discounted fabric-"

"We can't even spare a few bronzes," Mother cut in firmly, although her tone was kind. "We barely get by, and we certainly can't have such expense on something that will ultimately be a waste of time."

Nellie's face crumpled. "It's my inn, and my money. You can't keep me from it!"

The rest of us looked away, and Mother said what she'd said many times before. "Your father's will left me as your guardian and in control of this inn, and what little money there might be. Besides, only half of it is yours. The other half will be James's once he's old enough, and it still needs to take care of the rest of us, too. This isn't just about you, and you know that."

Nellie did know that, but she was still tight-lipped, her eyes wet. "I wish that I could get away from here, from this place, and from all of *you*. I'm better than this! Some way, somehow, I'm going to prove it."

Ouch. Mother turned away, and just then I saw out of the high window a shooting star streak across the sky, and the words came unbidden. "I wish you the best of luck," I told her angrily. "I wish that you would go away and leave us alone, even marry the prince, just stop being such a *burden*."

"A burden?" Nellie hissed, and now she did cry, then turned and ran for her attic room. We *all* had attic rooms – the better ones were for the guests – but no, poor little Petronella was the only one to suffer, just like always.

"Viola," Edwina scolded lightly. "That wasn't very nice."

I turned away, frowning. "I just agreed with what she said. And she *is* a burden. She wants everything done for her, thinks she's so much better than us – she just said it! And in case you haven't noticed, she's turned the whole town against us. Everyone thinks that we use her like a workhorse because we're *jealous* of her."

"Oh, that can't be true," Mother said slowly, but James piped up.

"Last time I was out, Nathan the butcher's son said that he felt sorry for me, because my mother and sisters were so mean to poor Nellie, and because I had ugly white hair like my ugly family." He frowned. "Do you really think it's ugly?"

"Of course it's not ugly," Mother assured him. "It's just unusual for here in Delmany, and it will darken in time. Mine did, and so did Viola's."

Mine had darkened from Cristonian 'white' hair to a very boring light brown, but I was still 'ugly', apparently. Feeling anger spike through me, I stomped over to the sink and began to wash the pile of dishes that was there as always. It was Nellie's job, but somehow I doubted that we'd see her again tonight. Besides, the effort involved getting her to do her chores usually outweighed what it would have taken to simply do it ourselves. "I really wish she would go," I muttered. "It would make our lives so much easier. Maybe we could finally make something of this inn."

"Or sell it and move back to Cristonia," Edwina suggested quietly, and we all turned to stare at her. Wide-eyed, she continued, "The living's cheaper there, and besides, there's all your family, Mother. Even if we got just enough to move and start over, I think we could do well."

It wasn't the first time it had been brought up, and just like last time Mother brushed it off. "This is our home now," she said firmly. "Besides, I couldn't go back...like this."

Meaning that she'd left all hopeful and bright-eyed with the two of us, heading off to make something of herself with her new Delman husband, but she would come back with an extra child, poorer and widowed for a second time, and unable to walk properly. Something of a blow to her pride, I imagined, but she had a point. For all of this place's flaws it was home now, and I barely spoke Cristonian anymore. Edwina was the only one who really wanted to go.

The next day I went into the market with James to get groceries, Nellie having refused to leave her room. He got distracted by some friends playing nearby, so I let him. These trips out could be a break for both of us, even though I knew that any work I avoided by being here would be waiting for me when I got back.

The market centre of Fortrente was larger than you'd expect for such a small town, but it was also one of the key routes towards the mountains, and was right across the river from Delmany's capital, Ostraime. There were dozens of stalls set up in the cobblestoned area, each specialising in their particular produce: meat, fish from the nearby river, leather or metalwork, fabrics or fruit.

As always, I headed straight for the pumpkin stall. The stallholder's name was Nancy, and she was one of the few here who I felt never judged me for what Nellie had said about us. She was an older woman with a leathery face and a slight orange tinge to her skin (too much of her own produce would do that) and she had the most open manner I'd ever known. She didn't smile much, and it had taken me a little while to realise that her deeds showed her kindness rather than her tone or expression.

"Miss Viola," she called gruffly as I approached. "You haven't been here in a good week. What have you been doing with yourself?"

"Lazing about while poor Nellie does all the work," a nearby man grumbled, and Nancy turned on him.

"Does that lass there look like she's done a day of lazing in her life? Bogger off, Derrick you old fool, and take your silly words with you."

Derrick did indeed leave, and Nancy turned back to me. "Sorry about that, love. If that man had an ounce of sense he'd see the truth. Any of them would. How would someone like you, all skin and bones, ever be lazin' about?"

Ouch. She didn't even realise she'd insulted me, but I kept my face straight. After all, it was true. My limbs were long and thin, I was as tall as most men, and the angles of my face were sharp. Perhaps if I had richer food and the chance to 'laze about' I might look different, but I didn't waste time thinking about it. "I just need a couple of the big orange pumpkins, and that grey one that's shaped like a pear," I told her. "And any news, if you've got it."

Yet another reason to visit Nancy first. Her ears were always open, and she knew all the good gossip that was brought into the town by those travelling through, even before we did at the inn. Many of those who stayed with us weren't inclined to talk.

But Nancy was still annoyed by what Derrick had said, even though it was an incorrect opinion that I'd heard many times. "Aye, but if those fools could only see that you and yer sister are doin' all the work while Nellie takes any damned chance to swan off to the capital whenever she can-"

"Anything I *don't* know?" I cut in. It wasn't quite fair what she was saying about Nellie, since as far as I knew she'd only been to visit the capital once, three months earlier with some neighbours who thought of her kindly. I wasn't angry anymore over last night's exchange with my stepsister, but I certainly didn't want to talk about it. "Nellie says there's to be a royal ball, but I don't care about that. Is there anything else?"

Nancy shrugged. "That's all the big news. There have never been so many people invited before. It was basically an open invitation! Why, even you could go lass, if you had the dress."

"In case you've forgotten, I'm not Delmany-born, nor a landowner," I retorted dryly, barely holding back from rolling my eyes. "Besides, what would I do at a ball?"

Nancy laughed. "Same as any of us, love. Eat as much fine food as we could fit in our bellies, and stare at all the toffs in their fancy dresses."

I laughed too, and a quiet voice piped up from beside me. "But it's a royal ball. Wouldn't you like to go to a royal ball?"

It was an unfamiliar woman who'd spoken: grey-haired and round-faced and round-bodied and reminding me a little of a cheerful gingerbread woman. She was accompanied by a quiet, handsome young man who surely had to be her son, and she was looking at me expectantly.

I couldn't help smiling. "Doesn't everybody? But when midnight strikes, you still have to come home."

"Midnight, eh?" Nancy commented. "Is that when it ends?"

"I've no idea," I admitted. "I was just winging it." But the round woman had vanished along with the young man, and I turned curiously, looking for her. "Did you see her leave?"

Nancy didn't look up from where she was sorting through the pumpkins, choosing the largest. "Who?"

"The woman who I was just talking to. She just disappeared."

"Didn't see anyone but the air," Nancy countered. "And that'll be one bronze, thanking you."

I handed over the coin, bemused as to what had happened, and that was when the soldiers arrived. Four of them all dressed in the grey of the royal guard, walking into the market centre – clearly none of them high enough ranked to rate a horse. Otherwise it was a three hour walk from Ostraime, and judging by the sweat on their faces, they'd done it. The hum of noise reduced as everyone watched them curiously while pretending not to be watching, and the first of the soldiers walked over to the wooden wall that served as our notice board, lifting up a piece of parchment and hammering it in place.

News was always interesting, so as people moved over to see what it was, he raised a hand. "Attention! There has been a theft from the temple of the Dragi in Ostraime, a series of small gold figurines in the shape of elephants. If anyone knows anything about this and can give information leading to recovery of the items, there will be a reward."

"Odd that it should be elephants," Nancy murmured. "Aren't the Dragi snake worshippers or somewhat?"

"Dragons, I heard."

"Either way it's a nasty mess I wouldn't touch with a ten-foot pole. Can't trust those kinds of people as far as you can throw them."

She probably had a point since the Dragi had a reputation for being rich, powerful and mysterious, and therefore untrustworthy, but I was thinking about something else – the reward. If the figurines were worth more than the reward, why give them back? Mercenary, and I'd never follow through, but I wasn't the only one to realise that.

"How much is the reward?" someone called from the crowd.

The guard paused, and I realised that he was younger than

I'd first thought, perhaps not more than nineteen or so. He was also quite handsome: dark-haired with a long, interesting face and a strong chin. "I don't know," he admitted finally. "But if it's coming from the Dragi, they'll be generous." A hum arose in the crowd, and he had to shout the rest: "I should also say that the stolen items are cursed! Whatever the reward is, it'll be better than whatever curse keeping them would bring!"

Now *that* brought conversation, and I shook my head, amused. Not only were the Dragi a rich, secretive cult that I truly wouldn't touch with a ten-foot pole, but anyone's chances of finding the figurines were as good as Nellie's for going to that royal ball. It wouldn't happen, and I said as much to Nancy.

"Even if the thieves have come through here, and I doubt it, then why would they stay long enough for curious townsfolk to go through their things?" I said reasonably. "They'll be long gone. Or at least I would, if I was a thief."

Nancy's eyes widened a little, and I turned to see the young guard who'd pinned up the notice standing there right next to me, his dark eyes narrowed. "And you know the thinking patterns of thieves, do you Miss?"

Flustered, I raised my chin. "Well, no, but it just seems a reasonable thing to do. If you were to steal a valuable item, why stick around to be found?" The guard's eyebrows raised, but he didn't look surprised, and I realised he'd been teasing me. "Oh. Well, good luck with finding them."

"Thank you," he replied wryly. "But you can do more than wish us luck. Where is the nearest inn?"

"You've come to the right place," Nancy said bluntly. "Viola's family runs the Bluebell. It's the only inn here in Fortrente, but then people seldom stay here when they can stay in the capital."

And that was our inn in a nutshell. I raised an eyebrow back at the guard, shrugging. "Well, do you want me to take you there?"

"If you don't mind," he said politely.

Of course I didn't mind, but even if I had, I still would have offered. After all, he was a royal guard, and I didn't want to get on the wrong side of people who could arrest me on a whim. I'd never personally been mistreated by any guards, but I had heard stories.

I led the young guard along with a slightly older, fair-haired guard to the inn, carrying the pumpkins with me. As I was planning to come straight back I left James in the market, and the young guard gained some favour with me by offering to carry one of the largest pumpkins. I let him; they *were* quite heavy.

"The Bluebell," he mused as we approached the inn's familiar, blue-trimmed front. "It sounds familiar. Do you advertise in Ostraime?"

I laughed, I couldn't help myself. "We don't advertise anywhere except by word of mouth in the marketplace. Besides, the place needs a good spruce up before we start telling all the toffs about it."

"Toffs?" the fair-haired guard asked.

I glanced at him sidelong over my armful of pumpkin, noticing that he had a gleam in his eye I didn't appreciate. Guarding my tongue, I explained, "It's a casual word for nobles and wealthy travellers. Perhaps you don't use it in the capital?"

"Of course it's used," the young guard cut in. "It's just not very polite, and it wouldn't pay for us to be using it in regard to our betters."

His betters, meaning those who paid him. I secretly agreed with the fair-haired guard's scoff of derision, but I didn't say anything in reply as I led the two of them in through the front door amid interested stares from our neighbours. Inside Mother sat behind her table to the direct right of the doorway, and she looked up in surprise. "Is everything alright, Viola?"

"There's been a serious theft in the capital," the young guard explained before I could say anything. "We've been sent to visit all the possible places the thieves could have gone, including all the inns within two days' journey. Hence our arrival here."

He was perfectly polite, and I saw Mother's manner warm slightly. She always appreciated good manners in a man before wealth or position. "Forgive me if I don't get up, my legs aren't what they used to be, but I'll be happy to answer any of your questions. I am Madame Hazel, and my family owns this inn."

The guard nodded briefly. "Captain Franco of the Royal Guard. Can you tell me if anyone new has been through here in the last couple of days? Anyone at all."

"Well, there's only been John Tailor, but he comes through

every week," Mother replied thoughtfully, "and he left this morning as usual on his route into Ostraime. He comes from the mountains to the east."

A captain, was he? He looked very young for his rank. But he dismissed John as an option. "Anybody else?"

Mother looked hesitant. "The only others who've been through last night also left this morning, but I truly doubt they're what you're looking for."

"We must address every option," the captain said politely. "Who were they?"

"Well, just two young women from Brelfne on their way to visit family a few towns over," she replied. "Sisters, and very religious, just like most are from that area, and they wore headscarves the whole time, even at the table. Quiet, well-behaved, paid without any trouble."

As I'd expected, the guards dismissed those as well. "If there's anything else, let us know," the captain said, but it was clear that we wouldn't be hearing from them again. After all, why would they have reason to come through here? For some reason, I found myself a little disappointed.

Just then Nellie came into the room, dragging a small bucket of water as if it weighed a ton, and with a mop tucked under her arm. She looked like some voluptuous, ill-treated saint with her lovely face and her expression that cried 'It's hard work, but somebody must do it', and both men's eyes shot straight to her.

"Ella?" the captain burst out in surprise.

Nellie looked up, and her eyes widened, a bright smile dawning on her face. "Franco, is that you? What are you doing here?"

The captain flushed with pleasure, suddenly looking very much his age. "Official business – nothing to do with any of you, it seems, but I'm very glad that it's brought me here. Is this the inn you told me about?"

It was a silly question, because what other inn would there be? But as if there was no one else in the room, Nellie beamed at him. It was the same sweet, brilliant smile she used for every person who didn't know her well, but I could see by his dazed expression that he was infatuated.

Typical.

"Yes, it is," she replied sweetly. "The Bluebell was built by my father's father, but now my stepmother runs it." As usual she didn't say anything I could point out as wrong, but there was something in her tone that made the guards look at us narrow-eyed.

"This is your family, then?"

"Stepmother, and stepsister," Mother interrupted crisply. "*Nellie,* I didn't realise you were acquainted with any royal guards."

"Oh, Franco and I met a few months ago when I visited Ostraime with the Smiths, do you recall?" She smiled once more at the captain.

"Ah, yes," he agreed. "But I thought your name was Ella?"

She looked down sadly, her voice lowering. "It's Petronella, but my family calls me Nellie. Please do call me Ella, though, as I prefer it."

That was news to me. Of course that made it sound like we had purposely called her by the name she disliked, and Captain Franco gave us dirty looks. Behind him, the fair-haired guard looked amused.

The captain indicated towards the bucket of water. "Perhaps after you've finished your work, you might come out for a walk? It's a lovely day."

"Oh, I couldn't," Nellie replied softly with a sad little smile. "I'll be working all day, no doubt, and you must finish your duties. You said there was a theft, is that right?"

I realised then that if they'd met that one time she'd gone into Ostraime with a neighbouring family, then who knew what she could have told him? Captain Franco looked even more displeased at this reminder of 'Ella's' work situation, but he nodded. "Five small gold figurines were stolen from the Dragi temple in the capital. They're valuable in themselves, but they're also cursed. Whoever stole them is going to be sorry."

Nellie looked suitably appalled, and the captain added, "Perhaps tomorrow? We shall be staying in the woods tonight as an antidote to the bandit problem, and if you were free then...?"

He was so, so keen it hurt to see, and the rest of us were just awkward bystanders. Nellie of course wouldn't be interested, not in some poor soldier, but she'd string him on for weeks if he wasn't careful.

But Mother put an end to it. "She won't be free," she said firmly though respectfully. "My stepdaughter does not go for walks with men, especially ones I do not know. You understand my position on this, of course."

The captain still looked unhappy, but he nodded, taking a step towards the door. But he couldn't resist one last glance towards Nellie. "Good day, Miss Ella. I hope to see you again soon."

She gave him a brilliant smile once more, then turned back to her mop as if it was a long lost lover. The last expression on Captain Franco's face was a definite one of displeasure, and the unnamed fair-haired guard was smirking. I couldn't help agreeing with that second emotion.

The moment they were gone I turned to Nellie. "Since when do you prefer to be called Ella?"

She shrugged carelessly, plunking the mop into the soapy water so that it splashed out on the stone floor. "I went through a phase. But don't you think it's prettier than Nellie?"

"Your father called you Nellie," Mother cut in, looking weary. "What's wrong with that name?"

Nellie shrugged again, beginning to swirl the mop around in a way that left puddles of water and wouldn't make the floor any cleaner.

"He was infatuated, poor boy," I couldn't help saying. "How much did you talk to him when you first met him?"

"Oh, it was just a brief meeting," she replied, eyes fixed on the stone floor. Clearly our argument of the previous night was forgotten. "He's nice though, isn't he? Useful."

My eyes narrowed. "Useful how?"

"Well, he's a captain, which of course is never a bad thing, and they say that he got his promotion so young because he saved the king's life once." Her lips curled at one side, a genuine smile for once. "But I know the real reason. He's one of King Barrick's bastards, and the old man can't stand to see his offspring as a mere guardsman."

"Good grief," Mother burst out. "Language, Nellie!" Then a moment later, "How do you know that's true?"

Yet another careless shrug. "The Smiths told me. It's common knowledge, or at least commonly suspected. He looks an awful lot like the king did when he was young, you see, and his mother was apparently a chambermaid in the palace twenty years ago."

Interesting, yes, but it was also gossip. "Good for him," I said bluntly. "But did you have to make us seem like we were working you to death, Nellie?"

"What are you talking about? I just told them I had to work."

"Like we all do," I countered, then sighed. There was no point. We'd been over and over this many times, and she could never seem to understand (or chose not to understand) that it was her tone and body language that caused the trouble, not her words. "Never mind. I'm going upstairs to clean."

I headed up to the rooms that the sisters from Brelfne had recently vacated, changing the sheets and checking for bedbugs and lice left behind by the guests – not very nice, but unfortunately not unusual. I spotted a couple, so I quickly moved over to the nearby hall closet, looking for the bottle of Essence of Terebinthia we kept there for such cases.

The small wooden crate sat at the bottom of the closet, accompanied by countless other boxes of useful bits and pieces, the mops and brooms, and an unfamiliar cloth bag. It was dark blue fabric, about the size of a pillow case, and stuffed off to the side of the box so that I almost didn't notice it. When I picked it up it was very heavy.

"Odd," I murmured. "Who would have left this here?"

Inside was an assortment of items. The first thing I pulled out was a small, leather-bound book of the kind Mother used to keep track of our income; its cover a simple, time-worn dark brown. I flicked through its pages, looking for a name that might hint at its owner, but there wasn't one. It appeared to be a diary.

Besides the book, the bag contained a series of small shapes. I pulled out the first one to see that it was a plain dark green figurine, in the shape of a stylized, fat elephant and about the size of my closed fist. It was very heavy, but I still didn't realise what it was.

Footsteps clomped up the stairs behind me, and a moment later Edwina appeared, carrying the still full bucket of water. Nellie followed behind her with the mop, most likely having claimed that she couldn't manage to carry the bucket alone.

Couldn't be bothered, more like. They both looked curious. "What's that, Viola?" my sister asked.

I studied the thing, turning it over in my hands. "I don't know. After what the guards said…well, this can't be it, right? It's *green*."

"Let's see," Edwina asked in interest, leaning over to pick up the bag. She tipped the rest of the contents out on the floor, eyes widening as she saw that they were all the same. "Oh…do you think…?"

"The missing figurines are gold, Edwina," Nellie said with an eye roll. "Like Viola said-" She reached out to pick up one of the figurines herself, knocking my elbow as she did so. I dropped the thing on the hard floor and it landed with a crunch.

"Ah!" It wasn't damaged, not really; but there was a wide scratch the size of my nail, revealing a bright, white-gold metallic surface.

The sisters from Brelfne had always worn headscarves, even at the table, and I'd assumed it was because they were devout. But there was another reason that you might cover your head, and partially cover your face.

If you had something to hide.

It looked like the sisters from Brelfne weren't so innocent after all.

2

A Fitting Reward

"**I**t *is* the stolen treasure!" Edwina exclaimed, and I scratched at the coating of what seemed to be paint. Underneath wasn't the bright yellow gold I would have expected, but it certainly seemed to cover the whole object. "Shall we call the guards?"

"No," Nellie said abruptly, and we both turned to look at her in surprise. She was staring at the figurine wide-eyed and pale-faced, and her voice came out very serious and quiet. "Don't tell them, or we'll never see that reward. We'll have to take them ourselves."

I felt a chill up my spine as I looked back at the supposedly cursed gold figurine, then back at Nellie. All our previous arguments seemed to be forgotten – we could get a *reward*, and money meant change in our lives, finally.

"But it's a three hour walk to the capital," Edwina whispered, taking in the gravity of the situation. "That's each way, and through the forest too! How are we supposed to go without Mother or the guards noticing?"

"It's only midday," Nellie countered. "We could be back just after dark – or one of us, anyway. I know I can walk fast," and she spoke over any arguments we might have had, "and it isn't just for me, you know. We get that reward and I can go to the ball, finally get noticed by a decent man, and the rest of the money can go to the inn, to make it what you lot are always talking about. A good living for you, and a good inheritance for James."

Except for the bit about her taking the figurines, she'd had my attention until she mentioned James. I swore. "Would you believe I've left James in the market?"

"He won't even notice," Edwina soothed. "I expect he'll be playing." Then her eyes brightened. "But if you said you had to get him, then that would be a good excuse to leave the house, wouldn't it?"

"Wait, I thought I was going," Nellie interrupted. "Everybody likes me-"

"Everybody notices you," I countered. "Do you think you could walk through that forest alone without being accosted? Me, on the other hand…"

"I don't know," Edwina said doubtfully. "You're still a girl, Viola, even if you're tall. Maybe two of us should go."

I shook my head, shoving the figurine back into the cloth bag and standing up. "Whatever we do, I want to talk to Mother about it." Nellie would have argued, but I wouldn't relent. "She wants us to succeed as much as anyone, and I won't lie to her."

"Viola will go," Mother said firmly, ignoring Nellie's protests. "She's street-smarter, and she'll be safer, too. And no, not for the reason you think." She looked at me narrow-eyed. "Trousers, do you think?"

That cryptic comment meant that I ended up heading into the market with Edwina fifteen minutes later, all five figurines stuck very uncomfortably in my bodice against my skin with a loose shirt over top to hide them, as well as a pair of my late stepfather's trousers underneath my skirts. Except for being a little large around the waist, they fit just right. I carried the basket I usually used at market, and inside was my cloak and a boy's cap, as well as some sweet biscuits for the journey.

The plan was to pick up James and have him and Edwina accompany me through the back of the forest rather than the main road, just for the half hour it took to reach the bridge across the Silver River. Then I would change into the men's clothing, leaving my skirts in the basket in some to-be-decided place, and quickly move through the forest to reach Ostraime and the Dragi temple long before curfew. I would be back late at night, but if I succeeded, it would be worth the risk.

As we went back through the market to get James I saw the

captain speaking with the other three guards, and as he saw me pass he gave me a narrow glare. Clearly no matter what Nellie had said, what he'd *heard* was a different story. Jealous, mean stepfamily forces lovely young maiden to work like a servant…

I'd heard it before, and even though it was untrue, seeing that same condemning look from this person hurt. Foolish me, being attracted in spite of really knowing better. I should focus on the important things in life, the things that I could actually achieve – like making the inn a success. Maybe.

Everything went to plan up 'til we reached the bridge. I moved into a stand of trees, changing into my disguise and pulling up the corset so that it flattened my chest. Even though I was thin, I wouldn't want such small things to ruin our plan. I sat the cloth cap over my hair, tucking in as much of the distinctive pale strands as I could, then pulled the hood of the cape over as well.

"Don't do that," James objected, his nose screwed up in distaste. "You look like a villain for certain."

So the hood came down, but the cap stayed on. I took a deep breath. "I'll be back likely after dark, and if you don't see me, don't worry. I'll find a spot to sleep if I think I'll be back too late to be safe, alright?"

The other two nodded solemnly, then Edwina handed me something small and sharp: a paring knife. "Just in case."

Just in case I came across a situation that could only be resolved with violence. Praying that I would never have to use the knife, I slipped it into the pocket of my cape, then headed towards the bridge. It was just wide enough for a carriage and spanned the wide but shallow Silver River, its still water reflecting the often clouded sky. It had fairly regular traffic, and luckily there hadn't yet been a toll in place as we'd heard threats there would be. There was nobody about: just me walking alone towards the road on the other side where it disappeared into the thick forest.

I'd made it halfway across when a voice called out. "Halt!"

So much for thinking I was alone. Slowly I turned to see the young captain from earlier walking towards me, one of his colleagues left behind at the other side. He looked grim. "What is your reason for going this way?"

Now I could have done one of many things at that point. I could have made up a lie for why I was there and hoped he didn't recognise me, or I could have turned around and tried to go back, but I didn't. I panicked, and as he reached me I pushed him hard in the chest, watching his surprised face as he tumbled backwards over the bridge's stone wall towards the water not far below.

Perhaps a bad choice, but it was done. I ran for it, ignoring the shout from the guard on the other side of the bridge, and fervently grateful for both my long legs and the length of the bridge; and once I made it to the forest I ran right for the thickest part of it. All I could think of was to get away, to hide: to make sure they never found out who I was, and cursing myself as a fool a thousand times over.

The good news was that they didn't follow me. Probably they were just trying to pull the captain out of the water, his armour making him less than suited to swim, and certainly not to run. At least none of them had arrows, hmm?

At that thought I felt even stupider at what I'd done – attacking a royal guard! Did I *want* to die? – but I couldn't see what else I could have done in that situation. We'd only just spoken and he surely would have recognised me as Nellie's stepsister from the inn, and then seeing me leaving the town immediately afterwards in disguise would have been even worse.

Oh, and the bad news: I got lost. Not terribly, and not permanently, but I was walking through those woods for a good four or five hours before I made it through to the farmland on the other side, the city walls in the near distance. By this time it was late afternoon, and I revised my goal to just reaching the Dragi temple and getting the reward. Ostraime was a big city, ten times the size of Fortrente, and that would be a worthy goal in itself. Oh, and making it out before curfew at dusk...

Although we lived so close to the capital, I hadn't been here inside the walls in several years, since before my stepfather died. Last time had been a pleasure jaunt as much as anything else, but I still remembered the sense of noise and confusion, the busy streets and unfamiliar buildings, and the guards everywhere in their royal grey including at the entry gate. The last made me nervous, and I had to steel myself to walk normally between those high stone walls and try not to look suspicious.

Last time I'd been here the Dragi had had their meeting place, but it was only recently they'd begun to call it a temple. That didn't sit too well with most of the populace in Fortrente. We would listen to stories of the Dragi cult with fascination and perhaps a little judgement, our kingdom having been at least nominally Christian ever since the dark ages, but King Barrick allowed them to remain in the city. He'd even allowed his guard to pursue their missing treasures. Besides, they were rich and mysterious, and that was enough to keep them up and running.

As if the thought had prompted it, I felt a tingling in my corset where the figurines sat. I didn't believe they were cursed. I thought that was just an excuse the captain had given for why people shouldn't keep them. Nonetheless they had significance to the Dragi, and the sooner I could get rid of them the better.

Realising that I wouldn't find the temple without help, I stopped a nearby woman who was pushing a barrow full of grain. "Excuse me, could you direct me towards the Dragi temple?"

Her eyebrows shot up. "What would you be wanting with that place?"

"I need to talk to someone," I hedged. "Do you know where it is?"

"Talk to someone, eh?" She looked unimpressed, and I realised that if the news of the theft had gone as far as Fortrente, it would certainly be known here too. But still she lifted her arm, pointing across the busy street. "Right there. That green gateway."

There wasn't a sign, but there was a high stone wall, high enough that I couldn't see over it, and just past that I could make out the neat slate roof of what was probably a large building. The gate she'd referred to was indeed green. It was high and ornate, likely iron, and painted in a similar colour to the figurines I held.

I thanked her, heading over to see that not only was the gate locked, but it was unguarded. Through the iron framework I could see a series of wide, flat stairs leading up to a beautifully carved door, but not a person in sight. I frowned. How was I going to get their attention?

But I didn't have to worry, because just then a guard in a

shiny steel helmet approached from the other side of the gate, a long spear held casually in one hand. He was also wearing green. "State your business."

A little intimidated by his cold manner and large size, I began shyly, "I need to talk to someone in charge. I have…I have information about the theft."

He stared at me, leaning forward with flared nostrils almost as if he was smelling me. I couldn't help stepping back in dismay, but then he turned and disappeared inside a side door. A moment later he reappeared with a woman. She was smooth-skinned and attractive, with silver-streaked straight black hair and dark eyes, and her air of authority was as obvious as the cost of the lovely green and gold dress she wore. It was made of gorgeous lace over shining silk, its beauty belied by its modesty – the long sleeves covered her wrists and the neckline came right up to her chin. "Let her in."

Her? It seemed my disguise wasn't good for much, and as if seeing my surprise, the woman smiled thinly. "Trousers don't make the man. Now come in, or stay out. It's your decision."

Impatient, much? I'd only been standing there five seconds before she'd scolded me, but I stepped through the gate, following her up the stairs towards the double doors. But as I drew closer I found myself more and more reluctant to go inside the building. This whole place disturbed me even though I couldn't say why. It was like the chills you got in a graveyard, or perhaps the opposite of the peace that was felt in many churches or on a beautiful spring day.

"I'll talk to you outside, please," I said abruptly, stopping before I went through. "It won't take long."

The woman looked at me narrow-eyed, but nodded. "Very well. I am Theodora, priestess of the Dragi, and I charge you now to tell me the truth of who you are and why you are here."

I was so startled by her words that I found myself blabbing out the whole story, right there outside the doors of the temple. "I'm Viola of Bluebell Inn in Fortrente, and my family and I found five gold figurines which we thought must be the missing treasure, but I brought them here to the temple rather than giving them to the guards because I wanted to make sure we got the reward."

Too honest, maybe? I put a hand over my mouth in dismay, and she raised an eyebrow. "Indeed. Give them to me."

A little embarrassed, I turned my back to the street and stuck my hand under my corset, pulling out the figurines one by one and passing them to her. The scratched one had lost even more of its paint while pressed against my skin, and its white-gold gleam was obvious.

The priestess's eyes widened very slightly as she saw them, and she took them in satisfaction with a gloved hand, passing them to an acolyte who had approached quietly enough I'd not noticed him there. After all five had been produced he disappeared, and she turned to stare at me, slipping her hands together in front of her. "So, Viola of Bluebell Inn. You wish for a reward, do you?"

My mouth suddenly dry, I nodded. This wasn't just for me, it was for my whole family – something that might change our lives forever, and I needed to be bold. "Yes, please. The guard said there would be one."

She stared at me for long enough to make me uncomfortable and for my eyes to slide away from hers, then she clapped. Just once, and abruptly enough to make me jump. "A reward. Yes, a fitting reward. Viola of Bluebell Inn, may you and your family receive everything you deserve."

A cool breeze tickled the back of my neck, and I couldn't help taking a step backwards even as she turned away. "Was that...was that it?"

Theodora paused halfway through the door, and her gaze on me was cold. "Were you expecting more? A blessing from the Dragi is a blessing indeed. You should not scoff at it." As I began to say that I wasn't scoffing, had just been expecting a little more *materially*, she cut in. "Take what you have been given, before worse comes to you."

She turned her back on me and walked through the door, closing it after her, and the big guard who'd let me in opened the gate, holding it for me to leave.

For a moment I just stared at it numbly, processing what had happened. They'd just taken the treasure from me. There was no reward, only a threat of worse treatment if I didn't accept it. And what could I do? I was just a girl not even well-disguised as a boy, foreign-born at that, and without beauty or even charm to turn anyone to my cause. Oh, and let's not forget I'd assaulted a captain of the royal guard earlier today, so I couldn't ask for *their* help.

For a few seconds I just stood there, then I forced myself to move towards the gate. I stepped through, and it clanged shut behind me, the sound so very final. No more chances, no more hope. I could see the merchants and barrow-sellers beginning to close up their stalls and go home. The sun was very low, and no doubt curfew would be very soon. I had no money and no connections here. The last thing I needed was to be stuck inside these walls illegally – I'd probably end up in prison under the vagrancy laws.

Numbly I stumbled back towards the city gates, my body remembering where to find the exit better than my mind. The guards were beginning to close it, two of them on each heavy wooden door, and seeing that I began to run, calling out in a panic. "Please, let me through! I need to get back home!"

At least one thing went right for me today, and the guard held back one side, letting me through and then shutting it after me. I heard the thud of the heavy block coming down to hold the doors shut, and then after that the clang of the iron portcullis. A double layer of protection for the city, but it just reminded me of what had happened at the temple.

It felt like I'd been robbed.

But the worst thing was, I couldn't even claim I'd been ripped off because I'd been dishonest in the first place. We all had, my family and I, because instead of handing the figurines to the guards as we'd said we would, we'd tried to get around them and get a reward for ourselves. What we would have instead was disappointment, and for me, a very long walk home in the dark. Nothing would ever change at the inn, not 'til that far off day when Nellie finally found a rich man who'd marry her.

The sky darkened as the sun dipped behind the mountains, and by the time I reached the edge of the forest it was fully dark. The moon was out, thankfully, and that cast a faint silvery glow over everything – just enough to create big black shadows under every tree, and for every movement to make me shiver. I walked quickly and quietly, praying for my safety and that any bandits in the woods might be taking time off. After all, who travelled at night except a complete idiot? And idiots didn't tend to be worth robbing, or so I would think.

After a while – fifteen minutes? An hour? – I heard a faint sound in the distance, one that made me stiffen in fear. See, bandits weren't the only danger here, no matter how much the royal guard claimed they were cleaning them out. There were also wolves. Just a few, and none had been seen recently, but you could still hear them occasionally. Oh, yes. I could hear them even now, their distant howls making the hairs stand up on the back of my neck.

I was looking for the nearest sturdy tree to climb when I saw the glow of a fire. It was just through the trees, orange and cheery and completely welcome, and I headed straight towards it in relief, stopping just far enough back that I could see who it belonged to. After all, with some people I might be better off facing the wolves.

I didn't recognise them at first. They were just sleeping shapes lit by the flickering orange glow, and it wasn't until I saw the one standing watch that I realised who they were. The royal guardsmen, here fulfilling their promise to stay the night in the forest. Four of them, which meant that the captain hadn't drowned when I'd pushed him off the bridge (wouldn't that have been a stroke of bad luck?) but it also meant that if they recognised me, they might be less than friendly.

Argh, what to do…?

My decision was taken from me when the man on watch saw me. He reached for his sword, calling out, "Halt! Who goes there?" as if guards never knew how to say anything else (maybe they didn't) and I realised it was Captain Franco. Oh, what *good luck*, I thought sarcastically.

Thankful that my cloth cap was in my pocket and I was instead wearing the more concealing cape hood, I stepped out into view, my hands raised to show I had no weapon. "I saw your fire," I said in a low voice.

He lowered the sword. "And heard the wolves, no doubt."

I gave a brief nod, and he frowned. "Well, come on closer. You can sleep by the fire – but any funny business and you'll be sorry."

He hadn't recognised me. I'd pushed him off a bridge (and that was *after* I'd earned his dislike by being Nellie's evil stepsister) and he still hadn't recognised me. The question was, how far could I push this? Could I huddle down by the fire and hope to get away early enough to avoid recognition?

I spent enough time thinking about it that the captain finally shrugged. "Or head off, suit yourself."

"I'll sleep," I said quietly, moving closer. "Thank you."

With my face turned partially away from him, I moved around to the very edge of the fire, several body-lengths from the other sleeping men, and sat down to find a comfortable spot, as if dirt could ever be called comfortable. But it must have been, because nobody disturbed me and I finally slept.

When I awoke the sun hadn't yet risen, but there was just enough light for me to see around me. The fire had gone out, and there were still three sleeping figures around its greying embers. Presumably there was still someone on watch, but I couldn't see them. My luck was changing.

Silently I crept to my feet, adjusting the cloak so it was more comfortable and slipping the cap back over my hair. I might have got lucky the night before without them recognising me, but my pale colouring and build were unusual enough that in daylight it would be a different story.

I headed away from the road, aiming to take a wide route which would take me back to the bridge and my still hidden skirts, but I'd barely walked two minutes before I was found. The fair-haired guard from back at the inn was on watch, and he cut across to stand in front of me, an unwelcome sneer on his face. "Sneaking off without saying goodbye, were you?"

I shrugged. "I had to use the convenience." So to speak. And it was true, but yes, I was also trying to sneak off without saying goodbye.

"You have to pay for your night's safety. You don't get it for free."

Was he serious? Unable to hide my disbelief, I held up both hands. "I have nothing," I said clearly. "I can't pay you."

His gaze flicked up and down my body. "Oh, yes you can."

It took a moment for me to understand what he meant, and when I did I was repelled. I was dressed as a *boy*, and even if I hadn't been… "I would rather have risked the wolves," I said in disgust, taking a step sideways to move around him. "Now leave me alone, or I'll see that your superior hears about this."

The guard laughed, stepping to block my path once more. "You mean the captain? He won't be so kind once he realises that you pushed him off the bridge earlier, will he?" As my stomach dropped, he added with a nasty grin, "No disguise can hide that face, girl. Besides, you're dear Ella's sister, and he already dislikes you. He won't listen to a thing you say."

"You might be surprised," came the captain's voice, cold and grim. We both turned, and I was equally relieved and horrified. The guard, on the other hand, simply looked taken back.

"Jonley, I told you what would happen if I heard about this sort of thing again," Captain Franco said grimly. "Go back to the camp."

Jonley the horrible guard (as I would now think of him) didn't argue; he turned and headed back towards where they'd been sleeping, and then it was just me and the captain, who knew exactly who I was.

"I'm sorry," I said in a rush.

His dark eyebrows lifted, but he didn't look amused. "What for, exactly? For ignoring my orders and pushing me into a river when I was in armour and you didn't know if I could swim? Or for hiding your identity from me because you are *clearly* doing something you shouldn't be?"

I was quiet a moment. "For pushing you into the river," I finally answered. "I panicked. Sorry."

He didn't look at all appeased. "You do realise that at the very least, I could have you put in the stocks for what you did? And that's not even considering *why* you were sneaking out to the capital overnight. Something to do with a certain reward, perhaps?"

Was I so very transparent? Seeing that I had nothing to lose at this point, I decided to go with the truth. "After you left, we found…well, something about the figurines you said were stolen. We thought we could get the reward if I took it straight to the temple."

"We?"

"My family and I."

"Hmm." Captain Franco watched me narrowly. "I'm guessing we no longer need to search for the stolen items, then."

I shook my head.

"And did you get a reward?"

I shook my head again. "No. They didn't give me anything."

He studied me a bit longer as if trying to find out the truth of that statement. "Mind if I take a look?"

Realising he meant checking me over, I stared at him in dismay. "Yes, I do mind!"

"Fine. Well, lift up your cloak then. Let me see your pockets."

I did so, flattening them against my body to show that they were empty except for a few crumbs from yesterday's biscuits. "See, I told you I didn't have anything." Then a little more hesitantly I asked, "Are you still going to punish me for pushing you off the bridge?"

The captain stared at me narrow-eyed a few moments where I died a thousand deaths imagining the potential shame, then finally shook his head. "No, on one condition."

"Oh?" It had better not be anything like what Jonley the Horrible had suggested…

"I don't want to ever hear anything again about you mistreating Ella," he announced. "And I don't want her caught up in any more of your schemes. If I hear about either, I'll bring up how you pushed a captain of the royal guard off a bridge, and you will pay the full consequences."

For a moment I was struck dumb, then by the urge to laugh. Mistreating 'Ella'? *My* schemes? "I suppose if I told you that Nellie doesn't work any harder than anyone else, or that the whole thing with the figurines was her idea, you wouldn't believe me."

Captain Franco stared at me, dislike evident in every inch of his face. "No. I would not."

I sighed, feeling remarkably depressed. "Well, with that sort of threat in mind, I wouldn't dare follow through with my plan to make her clean the roof tiles with her tongue," I said lightly. "I'll leave that for my crippled mother, shall I?"

"This is not a joking matter," he replied coldly. "If I hear one single thing…"

No, that was not a joking matter at all, because it would be a miracle if he didn't hear anything. Nellie could make being forced to do the dishes twice in a row sound like a terrible ordeal, and we couldn't do without her help, half-hearted as it was. I'd tie her mouth shut, except that would likely count as abuse too. "I'll do my best," I said finally. "Now if you don't mind, I've got to get home. There's a stack of chores waiting for me."

My basket of clothing was still hidden where I'd left it, and by the time I made it through the town to the inn the sun was well and truly up, and the day had begun for most people. So I just looked like one more early riser, and nobody gave me a second glance.

Mother was at her usual place as I walked into the inn, and I saw her face light up with relief and hope. "Viola, thank God! Where were you all night?"

"I slept for a while in the forest," I replied, purposely omitting the part about the guards. "I'm fine."

But my tone was flat, and she frowned. "What happened?"

I slumped down on the nearest stool, suddenly very tired, and let out a deep sigh. "The Dragi took the figurines and shut the door in my face. I guess we could have given them to the guards after all."

Mother's face fell, but she leaned forward, patting my arm sincerely. "I'm sorry that it didn't work out, and I'm certainly sorry that you walked all that way for nothing." She shook her head, looking rather sad. "Well, this can be a lesson for us not to be greedy. I knew it wasn't right to send you out there alone in such a hurry, but all I could think of was how the reward might benefit us. I'm so sorry, love."

And she didn't even know the full story. I slumped forward, hanging my head, and she said softly, "Why don't you go to bed? You look dead on your feet."

I shook my head. "There's work to be done-"

"It can wait an hour or two," Mother interrupted. "Go on."

I turned towards the door leading to the bedrooms, very tempted to follow through, and Nellie came rushing in, her eyes wide with expectation, and James and Edwina on her heels. "How much did you get?"

There was a long silence before Mother replied flatly, "She

got nothing. They took the treasure and shut her out."

There was a brief, frozen moment as that sunk in, and seeing the disappointment on my family's faces made me feel even lower. But Nellie wasn't just disappointed. "What do you mean, you didn't get anything? Did you even ask?"

"Of course I did," I replied, scrubbing my hand over my tired face. "I asked, and the damned priestess offered me a Dragi blessing, whatever in heaven's name that is." Mother didn't even scold me for my language, which showed the situation was truly abnormal. "And then when I asked for something more, she got angry and shut me out."

"This is unbelievable!" Nellie burst out. "I *knew* I should have gone. People like me, and they listen to me, and I *know* I would have got a reward. But no, you had to insist that it was big old Viola, and now look at us! We've lost our chance." Her face crumpled, and Mother spoke to her sternly.

"You wouldn't have been any better off. It was a dangerous journey anyway, and I'm *glad* you didn't go, Nellie. I certainly wish that Viola hadn't." She shook her head in self-recrimination. "I should have insisted that we give the figurines to the guards as we'd agreed to, and this is the result. Crooked vines bear no fruit, children."

I didn't know about the accuracy of that metaphor, but I agreed with the sentiment. I was also exhausted, and decided that I'd take Mother up on the offer of a rest. As I headed up the stairs towards my room, Nellie called after me. "And where are you going?"

"To have a quick sleep," I called back dully. "Wake me in an hour, will you?"

She stomped up the stairs after me, her pretty face twisted in anger. "Oh, so you're going to laze about in bed, are you, right after you just thwarted my chances of ever making a good marriage?"

"It wasn't on purpose!"

"Sure it wasn't! If you think I don't know why you really let that reward go, then you're wrong! You're jealous of me, and you want me to stay here at your level," she hissed, quietly enough that the others downstairs couldn't hear. "Well, I won't! I'll find a way out of here whether you help me or not, and then you'll be sorry!"

I just stared at her blankly for a moment, looking so furious as she stood below me on the stairs. She barely reached my chest when she stood like this, and I was struck by how surreal the situation was, and amazement that she really, truly thought this was about her. "Alright," I said numbly, then turned and went upstairs.

Our bedrooms were at the very top of the inn, in the roof, all except for Mother's which was on the lowest level as she couldn't make it up the stairs. James had recently been moved to a small storeroom next to hers just in case something went wrong and she needed to call out, but the three of us girls slept upstairs in the two smallest rooms. Edwina and I shared one, a narrow window looking out over the roof towards the town and two neat beds stuck side by side, while Nellie had what I had considered the best choice: a room on the highest level that was slightly smaller than ours but had a larger bed, and a lovely view of the forest.

Once I reached my room I closed the door after me, slumping down onto my mattress in exhaustion. Something prickly stuck into my back, and I realised that it was time to fluff up the straw once more or perhaps even change it, but I was too tired to think about it at the time. My head hurt and my belly itched where the figurines had been – likely just my head playing tricks on me rather than anything real – but still I managed to sleep.

My dreams were as intense and strange as they often were when sleeping during the day. I dreamed that I was a young boy, and that a great red dragon had taken over our town, insisting on being worshipped and given tribute. I was terribly afraid but I knew that I must not obey. Then as the dragon came by with its green-garbed acolytes I ran and hid myself in the closet, desperately praying that I would be overlooked, and somehow, miraculously, I was. Then the dream turned into the blurred images that often passed through my mind in sleep, and I woke up, too hot and confused.

Edwina was gently shoving my shoulder, and the sun was high in the sky. It must have been several hours. "Mother said not to let you sleep too long, or else you'd be awake all night," she said apologetically.

I grunted, swinging myself out of the low bed so my feet were on the floor. "It's OK, 'Wina. It was time to get up anyway." After all, the chores didn't sleep. "What needs doing first?"

"We've had a group come in from the mountains," she began, then launched into a quick description of what needed to be done today.

"Very well," I agreed tiredly. "I'm just going to change my dress. I don't feel so fresh."

Edwina just stood there a moment, and I knew she wanted to say something. Then finally, in a small voice: "I suppose there will be other chances, won't there?"

I knew exactly what she was talking about, but I didn't answer, and she added, "It was too good to be true, wasn't it?"

"Probably," I agreed finally. "Don't worry about it, alright?" As if words would ever make up for such a disappointment.

I began to undo my dress, itching again at the spot under my corset where the figurines had sat. It was just above my navel, and it was *so* ticklish. Wondering if there'd been a scratch of some kind, I finally pulled the corset open to have a look and recoiled in horror. On my belly, where the figurines had been hidden, was a scattering of silver spots. Or diamonds, more like, since each was almost the size of a four-sided coin – covering my skin where the figurines had sat. They didn't hurt, but they felt a little thicker than my normal skin, and suddenly I wanted to cry.

"King's crown," Edwina murmured in dismay. "What are those?"

I shook my head wordlessly. The metal must have caused a reaction, or else I'd got the plague…but I suspected the first. What odd shapes the lumps were, though.

Mother agreed with me when we showed her. "That'd be why they called them cursed, I'll bet," she said decisively. "Just be glad that covering had only come off one of them. Here, go get some evening primrose oil, and wrap it with rags. I'm sure it'll fade away within a few days."

I did so, unsure of whether it would actually work, but deciding not to think about it. Then I got on with the chores because they needed to be done, Nellie was nowhere to be seen, and Edwina and James were looking overwrought. Back when my stepfather had been alive, the inn had been a bit better off, and we'd been able to afford some extra help, but those days were gone.

I was returning the bucket and mop to the upstairs closet when in a strange repeat of the previous day, I found something unexpected. The diary from the velvet bag was sitting in the shadows off to the side where I'd left it, overlooked in favour of the heavy (and possibly toxic) figurines. I picked it up gingerly with my clothed hand just in case, and it fell open to show pages and pages of neat writing.

I flicked my way through the book to discover that it was almost completely full…and a closer look showed that there were many, *many* mentions of dragons. I was suddenly reminded of the odd dream I'd had earlier. It was just the situation, of course, and no doubt seeing the diary yesterday and visiting the Dragi had brought on the dream.

But if they thought I'd give them back the diary after what happened yesterday, they could think again! I was tempted to throw it straight into the privy, but then held back at the last moment. I might be able to read, but there was very little available *to* read. We only had a very plain family bible, as most who weren't completely impoverished did whether they could read or not, as well as a couple of pamphlets about horticulture from my late stepfather.

It was such a struggle to find the time to teach James to read and write when we all had to work so hard and he seemed to lack interest, but perhaps that too was something we could fix in the future. Being literate was useful, and I'd largely been taught by Mother before I'd come to Delmany, but in truth people could and did get by without knowing how to read and write.

So I sneaked the diary into my room, stuck it under my mattress, and resolved to take a better look later. If it seemed important…well, then I could pass it over to the wonderful royal guard, couldn't I? Or better yet, get Nellie to do it – because no one would tell *her* that she'd been remiss in not giving it earlier.

Speaking of Nellie, she hadn't been seen much all day, and we knew from experience that when she was in a mood she was better left alone. Still, she needed to eat, so by evening when she hadn't appeared Mother sent me up to see if I could find her.

I went straight to her room at the highest part of the inn,

not at all surprised to find the door shut. I tapped it a couple of times. "Nellie, dinner's ready." There was no response, so I tapped it again, harder. "Nellie-"

The door swung open, and I saw that she hadn't answered because she wasn't there. But that wasn't what caught my attention. Lying across the bed was a dress: the light green fabric clearly good quality, and the style distinctive.

It was a ball gown.

3
The Green Gown

I moved forward into the room, my attention fully caught by the gown lying across the bed. It was *beautiful*. The light green of a fresh apple and embroidered in a faint silver, it reminded me just a little of the priestess's dress from the previous day, except this was obviously intended for a ball. It had a full skirt, a tiny nipped-in waist that would never fit me, and small sleeves that would just cup the shoulders.

But when I got closer the first impression of beauty faded. The fabric, while far better than anything we would wear from day to day, was coarser and thicker than I'd expect from a ball gown; and the quality of the stitching was clearly poor. The dim light from the setting sun had fooled me into thinking it was better than it was.

Oh, dear. Where *had* Nellie got this? I'd never seen the fabric before, but that stitching was obviously her own. Out of all of us she was the shoddiest sewer, her stitches irregular and too large, clearly not strong enough to withstand much wear and tear.

I studied it again, noting in dismay the short distance from the waist to the bodice. It would be low cut...*very* low cut, and together with the fact it was green (the typical colour loose women wore, or so society said), she'd look like she was for sale, not for marriage – and that was assuming it didn't fall apart if she breathed too deeply.

Behind me the floor creaked, and there in the doorway was Nellie, her expression horrified. "What are you doing?" she cried. "Sneaking into my things!" She ran over and stood between me and the dress as if by hiding it now she could undo what I'd already seen. "I bet you're going to tell your mother now, aren't you?"

That last question had been in a nasty tone, but I could see her fear. "I'm not going to tell Mother," I told her crossly. "I came up because you didn't come down for dinner, and no one's seen you all day. We thought you might be sick." Actually we thought she'd been sulking, but she wouldn't like to hear that.

"I'm not sick, but you can tell Hazel that if you like."

She was still standing defensively in front of her badly made gown, and I had to say something. "Where did you get that fabric?"

"It was a gift."

"A *gift*?" I burst out in dismay. "Nellie, was it from a man?"

"No," she snapped. "Joan the miller's wife gave it to me this morning after you came back." When I just stared at her – because Joan didn't give *anything* away for free – she added, "Very well, it was a trade. I gave her my mother's pearl earrings."

I closed my eyes in dismayed disbelief. She had given away her one item of real value in exchange for…for this waste of hope and fabric. "You're obviously planning to wear that to the ball, but I don't really think you've thought this through."

Nellie lifted her chin. "Of course I've thought it through. You didn't even know about this 'til five minutes ago, so stop acting like you know everything!"

I sighed. "Very well, who's going to be your chaperone? Mother certainly isn't, and you can't walk all the way to the palace. Wait, do you even have shoes?"

"Of course I have shoes," she replied sulkily, her eyes sliding away from mine. "Besides, nobody will notice my feet in that dress."

"If it's as low cut as I think it is, then no, they won't," I told her flatly. "And you didn't tell me who's going to take you. Has someone agreed?"

"I was going to ask the Havensteys, since they've got two daughters-"

"Neither of whom are half as pretty as you," I cut over. "There's no way they'll take the competition, even if her dress isn't nearly as nice as theirs."

"It *is* nice!" Nellie argued hotly. "I based it on the design from that lady who came through the other week-"

"It would be nice if it fit properly, and if it was sewn properly," I interrupted, suddenly angry at her insistent stupidity. Couldn't she see that this wouldn't work? "It's not either of those things. It'll fall right off you. Those seams are as weak as hay, and besides, you don't have any jewellery now, do you? No gloves, no nice cloak, no decent shoes – no one to do your hair! A dress doesn't mean you can just go to the ball, Nellie! They won't even let you in the door looking like that!"

My words had been harsh but true, but she wouldn't give up. "They will let me in, I'm beautiful-"

"Not enough to make up for this sort of thing!"

"And it is sewn fine!" she burst out, suddenly turning back to one of my other criticisms. "It is, and you're just being fussy because you're jealous as always, because I'm going to go and you're not! And even if you could go, you'd never be half as pretty as me, and you're green with envy!"

I went hot then cold with hurt and anger. She was right, but so was I, and I would prove it. Stalking over to the bed I picked up the sleeve of the dress, giving it a tug. "Look at this, Nellie, it's pulling already-"

"Don't touch that!"

She grabbed the other side as if to pull it off me, and in horrible slow motion I saw the sleeve tear. It ripped away from the dress to hang by a thread, and I dropped it in horror. "Nellie, I'm so sorry…I can fix it…"

She turned on me, tears welling in her bright blue eyes. "Just get out! Out, before you ruin anything else!"

"I'm sorry," I said again in a low voice, moving for the door. "But what I said still stands. I can help you remake it, it could be your new Sunday best-"

"Just *go!*"

I left, and the door was slammed shut after me. I stood there a moment, listening to the sound of Nellie sobbing in her room, and I felt utterly miserable. I'd told her the truth, and if she listened it would save her being humiliated, and us by extension. What would she promise for people to help her this time, her firstborn child? And even if she did somehow manage to make her way to the palace in Ostraime, she would still be in rough shoes, without gloves or jewels and with her hair looking like it had been done by some servant girl (which basically it would have been) and with her generous bosom spilling out of that dress. She'd be a laughing stock. It would likely even tear at the seams throughout the night…

But the worst thing, the very worst thing, was this. I felt so miserable because she had been right too. I *was* jealous of her. I was jealous that she would always be far more beautiful than I, that people would always love her (at least 'til they got to really know her) and that her flaws would be overlooked where mine were pointed out, and that she could catch the eye of a prince where I couldn't even catch the eye of a middle-aged widower with no hair. I knew that although I'd spoken the truth my motives hadn't been at all pure, and I was ashamed.

That was why I told Mother that Nellie wouldn't be coming down, that she was still sulking over not getting any reward, and I didn't mention the dress or the argument. I suspected that they'd heard us shouting (the walls weren't stone, just oak unfortunately) but clearly the topic had been missed, or else the others wouldn't have stayed quiet. Besides, we had guests to attend to, and the day didn't finish until all the chores were done.

Dishes.

Hooray.

When I woke the next morning the odd, thick patches of skin on my belly had changed. When I ran my fingers over them I was horrified to feel sharp edges; solid and smooth and thick as diamond-shaped coins. Once I saw them I felt even worse: they weren't silver anymore, they were gold, and they certainly didn't look like anything natural. Holding back the urge to cry I picked at the edge of one, then was repelled as it came off as cleanly as an old scab, barely hurting at all. The skin underneath was silvery white once more, and there I was holding what looked like a gold coin, if gold coins were diamond-shaped.

May you receive exactly what you deserve, Viola of Bluebell Inn.

A gold coin. No. Surely not…?

In the next bed Edwina began to stir, my movement having shaken her out of her deeper sleep, and I froze in place. Then she slumped again, her breathing steady, so I focused again on the scab-thing. It *was* a scab, right?

But scabs didn't have smooth glossy surfaces that gleamed like precious metal, and the same consistency, almost bending when I put pressure on it. They didn't have one side as slick as polished gold, and the other almost as smooth, but lightly marked where it had been attached to my skin. Like a scale that had fallen off a giant, golden fish…or a dragon.

I raised it to my face, stared at it, smelled it. I'd only handled real gold once, when a rich guest had paid for his room with a single gold coin and had needed almost twelve silvers in change. Now that had been most annoying to deal with at the time, but it had given me a feel for the metal. Gold had a certain scent to it…or maybe I was imagining it, I told myself. Was I so desperate to see some improvement in my life that I saw treasure instead of trash?

But the rest of the spots were irritating me now, almost as if they needed to be removed too, so I carefully picked off each of the other six gold scales and pushed them into a pile in the middle of my bed.

So…*shiny.*

When Edwina woke up I was still sitting there, staring at the pile. She watched me muzzily for a moment, then looked at the pile, then back at me again. "What's this, Vee?"

It was so much like what I'd asked Nellie the night before, but my response was very different than hers had been. "I don't know," I admitted softly. "Looks like gold, doesn't it?"

She scrambled off her bed, open-mouthed, and crouched to stare at the small pile of discs. I'd layered them into a tiny pyramid, and they'd made the rest of the bedding look old and dingy in contrast. "But you said that the Dragi didn't give you anything."

I shook my head, still staring. "Perhaps I was wrong."

We carried the scales down to Mother's bedroom and tapped quietly on the door, but didn't even wait for a response before going in. Once awake, her reaction was very much like ours had been. Shock, and amazement. "What…this *grew* on your skin, Viola? How is that possible?!"

"Some kind of enchantment," Edwina breathed. "It's the

reward, surely. It must be!"

I still held the perhaps-gold warily, as my memories of the Dragi temple were unpleasant. They'd said the figurines had been cursed. If I had rubbed the gold on my face, would I now be growing scales there? I couldn't see that anything truly good could come from such a place. "Wait a second, we don't even know if it is gold," I countered. "It might just be...I don't know, a look-alike."

Mother turned a piece over in her fingers, bending it slightly. "It's soft. Pure. If this isn't gold, then I don't know what it is."

"Even if it is, we can't use in the local market," I said reasonably. "People will want to know where we got it. This town is full of terrible gossips."

"Not everyone will gossip," Mother replied. "Not if you offer the right incentive..."

And that was how I ended up at one of the local merchants, showing one of the scales to the practically slavering jeweller who also acted as the village money-changer.

"This is pure gold," he declared. "Some of the finest I've ever seen. Where on earth did you get it, Viola?"

"I told you, Athelbert," I replied, doing my best to hide my elation. Gold, real gold, and it was all ours! That horrible walk had been worth it after all. "It was a gift fairly given, but you aren't to ask for any more details, or next time I won't bring it to you. Now how much will you give me for it?"

"Nineteen silvers," he said quickly. "And promise to bring me any more that you find."

Now I knew that a standard gold coin of about the same size was worth twenty-two silvers, but it was close enough that I was satisfied. Athelbert was known for the fine quality of his work and the tightness of his lips, closely matched by the tightness of his purse. It would be worth the discount in exchange for his silence. Still, nineteen silvers...that was as much as we earned in a month.

Slipping my hand into my pocket I pulled out the other one I'd brought with me; the other five being hidden in Mother's underwear draw where *no one* was going to find them. "Can you break this into a few bronzes as well?"

He nodded knowingly. "Don't want people to know you've come into money, hmm?" I smiled at him tightly, taking the offered change and going to leave. He called after me, "Do you even know what these are, girl?"

I glanced back over my shoulder. "I suspect you're going to tell me."

"Dragon scales," Athelbert enunciated, a satisfied smile on his face.

"Dragon scales?" I echoed in disbelief. "I thought dragons had hides like iron."

"Except for their bellies," he said knowingly. "The stories say they lie on hoards of gold, but they don't often say that the gold has grown on the beasts themselves. They're jealous of it, I hear, because it shows their weakness, and because they love the smell of it."

I stared at him suspiciously for a long moment. He seemed sincere, but this was a tale I'd never heard before, and I wasn't sure how much I liked the idea of dragon scales growing on *me*. "And you're certain that these are such?"

He nodded. "Aye, they're dragon scales, and they're rare as hens' teeth. I don't know where you got them from, but for your sake, I hope you came by them honestly."

I paused. "Rare, eh? How rare?"

"Not that rare," he said hastily. "Never mind where you got it. You bring any others to me, understood?"

I did understand, and I also resolved to ask around whenever I got the chance to go back to Ostraime. If they really were that rare, then perhaps we could do a lot better than nineteen silvers.

But *dragon* scales? I'd heard that dragons loved gold, not that they were *made* of gold.

Back at home the others were busy doing their chores, and I quietly pulled Mother aside to show her what I'd been paid. She was so stunned that she just stood there silently for a moment, her eyes round and face pale. "My word," she breathed finally. "That's certainly enough to redecorate the inn, and it's not even half of it!"

"Maybe you could go with James to visit your family in Cristonia," I suggested quietly. "You said your sister hasn't been well."

She nodded slowly. "Yes. Yes, I should do that. But there's one thing I want to do first."

"What's that?"

"I want all of us to have new clothes. Nice ones, nice enough to attend the next local ball." She smiled up at me, a twinkle in her pale blue eyes. "We'll be a bit too late for the Royal Ball, but I daresay you'll be able to withstand the disappointment."

I would, but I didn't know about Nellie. The ball was tomorrow night, and after last night's fiasco I didn't know if she'd give up on the idea all that easily. "What about Nellie?" I asked.

"What about her?"

"She really wants to go the ball. Perhaps…"

"We could spend all this on a horse and carriage, a splendid pre-made dress and jewels just so she can pretend to be a noblewoman for one night?" Mother looked at me with raised eyebrows. "Perhaps we should go as her servants, since none of us are Delmany-born. How about that?"

I looked away. "You're right. It's ridiculous, and not fair to the rest of us. She'll be disappointed, that's all."

"And she can bear the disappointment," Mother replied gently. "I daresay if she'd had a few more disappointments when she was younger, she'd be a bit easier to live with now. But she won't know, Viola. I don't want you to tell a soul about this money, not until we decide what to do with it. We can't have the town knowing we've suddenly had a windfall, they'll want to know why, and I won't want to tell them."

I'd have to tell Edwina, of course, but I could see the wisdom of it. The money was greatly appreciated, but it certainly wasn't unlimited, and it wouldn't go far if we started to live above our usual standard.

But in spite of the secrecy I was elated, going about the rest of my day with a sense of jubilance. Things were finally improving, and the 'genie' list might finally get attended to. Oh, and we'd get new gowns, all of us; nice enough to show our faces at the next local ball and not be ashamed. Now that was a long time coming.

Nellie and I barely spoke all day, not that I saw much of her. But the few times I did see her, she looked so down, so depressed, that I wanted to tell her what had happened even though I was still angry with her for the things she'd said last night. But I didn't. Instead I just did what needed to be done as always, and the tiny treasure trove stayed hidden half in Mother's underwear draw, half in my pillow.

However, I did know that any improvements to the inn would only really benefit Nellie and James since they were the ones to inherit, and Edwina and I would have to rely on the two of them to look after us in our old age. Ha. We'd be far better to put a little aside for dowries if we could, perhaps in the form of jewellery. I could definitely see Edwina getting married one day, although I wasn't sure about myself, and that would be a lot easier if she wasn't going in stone broke.

The next day went on as usual. Nellie was still too quiet, still not talking to me, and as evening came around I saw her slip off to her room, her head hanging low.

"Call her back, will you?" Mother told me. "We need the last pumpkin cut up for tomorrow's soup."

"I'll do it," I replied, even though I still had several other chores to finish. "I'll be faster." But by the time I finished everything else and the sun was growing low in the sky, I couldn't find the pumpkin anywhere. It was one of the big grey ones with flavourful flesh, and I couldn't think where it might have gone. I asked Edwina as she sat near the fire mending torn sheets, and she shrugged. "Ask Nellie."

I didn't want to. I didn't want to see her at all, so I decided to take a second look in the kitchen. Perhaps it had been put outside to save space?

Outside the back door was an alley that looked right out onto the street, and towards the busiest part of the village. Across the road I saw two beautifully-dressed women climb into a neat, plain carriage. I recognised them as the mother and daughter of one of the wealthier local families, clearly having saved money on transport in place of clothing. The daughter, Alexa, was quite pretty, not like Nellie of course, but she'd cleaned up well tonight in her full pink-skirted ballgown. Even though she probably wouldn't snag a nobleman, then at least she'd have a night to remember. Not everyone got to go to a royal ball.

I wondered absently if I would have looked less plain

dressed in such a way, then at the pang of hurt that brought on, I pushed the idea aside. I knew it would be foolish and a little sad to think that way; but still I watched the carriage drive off, seeing the outline of the women's plumed heads silhouetted in the tiny windows. They were cutting it fine if they wanted to get to the palace for eight o'clock. I'd bet the line of carriages would be huge, and it was probably a two-hour journey even by horse, since the road needed repaving. King Barrick didn't believe in spending money on roads he didn't use himself.

Just then a new carriage drove up right outside the front of our inn, just in front of the alley. I stepped back into the shadows, determined to be unnoticed, but curious as to who this would be for. The carriage wasn't plain and sturdy like the previous one. No, this one was rounded and elaborate, painted in a silver-white that shimmered slightly in the dim light, and which matched the uniform of the footman who moved forward to open the door and help the ladies in.

The first one was short and round, and although I saw her only briefly as she stepped inside, I recognised her as the woman I'd spoken to in the market the other day. The one who'd asked if I wanted to go to a royal ball.

How odd.

But then the next lady stepped inside. I'd never seen her before, but she seemed to be coming from our inn. At first all I saw was her dress: full-skirted with lovely fabric that shimmered even more than the carriage, and which perfectly flattered her tiny waist and curvaceous figure. She was wearing gloves that rose above her elbows, almost the same shade as her fair skin, and a series of diamonds adorned her ears and neck, and were set in her golden hair, pinned in a high mass on the back of her elegant head. A noblewoman surely, because who else could afford such finery?

Then the lady turned, and I recognised that perfect profile immediately. It was Nellie, and she was smiling as if the sun itself shone from within her, and I had never seen her looking so beautiful. I couldn't take my eyes off her. I don't know if I gasped, or if I made some other sound, but she must have heard me. She turned, just for a moment as she climbed into the carriage fit for a princess, and our eyes met. She didn't stop smiling, but I saw something in her expression.

Triumph.

I watched in silence as the door closed and the carriage drove away into the distance. Then I stood there for I didn't know how long, until I felt the evening chill hit my exposed arms. My mind was buzzing with confusion, but my movements were mechanical as I turned and went back inside.

"Did you find it?" Edwina asked.

"Find what?"

"The pumpkin, of course."

"Oh. No, I didn't find it," I replied numbly. "I'll go to market first thing in the morning."

There was a pause, and my sister gave me a strange look. "Are you well, Vee? You've got a funny look on your face."

I turned away, unable to shake the memory of my glowing, ethereal stepsister and that last look of triumph. *I win, you lose,* it seemed to say. "I'm fine," I murmured, heading towards the stairs. "Just fine, thank you."

I should be better than fine. The silvery spots on my belly seemed to be thickening again, and if I guessed rightly, I'd have another batch of 'dragon scales' to sell in two days' time. Not a limited source, after all. And what difference did it make to me what Nellie did? Hadn't I wished that she would leave and stop being such a burden on us all? There was no better way for her to do that than to show herself off, and catch the eye of some rich man who'd put a ring on her finger.

I made my way up the stairs to my room, lighting each taper as I did so. Then I sat my candle beside my bed in its holder and pulled out a 'precious' item from the drawer that Edwina and I shared. It was a piece of broken mirror, only half the size of my palm, and its edges were worn smooth by many handlings. Not by me, but by her – she didn't get her hair so perfect without having to check it somewhere.

The face reflected in the mirror looked nothing like the beautiful one in the carriage. It wasn't deformed or missing anything, but it lacked that perfect, delicate symmetry where a mere quarter of an inch here or there would be the difference between beauty and plainness. My eyes were big, but they were set a little too deep into my head underneath strongly arched brows that made me look perpetually stern.

The nose wasn't badly-shaped, but that was also too big, and not straight like Nellie's nor a snub like the rest of my family's, either. It was slightly hooked, just like my late father's had been. Mouth: too big, too wide, and in its resting state as stern as the rest of me.

Added in with my sharp cheekbones and jawline I was like a caricature of a girl, the sort that was set against pure beauty in those comic woodcuts guests would sometimes bring from the city. The wicked witch curses the heroine, or the greedy fishmonger's wife scolds her husband…or the ugly stepsister envies her lovelier sibling. That was what I was to people, wasn't I? Me and my family, all cast in a simple, twisted story written in the minds of our neighbours. It was no wonder we had no real friends, and me learning to smile and simper wouldn't change one single thing.

In that moment I hated my life, and perhaps I hated Nellie too. It wasn't a personal hatred (although I could very easily summon up energy for one of those if I tried) but it was the general hatred of a plain person for a beautiful one, a hatred born of envy and frustration that the world should be so unfair, should judge a person by their outward shell rather than their true self.

When Edwina came to bed not long later I pretended to be asleep, not interested in hearing her excited whispers about what colour she might choose for her new dress, and when we might tell James and Nellie. Soon enough the sleep was for real.

I dreamed fitfully, this time disjointed images of being chased by a dragon, of *being* a dragon; of standing in my underthings in front of a crowd, all of them pointing and jeering and calling me ugly. I awoke with a start, unsure of which of those was worse. To be honest I'd rather face a real dragon than that last situation.

A faint sound outside caught my attention, and I crept over to the window, pushing aside the thin curtain. Outside I saw a young woman in servants' clothing slipping through the street towards our inn, her skirts hitched up enough to show her bare feet. The moon was out, its crisp quarter enough to show her identity. It was Nellie, and while her beautiful gown was gone, her smile wasn't.

A few moments later I heard the groan of that creaky stair (one which I'd put on the genie list to be fixed) and not long after that, the sound of her door opening and closing just up the hall from my room. I didn't wait. Taking the snuffed candle from beside my bed I lit it on the torch outside my room, moved quietly up the short flight of stairs to Nellie's attic room, then gave a very light tap on the door. Where there'd been shuffling noises there was silence, and I tapped once more. "I know you're there," I whispered. "I saw you come in."

The door opened, and Nellie looked out at me, her wide eyes not hiding her happiness. She was wearing the same plain dress she had been all day, and her hair was a rumpled mess. "Are you going to tell your mother?"

Oh, for heaven's sake. Pushing my way in, I closed the door after me. "What did you do this time, Nellie? What did you promise for a dress like that?"

She lifted her chin defiantly, and I was reminded of two nights previous when we'd had that terrible fight. This wasn't going to be the same, but I had to know. I'd never be able to sleep otherwise.

"I promised nothing," she replied triumphantly, forgetting to keep her voice low. "It was a gift from a Wyse woman." As my jaw dropped in disbelief she hurried on, "She said that she'd been going through the land, looking for a beautiful and virtuous girl to bless, and she found me crying because I couldn't go to the ball. So she helped me to go!"

Beautiful and virtuous. A Wyse woman picked *Nellie* as the most deserving of such a gift.

The Wyse were named because they were knowledgeable, cautious, well learned, and mysterious. Some of them even had wings, and the power to make real differences in people's lives. Kind of like the Dragi (except for the wings part) only with a far better reputation. I'd never met one, but I'd heard stories, and until now I'd always thought the Wyse were somehow…special. But at that moment I wondered if either I had missed something monumental in Nellie's character, or perhaps the world was even more unfair than I'd realised. "Helped you…?"

Nellie shrugged, still looking wonderfully happy. "Made me a dress, got me a way to the ball – but you saw that, didn't you – and the only problem was that it only lasted 'til midnight. Heavens, I was having such a good time that I only saw the clock at quarter to twelve, and then I barely made it out in time." She shrugged, for the first time looking disgruntled. "At least the Wyse spell brought me back here, or else I would have had a long walk. I don't know who came up with such a silly idea, the gift only lasting until twelve. Everyone else was still dancing."

I couldn't see how or why she would lie, but still the whole story seemed fantastical. Sure, the Wyse people existed, as did all sort of weird and wonderful non-humans, mostly off in foreign lands. But I'd never met one, nor spoken to anyone who'd met one, let alone heard of a Wyse woman selflessly helping a human for nothing in exchange!

Nellie. Out of everyone she could have chosen, she'd chosen Nellie.

"And Prince Royce danced with me," she added almost defiantly. "All night, almost, and he said I was the most beautiful girl he'd ever seen."

"Of course he did," I replied numbly, still trying to take it in. "Did you tell him who you were?"

She flicked her rumpled golden hair. "Of course. Well, sort of. I told him my name was Ella, and that my father was the Count of Novantine."

My gaze shot up in surprise. "But Nellie, there hasn't been a Count of Novantine for what, sixty years? King Atticus abolished that title years ago. Surely the prince will know that."

Nellie shrugged, seemingly unbothered. "When he takes the trouble to find me, then he'll know what I meant. My mother's grandfather was supposed to be the Count, you know."

Yes, I had heard that tale before, but I hadn't put much stock in it. The Count's lands had been situated around the village of Novas just down the river, and there'd been an inheritance dispute, with no legitimate sons and about half a dozen bastards all trying to claim the title. King Atticus had just abolished it in the end, not at all adding to his popularity.

I thought about it for a moment. The prince surely wouldn't find her, not with such poor information. And there must be dozens of beautiful golden-haired girls in the kingdom, titled nonetheless, so that he wouldn't come looking for some innkeeper's daughter. I hoped for Nellie's sake that he didn't. He surely wouldn't marry her when he found out her true rank.

But my silence told my opinion, and she turned on me. "He will come! I *know* he will, even though you're jealous and you don't want him to. He said he loves me. So there!"

I stared. My stepsister could stretch an inch of truth into a foot of fantasy, but this was a whole new level. "How many dances did you have again?"

"Four," she snapped defiantly. "And three of those I said I was feeling faint because I didn't know the steps, and so we went out onto the balcony. So there," she said again.

"Wait," I said slowly. "After four dances, Prince Royce of Delmany said he loved you. Love. Those precise words. Ella, I love you. Like that."

"Well...not *exactly* like that. He said 'I think I could love a girl like you'. It's pretty much the same thing."

Well, that made the prince only slightly less stupid than I had imagined. "It's not the same thing."

"It is!" she insisted. "And he *will* come! I'll send him a message, tell him where to find me."

Realising we were getting loud, I lowered my voice, making my expression as calm as possible. It was imperative that I got her to understand me. "Alright, Nellie. You say that the prince loves you and will come find you, and maybe you're right. But let's test it, shall we?"

She watched me suspiciously. "What do you mean?"

"If Prince Royce really loves you, if he really wants to find you-"

"He does!"

"Fine, then he *will* come find you. After all, how many Ellas can there be in the Novantine area, especially ones who look like you? But if he doesn't really care for you, then he won't try, and he won't come. But will you leave it for a month, Nellie? Just a month without sending a message, so that you can prove to me that he cares for you enough to look. Like you said, it can't be that hard."

I was beginning to even convince myself, and I saw her soften. "A month is too long."

"Two weeks then," I said hastily. "If he hasn't come in that time, then you can send a message."

"He will come," she assured me. "But I'll do what you ask, just to prove that I'm right on this. And in exchange you won't tell Hazel where I was."

"Not until- *if* you send a message," I promised, thinking that the prince would never come to find her. It was too much of a long shot – he might try to look, but doubtless he'd give up the moment he realised there was no Count of Novantine. "Then we can tell her, because it wouldn't be fair for the prince to show up on our doorstep without warning her first."

Nellie nodded, and in spite of our argument I could see she was still glowing from her evening out. In spite of myself I was interested. "Was he handsome, then? The prince?"

"Very. Everything a prince should be."

Naturally. "And did you see anyone you knew there?" A horrible thought occurred to me. "Lord above, did anyone see *you*?"

She looked taken back for a moment. "I've really no idea," she confessed. "I was too...enthralled by the wonder of the occasion."

How nice for her, I thought dryly, knowing that I *was* feeling just a little jealous. I didn't need to be the centre of attention, but perhaps one small part of me would liked to have attended – to sit and stuff my face with delicious food, and watch all the toffs in their finery, as Nancy had said.

4
Spun Gold

The next day Nellie was visibly happy, even doing her chores with the minimum of complaining. Edwina was so surprised she even asked me if I had told Nellie about the gold, but I told her no. Perhaps she'd met a handsome new boy. I hated lying to my sister, but I had promised Nellie, and I would keep my promise. Later, when this all blew over, then I could apologise.

"Are you sure she hasn't found out somehow?" my sister asked dubiously. We watched as Nellie carted an armful of linen up the stairs, a little smile on her face. "Look at her. That's not normal. I don't like keeping things from her, anyway…"

"Mm." Time to change the subject. "Speaking of the gold, it seems to be growing back," I said in a low voice. "And it's spread. There are eight patches now." They were closer together, and I almost hadn't noticed at first.

"Eight? Are you sure you didn't just miscount the first time?"

I shook my head. When you were talking about extremely valuable gold pieces, you didn't miscount. But just then some of the guests came into the room, and the conversation had to be left.

That evening Edwina and I were in the kitchen cleaning up after dinner when Mother came in, the poorly healed bones of her legs making her limp as always. "I got another letter from Melicia," she said, referring to her sister. "She hasn't been well and wants to know if we can visit soon." She paused, for the first time not adding, *but of course we can't afford it.*

"You should go," Edwina said. "Take James with you, wear

a new dress. Why not?"

It was a generous thing to say considering how much I knew my sister had wanted to go as well, so I added in, "Or take 'Wina with you as well. I can hire a couple of girls to help us while you're gone, and you know I can run the inn by myself if I need to."

Mother seemed to think on it. "You've been helping me with the books for long enough," she admitted. "But are you sure you don't want to come as well?"

"Maybe some other time," I said firmly. "But you must go, Mother. After all, Aunt is sick, and she's older than you anyway."

"Mm. Perhaps."

But within days 'perhaps' had turned into definitely, and they were making quiet plans for a visit. Unsurprisingly the prince didn't come, and I started asking around in the market if anyone would be interested in taking on work. While I got several snide remarks about how overworking and underpaying people, a young brother and sister seemed interested. Wallace and Maria's parents weren't at all well off, and they seemed to have good character, so I made plans for them to come the next day.

I traded a couple more gold pieces for smaller coinage, and then hid the rest of the gold in three separate locations. Besides in Mother's underwear draw we put some in Edwina's old pair of boots that we were keeping for James to grow into (too horrible for anyone to dare touch) and some more in my pillow. Even though I didn't like having it so close to my face, I was terrified that someone would find it, confront us and try to take it. I couldn't bear the thought of being so close to freedom and then having it taken away again.

The gold scales kept growing with no sign of disappearing, and eight seemed to have turned into ten, if those grey shadows were any sign. They weren't spreading over my belly, just getting closer packed, more like real scales, and my excitement was mixed with a little dread. What if they kept growing? What if I got covered in them? Heavens, it would be awful to be known as the girl who grew dragon gold; I'd practically be inviting a kidnapping.

The diary was no help. It was mostly descriptions of some

dragon, almost loving in their detail. *Its body is huge, as long as ten oxen laid end on end.* And how had they measured that, hmm? *I long for it to wake even as I dread it. Its bright, almond-shaped eyes with those slitted pupils, the deep orange-red of its hard, beautiful scales...*

Quite frankly I found the writing style disturbing, and didn't want to read it in any detail. I could have understood keeping the damned beast around just for its scales (now there was a way to grow rich quick and die young; harvest from a sleeping dragon) but the writer seemed to *love* it. I would have given up completely except on the fourth page the writer put that this dragon had been the same one that ate King Atticus, and that was interesting enough to keep me reading.

See, King Atticus had been well known for his greed and his poor character. He had come to power almost as a child, ruling from the age of fourteen, and as Mother always said, too much power too young couldn't help but corrupt. She'd been referring to Nellie's manipulation, but the same applied to our late king. He had ruled for many years, and wealth was his obsession. He wasn't married and didn't have any children, instead focusing on collecting gold and jewels at a massive speed. Nothing else would get in the way, and he even had little children sent into mines because they could better fit into the small spaces.

However, Atticus was most notorious for something that happened when he was in his late thirties, which would have been forty or so years ago. He'd been finally looking to marry, and a rumour came to his ear of a very beautiful peasant girl who could spin straw into gold. Esme, I think her name was, not that it mattered to the story. It was all nonsense spread by her drunken father, but the king had listened. He had ordered the girl brought to him and had her locked into a room full of straw and with a spinning wheel, saying that if she didn't have the straw spun into gold by morning, she would be executed.

Now, to me that was a strong sign of his twisted character, because I couldn't imagine any beautiful girl actually being *killed* because they failed to live up to a ridiculous challenge. Nellie would only have to cry a single tear and then anyone would give her whatever she wanted, let alone execute her. But perhaps this peasant with a drunkard for a father wasn't as clever, because she found herself locked in, and with death surely coming the next day. She was *not* an alchemist, and she couldn't change anything into gold.

So there she was crying when suddenly a dwarf appeared in her cell, thus proving that beauty will always find a white knight, regardless of what size. He *was* a power user, and he promised that he would weave the straw into gold in exchange for something to be agreed on later. Or I forget exactly what happened, except that the dwarf did do as he promised, and spun the straw into gold.

Naturally, once greedy King Atticus saw the gold he wasn't satisfied. He had Esme tossed into a larger room full of even more straw, with the same threat. Same story. The dwarf showed up, helped out the girl, everyone was happy. But of course the king wanted more, and this time he said that if she could do it once more, he would marry her.

The straw was spun into gold, the king married Esme, and then everyone seemed to be happy…until a year later when a certain dwarf showed up, demanding payment. See, it seemed that the girl had promised that in return for saving her life, she would give the dwarf her firstborn child. And considering she'd just had a child (with King Atticus, of course) the dwarf was ready to collect.

The king was furious, and at first everyone thought it was because of the dwarf's request. Later, though, it was discovered that he was angry at Esme, for lying to him in the first place. What surprised me was that he hadn't tried for more gold since, but perhaps even his greed was limited. He'd been boasting that his wife was a power user, apparently, and was worried about looking foolish.

But in spite of the initial stupidity, the new queen was quite clever as well as being beautiful. She managed to trick the dwarf into agreeing to a challenge: if she could guess his name, then he would have to leave without payment. He accepted, saying that no one knew his name nor ever would, and of course that was like asking for trouble.

Through a strange series of events, the queen *did* manage to find out the dwarf's name. It was Rumpelstiltskin, and while no one ever found out what he'd wanted with the baby, he'd had to leave. Everything seemed to be alright…for a while. It seemed King Atticus's greed was unending, and he was very unhappy with his poor wife. Unknown to anyone, he contacted Rumpelstiltskin, saying that in return for what *he* wanted, he would give the dwarf the child.

Or so I heard. I didn't know what really happened, except that the queen and the child both disappeared suddenly. People were making accusations behind the king's back, saying that he was somehow responsible, but no one could confront him. And then one day along came a dragon, who ate Atticus and burned down the palace, and then disappeared to who knew where. And no one cared. They all celebrated once the dragon vanished, and then gave the kingdom to Atticus's young cousin Barrick, our present king. I didn't think much of him, but at least he wasn't trading his firstborn for wealth.

Anyway, when I saw in the diary that the dragon described was the same that had killed Atticus, I was very curious, and even more so when I saw that apparently the dragon was *sleeping* somewhere. Ugh…

Well, it could be anywhere, couldn't it? And the diary could be ancient, as old as the story itself. Or I liked to think so. As it was, I stuck the diary back under my mattress and tried to forget about it.

The prince didn't come, and I saw Nellie's determination waver a little as two days turned into five. We'd told her that Aunt Melicia had sent money for Mother to come visit, so she didn't question the packing going on, but even I started to feel a little bad for her as the days went past with no response.

That was until we heard about the shoe.

I was in the market six days after the royal ball, buying the usual range of grey and orange-skinned pumpkins. We could afford to get better now, but I didn't want anyone to know that our situation had changed. Besides, I liked them, and I wanted to talk to Nancy. There was a buzz in the market, something about a shoe, and as usual, she was the one with the news.

"What, you haven't heard about the prince and the shoe?"

"No, I haven't," I replied a little irritably. "It sounds like the beginning of a rhyme, but I've no idea what it actually means."

Nancy's leathery face creased into what was for her a smile. "Seems that at the royal ball the prince met a lady who took his fancy, but she left all of a sudden, leaving just her shoe. He's going 'round looking for whoever will fit it, and that will be the girl. Or so the rumour goes."

I stared in disbelief. "That's mad. Surely any number of girls could fit a *shoe* unless it's for a dwarf or a giant. And what, has he forgotten her face?"

"Don't be disrespectful," she replied tartly, sorting through the small grey gourds and selecting one of the nicest for me. "You don't know who might be listening."

I looked back over my shoulder, and as if he'd arranged it, standing not ten feet away was Captain Franco of the royal guard: possibly the king's bastard, definitely in love with Nellie, and most certainly not a fan of mine. He was watching me with narrowed eyes (but then perhaps his eyes always looked like that, I thought uncharitably) and when he saw I'd seen him, he simply stared for a moment longer, then turned away. Rude, but really, it could have been worse. He could have told everyone how I'd pushed him off the bridge, and then I'd *really* be in trouble.

At home I passed on the news about the prince searching for the girl who'd fit the shoe, watching carefully for Nellie's reaction. Her eyes widened, and then she looked at me in triumph, luckily not saying anything.

"How odd," Mother commented. "You would think he would remember the lady's face, if he was really that taken with her."

"Exactly what I was thinking."

But when I looked back at Nellie, she'd left the room. I wanted to talk to her in person, but there were visitors to serve, animals to feed, dishes, washing, floors to clean, food to prepare. A normal day.

It was early afternoon when the coach came. In fact I'd barely heard it rattle to a halt when Nellie came charging down the stairs, her cheeks a little flushed from the exertion. "It's them," she whispered in excitement. "Do I look pretty, Viola?"

She was wearing the usual red and white dress we wore for housework, but today it was very tidy with the waist cinched tighter than usual, and her hair was carefully curled around her face. "Of course. But who-"

"The prince, of course! With the shoe."

Oh king's crown, so it *was* her. "Shoe?"

"One of the slippers I wore to the ball," she said excitedly. "I left it behind by mistake, and it didn't disappear, because I've still got the other one. Oh!" Then suddenly she turned and ran back up the stairs, and I was still standing there stunned when Mother came in.

"New guests?" she asked, just as the heavy oak door swung open. In came first a royal guard in grey, one I didn't recognise, then a tall, slim older man who was very well dressed, although not royally so. He carried a notepad and something tucked under one arm, and was followed by a guard I *did* recognise. Captain Franco.

"Is this the place, Captain?" the man asked dismissively.

Franco nodded. "This is the one."

The man turned to Mother. "I am Felix, chief secretary for His Royal Highness Prince Royce Lyndon, and I am looking for a lady by the name of Ella. I am told she resides here."

"Ella?" Mother asked in surprise. "Do you mean Nellie?"

"Don't pretend you don't know her or that she's not here," Franco said hotly. "I know she is. She came to talk to me this morning."

So that was where she had gone. Mother was still stunned, and I was beginning to seriously regret not telling her about Nellie's outing to the ball. But then who could have known this would happen? I stepped forward, speaking softly. "I'll go get her."

I'd just made it around the corner of the stairs when I heard thundering footsteps in the other direction. Nellie was racing towards me, and we had a moment of hushed, frantic discussion in the hall before she managed to push past. Her: "I told you, didn't I? Ha!"

Me: "Oh, for- Nellie, just be *careful* with this one-"

But she'd pushed past towards the stairs, slowing down to a stately pace as she reached the last flight, and I never got a chance to say what I really thought. Surely, *surely*, a prince would never marry a commoner after only an evening's acquaintance, no matter how beautiful she was. I could only see it leading to pain for her in the end.

By the time I came down the stairs back into the main

room, Edwina and James had joined us, along with a couple of the more curious guests. I was in a perfect position to see the look of slavish devotion appear on Captain Franco's face as my stepsister appeared. Even in such plain clothing she was still lovely, and even the snobbish secretary looked surprised. "You are Ella of Novantine?"

"My family is descended from the Count," Nellie replied graciously, a dimple appearing on one cheek as she smiled. "My name is Petronella, but I go by both Ella or Nellie."

"She prefers Ella," Franco interjected, looking only a little embarrassed when the others stared at him.

Felix scanned her over quickly, nodding. "Well, you look the part. I presume you know why I'm here?"

Even as Nellie nodded, Mother spoke up. "Well, I have no idea, I must say. Nellie didn't even go to the ball..."

But her words faded out as Nellie sat down, extending one dainty foot. It was clad in a simply beautiful slipper: silvery and studded with diamonds so that it shone like a glass window covered in dewdrops. "Oh, I'm sorry," she said sweetly. "You'll want the other foot." She lowered the slipper and raised her other foot, clad in what I knew was her best plain white stocking.

Everybody stared for a long, silent moment. "Well," the secretary said in surprise. "I suppose this is just ceremony then." He pulled the other slipper out of his bag, bending down to put it easily on her small foot. It fit perfectly, of course. "That's it, then. If you will stay here, my lady, I shall get the prince."

"The *prince?*" Edwina breathed from beside me. "Nellie, what's going on?"

But it was James who spoke the honest truth. He said in his loud, piping voice, "But Nellie, you didn't even go to the ball. We didn't have any money for a dress, Mother said."

Nellie glanced away coyly, her smile telling the whole story, and once more I felt terrible guilt. I should have said something earlier. I had never been more sorry to be wrong. "Sometimes life comes through for those of us who are deserving," she said softly, looking down at her silver-clad foot.

She was the picture of demureness, but I could feel the shock and disbelief from the rest of my family. As for me, I couldn't move. I felt like I would throw up.

Mother was white-faced. "Viola, did you-"

Did I give her money? "No," I said abruptly. "I didn't. It was a Wyse woman, would you believe."

"A Wyse woman…" Mother echoed faintly.

Just then a trumpeter in bright purple and green entered the room, blowing a short fanfare. "Bow for His Royal Highness, Crown Prince Royce!"

As one, everyone in the room bowed or curtseyed low, Mother struggling with the dip with her bad legs. I moved quietly over to her side to aid her, and I could see the absolute shock on her face. "Viola," she murmured, but anything else she would have said was cut off.

The prince came in. He couldn't be anyone else: not with those lavish clothes and that expression of complete arrogance. He was perhaps only average height, slim and well built, but his chin was lifted so high I was surprised he could see where he walked. Except for his rather lovely red-gold hair, he did resemble Captain Franco: handsome, with a long face and rather narrow eyes as though he viewed the world with suspicion. As I glanced up through my eyelashes, I saw that his expression softened as it rested on Nellie.

"This is her."

Funny, he was a royal prince yet he had a very normal voice. But then a prince was just a man who had…everything…

And the man who had everything moved over to Nellie, taking her arm and lifting her gently to a standing pose, smiling down into her awestruck face. "I'm sorry I took so long to find you," he murmured. "But you left rather suddenly, didn't you?" To the rest of us he said in his normal tone, "This is Ella of Novantine, my bride-to-be, and she is to be treated as a princess." There was a pause, and he added, "That means bow."

Most of us had half begun to rise (as extended bowing and curtseying becomes painful) but we crouched down again, bewilderment written over my family's faces. "But Nellie," Mother said almost in a whisper. "I didn't know you'd even met…"

Nellie opened her mouth as if she would answer, likely something very sweet and soft-voiced that made her actions seem utterly reasonable, if I knew her, but the prince spoke over her. "Why should she explain herself to you, woman? You who have treated her like a servant all these years, the sweet, gentle girl who has deserved so much better, the true owner of this inn and a descendent of good Delmany nobility! You deserve no explanation except to go fetch her things now, and not keep us waiting in here any longer."

I felt the blood drain from my face, and I saw the same in Edwina's opposite me. Mother looked horrified. "Treated like a servant…?" she whispered.

The prince stared down at her coldly, and behind him I saw an almost identical expression on Captain Franco's face. "I have been told everything by trusted advisers," he continued. "Of course dear, sweet Ella would never complain, but there are those who would be more open. I know everything, from the early mornings to the smallest attic room to her many washings of this very floor. I know her weariness and her refusal to complain,"

And that, in my opinion, was the biggest lie:

"…and how notorious you and your *ugly* daughters are for your behaviour towards Ella." This made Edwina gasp with dismay, clearly on the edge of tears, but the prince kept on. "You are lucky I do not give you all what you deserve and send you back to Cristonia with only the clothes you wear. Now, although it is a poor recompense for years of mistreatment, you will apologise to Ella."

There was a long silence, filled by the sound of Edwina's gasping tears. Lord, that those ridiculous stories of how we treated Nellie had got to the *prince*…We even had an audience. There were half a dozen customers in the background, no doubt all gaping and taking in every word.

Nellie broke the silence. Her voice was very small, and I could see the guilt on her face. Finally, finally something had got through to her, but that didn't help us now. "We all worked, Your Highness. All of us. They don't…they don't need to apologise."

Prince Royce waved that off with a brush of his hand. "Enough, dear. I know the truth, and I would hear the apology, unless this old bat wishes to be cast out into the street along with her two horrible daughters. From you, woman, who should have loved this angel as though she was your own child. Apologise now."

I heard a whimper that could only have belonged to James, and I knew that whatever had happened, the prince didn't know about him. I opened my mouth to speak (because what else could I do?) but Mother finally spoke up. She was shaking as she crouched there, as much from her crippled legs as from anything else, and her face was bloodless and stunned.

"Petronella," she said finally, and her voice was barely above a whisper. "I...am *sorry* that I made you work. I am sorry that it has brought us to this place. I...I should have known that you were not the sort of person to work, that your hands and your character were too soft and sensitive for such things."

King's crown, I thought desperately, it was an insult, not an apology. But the others hadn't seemed to notice.

"I should have seen your...beauty, and known that you were to be treated like a precious jewel," she continued on, her eyes tearing up with what I knew had to be rage and pain. "I should not have treated you the same as my daughters, I should have treated you better, and I am sorry for that."

It was absolute hogwash voiced in an almost inaudible tone, but the prince seemed satisfied. Perhaps he was accustomed to such nonsense and so took it seriously. He lifted his chin, taking Nellie's arm as though he would lead her out. At the door he paused. "This place will be under new ownership from tomorrow since you have clearly fared so poorly with Ella's inheritance, not that she will need it any longer. I expect you to be ready to work, or else to be out. Don't bother bringing Ella's things. I doubt that they're worth having."

He left, the last I saw was Nellie's wide-eyed, horrified glance before the guards blocked our view and they were all gone. Inside the inn was complete silence, except for the sound of Edwina's crying. A moment later James started to cry too, and suddenly stiff, Mother fell sideways towards the ground. "My legs..."

I rushed over to help her up, and I knew that her stunned face echoed the same shock that we all felt. All around us there were whispers and staring faces: mostly shocked, a few gleeful, one or two kind. Ignoring the staring customers and the tears stinging my throat, I whispered urgently, "Come on, let's get out of here."

We moved into the kitchen, all of us stunned. Mother could barely speak, and James kept saying, "But the inn is mine too, isn't it? Isn't it?" Poor little thing, he'd been often overlooked because he was so much younger and didn't look at all like Nellie, but this was very much his inheritance as well.

Edwina was sobbing openly now. Just fifteen, and she had been called ugly and horrible by the crown prince. So had I, mind, but she wore her emotions much more openly. Besides, in some small way I had already seen it coming. I *should have* seen it coming.

"I hate her!" she said viciously. "I want to leave now. Mother, can we leave now, please?"

I moved over to where the half-peeled potatoes were sitting on the workbench, numbly picking one up and beginning to score it with the small paring knife. I was still in shock, unable to even formulate words. *It was my fault.* No, how about, *I knew that she'd been to the ball, I could have warned you.*

Finally I said hollowly, "I saw her the night of the ball. Dressed up like a princess. I thought…I thought that the prince would forget her, so I promised I wouldn't say anything. After all, she's just…just a commoner…"

"A Wyse woman," Mother said, eyes wide and staring at nothing. It was as if I hadn't even spoken. "My God, why would a Wyse woman visit Nellie?"

"Because she's beautiful, and the Wyse are apparently as stupid and shallow as anyone else, never mind their name," Edwina snapped. Her temper wasn't often seen, but if there was any time for it, it was now. "She didn't even stand up for us. Did you see that?"

"But I didn't tell you I knew she'd gone," I said again. It was as if I couldn't stop myself, not until they turned to me and condemned me as much as I was condemning myself.

Finally Mother turned to look at me. "Why *didn't* you say anything, Viola?"

The tears stinging at my eyes threatened to overflow. "Because I thought she was in the middle of some bloody fantasy," I whispered. "I thought it would never happen, and I promised her that if she didn't message the prince, then I wouldn't tell."

"Oh." It was a sign of the circumstances that she didn't correct my cursing.

Hesitant footsteps approached the door. It was John Tailor, one of our regular customers. Average in height, plainly dressed and just a little portly, he looked very apologetic. "I'll be just leaving now, sorry to say. Thought I'd best let you know."

Mother might have been shattered, but she still had her manners. "Thank you, John," she replied hoarsely. "I can't say if we'll see you again, but we wish you well."

He nodded, looking as if he wanted to say something else, and finally did. "I know that's not true, what the prince said," he said in a low tone. "But some of the fools out there think it is. You might find yourself with some trouble by morning. With your reputation, I mean."

I laughed aloud, cold and humourless. John clearly didn't get the joke as he left hurriedly, but I turned to the others. "As if our reputation has been sterling before now. I think Edwina's right, Mother. We should go. You were going to go next week anyway, why not go earlier?"

She nodded, staring into the mid distance. "They think I mistreat her. My own stepdaughter," she half-whispered. Then to us, "Yes. Yes, I think you're right. This isn't going to get any better. They're sending someone to run the inn, did you hear? We should go before we're run out of town."

"If we left now we could reach Strenley by sunset," Edwina said, referring to the next town towards the Cristonian border to our east. She'd stopped crying, but her eyes were very red and puffy. She looked very much her age, just halfway out of childhood. "We can stay at an inn for the night, not have to put up with any gossip."

Mother looked tempted for the barest moment, then shook her head. "No, no. I believe we are going to have to ride this out, just for the night anyway. We might have the wagon and the mule hired for the journey, but we're not packed yet. And then there are the animals to think of."

We had a half a dozen chickens and a milk cow, all of which needed tending. "Pack tonight then," I suggested hollowly. "Leave at first light. I'll stay and meet with the new steward, then come meet you at the next town."

Mother paused, then shook her head. "No. No more travelling by yourself, Viola. You're not so ugly that you put off anyone from attack, no matter what some idiots might say." Suddenly fierce, she shook her head. "Heaven above! How can people be such fools? Why can't they see that character is more than sighs and pretty smiles?"

Well, they couldn't, and it didn't seem like they ever would. Finally finished with the potatoes, I put them into the stew that had been cooking all afternoon. "I'll tell the guests that dinner will be at six, shall I?"

"I think you should go at first light," Edwina said suddenly, referring back to the previous idea. "We can buy another mule, or even a horse with Viola's gold, then come and catch you up. You'll move so slowly with the wagon…I don't like to think of you leaving late."

"I'll ask Wallace to come along with you," I suggested. "He can accompany you as far as the next town, and then we can hire some men to come along as guards. It's not a safe trip for us to go alone."

"Guards for a wagon?" Mother scoffed. "No, we'll hire a carriage in the next town. We should have one anyway, except that we've been trying to hide our increase."

James was watching Mother, then Edwina, his eyes wide and dark under his shock of pale hair. "Gold?" he echoed, proving that while small children might not understand everything, they *heard* everything.

Poor boy, I thought again. He wouldn't understand why the village would be laughing at him the next day.

In the end Mother and James left at dawn, the well-packed wagon trundling off along with Wallace and his older brother Thomas, a beefy-looking eighteen-year-old with a solid wooden cudgel. They would come with us to Strenley, then we would discuss whether they came as far as the Cristonian border. It was a day's ride away, or perhaps two on a very slow wagon, but it would be a long way for the boys to return alone.

As for Edwina and I, we had bought a horse to take us to the next town. Yes, an actual, expensive horse, not even a mule or a donkey. We told the seller that the money had come from our aunt, and decided that once we were done with it, we'd either resell it or else use it for our carriage – I didn't care, as long as we got out of here.

Word of the prince's visit had spread quickly. Wallace's young sister Maria had come to help with the chores, and we'd paid her in advance. She'd also got a friend of hers to help, but the two of them spent more time gossiping and staring than working. Edwina was out the back saddling the old horse we'd bought as we were to leave imminently, and I was at Mother's old writing desk, making a list of everything that we did each day. The washing could wait, of course, but the animals had to be fed, and I couldn't bear to think that any of them would be missed by mistake.

I tried not to think of Nellie, but what had happened the day before played over and over in my mind. Could I have done anything differently? Could I have stopped that humiliation for my family? Perhaps not. It seemed like that scene was the culmination of years and years of gossip, half-truths and poor reputation, all coming together in one awful moment.

Nellie was so *selfish* that sometimes I felt like I hated her enough to hit her in the face with a brick and ruin her pretty looks, but those intense feelings were quickly followed by shame and numbness. No, that horrid scene with the prince had been a result of many years of people choosing to believe the worst, passing around those stories about us. Nellie herself could have been a better person had she not been so spoiled, but there was no point musing on that now, was there? She was going to be a princess, and we...we were going to leave.

The sound of hooves and wheels approaching caught my attention from a distance, and I glanced out of the small front window to see what looked like a covered wagon, dark and rough, and three unfamiliar guards at the front. It took a moment to realise what it was, since I'd never seen one outside my infrequent trips to the capital. It was a prison wagon, a transport to move criminals around – and it was pulling up towards our inn.

Standing abruptly, I turned and ran for the back door, slamming it open. Edwina was standing there with the horse, stroking its slightly worn-looking neck. It was an old beast, grey with a darker, white-streaked mane, but placid and obedient. "What is it, Vee? Are you finally ready to go?"

In that moment I made a decision. "There's trouble," I said tightly. "I need you not to argue now, 'Wina. I need you to leave right away for Strenley. Take the back streets – don't let them see you at the front of the inn, and if I don't arrive by tonight, then all of you should go on to Cristonia."

"What? No, I'm not going without you," Edwina began to protest, but I shook my head, urgency filling my tone. She *had* to listen.

"We've got about thirty seconds. I'm going to go stall them-"
"Who?"

"The guards!" I cried out desperately, moving forward to help her onto the horse. "I'll stall them enough for you to go, and you know I can afford to get another horse if all this turns out to be nothing. But you have to go!"

Through several open doors I heard heavy footsteps enter the front room, and I hissed at her. "You do this right now, or I'll never forgive you!" Her eyes were wide and scared, and I lifted my chin. "I love you, and I'll come find you at Melicia's if need be."

Copying something I'd seen a nobleman do once with his horse, I slapped the horse on its grey rump. It jolted, startled, and then began to move forward. Edwina called after me, but I turned back to the door, quickly moving through it and closing it tightly.

"Innkeeper!" The bellow came from the other room, and I called back, "Coming!" even as I carefully locked the back door, then slipped the key into a barrel of flour. It wouldn't slow them down much if they were determined, but I prayed it would be enough for Edwina to get out of town.

My hope that all of this was just my own paranoid imagination died when I came into the main room. Four, not three guards stood there, including none other than Captain Franco, who had seemingly turned into my chief tormentor. He stood at the back, though; he wasn't the highest-ranking man here. Another, older man with a brown moustache stepped forward. "You are the innkeeper's daughter?"

"My half-brother is to inherit, yes," I replied, hedging a

little. "I am Viola."

The man flicked his gaze over me, seeming completely unimpressed. "Where is your family?"

I swallowed, keeping my face even. "They all left last night for Cristonia. I'm to follow them today after I've spoken to the new steward."

I saw the moment when he believed me. "Cristonia. Hmm."

"They'll have made it almost to the border by now," Captain Franco said quietly. "There's no point following, not now."

In that moment I blessed him, just a little. If the guards wanted to follow and retrieve my family, then they *would* catch them up. They would only have just reached Strenley now, and didn't know enough to keep moving.

"What do you want?" I asked bluntly. "The prince made his opinion more than clear yesterday. What little reputation we had is now gone."

Behind the moustached guard, the captain's eyes slid away from mine, and the moustached man spoke. "The king wishes to speak to you in person."

I felt the blood run out of my face, and I was *so*, so glad that Edwina had gone. *Please, God, may she make it away in time. Please…* And please may my stupid, loyal family not wait for me! "Very well," I said, my voice shaking just a little. "Might I go get changed?"

I was wearing travelling clothes, rough and sturdy, and even I knew that they weren't at all flattering. If I was going to see the king (and I knew it couldn't be good) then I would like to at least not look like a vagrant.

He nodded. "Go on, then."

Ten minutes later I was back downstairs, my travelling gear having been exchanged for my Sunday best, not that that was saying much. The guard scanned my worn blue gown in distaste. "That's it?"

I lifted my chin. "Were you expecting cloth of gold?"

He scoffed. "Come on, then."

Getting into that closed wagon was worse than I'd imagined. We'd amassed quite a crowd: a good thirty or forty people who watched me come out of the inn and into that vehicle. They were jeering, most of them, and I felt so humiliated that I almost couldn't move. It was as bad as that dream where I'd been in my underwear in front of such a crowd, except I knew all these people…and they all hated me.

Someone gave me a not ungentle shove and I finally managed to climb into the dark, slightly dank-smelling interior, and a few moments later the captain climbed in after me. The doors closed, and then we were moving: rattling along and I could still hear the sounds outside. *Yer getting what ye deserve –* that sounded like Derrick, perhaps, but could have been anyone who was stupid enough to believe gossip. I also heard Nancy, stringently arguing with someone that I didn't deserve this, but soon that too faded into the distance.

5
The Ugly Stepsister

After a moment the captain spoke. In the dim light of the covered wagon his face looked even harsher; too harsh for someone so young. "You won't be harmed."

I just stared at him.

"Ella wouldn't want you to be hurt," he continued. "She was very determined about that."

"Wouldn't want me hurt?" I echoed after a short, stunned pause. "King's crown, I would rather be beaten than have to go through that humiliation again, and you say I haven't been hurt?"

"You are simply getting what you deserve," he said icily. "Do not try to get sympathy from me."

Better to get sympathy from a snake than this one. But I sat there in the almost dark for a few minutes before things finally began to make sense. "It was you, wasn't it? The trusted advisor who told the prince about what we supposedly did to Nellie?"

"Someone had to tell the truth. Ella wouldn't."

"*Nellie*," I cried out in sudden fury, "wouldn't know the truth if it hit her in the face. She's a selfish little flirt who was spoiled by her father and by her looks, and it's idiots like you who take everything she says at face value that keep her that way!"

"Do not speak of her like that!" the captain thundered back. "She's worth ten of you! It's only out of kindness and respect for Ella that I didn't tell of how you pushed me off that bridge, but I still could, you know. Then, with the way the prince has been feeling, you'll likely end up hanged! And only Ella would weep

72

for you."

Hanged. Oh, God. I slumped back against the rough wood of the wagon sides, suddenly breathless. No, they wouldn't *hang* me, surely? Whether it was true or not, making someone work too hard wasn't a *hanging* offence.

"They're not going to hang you," Captain Franco said abruptly. "I am certain of that. I was just…I was trying to scare you."

Well, it had worked. "You're the prince's brother, aren't you?"

Pause. "Where did you hear that?"

I turned to stare at him, fear and hurt making me spiteful. "Nellie told me after I led you to the inn the other week. She said you were handsome," – and here I saw his face light up – "and useful, because you were the king's bastard, and that was why you were a captain already even though you look barely twenty."

He glared. "*Ella* wouldn't talk like that, and if you have only lies to tell, you may be silent."

Here was what had happened over and over. I used to try to counter the rumours that would spread about my family, but no one ever listened, and it simply made me furious. But now I was scared, so scared, and so angry, and I felt reckless. All my fear and anger targeted this one 'useful' young man.

"Here's some truth, Captain. I might be plain and have a ruined reputation, but your life will never really be any better than mine. Everyone knows you're a bastard, the result of a liaison between a king and a chambermaid, and no one of any worth will ever give you the time of day. Not truly. My stepsister would never look twice at you except for your usefulness, and you'll always be on the outside looking in, wanting what your brother has, and never getting it." I smiled icily. "So we're two of a kind."

I saw his face pale and then harden. "You're as ugly on the inside as you are on the outside."

Now that hurt, but I just lifted my chin and turned away. Not long after that, the captain got out and travelled at the front of the wagon, and I was left to my own thoughts. They weren't happy ones, and I don't want to dwell on them now except to say that I was scared, angry and felt dreadfully betrayed by Nellie, my village, and God. After all, he was in charge, wasn't he? I had tried my best to do good, to treat others how I would like to be treated, but he hadn't seen fit to give me looks or charm, and my life seemed to have gone straight off a cliff, to so speak. Unlike Franco the Bastard seemed to think, people did *not* get what they deserved. Careless, cruel people flourished, and the meek were trodden on.

I could see through the bars at the back of the wagon as we finally entered Ostraime, and it was quite a different view of the city than last time. People would turn to stare as the wagon went past, although luckily they couldn't see me, and then I heard the sounds as we entered the palace. The *palace*. I caught a glimpse of those high, solid stone walls, seen for the first time from inside the gates. I was hungry, thirsty and needed the privy, but I didn't dare to ask for anything.

The wagon stopped in a grim grey courtyard and the captain got out. I stayed there in the back for some time, shivering, but perhaps it was from fear rather than the cold. I had never been so afraid in my life. Strangely, the captain's promise that I wouldn't be harmed was like a lifeline to me now. They wouldn't kill me, and they wouldn't beat me…probably. Unfortunately, that left a lot of other, unpleasant options.

I was taken to a small room in the lower regions of the palace. It wasn't a dungeon, reminding me more of an unused washroom. It *did* have a chamber pot – thank God for small mercies. Several hours later someone came for me. It was yet another unfamiliar guard…and Captain Franco. Perhaps he had asked to come, especially after the last, nasty thing I'd said to him.

I was led along a series of halls, then up several staircases until the decorations began to change. The walls became smoother and painted, then covered with what looked like wallpaper, something I'd only ever heard about. Carpets appeared underfoot on the polished stone floors, and we began passing beautifully dressed courtiers as well as servants in immaculate grey and white. Some of them turned to watch us pass, and my fear that they knew my identity was proven correct.

"That's her," I heard a richly clad woman whisper to her

equally well dressed male companion. "That's the ugly stepsister, isn't it?"

I felt my cheeks heat even as my jaw ached with the urge to defend myself, but then we'd passed them. But there were more people here in these wider halls with their lovely lead-light windows and high, carved stone archways, and they were all watching us. All of them.

I bit my tongue and ignored them, but inside I was burning with shame and humiliation. "Where are you taking me?" I asked finally, and my voice came out roughly rather than cool and confident as I'd intended.

"You'll see soon enough," the second guard said. Franco didn't answer.

But then we came to a new set of doors. These ones were as high as the painted ceiling, and were guarded by two men in royal grey. They paused when we approached. "This her?" one of them asked.

"Obviously," Franco said shortly. "Let us in."

But instead of opening those two enormous doors, one of the guards moved over to the richly decorated wall, and turned a previously unseen handle. A much smaller door opened, and after the briefest pause I was led through.

On the other side was a room about the size of the Bluebell's entry parlour, except presumably much prettier. I hardly had time to take it in, only registering the dozen occupants, because the hum of chatter silenced even as we entered.

"Your Majesty, Your Highnesses," Franco said in what might have been for him a respectful tone. He bowed, and startled, I slipped into a deep curtsey. "Miss Viola Cadence."

Now the chatter started up again, but quietly. Even though I wasn't chained, I felt frozen with fear, and it was all I could do to keep my crouched posture as a man stepped forward out of the crowd. He looked to be in late middle-age, was solidly built with a neat grey beard, and had familiar, narrowed dark eyes. Crown? Yes. Gorgeous red and purple tunic, trimmed with sable? Yes. Looked a bit like Franco? Yes, definitely. It had to be King Barrick.

He was also staring at me as though I was some sort of previously unknown insect that had appeared on his breakfast plate. Next to him stood the golden prince, expression much the same, and another.

Nellie.

She wore a beautiful gown of deep red trimmed with golden thread, but the beauty of her garb couldn't hide the clear expression of misery on her face. She met my eyes with hers, beseeching, as if she wanted to say something. But she didn't. Not a single word.

A wash of anger and sorrow came over me, and I looked down at the carpeted floor, each strand clearly finer than anything I'd ever walked on. In my peripheral vision I could see the slightly curled boots of the king and prince, and the skirts of Nellie's beautiful gown, and I heard the sound of people leaving until it was just those three, and the guards and I. Everything sounded like it was coming from a great distance, like it didn't really touch me, and I just waited.

"So here we have the stepsister," the king said. He sounded very much like his son: terribly normal to have such power. Not smooth-voiced or beautiful at all, but he held my life in his hands. "Hmm."

A moment later I felt his hand under my chin, lifting my face towards him. I couldn't meet his eyes as he studied me – why was he studying me!? – and I found myself catching Nellie's eye again. Nope, that was worse. I glanced away.

Finally he let me go, and I felt him move back. "Based on the rumours, I thought you'd resemble a mountain troll," he said dispassionately. "And here we have just a plain, ordinary girl. You may leave."

My eyebrows shot up. Leave, already? But he hadn't been speaking to me. I heard the two guards move away on either side of me, and Nellie moved towards the door, hesitance clear in her posture. The prince was slower to move. "But Father-"

"Leave," King Barrick snapped. "I'll speak with her alone. I *am* the king, am I not?"

King's crown, king's crown, king's crown. *Why?*

"Yes, Father." Prince Royce sounded as reluctant as Nellie looked, but he too left.

Then finally the door closed, and I knew it was just the two of us. I swallowed, finding my mouth was exceptionally dry, and my heart was beating double-time, so loudly it seemed to echo in my ears.

"Hmm," the king said again. "You're the one who found the Dragi treasure, aren't you?"

My head shot up, and I actually met his eyes for a moment, my shock overcoming my fear. "Yes…yes, Your Majesty." How had he known about that? Why would he even care?

"I understand you found them in a closet."

Nellie must have told Franco, who would have told the prince, and so forth. But why would he even bring it up? Surely I hadn't been brought here just to discuss the stupid cursed treasure… "Er…yes, Your Majesty."

"And did you return *everything* you found?"

"Of course," I said in surprise. "They were cursed. I wouldn't keep them." I'd hoped for a reward, but of course *that* hadn't happened. Instead my life had turned to horse pellets seemingly overnight.

"Hmm." There was a long, awkward pause where I debated if he knew how to say anything else, and tried desperately to figure out why I was here – I was in trouble, right? – but then he finally said, "Well, you've certainly got a reputation. And because Petronella is marrying my son, and because half the kingdom despises you,"

They did?!

"…something must be done. You'll stay here at the palace, working as you made Petronella work, until you're told otherwise. And if your mother or sister are foolish enough to return to Delmany, then they shall do the same. Consider it mercy."

Working in the palace? I tried to take in what he was saying, but I could see him moving past me in his red and purple, until he'd reached the outer door. A moment later it opened, and I heard him say, "Take her to the kitchens."

I finally stood up, my knees aching from holding a curtsey for so long. Captain Franco was standing in the doorway, and his expression was completely unimpressed. The second guard seemed to have disappeared. "Come on. It won't do you any good to delay."

"Just getting the feeling back in my legs," I told him, my

tone a little snappish. I was still stunned, unbelieving of what had just happened. The king had asked to see me privately – and then had asked a few odd questions, and had condemned me to working in the palace just like I'd made Petronella work. Seriously?

Like I'd made *her* work. Ha. The wording was so…so *stupid,* that I found myself snorting out a half-laugh.

"What's so funny?"

I glanced across at Franco, whose dark eyebrows were drawn low over his eyes. "Funny?"

"You just laughed. You've been brought to the palace in shame as a consequence of your behaviour, and you spoke privately with the king, and now you're laughing!"

He sounded genuinely irritated with me, and in spite of the circumstances – or perhaps because of them – I laughed again. "Because this all makes no sense. Making me work at the palace as some kind of punishment? I've worked in the worst parts of the inn ever since I was a child. This is a step *up.*" Except for the humiliation angle. I could have done without that.

Franco scoffed. "Save your lies for someone who's stupid enough to believe them."

"No one ever believes them," I said, hearing the slight sadness in my tone. Then I realised what I'd said. "And they're not lies! I'd say ask Nellie, but she'd somehow end up implying that I eat grapes all day while she cleans the privy."

He scoffed again, more loudly this time, and I went silent. I wouldn't waste my breath.

If the exit from the inn to the wagon had been terrible, then this walk down to the lowest parts of the palace was the complete opposite. I had a few curious glances, but nothing out of the ordinary. If I hadn't been escorted by a clearly grumpy captain, then perhaps I would have been ignored completely – and the inattention was most welcome.

Finally we reached an area where the walls were plain stone, clean but unimpressive, and the people quickly moving about were all wearing that grey and white. Servants, all of them, and so many! I counted dozens, carrying trays or buckets or even a couple pushing wheeled trolleys. I studied those curiously – they'd be helpful at the inn, if ever we got it back – but then we were in the kitchens. They were ten times the size of the Bluebell's, filled with noise and food smells, some good, some bad.

We gained a few more curious glances, but then Franco brought me to a halt in front of a thin, middle-aged woman who appeared to be loudly directing some of the others. She stopped mid-shout. "Yes, Captain?"

"Salina, this is Viola Cadence. She'll be working here indefinitely, at the king's express order."

Salina's fine eyebrows shot up. "Anything in particular?"

"Whatever needs to be done, but don't let her slack off," Franco replied ominously. "She needs a close eye kept on her."

Now that caught people's attention, and feeling those eyes on me, I said quickly, "No, I don't. I'm a hard worker. *He* just listens to gossip."

"And a liar too," Franco snapped. "Good luck, Salina. You're going to need it."

He finally left, and then it was just me with my red-hot cheeks, the curious-looking Salina, and another dozen servants all gathered around. She turned on them with her hands on her hips. "Well? Get back to work!"

"Thanks," I said gratefully.

"Don't thank me," she retorted. "What did you do to upset someone so much?"

"Please don't ask." *No really, please don't.* She'd find out soon enough anyway, if things were as bad as King Barrick had implied.

Half the kingdom despises you.

Ouch.

She raised an eyebrow. "Very well. Viola, was it? Pretty name. You'll be peeling potatoes."

I peeled potatoes for hours, until my hands were red and my fingers ached. Then I peeled carrots, then parsnips, then some fat, round root vegetable that I didn't recognise, but which Salina told me was called a 'swede'. As the day passed, the whispers around me increased.

The ugly stepsister.

Really? What's she doing here?

She's not that *ugly.*

Damn. That meant the gossip had reached the kitchens. I felt my face heat with embarrassment and anger, but I just put my head down and peeled, peeled, peeled. Finally, when the natural sunlight through the small windows had faded and the large kitchens were now lit by torchlight, Salina finally tapped me on the shoulder. "Have you eaten?"

I kept peeling carrots. "Not since breakfast."

"Hmm. Well, you can't afford to lose any weight. Come eat, then you can finish up and go to bed."

'Bed' ended up being a small pallet in a very small attic room at the far reaches of the palace. Ironically it wasn't any smaller than what I was used to already, even though it was shared with a cranky old maid called Imogen. (By which I mean she was elderly and worked as a maid. I make no judgements on her romantic history.) I slumped onto the lumpy mattress, feeling exhausted and depressed by the day's events. That made it easy to ignore her complaints that I was making too much noise.

The next few days were better and worse at the same time. I wore a plain grey smock over a white dress, the usual costume of the palace servants, and worked as hard as expected. I didn't mind that at all; it was the behaviour of those around me that was harder to bear. It felt like I was being watched the whole time, judged by curious and suspicious eyes of people who'd heard the rumours.

It was like Fortrente all over again, with a new batch of locals and again no chance to defend myself. No one asked for my version of events, so I just kept my head down and seethed... and plotted my escape. Yes, this situation was ridiculous. No, I didn't understand why I was here, since Nellie sure wouldn't expect it. So why should anyone care? But I consoled myself that my family had probably escaped, and it didn't seem like King Barrick cared enough to chase them.

Hopefully he wouldn't care enough to chase *me* once I took the chance to leave. I'd decided to wait a few more days, maybe a week, until I felt those suspicious eyes on me relax a little. By that time Mother, Edwina and James should have made it over the border into Cristonia, even if they'd waited for me at Strenley longer than agreed. It wasn't as if I could send them a warning letter. I could only hope and pray that they'd be alright.

A few days later I'd been sent up to the upper servants' halls to scrub the floors, a job I didn't mind because it meant I was mostly left alone. So when I heard light footsteps I ignored them at first. They paused just behind me, and I felt myself tense, resolving not to turn around.

"Viola?" The voice was tentative, but unmistakeably Nellie's.

Now I did freeze, but I still didn't turn around. I didn't want to look at her.

"Viola, it's me, Nellie."

Slowly I turned to face her. She stood there in a lovely light blue dress, rather like a much nicer version of my old Sunday dress – no doubt in the palace rag bin by now. Her hair was pinned around her face in elaborate curls, and she wore a neat pearl necklace. Except for her 'kicked puppy' expression, she looked lovely. Like a princess...or a princess-to-be, since the wedding was next weekend.

Various feelings skipped through my head – anger, hurt, weariness. "What do you want?"

"I want to talk with you," she pleaded. "You have no idea how these last days have been, Viola. I had to sneak away to see you, you know, because I'm surrounded by ladies-in-waiting all the time. I'm so miserable, and I can't stop thinking about what happened..."

I dropped my cloth into the bucket, staring at her in disbelief. "King's crown, Nellie! Look at you here, dressed like a princess, and then look at me. I've been *humiliated*. They took away the inn, and Mother and Edwina and even poor James have had to flee the country, and it was half his! If anyone even sees you here talking to me I know I'll be the one blamed, and you're complaining about your situation? I can't believe you have the *gall*."

Nellie's perfect pink lips quivered, and her blue eyes grew glossy with tears. "But I didn't mean for any of this to happen! I was angry at you but I never wanted it to be like that! They wouldn't listen to me when I tried to say what really happened!"

Suddenly boilingly angry, I glared at her. "They *did* listen to you, Nellie, and that's why this all happened. They listened to exactly what you said without realising that most of what you say are blatant exaggerations because you're so bloody led by your emotions, and they haven't seen past your angelic face to realise that. This has happened because of *you*. Can't you see that?"

"It wasn't like that," she pleaded. "I'm so, so sorry about what happened, but can't you see that I didn't mean for any of it to end up like this?"

"If you're really sorry, then help get me out of here," I retorted, not caring that now she was truly crying. "I won't be able to do it myself." Or at least not without a lot of bribery that would risk my golden secret being let out.

"I can't," Nellie wept. "King Barrick wants you to stay, and I can't go against him. No one can."

"Why does he want me to stay?" I asked, my voice suddenly hoarse. "Is he so offended on your behalf?"

"I don't know, I don't know, and Royce is *so* upset with you. He won't listen to me…"

"You're the only one they *would* listen to, Nellie! You need to ask again!"

She shook her head, still weeping. "I can't. I just *can't*."

Now I wanted to cry too, but I didn't. Instead I stood, picking up my bucket and wash cloth, and looked down at the top of her golden head. "Then you're of no use to me," I said crisply, turning to walk back down towards the kitchens. I'd finish the hall later.

And that was when I saw Captain Franco. He was dressed in plain clothes almost like a low-grade courtier, and he'd clearly witnessed the entire conversation which had left darling Ella in tears, and the horrible stepsister Viola stalking off back to her lair. Oh, well. Surely at this point nothing could make him think any less of me, and I was determined not to care.

Later that day I stood at the back door of the kitchen, emptying the piles of parsnip peelings to the pigs. There was a clear path between some buildings towards the palace wall should I have wanted to escape. But assuming I would even have tried it, I knew that Salina was watching me from behind with an eagle eye. No, when I did try to leave, I would do it at night. Wait 'til Imogen the Old Maid was asleep, then creep either out of the window or down the hall…

I was lost in my fantasy of how it would go when I saw the men. They were walking together at the end of the building, clearly deep in conversation, and I watched them idly as I shook the scraps from the bottom of the bucket. I didn't recognise either, but one of them was quite tall and solid, wearing green garb with gold trim that reminded me of the guards at the Dragi temple. As if he could feel my gaze, he suddenly turned to stare at me, and even across the distance I felt uncomfortable.

Turning back to my pails, I picked up the second one and tried to shake it out, but the peelings were stuck. When I finally looked up again the green-clad man was standing right in front of me, staring at me. Or staring at my chest, rather: or perhaps my abdomen, and he was leaning forward, sniffing…

King's crown, did he know about the scales?

I jerked back just as Salina stepped outside, staring coldly at the man. "Come in, Viola," she said sharply. "You've taken long enough."

I quickly shook out the rest of the peels, then picked up the pails and followed her in gratefully, feeling the man's eyes on my back the whole time. We didn't speak until after the door had been closed.

"You must never be by yourself with a man," she told me firmly. "Not with anyone, and especially not with Dragi like him. With your reputation, some men will think that you no longer need to be respected, and you must take care to see that doesn't happen. You can still sink lower, you know."

So he was Dragi, then. Her words were meant kindly, I knew, but she had no idea what she was talking about. Had she thought the man was staring at my unimpressive chest? I knew better.

As if they read my thoughts, one of the other scullery maids piped up. "A Dragi, was it? One of my friends went out once with one of their guards, and she said that he was very strange. Kept sniffing her, said he could smell if she'd been wearing gold, can you believe it. A very odd bunch."

Smelling *gold?* I thought about how this morning I'd found not eight but eleven diamond-shaped scales on my belly, becoming more and more tightly packed like real scales. They were beginning to itch even under my clothes now, showing that they were almost ready to come off again. As if I didn't have enough problems already, without needing to hide almost a dozen very valuable gold pieces that apparently some people could *smell*.

In the end I did the old cliché and hid them in my mattress, pulling them off in the middle of the night while Imogen snored and then shoving them into a piece of cloth and then into the middle of the straw I lay on. I knew it was a risk, but then wasn't anything? I couldn't keep them on me.

The following day I was scrubbing yet another floor in a different servants' passage when someone walked past, dropping a square piece of paper as they went. It fluttered to the ground right by where I knelt. I glanced up to see Franco, once more in plain clothes, but he barely looked at me before turning the corner. I picked up the paper curiously. It was the size of my palm, and scrawled on one side were the words, *meet us in the third laundry room in five minutes.*

Seriously? It would be empty as almost no one used it, but the subterfuge... And what did he mean by 'us'? Nellie, surely. I debated my response for a few minutes before finally standing, picking up my pail and moving down the hall.

They were already waiting in the room, both of them with solemn faces that made me pause. "What's so important that you come all the way down here with company, Nellie?" I looked pointedly at the captain, and he just looked back, his expression so very serious. "Oh, no... Is someone dead?"

"Nobody's dead," Nellie said. Her face was unusually pale and her large eyes round with what looked like fear. "But we found out something new."

There was a long pause and she didn't say anything else.

"Are you going to tell me what it is?" I asked finally.

"Haven't you wondered why the king wanted you here?" Franco asked abruptly. "Why he didn't have your family followed and brought here too if he truly felt so badly about what happened to Ella?"

"Yes, of course I wondered, but *Ella* said she didn't know why the king wants me here." I'd also been grateful that he hadn't pursued the others. I'd be the scapegoat...as long as I could get away later.

"He doesn't want them, Viola," Nellie told me urgently. "He wants you. This is all about *you*."

For the first time ever, Nellie was admitting something wasn't, in fact, about her. I just stared at them for a few moments, then turned to Franco in disgust. "You told him about the bridge, didn't you?"

"The king doesn't care about anything you did to me," he retorted impatiently. "It's about the Dragi figurines you returned, and no, I *didn't* mention that you took in the reward, even though I can see that you're thinking that. I'm pretty sure it was Jonley who told him. But that's why King Barrick had you brought here. It's nothing to do with Ella, not really. That was just an excuse."

For a few moments I couldn't speak. It seemed the Dragi 'blessing' had brought me nothing but trouble. "He did ask me about that," I admitted finally. "I figured you'd told him, or maybe Nellie told the prince earlier. But what difference does it make, and why would the king even care about those stupid figurines?!"

Franco opened his mouth, but Nellie spoke over him. "*I* didn't tell King Barrick about the treasure. But I told you he wouldn't listen, Viola. After you shouted at me, I went back to him, I kept saying that you were fine, that you should be left with the inn. I even told him that it was James's inheritance too, and he wasn't interested! Even Royce said he didn't care if you got it back, and that if I was happy then he was happy, but King Barrick insisted that you had to be punished for what you'd done, even though I kept saying not to." Her fair eyebrows shot up, and her tone was urgent. "It didn't make sense!"

"Then she heard them talking," Franco added. "The king and one of the Dragi. They said that if you knew their secrets, then you had to be dealt with."

"But that made no sense!" Nellie insisted again. "What could you possibly know, Viola? They didn't even give you a reward!"

She didn't know about the gold. She didn't know anything, and king's crown, I was so relieved that she didn't. I stared blankly at the wall, thinking of all the ways this could go terribly wrong. The scales were a part of me, for a brief time, anyway. I couldn't hide them, not if anyone really looked.

"They said something about a book," she continued. "But there was no book, was there? I saw the bag."

The diary! I suddenly realised that when King Barrick had asked me if there was anything else, I'd said no. I'd replied honestly at the time because I'd plain forgotten about the diary, but had that been what they'd wanted the whole time? Some silly book full of demented scribbles?

The diary had been left off to the side of the dark cupboard, and was even now sitting in Edwina's saddlebag – hopefully all the way in Cristonia by now. In that moment I desperately wished I had tossed the bloody thing in the privy as I'd first been inclined. I wished I'd never found the things. "I wish I hadn't listened to you," I said hoarsely to Nellie. "I wish we'd just given the figurines to the guards like we were supposed to."

Franco looked like he would object to that accusation, but Nellie seemed unbothered. "Well, you didn't have to listen, did you? And I wanted to take them, not you, but Hazel wouldn't let me. But this book-"

"Was it your idea?" Franco interrupted.

"What?" Nellie asked irritably.

"Taking the figurines to the Dragi temple yourselves instead of giving them to me. Did you think of that, Ella?"

For a moment she looked nonplussed, then shrugged. "What does it matter? It would have made no difference to you."

"It makes a difference," he said softly, looking away.

"The book," Nellie said again, insistently this time. "Do you know what they're talking about?"

In that moment I could choose whether to lie flat out, or whether to tell a truth that could only cause more trouble. What was in that diary that was so important? Besides the fact that the dragon that killed Atticus was probably still alive... King's crown, I couldn't think on that now, so instead I hedged. "If I did, would it make things worse or better?"

"It wouldn't change anything," Franco said woodenly. "They already think you know too much, although about what I have no idea. If you're going to leave, you need to do it now."

"And how am I supposed to leave?" I cried. "I'm watched all the time, even when I go to the bathroom. And what about you two? What happens if people find out you helped me?"

Nellie tossed her perfectly coiffed golden head. "I'm going to be a princess, Viola. Next week. And everybody loves me. I'll be fine. I'll just say you tricked me into helping you, and they'll believe me."

"What about you, Captain?" I said sardonically. "Will your *connections* keep you safe?"

Franco had been watching Nellie like he'd never seen her before, and when finally he turned to me he laughed without humour. "You mean my vague resemblance to the king?"

"I mean your friendship with the prince," I elaborated. "You're one of those trusted advisors who told him all about how my family treated Nellie, correct?"

"Ella," he corrected almost absentmindedly. "And no, not really. It was village gossip, mostly some man called Derrick, but there were plenty of others who happily joined in. And if you think I've got a relationship with Prince Royce, then you're seriously mistaken. As you said, I'm just a bastard from an old liaison with a chambermaid, and while the queen was alive, to make it worse. They're *embarrassed* that I exist."

It was an incredibly honest speech, and one that seemed at odds with the person he'd taken care to show himself to be. I wasn't sure of how to feel about it, except perhaps to dislike him just a little less. "So what will happen to you, if you help me out?"

He shrugged. "I've no idea. Perhaps they won't find out."

Or he might really get in trouble. But he didn't say any more, and considering that I still blamed him in good part for my circumstances, I didn't argue. "When can I go?"

"Now."

"What?" I cried. "Now? I'm not ready…"

Nellie bent down and picked up a cloth bag that I'd not noticed earlier. "Workman's clothes," she said. "We'll sneak you out like that."

"We mustn't wait any longer," Franco added seriously. "I'm surprised they haven't confronted you already over what they think you know."

"But…" *But I've got gold dragon's scales hidden in my pillow,* I wanted to say. That wouldn't matter soon enough, would it?

They'd only have to look at me in a couple of days to know the truth. Perhaps grumpy Imogen would find herself wealthy in her old age. "Very well," I said finally. "What do I need to do?"

Two minutes to get changed into the rough, loose workman's clothes, another ten to wait for the halls to clear. Five more for Nellie to distract the servants, pretending she had got lost in the winding halls of the palace, and another three for Franco to sneak me past, pretending I was a real worker that he was directing to the back of the palace.

Less than half an hour after that meeting in the laundry room I was standing outside the palace gates, my loose cap pulled down over my hair and shadowing my face. To anyone watching Franco would have seemed to be giving me directions, and so he was.

"Go, take the first barge you see that's heading down river. It'll cost you about two bronzes to go as far as Novas, or perhaps you can go all the way south, if that seems easier. But I'd recommend you get off and use the roads instead. They'll be expecting you to use the river from here since it's so direct to Cristonia, and you'll be watched more carefully."

Two bronzes from the small bag they'd given me. Apparently Nellie had sold one of her fancy pieces of jewellery to one of the maids. I thought once more of the eleven dragon scales in my pillow, but nodded. And then, because I had been taught good manners; "Thank you."

"I'm not doing it for you, I'm doing it for Ella."

As if I didn't already know that. He looked as though he was about to say something more, but something over my shoulder caught his attention. He cursed softly. "Someone's watching. Act casual, and follow me."

But I could already feel the tension knotting my body, and I didn't turn as I heard footsteps approaching from behind. Instead I followed Franco as he walked briskly away from the palace, heading into the crowds.

"Captain," someone called.

Franco acted like he didn't hear, and it was noisy enough that it might have been believable. But the footsteps behind us picked up, and when a heavy hand fell on my shoulder, I jumped.

"Captain," the voice came again. "Who's this?"

I turned, trying to shrug the hand off me as I imagined a real young man might do, while still trying to hide my newly dirty face. Under the shelter of my cloak I could see my accoster was a guard, a youngish man with plain brown hair and features, and a very suspicious expression. I didn't know who he was, but he seemed to know me.

"Just a boy who needed directions to the Dragi temple," Franco replied casually. "He barely speaks Delman and had ended up in the palace by mistake."

I could feel the unknown guard's eyes on my face, studying me, and I stared at my feet as guilelessly as I could manage. It was what I called the 'clueless child' expression, and I'd seen it performed many times by Nellie to get her out of sticky situations. It usually worked.

"He's not causing any trouble?"

"Not at all," Franco replied. "It's my day off, so I was taking the chance for some fresh air."

The guard harrumphed, but finally moved his hand off my shoulder. I turned immediately, heading toward where Franco had told me to go. I'd walked only a couple of blocks, trying to scan the streets for directions to the barges, when Franco caught up. "We'll have to go faster," he said in a low voice. "Humphrey will certainly tell someone. He doesn't have the seniority to question me, but I'm sure he recognised you."

Curse my 'distinctive' features. I swallowed, nodding even as I picked up the pace, my long legs eating up the distance. "But what about you?"

We came out into a busy space where there was a gap between buildings. It was just enough to see that it was a river port: dozens of barges and boats lined up along either bank. I'd never seen the Silver River like this. Up in Fortrente it was much, much quieter, definitely prettier, and smelled better too.

He still hadn't answered my question, instead leading me to the nearest barge that was even now being unhooked from its mooring. He stepped neatly across the small gap of water and I followed him, ignoring the complaints of the owner. "This is a coal barge, you fools! You want a ride, go to one of the others."

"You want two silvers upfront and again at the end of the journey, you take us along now," Franco countered quickly.

The man was short and solid, covered with the stain of his cargo, but he wasn't stupid. He pocketed the coins offered. "In some trouble, are we?"

"Not at all," Franco said casually. "Except that my cousin here got on the wrong side of a jealous husband. Foolish, since he's barely old enough to even look at a woman twice, but we have to leave straight away."

The bargeman scoffed, glancing over me. "How old are you, kid?"

"He doesn't speak Delman," Franco interrupted. "And he's sixteen. Tall for his age."

"Then he's old enough to do more than look," the man countered, but didn't seem interested any further. He had his money, that would be enough to buy his silence. Instead he focused on pushing the barge out from the shore with a long pole, moving it into the current near the centre of the wide river. It slowly began to pick up speed, but it still couldn't compare with the pace of the smaller sail or rowboats.

Franco moved to sit in the shelter of the small cabin, partially hidden behind the huge pile of coal. A moment later I moved to sit near him. After all, it was the safest place to avoid being seen from the riverbank. I couldn't stand the guy, but I couldn't forget what had just happened. It seemed like by helping me, Franco had just burned his own bridges.

"Thank you," I said finally.

"I did it-"

"For Ella, I know," I interrupted with barely a sigh. "But it still remains that I've been helped, and at a real cost to you. What will happen when that other guard tells what he saw?"

Franco shrugged, his strong features serious as he pulled his knees in towards his chest. It was a surprisingly childlike posture for someone like him, and told a lot about his state of mind. "I don't know. I suppose I'll find out."

I hesitated. "They won't...kill you?" After all, going directly against the king's orders might count as treason, and that was worthy of capital punishment.

Now he smiled, a crooked sneer that nonetheless had some

humour in it. "I don't think so, Viola. I *am* still the king's son. I'll just explain that I was doing a favour for the sweet princess-to-be, and thought that the king wouldn't care, that your humiliation was the true punishment. I'll still be in trouble, of course, but I doubt it will be fatal."

It was the first time he'd openly called me by my real name, and it felt strange coming from those previously hateful lips. Feeling a little disconcerted, I tucked my own knees into my chest and wrapped my arms around them, echoing his posture. "Do you think they'll come down the river after us?"

"Depends how badly they want to find you." Now Franco glanced at me sideways, those narrow brown eyes made even narrower by suspicion. "Ella's gone. If there's anything you need to tell me, it should be now. Did the Dragi give you anything?"

I couldn't tell him about the scales. Nobody could know about those. "As I said before, no. The priestess said something like, 'I should have what I deserve', but she didn't give me anything. When I asked about a reward she basically chased me off."

"Have what you deserve?"

Suddenly I realised how that must sound to him. He didn't know about the gold, only about my humiliation. "I suppose you think I deserved what I got from the prince and king," I said in a clipped tone, still not looking at him. "I don't suppose there's any point saying that things aren't always as they appear."

But this time Franco was slow to answer. "I suppose they're not," he replied casually. "But I'd rather not talk about it anymore." Then a moment later, belying his words, he mused, "Even the best of people have flaws, don't they? Nobody's perfect."

I turned to look at him curiously. He was staring out past the pile of coal to the smooth, slowly passing water, but there was a definite frown on that face. Was he talking about Nellie? I decided not to test it. "And even the worst people can have virtues," I countered lightly. When he turned to look at me I glanced away.

As if I hadn't spoken, he continued on. "I suppose that a virtue could become a flaw, if it was allowed to go too far. For example a very sweet, gentle person could get walked all over if they didn't learn to look after themselves properly."

Damn, he was talking about Nellie. I didn't point out that only the king himself could walk over Nellie, or the fact that Mother had always claimed that *I* was naturally sweet and gentle, but was forced to be stronger because of my circumstances. I could just imagine the laughter if I ventured that opinion, so I just let Franco sit there and work out some way in his own mind to keep Nellie as his heroine. What he thought about me at this point shouldn't matter, and I resolved to act like it didn't, even though there was a twinge of pain somewhere in my chest at the thought of his disdain.

About an hour later we'd made it quite a way down the river, although not nearly as far as we would have liked. The water was deep here, with the city extending down one bank and forest on the other. Each bank was artificially built up with large stones and the occasional brick, and the river was absolutely packed with other barges and watercraft. It seemed everyone was in a hurry to go somewhere, and no one was interested in letting us through. The coal barge was forced right up close to the steep, forested bank as the driver waited for space to open up.

Moving silently, Franco stood and beckoned for me to follow. He lightly stepped across the gap onto the nearby forested riverbank, and after a brief pause held out his hand to help me across.

A good thing I took it. As I stepped off the barge it moved suddenly, and I jolted and almost tripped right into that still, dark water. Franco moved fast, gripping my hand tightly and pulling me hard. We both fell, him backwards and me halfway across him, hitting one knee hard on the turf, and the other finding a softer landing spot.

"Ouch," I muttered, quickly shoving myself to my feet. I could feel my face flushing with embarrassment.

"Ouch?" he echoed, his own face twisted in pain as he crouched forward. "Have you sharpened your knees or something?"

I'd landed right in his sensitive areas. "Sorry." And now I was flushing even more. I was skinny, but even so, who had soft kneecaps? We weren't rag dolls.

"I'm alright," he lied, struggling to his feet. "Let's get out of sight before the driver realises we're gone. I don't trust him not to give us up the first chance he can."

I quietly moved further into the forest. It was the sort with large coniferous trees that scattered the ground with sharp pine needles and little else in the way of undergrowth, and it went on for miles without any roads or landmarks that I could see. We moved inland further still, just enough to be out of sight of the river, but not enough to lose its guiding sound. It would be easy to become lost in a place like this.

We walked in silence, Franco with an ever-present scowl, not that I could blame him. Here he was, risking everything for someone he couldn't even stand. That was what it came down to. He did it for Nellie, but I was the one who benefited, never mind that my situation was mostly Nellie's fault in the first place. And what would he get out of it? A sore crotch and a possible sedition charge, unless he was *very* lucky.

As for me, I'd lost the only home I remembered, and here I had to thank someone who hated me for saving my life. I was thinking about that and how awful it would be if Mother and the others got caught en route, or if I never made it back to them, and that was when something strange and very terrible happened.

6

Tears

It started slowly at first, so slowly I didn't even realise it was happening. And then it was full-on. I kept walking, but my eyes were burning, my nose and throat clogged, and it was a good thing I didn't count on my beauty to get me anywhere, because right now I was *not* beautiful.

Franco had been walking almost silently just ahead of me, but even he couldn't overlook the noise after a while. He turned and stared at me in what looked like disbelief. "Are you *crying*?"

"Of course I'm not crying," I tried to say loftily. "My eyes are running. It's the pine needles, they always do this to me." But the last few words dissolved into a sort of snuffle, and I couldn't seem to stop myself. How *humiliating*, to cry in front of my enemy like this. I'd held together before because tears never fixed anything, but now it seemed like this all had become too much for me. I turned away from him, hunching my shoulders in an effort to hide my face. "Just keep walking, alright?"

Only it came out more like 'Juff kip wahkm, arright?'

I wasn't looking at him, but I could feel his eyes on me. "Crying's not going to help anything, you know. It won't get you sympathy from me, and it won't change the situation."

Beastly man. If it wasn't for the slight panicked tone I could hear, I'd be very angry with him. But instead I ignored Franco, picking up my pace and trying to outrun him. But he kept up easily, still talking in an agitated tone. "We got away, didn't we? You don't need to cry. You'll get to Cristonia safely, I promise."

He might have said something else, but I wasn't really paying attention at that point. We just walked and I sniffled and

94

cried until finally I stopped – not really sure how long that took – and then my eyes were swollen and I needed to blow my nose, and Franco had gone mercifully quiet, walking just behind me along the riverside. I'd moved closer towards the sound without meaning to, and now I could see that it was different. I swore.

Franco came up behind him, and I knew the moment where he saw the problem, because he swore too. Somehow as we'd moved away from the water, we had gone upwards on a slight slope as the water had gone downhill. The river was now substantially lower than the place where we stood. It was almost a gorge, deep and rushing white, and the slow, safe river that the barge had travelled on was nowhere to be seen.

"We've followed one of the branches instead of the main river," he said resignedly. "We'll be headed in the wrong direction completely, into Brelfne if we're not careful. We need to cross over."

I looked down over the gorge's edge towards the frothing water below, unimpressed. "Do we need to go back, do you think?"

"How should I know? I've never been here before."

I gave him a look. "Fine. I'll keep going this way downhill, and you do whatever you want." He could jump off the cliff for all I cared.

I stomped away further down along the edge of the gorge, and after walking in silence for a while – which gave me plenty of time to calm down and feel embarrassed – I found a path that wound down to the water's edge. Here it was narrow and the water rushed white down between large rocks, but I could make the distance. Franco had followed me, although I'd half expected that he might give up and let me travel alone. I had to admit that having a man around (not just a fake one like me) was a good thing, especially one who had a weapon *and* knew how to use it.

The river had indeed forked off into two branches. Now we were walking along the middle section, which might have been a kind of island covered in trees, then eventually came to yet another body of water. This was flatter and quieter, wide enough to carry a good-sized boat or even a barge. Just ahead I could see a watercraft disappearing off into the distance.

Franco finally spoke. "See that plume of smoke up ahead?"

I nodded.

"That's got to be the town of Novas, unless we've missed it entirely. I think we should go around it, though. Try to avoid any settlements until we reach Cristonia."

I turned to look at him. "But that could take days! We don't have any food, and I doubt we're allowed to hunt in these woods even if there was something to go after." Usually the woods either belonged to the king or else other wealthy nobles, and hunting without permission – AKA poaching – could get you shot on the spot, or else hung. It seemed that rich people didn't like to share, even a hare that might feed a starving family.

He was quiet for a moment. "How are you with fishing?"

As it turned out, I wasn't very good at fishing, but I certainly didn't mind eating fish. We caught two small silvery cod and a long, skinny thing that wriggled madly on the end of the makeshift line and then managed to escape with a splash.

"Eels don't taste that good anyway," Franco told me. "At least, I've never liked them."

So *that* was an eel. At Fortrente we were close enough to the river that we got plenty of fish, but nobody ate eels. I'd never even seen them for sale. The fish we *did* eat were lightly flavoured and full of bones, but perhaps my hunger made them tastier than they would have been otherwise. We cooked them over a small fire further into the woods, under the shelter of a partial cliff.

By this time the sun was growing low in the sky, and so when Franco suggested that we settle for the night, I didn't argue. It reminded me a lot of that other meeting that seemed like an eternity earlier, the one where I'd so carefully hidden my face after that long walk in the dark back from Ostraime – not that it had done me any good. Luckily this time I wasn't trying to hide my identity from him, I couldn't hear any wolves, and there was no Jonley the Horrible to attempt blackmail. I'd be thankful for small mercies.

We settled in silence around the gently flickering fire, and the quiet dragged out long enough that I thought Franco wouldn't speak again. I didn't want to talk – well, I did, but not here and now. I *did* want sympathy, and like he'd said, I wouldn't get it from him.

I was just drifting off to sleep when he finally spoke. "Why did you cry?"

"What?" Tiredness made me less than polite.

"Before," he persisted. "Why were you crying?"

It seemed a genuine question, but it was a damned stupid one too. "Because I was upset," fool, "and if you can't guess why then you're not as bright as I thought you were. But what is it to you?"

There was a pause. "I'm not a monster," Franco replied quietly, and I couldn't tell his feelings from his tone. "I just didn't think you were the sort to cry, that's all."

"Because I'm tall and plain and too tough to have feelings? I've just lost everything, *Captain*. And while I don't normally cry because it doesn't fix anything, I suppose I ran out of stoicism." He didn't respond to that, and I felt suddenly angry. "And if you say that I deserved what I got, I swear I'm going to punch you in the nose, whether you've helped me or not. You played a large part in getting me to this place, you and Nellie, and I haven't forgotten that."

"I can't figure out whether you mean for good or bad."

Again, not as bright as I thought he might have been. But he was just a boy in a man's job, and one who had an uncertain status and a poorly chosen infatuation at that. I huffed out a sigh, turning over so that I faced the fire. The burning sticks were glowing red, breaking into the sections that said that the fire would need fuelling shortly, and even when I closed my eyes I still saw them.

I slept fitfully. Probably that was just a mix of the hard ground and the hard circumstances, but when I woke early the next morning, the light of day barely touching the sky, the embers were still red in our small fire. Franco must have put more wood on during the night, because I hadn't thought to, nor even to gather more wood.

I found a private spot for morning rituals (you don't need to know the details, except that it involved grass and a scratchy leaf, ouch) and when I came back he was just wakening. His dark hair was standing up on the side of his head, and the bleary expression made him look rather less threatening. It reminded me of James first thing in the morning, and it almost made me smile. *Almost.*

When Franco saw me he nodded. "You got up to find more wood? Thanks."

"What?" I looked down at my empty arms. Why would he think that?

"The fire's still going."

I looked at him curiously. "I thought you did that. I haven't touched it all night."

He frowned. "Well, I put wood on just after you fell asleep, and haven't touched it since." He shrugged. "Must be funny weather, or hard wood. It doesn't matter."

True. So we started walking again, reaching the town of Novas within an hour. It was the place which Nellie had claimed her father was Count of (as it used to be called Novantine) and it had a decent-sized market. Franco and I did a little clothing swap, with me giving him my jacket and hat in place of his distinctive guard's uniform, and he went in just long enough to get food for our journey. He came back with a small bag of provisions and a serious expression.

"Were there guards already?" I asked in dismay.

"There are always guards in Novas," he replied, "because of all the boats and roads leading through. No, it was the others that bothered me, and I couldn't get more than a couple of loaves."

"The others?"

His lips tightened. "The Dragi."

I went cold. I'd hoped that the incident with the Dragi outside the palace would be forgotten, or that it wouldn't mean anything. "Are you sure they're after me?" I whispered.

"Do you want to take the risk?" he countered.

I was silent for a moment, then shook my head. "I suppose we should go."

We began to walk briskly along the riverside, once more going further into the woods to be less visible. Franco passed me half a loaf of seed-topped bread, and we ate as we walked. All I could think about was the king's hostile expression, and the Dragi, and the gold scales on my chest that even now were itching to come off.

"Do you think-" he began, then stopped.

I turned to look at him. "What?"

"Ella. Nellie." Then it all came out in a rush. "What she said that she heard the king say about you – how much can we trust that to be the exact truth?"

I was so stunned by what he was implying that I couldn't speak for a while. I just kept walking.

"Viola?" he said again. "Well? Because if it's not true, then I've just left my post for no reason at all."

There were so many things that I could have said then. What I most wanted to know was why he had suddenly lost faith in Nellie – why he had suddenly considered that she *might not* be telling the whole truth. But I settled on an unimportant point. "Since when do you call her Nellie?"

Franco looked disconcerted. "You call her Nellie. Why shouldn't I?"

Because you're tragically in love with her and will say whatever she tells you to say. But instead I shrugged, keeping up my pace. "Doesn't matter, I suppose. I'm just wondering why you would ask that question. You've never doubted her before."

"I'm not doubting her." He paused, gathering himself. "It just occurred to me that the way she told it...might have been affected by her panic over the situation." There was another silence, and out the corner of my eye I saw he was looking even more uncomfortable. "She's a beautiful girl. So sweet natured and just...lovely, but that doesn't mean that she's unbiased in every situation."

Oh, I was enjoying hearing this. Amongst all the usual blabbered compliments was a true admission that Nellie wasn't perfect. It was a good start. In the interests of sounding unbiased myself, I replied lightly, "No, what she says is usually strongly coloured by how she feels at the time. She doesn't lie – or at least I think she doesn't – but it's her tone, the things she says or doesn't say, that tells a whole new story that is often not at all true." I could see him frowning again, so I quickly added, "But in the case of what she said about overhearing the king, she wouldn't have slanted it. Not with something so important, not when she was so scared."

"Thank God for that."

There was a silence filled by our footsteps and the occasional munching of bread, and then I gave in and asked. "What exactly was it that made you wonder?"

Franco was quiet a moment before he answered. "Actually, it was your hands."

I looked down at the items in question. Even dressed as a boy they seemed to fit well enough; long and skinny and work roughened, and almost white from the cold and my pale skin.

"When I helped you off the barge, I realised that someone who lazed around all day wouldn't have such rough hands. They'd be soft. Ella's hands…"

Were much softer than mine, although not lady-soft. We'd avoided giving her the hardest jobs like scrubbing the floors because she complained so much and wouldn't do the work properly. Edwina did most of the cooking, a hard enough job in itself, so I ended up with scullery duty. Not a recipe for beautiful skin, although in this case it seemed to work to my advantage. Even though mine were no worse than most servants, I still blushed at the thought he had noticed my hands' roughness so quickly.

"I shall have to buy more expensive moisturisers," I said lightly. "My current ones are clearly letting me down, unlike Nellie, whose purity and gentleness are enough to keep her hands baby-soft no matter how much floor scrubbing she does."

Franco scowled. "I'm not saying that I believe you over her, alright? I just think that you've had a bad deal. You're clearly not lazy."

"Gee, *thanks*, Captain. Is there any other body part you'd like to come to conclusions about?" A moment later I realised how that sounded, and in the awkward silence I added, "Or perhaps not."

Embarrassment was a good conversation stopper, and I skipped ahead, moving through the bushes alongside the river. Here the trees were growing close to the waterside, the terrain became steeper and the sound of rushing water grew louder until I reached a good-sized waterfall that poured off a cliff right by the river. Gorgeous, but how were we supposed to get past it? It had completely blocked our route.

I stood there staring at it a while before a cough caught my attention. Franco knelt before me in a small rowboat, a single large oar held capably in his hands. "A lift?"

Well, I wouldn't say no.

"I didn't mean to knock you out of the boat," I said once more, putting as much sincerity into my tone as I could manage. "I didn't realise how much it would rock once I climbed in."

"You live right by a river," Franco said irritably, squeezing water out of his jacket and socks. Our funds had dropped quite a lot, since he'd left half the remaining money in the boat dock for whoever owned this rowboat. But he was still annoyed with me. "I can't believe you haven't ever been in a boat."

"Well, I haven't. And I'm sorry that you're all wet."

"I'd believe that a lot more if you hadn't laughed so hard when I fell into the river."

Even the memory of how he'd looked so surprised as he toppled backwards made me smile once more, and I had to turn away to avoid irritating him further.

"See! You're still laughing!"

"Am not."

"Yes, you are, Viola," he retorted, but now he seemed a bit less angry about it. "Did you think it was this funny when you knocked me off the bridge back near Fortrente?"

"Actually I was horrified," I replied seriously. "I thought I was going to end up in the dungeons, or at least the stocks."

Franco looked thoughtful. "Probably the stocks for assaulting a royal guard, or perhaps a flogging, depending on how annoyed the guard was. You're lucky it was me."

"I'm lucky that you knew who I was to Nellie, and that you cared what she thought," I countered. I felt cold at the thought of what could have happened. Not all guards were as principled as this one, even though he was annoying and prejudiced. Just look at Jonley for example.

At the reminder of his one true love, Franco slowed a little, his expression serious. "I suppose you're right about that." There was another pause as he seemed to search for words. "Did she really say I was useful?"

I felt guilt shoot through me. He'd obviously recalled the nasty things I'd said last week in the wagon, and no matter what my circumstances had been, I'd been raised better than that. "I'm sorry I said that. I was angry, and it was the worst insult I could think of at the time."

"But was it true?" he persisted. "Did Ella say those exact words?"

I debated between honesty and kindness, then settled on both. "She did," I said carefully, "but not in the way I made it sound. She's not malicious, but she can be careless. And she did say you were handsome."

"I suppose she did," he agreed, but his face had closed over again.

We walked in silence towards the next town, having left the rowboat far behind. This town was the fork between two different routes to Cristonia: the river, and the winding route through forested hills. It would take far longer to walk that way, and almost nobody travelled it unless they had to since the river was so much more direct. I'd decided from the time Franco had mentioned it that I would take the forest route, and I'd do so alone. It was time for him to go back.

The town drew closer, its walls high enough to block our view of all but the tallest pointed roofs inside. The town gates were armed with a rather relaxed-looking guard who barely looked at us as he waved us inside. "Sloppy," Franco muttered after we'd moved out of hearing range. "If I was in my uniform…"

"You'd give him a scolding?" I asked. "Even though he's a good ten years older than you?"

"He deserves it," he countered. "He didn't even check us for weapons or ask what our purpose was. Yes, we don't want to be noticed, but it's no good for the town's safety."

I shrugged. "I'm just surprised that you've got the authority to do it. You're young to be a captain."

"Had the authority," Franco murmured. "And the king couldn't have me as a mere guard, could he?"

As we wound our way down cobbled streets towards the town centre, which was marked by a tall flagpole with the red and yellow flag of Delmany, he stopped and pulled out the coin purse that he and Nellie had originally given me. But now there was something else in it. "There's not enough left in here to get you the full distance to Cristonia, so here's one of Ella's hair combs. She gave it to me to give you."

The comb looked gold-plated, with tiny ruby flowers

arranged down its length. Pretty, valuable, and easily sold. Much more easily sold than my gold scales, but still I hesitated to take it. "What are you going to do? You might need this more than I do, because I'm going to my family."

"Ella wants you to have it," he told me firmly. "So you must. I can look after myself."

I took the comb and put it in my pocket, watching him seriously. "You're going back?"

"Of course."

Oh. Even though I'd known it was coming – had planned for it – suddenly I felt bereft. Even Captain Annoying was better than no company at all. "Of course," I echoed.

"You should darken your hair and eyebrows," he said suddenly. "It'll change your appearance enough that you won't be so easily recognised."

I reached my hand to touch my hair, ash blonde in the sun now that Franco wore my hat. Yes, it was distinctive, but I'd never imagined doing something about it. A sudden image of me with nut-brown hair popped into my mind, or else with golden hair like Nellie. I immediately brushed it off. Badly-dyed hair looked dreadful, and was trashy as well. Decent women didn't dye their hair, at least not in this part of the world. But still… "I might do that."

Franco nodded. "Good."

We walked into the market, pausing to buy enough lunch for both of us. I added a couple of loaves to my small bag for later, and just as I was putting the change back in my purse, Franco came up to me. He nodded towards a caravan set off to the side of the market, a large crowd of people standing nearby. "That's a family group headed to the south of Cristonia. I explained that my young cousin has to travel alone, and they've agreed to take you with them as far as you need to go."

So he was going to leave now. I knew it was the right time for it, but it still felt like a sharp change. We'd only travelled together overnight, but I'd subconsciously begun to rely on him. On Captain Difficult. How awkward. "I know you did this for Nell…Ella," I said once more, "But I know what you've sacrificed, and I know that I've benefited. So I'll say it one more time. Thank you."

He looked like he wanted to dismiss my gratitude, but finally nodded. "You're welcome. Now shall I introduce you to this group?"

I met the leaders of the group, an older widower named Gus, along with his sister Tildy. They were travelling with Gus's children and assorted other family members to go back to their home in the south of Cristonia. Upon hearing their situation, I realised how similar it was to my own. They'd come over two years earlier to make a new life, as back then the economy in Delmany had been better than at home, but had found that they couldn't really fit in.

Gus told me in broken Delman about what had happened, and he would switch occasionally back to the quicker, more melodic tones of the South Cristonian dialect to talk with Tildy. The two languages weren't so different, but I found myself picking up words here and there. It was a language I'd barely spoken or even heard for a good decade, Mother having stopped speaking it once we moved. She'd said she was trying to help us fit in better, but hearing it again now made me feel wistful and perhaps even lonely. I missed my family, and I just felt out of place.

I never got to say goodbye to Franco. I'd got talking to Gus (who could talk, and talk) and then when I finally managed to turn and look for Franco, he was gone. One of the others said to me in broken Delman that he'd had to go, and seemed surprised that I hadn't noticed he was missing. But then they didn't know the truth, did they? I resolved not to be stupid enough to miss him, and threw myself into the company of the people around me.

The trip home took a solid week, but felt quicker. After three days Tildy came over to talk to me, her lined, narrow face set in a curious expression. "You're a girl, aren't you?" she asked without much preamble. "Oh, don't worry, most of us have worked it out already. It's not even safe for a lad to travel alone, let alone a girl like yourself, even if you are tall."

I looked down at myself self-consciously. I didn't look very female, not in this loose, ugly shirt and trousers, but then I supposed I wasn't exactly muscular, either. "How could you tell?"

"Besides your face? Your habits, dear. Lads will just stand at the side of the road and do their business. No lad needs to take as much time as you do."

But I was caught by the first thing she'd said. "My face? What do you mean?"

Tildy gave me an odd look. "I mean you look like a girl. What else could it mean?"

I didn't have a response to that, but her words stuck with me. *I look like a girl.* It seemed odd, but I'd never put it into words before. I'd never felt pretty – king's crown, I'd never felt *feminine.* But Tildy thought I looked like a girl. Huh.

But for the rest of the week, I found myself being just a little more careful with my hair.

We finally came out of the forested mountain path to rejoin the Silver River as it moved into Cristonia. It was narrower and faster here as the land sloped, and the few boats that travelled along it were designed to handle the slight gradient.

There was no sign of my family in the first town we reached, although the innkeeper recalled seeing them. "There's something here for you, I think." He handed me a small parcel. It was a letter, wrapped in oilskin and dated a week earlier.

V, we had to move on. You can find us at Aunt M's house where expected. Lots of love, H, E and J. (P.S: E reached us without any trouble. You take care of yourself!)

I was disappointed that I hadn't had the chance to see them, but was also pleased that they'd travelled on to a safer location, and that they'd also kept names and locations secret. "Has anyone else seen this?" I asked.

He shook his head. "Just you."

"Thank you."

We reached the Cristonian capital just a few days later, and I left the group, giving them the rest of the money from the sale of Nellie's hair comb in thanks. I had a good-sized bag of scales by this point, and after a little hesitation I tossed a couple into the bag with the small change, telling them not to open it until they reached their home. I knew there was a risk of the Dragi tracing me by the sale of the gold scales if they were dedicated enough to look, but I figured a couple of them lost in circulation in the Cristonian south wouldn't matter too much.

Besides, the safety and companionship these people had given me felt like a Godsend after the hatred I'd been exposed to back home...or where my home had been, anyway. I'd made a point of speaking in Cristonian as much as possible, and the old sounds and ways of speaking had begun to flow back. They would laugh when I got a word wrong or mangled a sentence, but it was never nasty laughter. They'd been kind, and I would always remember them for that.

It was strange coming back to Cristonia after so much time away. The architecture looked different than I remembered: the buildings of this small country being so unlike those back in Delmany. There, they tended to be made of the local grey stone, cut into blocks that formed solid, slightly heavy-looking buildings. But here the local stone was limestone, and the palace that rose in the centre of this unwalled city was tall and graceful, its towers topped with white spires.

Ironically this was the hardest part of the journey. I hadn't been given an address for Melicia, and all I remembered was that she was married to a fabric merchant and lived in a tall, narrow townhouse trimmed with red paint. There had been matching red flowers in boxes by the slatted windows, but that had been over ten years ago.

"Sorry love, haven't heard of a Melicia," the first person I asked told me. They seemed amused by both my accent and the sparse details I could give them, although they weren't unfriendly. "But there are at least four fabric merchants I can think of off the top of my head. At least two of them have been here ten years. I can give you the addresses if you like."

"Yes, please."

I wandered the pale, winding streets for what felt like hours. But it must have been clear I was lost, because enough people gave me directions that finally I reached Melicia's townhouse. It was the second address I'd tried, not quite the same as in my memories, but still vaguely familiar. The building still had its red trim, but the window boxes had been removed to be replaced with patterned wood. More expensive, and also more permanent. Auntie's husband was clearly doing well.

When I knocked the door was answered by a tall young boy

with white-blond hair. I did a double-take – could James have grown so much?! – then realised this must be a cousin. He stared at me for a moment until I took off my hat and asked in clumsy Cristonian if his aunt or cousins were there. The boy stared some more, then turned and ran back into the house, shouting "Mama!" and leaving me alone at the door.

Thanks a lot, Cuz.

But I wasn't alone for long. Next thing Edwina came into sight, and then James and finally Mother, moving slowly with her crutch tucked under one arm, and followed closely by a gaggle of fair-haired people who were all talking at once. There were tears on all sides, especially on mine, and then I was being hugged and pulled inside, and scolded me for not contacting them earlier.

"How could I have contacted you?" I asked reasonably. "I was stuck at the palace, then I was in the middle of nowhere."

"Well, *I* thought you were going to be trapped in the dungeons forever," Edwina told me, sounding almost angry. Then she burst into tears and hugged me again, showing that anger and fear really could look similar at times.

"Just the scullery," I said lightly. "It wasn't so bad." And it hadn't been, although it could have been much, much worse.

"The scullery!" one of the cousins shouted. (I didn't know her name; as we were yet to be introduced.) "With dishes and laundry and cooking? You were practically a slave!"

Edwina, Mother and I all paused in unison, turning to stare in surprise at whoever-she-was. I thought again that Aunt Melicia must *really* be doing well, if the children didn't have to help with basic chores.

"She'd get on well with Nellie," Edwina muttered, agreeing with my unspoken thoughts.

But that comment set off a flurry of unhappy chatter, and it took a while for us all to calm down enough to really talk about what had happened. They told how Edwina had caught up with the others in Strenley as planned, and although they'd been worried for me, they'd taken my warning. They'd travelled over the border as quickly as they could manage, the whole time in fear of being pursued by soldiers in Delman grey. But no pursuit had come. So they'd stopped in the first Cristonian town they reached, and had waited for a week before finally leaving that message with the local innkeeper.

"What about you, Viola?" Mother asked. "What happened between the soldiers taking you away, and you ending up in the palace kitchens?"

"And then getting here?" one of the boy cousins piped in. "You're wearing trousers!"

"It's becoming a habit," I muttered. But then I quickly ran through the events of the past two weeks, from King Barrick's 'punishment' to Franco and Nellie helping me escape, to the barge trip and the long walk with Gus and Tildy. I skimmed over the part about the Dragi possibly-probably trying to catch me/kill me, because it might not be true (please, please let it not be true!) and besides, my family would get rather upset about it.

As it was, they were upset enough with what had happened. "I never liked that King Barrick," Aunt Melicia said decisively in quick Cristonian. "I saw him once many years ago when he visited our palace. The other girls thought him handsome, but he didn't have a single smile for anyone!"

He hadn't changed much over the years, then.

"We were lucky that the soldiers hadn't been sent out for the rest of us,' James said in a rare moment of adult understanding.

"You're right," Mother told him firmly. "Now Viola, let's get you to a nice warm bath, and some proper clothes."

She took me by the arm, leading me away from the crowd to a side room that was hung with laundry, and where an empty bathtub sat, half-obscured by tall privacy screens. A laundry/bathroom, clearly.

My sister and brother followed, and once we were alone, Mother's voice dropped to a whisper. "Was that really the full truth, love? Was King Barrick just trying to punish us for making Nellie clean windows and so forth, or was there more to it?"

My lips tightened. Of course she and Edwina at least would realise I hadn't told the whole story. I ducked my head, sucking in a fortifying breath through my nostrils. "Nellie overheard the king talking to the Dragi. They *were* after me, not you lot, and it wasn't anything to do with Nellie either. It was about the figurines, and he's involved with it somehow."

There was a long silence where Edwina's eyes widened, and

James just looked puzzled.

"Oh, you poor love," Mother said finally, putting her arm around me. "You've been the scapegoat, haven't you? Do they know about the…" Her tone dropped again to the barest whisper, and she glanced down at my front. "…The *other* things?"

The scales, she must mean. I shook my head mutely. "I never said anything to Nellie or the captain. And I never will."

"Ah."

"What other things?" James asked. Before we'd fled Delmany we'd told him about getting some gold from the Dragi, but not exactly how we'd got it. It had seemed safer that way.

"Personal girl things," Mother said firmly. "Now come with me, we'll get some hot water for your sister's bath."

They left, then it was just Edwina and I, so I spilled out the rest of the story even as I undressed. After all that time travelling, I needed that bath. "It's about the diary," I said in a low voice. "I found it in the bag along with the Dragi treasure, but it seemed like nonsense; nothing important. But the king was asking about it, and apparently so are the Dragi. Do we still have it?"

Edwina's face paled, and she nodded. "It's in the bottom of your bags. Mother said not to unpack them, not 'til you came. I haven't really looked at it."

Now my sister was scrupulously honest, so the fact that she'd said that at all caught my attention. "Haven't *really* looked at it? So you have looked at it a little?"

She flushed, shrugging a shoulder and handing me a quilted robe. She was looking good, better than I'd seen her in a while. The dress had to be new, no doubt from my aunt's shop. "Just a glance, but I didn't see much. I was too busy."

I nodded absently, scratching at my thigh absently even as I took the robe. I could feel a thickness in the skin that indicated another scale was on the way, and the thought made me cringe. Ugh. I didn't want to look at myself when I was like this, and I could see Edwina trying to not stare at the same time. I turned away from her, slipping into the long-sleeved robe and wrapping it as tightly as I could, but she'd already seen me.

"There are more scales. Viola, they go all the way to your neck!"

"And halfway to my knees," I agreed sadly. "Forty-three of

them now."

Her jaw dropped. *"Forty-three?* What on earth are you doing with all that gold?"

I shrugged glumly, moving to sit on the small stool next to the tub. It'd take a while before the water was heated over the kitchen fire enough to be used. I'd filled plenty of bathtubs in my time, but I wasn't used to anyone doing the same for me. Maybe I'd make an exception for today. "Collecting it, mostly," I replied. "Maybe I'll have to start burying it."

"Like hell you will!" she exclaimed, and I turned to stare at her in shock. I'd never heard my gentle sister use such language. "Viola, we're going to *use* that money, and we're going to take back everything that was stolen from us! Except here in Cristonia," she amended a little more gently.

"How will we explain the source of the money?"

"Who cares? We'll tell them it was a blessing from the Wyse people. Close enough, right?"

I scoffed. "The Wyse only bless good and kind people. It's some kind of mandate from God, so I've heard, and no one would believe that of us. Not at all."

"But nobody knows who we are here," Edwina persisted. "We can go by our old names, or by our Cristonian ones. I've already told the family to call me Elaina." The last was said almost defiantly, and I raised my eyebrows.

"Then I can start calling you Ellie, perhaps?" I said a little sarcastically.

"NOT Ellie." She paused. "Alright, you can still call me 'Wina, but just you. Everyone else has to say Elaina. And James is Jacobo, and you're…"

"You are *not* calling me Weola. I never liked that name." But her other words had resonated with me, and I smiled. A small smile, but still a real one. "A fresh start, is it?"

Edwina/Elaina smiled back, lifting her chin. "Yes, it is."

And it was a fresh start. James was rather quiet at first, but began to open up. Within two weeks we were beginning to recover from what had happened in Delmany, and starting to make plans for a new business. Or at least I was. I couldn't imagine life without some sort of occupation, even though the very mention of a new inn made Edwina blanch and Mother shake her head firmly.

"Forget about it, Viola. We're not going to slave away like we did before, and for what? To make a little extra on the side? We have all the money we need right here."

"But money doesn't last," I pointed out. "We have to use it sooner or later, and the kind we have now…that *definitely* won't last." My curse would be broken sometime. It *had* to be, and our supply of gold would vanish with it. "We have to plan for the future."

Mother huffed out a breath, and I could tell she knew I was right. "We'll sort that out later," she said finally. "For now, let's just rest."

I couldn't argue with that. I had years' worth of resting to do, if I judged by how much I slept in those first few weeks, and I could see the positive effects on my family too. The shadows under their eyes were fading, and even Mother's face looked less lined. I got to know my cousins a little, and began living what felt like an incredibly luxurious life. They had a whole three servants, and that meant very little hard work was required.

Bliss, but so very, very strange.

But there was one thing that wasn't so easy. The gold scales kept coming fast and thick, and every time I found a new scale I would weep on the inside at my slowly worsening deformity. Within a month of arriving in Cristonia I had to wear high-necked dresses to hide the scales that now scattered all the way up to my collarbone. They were even beginning to spot my thighs all the way down to my knees, and also my upper arms.

I didn't know any swear words foul enough to reflect how I was feeling. 'King's crown' just wouldn't cut it.

I started reading the diary again. I'd told Edwina that I would get rid of it, but when I held it over the fire, planning to throw it in, I found I couldn't take that last step. Not without finishing it, not without learning what it was truly about. So instead I hid it under the mattress in our shared bedroom, sneaking it out only when my sister wasn't watching. I'd get rid of it the moment I'd finished it, I told myself.

Really.

But now I was halfway through and no closer to finding out exactly what the diary was about. Someone recording their dreams, perhaps? It was almost poetic in places; descriptions of this apparently wonderful, beautiful, terrifying dragon the size of a house; and the diary entries seemed to be bleeding into my disturbed sleep. Every night I dreamed about fire and dragons and chaos, and the scales spread almost daily.

One night I dreamed about being in the quiet back streets of Fortrente. It was twilight, and a huge red and orange dragon pursued me through the village. It was wingless and had an enormous mouth full of razor-sharp teeth, stretched wide enough to swallow me whole. I fled, barely keeping out of its reach, with my dream-self's heart pounding in terror. Behind me I heard it roar, then a huge cloud of brilliant fire enveloped me…

I was woken by a panicked Edwina patting madly at my blankets.

"What? What happened?" I mumbled, my tongue still heavy with sleep.

"You were thrashing around, and knocked over your candle. It set your sheets on fire!" she told me angrily. "You're supposed to put it out before bed, Vee! You could have been burned to death!"

King's crown. Suddenly I was wide awake, and I stared at the candle in question, now looking harmless where it sat on my tangled sheets. There was no sign of the smoke curl that would usually issue from a recently snuffed wick, but then my bedclothes were still smouldering. "I thought I did put it out," I murmured in dismay. "I'll be more careful in future."

"Humph," my sister sniffed, but left it at that.

The next morning we were sitting at the breakfast table bright and early. James – who unsurprisingly hadn't wanted to be called 'Jacobo' – was arguing animatedly about horses with his almost-twin cousin, Sam, and Mother and Melicia were discussing when our purchase of the house just down the street was going to be complete.

The current owners had no objection to being paid in gold, and in fact seemed happier that way. It took an extra fifty scales on top of the asking price in order to forget what currency they'd been paid in – which just about cleaned out our stores, but there was plenty more where that had come from. The buyers and my aunt's family didn't know the gold's origins, but they did know that it was both legal and dangerous.

My cousin Aramanda was just a year older than me and was being courted by one of the boys who worked in the fabric shop, and who apparently liked to talk. This morning she was bursting with new gossip, having just come in from their morning stroll. "Did you hear about the fire?"

I went silent and looked at her in shock. Had Edwina told her? "It wasn't such a bad one," I argued defensively. "We put it out fast."

She gave me a strange look. "I'm talking about the ones up north, on the border with Delmany. The locals are saying it was a dragon."

7

Fiery Dreams

Adragon. 'Wina and I exchanged cautious glances, and I let out an awkward laugh. "Can they prove it? Did anyone actually *see* the dragon, or was it just the fire?"

Aramanda shrugged. "Who cares? The end result is a bunch of burned trees, and some superstitious peasants. You know those mountain folk are foolish about such things." She said it in an airy, condescending way, and I almost smiled. She might be older than me, but her life had been a lot easier, and she seemed quite young at times. Putting others down like that was a classic attempt to sound more sophisticated.

"I'm sure they are," her mother agreed dryly, seeming to note my humour. "But it's more likely that someone got drunk and dropped a torch, and is looking for an excuse to cover up their mistakes. Like Viola said, I'll believe it's a dragon when I see it." Thankfully she hadn't picked up cousin Sam's habit of calling me 'Weola', and what she said about the dragon made sense, except that *she* didn't know about the diary.

That afternoon I took a break from planning our next inn to look over the diary once more. I was more than halfway through, and the entries were becoming more and more disjointed and incomprehensible, although ironically the handwriting was perfect. But after reading a couple more pages I found a line that chilled me: *He woke up today. He was going to kill me, but Declan convinced him otherwise. Does he not know how I love him?*

If this writer, who I was growing more and more convinced was female, thought that a dragon could understand love, then I suspected there was a lot I didn't know about dragons. I skimmed the rest of the diary, trying to get any more practical information about it being 'awake'. But all I could find were more poetic, confusing descriptions of the creature, interspersed now with numbers. *Forty-six. Seventy. Eighty-three...*

And then on the very last written page, I read something that shook me more than anything else I had seen in this book. *More, more every day. I can't keep up with...*

With what? I flicked through the rest of the diary, trying to find an explanation for what the writer was referring to, but there was nothing. The rest of the diary was just blank pages, as though it had been taken away before the writer had finished with it. Perhaps it *had*. But what was in here that could upset King Barrick so much; that could make me the target of this unwanted attention?

It was a Dragi document, that much was obvious. But assuming that the writer was sane, I had to ask myself if it was even recent. There were no dates recorded, but if parts of it were forty years old, then probably any threat was gone...and probably some farmer's boys had gotten drunk on the border, set fire to their land and then blamed it on fictional dragons.

Oh please, please let them be fictional...

"It all comes down to the Dragi," I murmured to myself. "How long have they been around?"

There was a slight creak in the floor, and then Edwina was standing in the bedroom doorway staring at me, or more specifically, at the book. "You said you would get rid of that," she said accusingly. "You were almost killed for it!"

I hurriedly closed the pages, flushing with shame at being caught in a lie. "I wasn't almost killed, I was just..."

"Humiliated? Locked up?" My sister glared at me militantly, her hands on her curvy hips clad in her new red brocade gown. "You should burn it immediately! What if they're still after it?"

"You look nice today," I said, trying to distract her. "That dark red suits you."

"Don't change the subject! Viola, this isn't like you. You really need to get rid of it! What's in there that you need so badly?"

Finally I turned and looked up at her, my expression solemn. "Information about some dragon waking up around here."

Her jaw dropped. "No way."

"Kind of." I summarized what I'd read, finishing with, "I couldn't get rid of it when it might still tell me about the scales or about what I'm facing at the moment." I looked away glumly, reminded of how my nights had become so much less peaceful. And the way the writer had described 'more and more every day' – it had sent my mind immediately to my own rapidly multiplying scales. "I've been having the worst dreams, 'Wina."

She came to sit beside me on the bed, her fine brows creased in concern. "I bet it's because the book is cursed. The king wanted it enough to go after you like he did. You should get rid of it, Vee. I'll help you to burn it or drop it in the privy, or in the river. Anywhere, as long as if someone comes to find us, we can honestly say we don't know where it is."

I looked down at the diary hesitantly. Regardless of what was in it, books were expensive, and I'd never heard of anything good that came of book burning. Well, except for that one time when a book of wicked spells was burned in the Fortrente public square. It was a long time ago, back when I was a child, but I remember the sense of solemnity I'd felt upon seeing that. Words could be good, or they could be wicked, but to destroy something with fire was so very *final*. You couldn't un-burn a book.

In the end we went to Mother. I'd been tempted to get rid of the diary to protect her too, but I'd left her clueless about Nellie going to the ball, and look how that had turned out. Ignorance was no guarantee of safety.

When we showed her the book, and then I explained the extent of my dreams and the scales, she agreed firmly with Edwina. "Get rid of it, Viola," she told me. "How do we know it's not causing the scales to keep growing?"

I hadn't even considered that, but once she said it I couldn't think of anything else.

So we threw the book on the fire. I half expected it not to burn, being about dragons and all that, but it lit up like any other old paper would when put in flame, its edges curling then *whomph* being enveloped in orange. Within half an hour it was just ash, and I waited to see if it would affect my scales at all.

Unfortunately not. In the days that followed they grew steadily and surely even as we made plans to move out of Aunt

Melicia's and into our new home, and it got to the point where I'd be picking up new gold every single morning. It was all put into the same place, a safe that Mother had bought especially to be hidden in the floor of the new building. Rather more original than hiding it behind a painting, and certainly effective. If you didn't know where to look you'd never know it was there.

Or if you could smell it, a thought crept in, along with the memory of the Dragi outside the palace. But I dismissed that. We hadn't heard anything new about the Dragi or even that we were being pursued, and it had been a month since I'd arrived in Cristonia. News travelled fast between the two countries, brought along by merchants and travellers, and gossip travelled even faster.

The most popular topic was the Delman royal wedding. Nellie married her prince, arrogant jackass that he was. Part of me viciously hoped they'd make each other miserable after all the pain their meeting had caused us, but then I would remember Nellie's face and that we'd basically grown up together, and didn't want to think about her at all. She'd always wanted to be a princess, and now she was. According to the gossips, her official title was the Princess Petronella of Delmany, and she was already beloved of the people. When the merchant's wife went into detail about Nellie's wedding dress I zoned out. Enough about that, and I certainly wouldn't wonder about Captain Franco and his hopeless infatuation with my foolish stepsister – or wonder if his heart was broken by the marriage. His heart, his problem.

My heart, a quiet thought echoed, and I pushed it aside. I wouldn't think like that, not about him. It only led to pain.

The rumours continued to come about dragons in the north, and some of the city folk we spoke to seemed to believe it wholeheartedly. Others dismissed it as foolishness, but the fact remained that I knew that somewhere there *was* a dragon, or at least had been one. I also knew that I had a link to the Dragi that I certainly wouldn't have chosen, regardless of the wealth it had brought. If I was to get married, how would I ever explain why my body was covered in gold scales? And that was a big *if,* because I'd never really thought about marriage. Who would marry me?

Although my thoughts about that, about my looks, had begun to shift. I'd noticed that my cousin Aramanda looked a lot like me, tall and thin with strong features, but *she* was attractive. The difference, I decided, was that she took care of herself. She wore flattering clothing and did her hair just-so and wore, dare I say it, a bit of rouge. And that got me thinking…

So even though I felt ridiculous, I found myself borrowing Edwina's pot of rouge and sneaking up to my room with a small mirror. After the first attempt I looked like a clown with big, blotchy red marks on each cheek. I threw the pot down on the bedside table, feeling tears prick at my eyes. What was I thinking? But then I heard the sound at the door, and saw Mother standing there.

"Not like that, love. Let me show you."

Then rather than scold me or – God forbid – laugh, she took her handkerchief and simply wiped gently at my cheeks until there was just a faint blush remaining. "There you go," she told me. "Quite natural, and quite pretty."

Not pretty, I decided, resisting the use of that word in relation to myself. But not ugly, either. But something sparked in me. I didn't have to be the same, plain old Viola. And perhaps, rather than beauty aids being ridiculous, they could be…fun.

Over the next few days when I began to carefully (very, very carefully) use a little makeup, and then with Aramanda's help, even felt brave enough to put a honey-brown rinse through my hair and brows. It darkened it just enough to be noticeable, and I found that I *felt* different. I'd never be beautiful, not even with the layers of jewels and expensive clothes that I'd always found foolish, but I didn't have to be plain.

I'm a girl, I told my reflection in the hall mirror, reminded once more of Tildy's offhand words. *I do not look like a boy.*

The reflection's lips curved just a little, that tall, skinny girl in a tidy dress, and then walked away.

Another month passed, enough time to prove beyond doubt that the loss of the diary hadn't affected my curse. The scales now grew right up to my collarbone and down to my elbows and knees, as tightly-knit as real scales. They'd fall off every couple of days, but then they'd promptly be replaced. I felt tired all the time, tired and irritable from lack of sleep or too much sleep.

Sometimes I'd get into bed at seven or eight at night in our new home, then the next thing it would be nine in the morning and Edwina or James would be shaking me awake. I had gone from intense, terrifying dreams to none at all, and my sister had told me that more than a couple of times she'd found me standing out of bed, staring blankly out of the high window over the dark city, and she'd had to force me back to bed.

I remembered none of it. I was feeling disconnected from my own mind, from my self, and even James was starting to notice the difference in me. He didn't know the full details about the scales, only that there had been a curse involved with those Dragi figurines, and it had been part of the reason we'd had to flee. Poor thing. I could see that he was trying to reconcile his old life with his new one, but perhaps he was just young enough that in time, it wouldn't really matter.

As for my sister and my mother, I knew that even though we were outwardly comfortable now, there were still wounds from that treatment back in Delmany that would take a long time to heal. Edwina was looking better than she ever had before, but I knew she dreaded the locals ever finding out that the new Delman princess's 'wicked family' was in fact *us*. She tried to throw off that title of ugly stepsister with every curl of her soft hair, and with every carefully made gown, but some titles were stamped on the inside. Mother was the same. She was practical and seemed cheerful, but sometimes I'd see her with an expression on her face, a lost expression that I didn't like seeing there.

"Do you think Mother should get remarried?" I asked Edwina one day. She'd dropped the attempts to change her name to Elaina, thank goodness, but everything else seemed to have changed. "She seems lonely."

"As if two husbands wasn't enough," she muttered. Then she shrugged. "We'd have to find someone first, and she's not young anymore. She's almost forty."

"Hmm."

"I think it's you we should be worried about," Edwina said.

"Me? Married?"

"Well, maybe. But actually I was thinking about your...

little problem. I think you should visit a Wyse woman, see about getting it fixed. Aramanda said there were some Wyse living in the northeast forests, up by the mountains."

"Forget it," I replied, thinking of the round-faced woman who'd been good enough to grant all of Nellie's selfish desires, yet had left us in such trouble. "Wyse people cause as much trouble as they solve. Besides, it was power of that kind that got me into this. I don't want to use it to get me out."

"What about the church? Maybe the priest could exorcise you."

"Sheesh, 'Wina, I'm not *possessed*. And this…" I figured God knew what was going on, and probably how to solve it, but it didn't mean that the priest would know. He was just a man, after all.

But desperate times called for desperate measures, and so after the service on Sunday I found myself face to face with the man himself. Well, kind of. He was half a head shorter than me, small and slim with kindly eyes and deep lines carved beside his mouth. "What can I help you with, Miss…?"

"Cadence," I replied. "I'm Hazel's daughter."

"Ah, yes, I remember her. She left the country years ago, didn't she?"

"Mm. Well, now she's back. We all are, but I have a problem…" I summarized the curse as much as I could without giving away any detail, but that just left the priest looking confused.

"So, you unintentionally became involved with some sort of…cult? And now you believe you are cursed?"

I nodded. "There's no question of believing or not believing. It's a fact."

"Is it…" He paused awkwardly. "Is it something that could be mended with a trip to the apothecary?"

He thought I had picked up some disease. "Not at all!"

"Well, I'm afraid I can't give any advice without knowing the details, dear. I'm sorry. Can you tell me anything at all? The name of the cult, perhaps?"

"I don't think they'd consider themselves a cult," I hedged. "They're almost respectable back in Ostraime. They even have a temple."

The priest's eyebrows shot up. "The Dragi? You were involved with the Dragi?"

"Not on purpose!" I hissed, suddenly panicked. There didn't seem to be anyone within earshot, but even so... "Don't say it out loud! Please!"

"It's not as if it's going to call them up," he said reasonably. "But I shall remain silent anyway. They're a bad lot, those people. From what I've heard and who I've met, they're deep into darkness. I suspect that even any good they did would turn out bad in the end."

Like gold coins that created wealth instead becoming a curse. "Great," I muttered. "What they gave me was supposed to be a blessing, I think, but it hasn't ended up that way. What, do you think I should pray?"

"Prayer is vital for direction and change," he agreed amiably. "But chances are you'll have to take steps with this one as well. If I were you, I would both pray, and take wise steps-"

Loud footsteps sounded down the cobbled floor as a young boy came running in. "Father!" he exclaimed. "Mrs Galver's old man has just died. She needs you to come straight away!"

The priest turned to me apologetically even as he grabbed his cloak. "We'll finish this conversation later, perhaps? Will you come back tomorrow?"

"Sure." Wise steps, huh. He hadn't meant go see the Wyse people (or at least I didn't think he had) but that was all I recalled. Pray, and take Wyse steps...

But the next day, plans changed. I slept fourteen hours and only woke to someone beating me with what felt like a rug. Apparently my blankets had been smouldering again, and Edwina had found me about to catch fire, or so she said. "Didn't I tell you to check your candle?" she screeched.

"I didn't even have a candle," I muttered, pushing my hair out of my face. But the blackened area of the blanket was right by my face: if I hadn't been found, then I might have been the Ugly Stepsister for real. Burns usually left nasty scars.

But the town gossip was even more intense. The Cristonian queen (who I suspected was a bit mad) had finally allowed her poor son to actually betroth himself to a suitable girl, and that was after a long, long line of rejected princesses. Rejected by her rather than by him, I believe, but the whole city was in uproar.

So that was the good news. The bad news was that there was yet another rumour of a dragon, except this time it was a bit clearer. The people bringing the story this time claimed that they had seen it as it swooped in during the night to attack a town north of here, and that it had been green.

The one in the diary had been orange.

But aren't all dragons supposed to be green? I'd argued to myself. I was sure I'd heard that somewhere.

But the only picture I could find in the public library had the creature drawn as greyish-brown. It was the old story of George and the dragon, complete with huge teeth (the dragon, not George) and a pool of artificial-looking blood from where it had been fatally wounded. Apart from the huge teeth, George's dragon looked nothing like the one from my dream or the diary. Either the storytellers in the city square were making things up, or dragons came in all shapes and sizes.

"Did you get up in the night to go for a walk again?" Edwina asked me later. She hadn't yet heard about the new dragon stories, instead being fixated on doing up our new kitchen.

"What do you mean?"

"I woke up in the middle of the night to use the privy, and I couldn't see you in your bed." She shrugged. "I was too tired to come look for you, though. You must have got a candle while you were up." Referring to how I'd almost woken to my hair on fire.

But my night was just a blank, an empty gap between falling asleep and being woken once more. It all felt connected, the scales and the dragon and the embers, and I couldn't shake the feeling that I was being stalked. "Do me a favour, will you?"

"Sure. Anything."

We ended up putting a string across the bedroom door, with a series of bells attached. If I tried to get up and walk off, then hopefully the sound would wake me before I could get into any trouble. Which was a great idea, except apparently sleep-walking me was quite happy to dodge the bell string somehow and end up on the other side of it anyway.

At least I didn't set myself on fire again.

Three months later, we were comfortably settled in our new

house just down the street from Aunt Melicia's, doing nothing in particular, as the plans for a new inn hadn't materialised. Mother was out visiting old friends along with Edwina, so it was just James and I in the house. I sat in the downstairs parlour restitching a loose seam on one of my new dresses, and he was in the entryway playing knuckle bones. He said the floor there was smoother and less likely to cause blisters, but it also meant he had to answer if visitors arrived.

Then there was a knock on the door.

"James, will you answer that?" I called.

He sighed heavily, and I heard the tromp of his quick little footsteps, followed by the sound of the door opening and a brief murmured conversation. Then the door slammed shut and a moment later he was standing in the doorway of the parlour, his face white.

I looked at him in shock, guilt assailing me. "Who is it?"

James shook his head, numbly pointing towards the door, and my mind immediately leapt to the worst possibilities. *I never should have let him answer it. Is it the Dragi? The king's soldiers ready to grab me up and take me back to the dungeon? I should have known this peace was too good to last...* But as if in a dream I walked towards the closed door, then bent down to check through the peephole.

Hmm. It didn't *look* like soldiers. Not at all. Just some kid with a hood half-covering their face. So I opened the door, and they pushed back their hood to reveal they weren't a kid at all.

Oh no. The moment I saw that lovely face with those distinctive, wide blue eyes, I reacted on instinct rather than logic.

Slam.

I leaned against the now closed door, my eyes wide as James and I exchanged a shocked glance. "What's she doing here?" I hissed. "She's supposed to be a princess!"

"How should I know?" he countered. "You just shut the door in her face!"

Good point. And even now I could feel the hesitant knocks against my back, and could hear Nellie calling through, sounding increasingly agitated. "Viola? Viola, let me in! Please!"

I turned suddenly, pulling the door open and staring out at her as if my first impression would turn out to be a mistake. But it was definitely her, and the oversized, rough cloak had clearly done a good job disguising her on the trip here if she'd managed to get this far all alone…

…Or not. Another, taller figure approached from behind, this one also hooded and with a very serious expression. It was Franco, and he did not look happy.

Oh, *no*. They'd run off together.

8
Refugees

I wordlessly stepped back, allowing them both into the house. So many thoughts were swirling through my mind of all that I could say, but in the end I didn't need to say anything. As usual Nellie swept right in to fill the silence, bursting out the moment the door was closed.

"Oh, Viola, it's been so awful! The trip was so long and dangerous, and I couldn't show my face, and we had to sleep outdoors! And the boat trip was barely civilised, I mean, who travels with *gypsies* if they don't have to?" She ran a hand over the too-fancy-for-travel dress exposed once her cloak was removed. "We even had to sell them my jewellery for food, and I *know* that we didn't get nearly as good a price as we should have; it was so very pretty, and certainly expensive, but we didn't want anyone to know that we were leaving, and we knew that they'd not be reselling them honestly so we could probably get away with it-"

"Why are you *here*, Nellie?" I interrupted finally, my whole body stiff with tension. "You're supposed to be swanning around in the palace with that jackass of a prince, not sneaking off to Cristonia in a borrowed cloak!"

Nellie didn't correct me calling her husband a jackass, but she sniffed, her beautiful blue eyes wounded. "He's been so awful to me, Vee. He might seem kind on the outside, but inside he's really nasty, and so jealous! I practically had to flee for my life!"

"I never thought he was kind," James muttered from beside me. "Vee's right. He's a jackass."

And I couldn't even scold him for using that sort of

language, because I'd just said it. I sighed heavily, taking her words with not just a grain of salt, but a whole heapful. I turned to her companion, still silent and serious with his dark hood up over his head. "Why don't you tell me why you're here, if you please."

"But I just told you," Nellie began, but Franco cut across, his voice dull.

"It's what she said. She had to flee for her life."

My eyebrows shot up. "Funny, because here we heard that Princess Petronella was the joy of the masses in her pearl dress, or something. Why would she have to leave?"

Nellie, who'd flopped down in one of the parlour seats, interrupted. "I just told you. You're not listening, Vee! He was-"

"Awful and jealous, yes," I cut in. "And yet here you are, having apparently run off with a man who's been in love with you for longer than the prince knew you. And you wonder why he was jealous?"

"It's not what it looks like," Franco said flatly, and Nellie interrupted again.

"He's got no right to be jealous! Why, he *ignores* me most of the time, and when we are together he barely even looks at me. And I wouldn't run off with Franco," she added self-righteously. "I do take wedding vows seriously, unlike *some* people."

"And yet here you are."

"I told you-"

"Enough," Franco cut in, rolling his eyes. Clearly there was trouble in paradise. "Why we left will be irrelevant, because we're moving on. I told you we couldn't stay here, Nellie. It wouldn't be fair to your family."

Wait, he'd called her *Nellie?* What had changed in three months? "I don't think anyone's connected us with what happened in Delmany," I said. "But that won't last if you're here. If you've got a really good reason…"

Nellie turned towards me, her lovely face wearing a wounded expression. "Why won't you listen?"

"Because it sounds stupid and unlikely," Franco said, "and because she knows what you're like." Even as those harsh words shocked the rest of us, he lowered that big hood to reveal his face and neck. Then we saw that all the way down the right side of his face, leading onto his neck, was a harsh red burn scar.

Owww… I couldn't help but raise a hand to my own face in sympathy.

As he saw me looking, he grimaced. "As you see, Nellie would never run off with me. Not anymore."

Into the shocked silence came Nellie's petulant voice. "I never would have run off with you anyway. I married a *prince*."

"And left him, apparently," I said crisply, shaking off my dismay over Franco's injury. "James, why don't you run down the road and let Mother and Edwina know we have visitors? Don't say who it is, though."

"Don't," Franco countered. "Nobody can know we're here. Can you wait for them to get back?"

I looked at his exhausted, scarred face and nodded. "Alright, then. Do you want something to eat?"

"I would kill for a proper bath," Nellie admitted with a tragic sigh. "I wouldn't complain, but the conditions of travel *are* very rough."

Franco looked grim, and I raised my eyebrows. Of course she wouldn't complain. She never complained. Even so, I did understand what she meant. "There's a tub just off the kitchen. If you want a bath, I'll show you where the well is so you can heat some water. Else I can just get you a bowl and a cloth."

We had a well conveniently out the back of the house, and the water was always fresh and clean…when there weren't frogs in it. Having a proper bath was lovely, but we didn't do it often because it took so much work to fill even a small tub.

She frowned sweetly. "Do you not have any servants to help?"

"Since when have we had servants?" James butted in. "*We* do the work ourselves, just like always." Now he'd got over the shock of his sister's sudden reappearance, I could see how hurt he still was over what had happened. And then he took it a step further, adding, "*You're* the one who was always complaining about working too much, but you're just lazy."

Nellie's jaw dropped, and I stepped in. "No servants, sorry, but the house is small enough that we can run it ourselves easily enough. Nellie, if you come with me, I'll show you where things are. James, will you take Franco to the kitchen and get him something to eat?"

Nellie followed me down the tiled hall and down the steps into the kitchen, muttering under her breath the whole way. "Lazy, *me*? How could he even say that? Why, I always did exactly what I was told-"

"Enough!" I cut in, suddenly furious. I felt hot with the emotion, from my belly up my neck to the top of my head, and I knew that my fair colouring would be showing every inch of that anger-flush. "I'm not interested in rehashing old arguments, especially not after what you did to us back in Delmany, whether it was on purpose or not.

"No, I'm not finished!" I interrupted when she tried to interject. "Yes, you are lazy, and you are spoiled, and frankly I blame that on your upbringing and the way people will give you whatever you want. But now you have to take responsibility for your own actions! You can stay here for now, but I swear if you cause us any trouble, or if anyone finds out you're here..."

Amazingly Nellie wasn't arguing. She was staring at me wide-eyed. "Viola, I swear smoke just came out of your nostril."

I rolled my eyes. "Don't be silly. I don't smoke a pipe, and don't try to change the subject. Just...go get yourself a bath if you want one, and then come to the kitchens. But don't let anyone see you!"

"If I have to go to the well out back, mightn't the neighbours see me?"

I paused. "Put your hood back up." Although she had made me wonder.

Back in the kitchen Franco was sitting at the broad wooden table, a bowl of reheated stew in front of him. James was sitting saucer-eyed on the other side, staring.

Franco smiled, or perhaps it was a grimace. It was clear that strong facial expression hurt. "I would ask if there was something on my face, but it's clear that there is."

I poured a couple of mugs of small beer then pushed one in his direction, taking a seat next to James. "What happened? Full details, please."

He touched a hand to the side of his face gingerly, as if it still hurt. It probably did. "What, this?"

"That, and with Nellie. Why are you even here? And please

don't fob me off with what she said. Tell me the whole story."

And so he did. He started off slowly, hesitantly as if he was unsure of how much he should say, but then we were asking questions, and the whole story came out.

Franco had arrived back at the palace three days after we had left together, and his absence had been noticed, as had mine. The very day they'd helped me leave, the Dragi had come to the palace to 'talk' to me about what I'd found at the inn after the Brelfnean sisters had left. They'd found me missing, but it wasn't until Franco arrived back and various people put two and two together that they realised he had helped me leave. The guard back outside the palace had finally worked out that I wasn't Franco's cousin at all, and he'd let people know what he'd seen.

So Franco had been called in to speak with the Dragi priestess and with the king, who'd been furious at having his orders countered. Franco had done his best to avoid mentioning Nellie's involvement, but when the prince, who had been pacing angrily in the background, had asked how Franco could let dear Ella down so, Franco had admitted the truth. Well, some of it anyway, particularly the part where Nellie had begged him to help her stepsister leave because she couldn't bear to see her so, and hadn't she suffered enough already? Wouldn't Franco do it for *her* if for nothing else?

The prince had exploded at hearing that. 'If Ella needed something she should have asked me,' he had said, and then of course Nellie was brought in to confirm the story. And she'd looked so stricken, so tragically beautiful as she'd said that she couldn't *bear* to see poor Viola in such a position…oh, had she done the wrong thing?

They'd not punished Nellie for it, but Franco had been demoted to sergeant and sent out to the night shift; guarding the castle walls from non-existent invaders. A dreary and uncomfortable role. And he couldn't prove it, but when a vial of acid had been 'mysteriously' thrown over his face by a masked assailant one night, he'd known he was getting his real punishment. At least it missed his eyes, he said.

At hearing that I felt immense pity, but the closed look on Franco's face said he didn't want any. So I just raised my eyebrows and said coolly, "I always knew that prince was a fool. Too much power. But that must have been months ago, that attack. And Nellie still married him, right?" Or else we were getting *seriously* the wrong information here in Cristonia.

He nodded wearily. "And apart from…my face, it all seemed to be forgotten. I saw Dragi around the palace on occasion, but I didn't hear anything else about you. Have you seen any around here?"

"Dragi? No, thank heaven. There have been rumours of dragons in the north, although I can't see that would be what you're wanting to know."

"Dragons? Unlikely."

"I agree."

Franco shrugged, taking a sip of his ale. "Anyway, so I thought we'd got away with it, kind of." Except for the acid and demotion, presumably. "But then Nellie came to find me one night about three weeks ago. She was sobbing, and she begged me to help her leave. She said that the prince had been madly jealous through her whole marriage, and would barely let her leave their rooms if they weren't on official travels, which sounded true enough. I'd barely seen her since the wedding, not that she would seek me out any more. But she had these bruises, like rings of them round her upper arms, and she said that the prince had…had threatened to kill her that evening."

He frowned, shaking his head. "She said that he had never forgiven her for going to me for help instead of him, that he could have given you a real pardon, or something like that. She says she told him that she was in danger from the king, but he didn't believe her. Instead he got angry, and she was scared. So I helped her leave."

"Of course you did," I murmured. "I can't see you saying no to Nellie for anything." Even though the scandal of them running off 'together' would be enormous. No one would ever believe it had been just platonic, not when it was attractive young people involved, never mind Franco's burn. And for it to be the king's illegitimate son…that was a whole new level of drama. I wondered if there was any real danger to Nellie from King Barrick. Chances were she'd imagined that too.

He scoffed. "Before I had to travel with her for a whole three weeks."

Hmm. Interesting. By this time James had left the room, and I leaned in. "So the king got really angry that you helped me leave, and then what, just forgot about it?"

"I don't think he ever forgets about anything. Not like this, not when it's the Dragi who are connected as well. There's something going on there..." Franco petered into silence, sighing. "We can't stay here, I know that. Nellie's too distinctive-looking to hide for long."

The exact same could apply to me, yet I'd been fine. Mind you, I wasn't a princess, and they didn't seem to be looking for me too hard if I'd been here three months without any issues. But then I wasn't a royal offspring who'd taken off with his brother's wife. *That* wouldn't be overlooked, I imagined. "What are the chances that the prince just annuls the marriage and Nellie is forgotten about?"

"To the first, it's possible. To the second, unlikely."

He looked so dejected that I had to change the subject or else get very upset on his behalf. Funny, it seemed my grudge against him had faded with time and changed circumstances. "We can sort that out later," I said crisply. "Do you want a bath?"

He gave a wry smile. "I know I look like I need one. I'll take Nellie's when she's done, if you don't mind."

"Not at all. And I'll see if I can find you both a change of clothes, too."

"Thank you."

It was the first time Franco had said that to me rather than the other way around, and I stopped in place, giving him a brief nod. "You're welcome."

But I didn't leave, and he nodded towards my high-necked gown that carefully covered all those wealth-giving, cursed scales. "You look well. Much better than the last time I saw you."

"Where I'd been dressed as a boy? I'm glad to hear that."

"But I mean it. I'm...I'm glad that things haven't been terrible for you." He paused. "They haven't been, have they?"

I thought before answering, then I gave the truth. "People are kinder here. They don't know who we are."

"And your family takes care of you? If you've got this house..."

"Yes, Aunt Melly must be doing well if she could fund this,"

Nellie said, walking into the kitchen with her hair out, drying it over a gown that looked like one of Edwina's. James must have fetched it, because I sure hadn't. "Is she paying for the whole thing?"

Damn. How long had she been there? "It was from an inheritance we didn't know about," I said briefly.

"Wow, that's lucky."

"Yes," I said dryly. "We're known for being very lucky."

Nellie didn't pick up my irony, and I quickly got her some food, sending Franco out to bathe. I could borrow some of Uncle's clothing in the short term, or else buy some and claim it was borrowed. But the thought of adding lies upon lies made me feel ill.

Nellie finished her bowl of stew without complaining, then looked up at me. For the first time I saw the weariness on her face, and even sincerity. "I've missed you, Vee. Did you miss me at all?"

If she meant did I think of her at all, then yes, although mostly it was with resentment over what had happened back in Delmany. "I don't know."

"I missed you. I missed everyone I used to see. The palace… it's lovely, but it's so big and cold. I didn't have any real friends there, because no one cared who I was, just that I was Cinderella. Did you know they were calling me that?"

"I know they were calling me and 'Wina the ugly stepsisters, and Mother the wicked stepmother," I said. "Rather nastier than just Cinderella, don't you think?"

She looked away, stricken. "Can I ever say sorry enough?"

"I don't think you've said it all."

"Oh, I'm sure I must have! Many times, back at the palace… and I *am* so sorry it happened. It was terrible, what they did to you."

I shrugged. "Sorry's just a word. I'm sorry it happened too, but I'm not going to take responsibility for things that were beyond my control." I turned to look at Nellie coolly. "If you're accepting that at least some of what happened was a result of your behaviour, even if it was an accident, then yes, I'll accept that apology. It won't change anything, though."

"I'll have to apologise to your mother as well," she said

pensively. I'd never seen her so serious. "I just remember the look on her face when Royce was being so horrible…it was awful. I thought she was going to faint, and he was accusing her of the most dreadful things…"

"Where do you think he got those ideas from?"

"Not me!" Nellie blanched defensively. "I might have said something, just a little something, about the workload that my stepmother gave me, but I swear it was nothing like what he said! It was like I kicked a pebble on a hillside, and next thing there was a landslide, and I couldn't stop it. I couldn't get them to stop, no matter what I said, because they'd already made up their minds."

Just then there was the sound of footsteps, and James came rushing in. He was still deliberately not looking at his sister, and he exclaimed, "Mother and 'Wina are home!"

"Did you tell them who's here," I began, but it was too late. Mother was standing in the doorway, and she'd already seen Nellie.

I didn't know how it would go at first. My mother, who was one of the most gracious people I knew, had been so incredibly hurt by the prince's accusations that she'd barely said Nellie's name after that. And I knew that now, if Nellie did something foolish like burst into tears, there would be no sympathy.

Silence. Then Nellie said, very quietly and very solemnly, "Mother?"

I thought Mother was about to blow a gasket. But instead she gripped onto the doorway, and then Edwina was standing behind her, and she could see Nellie. "What's *she* doing here?" Edwina gasped.

Nellie looked like a doe caught in a trap, unable to say anything, so I spoke for her. "It's gone very nasty with the royals. They'll be leaving shortly."

"They?"

"Franco is here too."

"Oh my God," Mother muttered, a phrase I had never heard coming out of her mouth before. "You've brought trouble down on us again."

It took some time to explain what Franco had told me (along with Nellie's frequent interjections, which no one really listened to) and by the time I'd finished, Franco had come out from his bath. He'd put back on the same clothes as before since I hadn't had the chance to borrow any yet, and he looked incredibly awkward to be standing amongst us. The last time he had seen my family, he had been standing by as we'd been humiliated.

There was a pause, and then Mother said stiffly, "You helped Viola come here, and at great personal cost. Thank you."

Franco looked awkward, but at least this time he wasn't silly enough to say he'd done it for Nellie. "It was the right thing to do, especially considering I wasn't…helpful to you earlier. I'm sorry about that."

Mother shrugged, although tension deepened the lines beside her eyes. "What's done is done. Besides, you only believed what everyone else in the town did. And who's to say it wasn't true?"

I let out a grunt of annoyance. I hated when Mother talked like that. And then Mother saw me and frowned. "Have you been smoking, Viola?"

"Of course not!" And that was the second time someone had said that to me today.

We found makeshift beds, swearing Nellie and Franco to secrecy. They mustn't leave the house or even be seen at a window until it was time for them to go. Even Nellie going to the well the previous day had been a bad idea, Mother said. As for where they were going, Franco said that his mother's extended family lived further south in Sudante, and they'd go straight there. They'd have to change Nellie's name…

Later that night 'Wina crept into my room to talk. For the first time ever, we'd got our own rooms in this comfortable house. "I can't believe this is happening," she whispered. "Nellie, running off with Captain Franco? I wouldn't have thought she'd leave her prince short of an earthquake, and even then…"

"They're not 'running off' like that," I corrected. "He's helping her. By the sound of what he'd said earlier, he's got some idea of what she's really like now." And I couldn't shake the sneaky satisfaction that gave me. It was so hard watching people fawn over Nellie, assuming that because she looked perfect and pure, that she must be like that on the inside too, rather than just as flawed as every other human being.

"I didn't mean it like that. I can't see Nellie being in love with someone who's…"

"Illegitimate? He's still the king's son, 'Wina."

"Scarred, I was going to say. Vee, I was so shocked to see his poor face! I mean, he wasn't precisely beautiful, but now…"

"I think he's still perfectly good looking," I snapped back. "The burn will fade, and besides, it's only on the side of his face."

Wina gave me a knowing look. "You think he's good looking, do you?"

Flustered, I tried to backtrack. "I suppose so. He's not ugly."

"Hmm." But she didn't sound convinced, damn it. "How did you react when you first saw Nellie? I tell you, I wanted to pour a bucket of slops over her head and ruin that darned velvet dress. I can't believe she had the nerve to show up here, at our house!"

I shrugged, feeling weary rather than angry now. "Where else would she have gone?"

"Yes, but then she had to comment about how Aunt Melicia must be rich to give us this house-"

"She doesn't know about the diary," I interrupted. Now here was the biggest issue, the biggest lie that I'd been so carefully hiding. "That might be the reason why all of this happened, and she and Franco don't know about it, or about the scales. They might have to run for their lives, 'Wina." *So might we.*

"But we're in Cristonia now," she said uncertainly. "And the diary's gone now…"

"Of course," I said quickly. If they hadn't come after us yet, I couldn't imagine that they would. Surely it wouldn't be hard to find out where Mother was from, since enough people back in Fortrente knew about it. "I guess the biggest problem now is that Nellie is a fleeing princess, and she doesn't exactly blend easily."

"So dress her as a boy." Edwina scoffed. "You could even cut her hair, rub dirt all over her face. Say she's a twelve-year-old boy. I'm sure they could get away with it if they had to."

Yeah, a twelve-year-old boy with a hormone imbalance. "No one would ever believe that."

"I still think it would work," my sister said petulantly. "Alright, maybe I just want to see her with all her hair cut off. I can't forgive her that fast, Vee."

The concept of Nellie and forgiveness made me feel all hot with anger again. "I don't want to think about it."

"Fine, don't then." Edwina paused. "Oh, and I forgot to tell you because of all the fuss with our *visitors*, but apparently a dragon has been seen just outside the city. Aramanda's best friend's cousin said that he saw it when he was out riding. They say it took off with a sheep."

"Let me guess, it was the size of a house?" I asked wryly. I knew the descriptions that the diary had held, and there was no way that a dragon that size could ever hide in this area. There would be many, many people who had seen it, and it would have destroyed far more than just a single sheep. "The incredible power of suggestion. Remember a few years back when everyone at home was convinced that Friar Rendsoll was some sort of frogman?"

"And it turned out he just had one webbed toe, and people were fools or liars," she finished. "I know. So you don't believe the stories, then?"

I shook my head, sounding more confident than I felt. "Not at all."

"VIOLA!" The call seemed to come from a long way away, as if I was hearing it through water, and I tried to turn from it. "VIOLA!"

"What?" I murmured grumpily. I didn't like being woken, especially not to Edwina's worried face shoved right in mine. A pretty blonde was standing just behind her, and a moment later my memory caught up with me. Oh, carbuncles! Nellie was here. As if life wasn't hard enough…

"What's that on your chest?" Nellie whispered, pointing.

I looked down to see that my nightgown had ridden down just a touch, and I could see the edges of grey-gold scales creeping up over my collarbone. Definitely higher than the day before, and I jumped in panic, pulling the dress up to cover them.

"What are you all doing in my room?" I shouted. "I didn't give you permission to be in here!"

Edwina was staring at me with a seriousness I rarely saw in her expression. "Vee, you were *screaming*."

"More like roaring, if you ask me," Nellie corrected. She was still staring at my neck. "What's wrong with your neck? And why are your eyes like that?"

"Like what?"

Edwina cautiously handed me a small mirror, one we'd bought since arriving in Cristonia, and I lifted it to my face. Ignoring the usual morning hair and grumpy expression, I saw that I did look different. I could see the pale grey bruises which forewarned of more scales to come, scattering up over my neck in a way they never had before, but my eyes…my eyes had changed. Instead of their usual pale blue-grey, they were a brilliant speckled yellow…

I threw the mirror away from me in shock, and quick as a wink, Nellie stuck her arm out and caught it. "Careful," she admonished. "You don't want seven years bad luck."

"Seems like you've got enough bad luck already," Edwina retorted. "What's happening to you? You've seriously overslept again, and there's dirt all round your floor, and your eyes…oh, they've gone back to normal."

I grabbed back the mirror to see that she was right. My eyes were once again their usual nondescript blue-grey colour, but the scale marks on my neck seemed even worse. I quickly checked my arms and the back of my neck, to find that they'd extended there as well. "Oh no!"

"Why won't anyone tell me what's happening here?" Nellie complained loudly. "Viola, what's wrong with you? And what are those things all over-"

Edwina had already closed the door, and she turned grimly towards the two of us. "Nellie, Viola was cursed by the Dragi. Something to do with the figurines being hidden under her top, but it's a deadly secret, alright? Don't you dare tell!"

Nellie looked wide-eyed but fascinated. "Who would I tell?"

To me Edwina said, "Vee, we've got to do something about this. Next thing you're going to look like a lizard person, and you can't cover *that* up with a high-necked dress!"

"Or a dragon," Nellie piped up. "And you had the smoke coming out of your nose yesterday! I saw it! 'Wina, what if Vee is turning into a dragon?"

They exchanged appalled glances. "Well, it would explain why those stolen figurines were cursed," my sister said.

"Don't even suggest that," I snapped. "That's not physically possible."

"It seems unlikely," Edwina agreed. "Normal girls just don't turn into dragons, and there's a world of difference between a few cosmetic changes and actually shifting form. I wouldn't believe it unless I saw it."

"But this morning I heard about a dragon that had burned down a cottage at the edge of the city," Nellie persisted. "And here's Viola with dirty feet! What if she's been out there?"

"I think I would notice if my sister turned into a dragon at night," Edwina countered, but she looked shaken.

As for me, I couldn't speak. It was an idea that had been dancing around the edge of my mind but had never really surfaced enough to be judged as true or false: that the scales were more than just scales, and that the stupid stories of dragons were connected with me in a way that went further than my imagination. The shock over Nellie and Franco's arrival seemed to have sped things up, and soon the changes would be enough that only a sack over my head would hide them from the public.

"We have to do something about this immediately," Mother said when we all told her. "Viola, dear, this isn't going to go away. What did the priest say when you spoke to him?"

I struggled to remember exactly what had happened. The conversation had been cut short, and I shrugged miserably. "Prayer and wise steps, he said, but he didn't explain exactly what that meant."

"Go to the Wyse folk, then," Franco said from the other side of the room. We'd filled him and even James in with only the very barest of information, that touching the figurines had cursed me and now I seemed to be changing. "I hear there are some living in the forests north of here. If anyone could help you, it'd be them."

It was almost exactly what Edwina had said, and I reacted just as predictably. "No way. Wyse folk can cause just as much trouble as they fix, and besides..."

"Besides what?"

"They probably wouldn't help me anyway," I muttered. "Wyse folk like little, pretty girls, not great big skinny ones with noses like hatchets."

Mother and Edwina looked at me in dismay, but Franco let out a laugh. When we turned to stare at him he said, "What? Surely you weren't serious?"

Mother turned to Nellie, who had been sitting very quietly ever since the Wyse folk were mentioned. "Petronella, what was the name of the Wyse woman who…helped you?"

Nellie blanched at having all our attention on her. "Her name was Gerelda. But she didn't really help me, did she? I haven't had a happily ever after!"

"Nobody gets a happily ever after," Mother said crisply. "In the end we all die, and some sooner than others." It was the first time I'd heard her sound so bitter over her situation, but she had a point. As far as I could tell she had loved both her husbands, and both had been taken from her early. My and Edwina's father through illness after only a few years of marriage, and James's father through the same accident that had damaged her legs.

But then Mother added a little more softly, "But life doesn't need to be full of trouble if we can help it, does it? I'm sure that anything you can tell us will be useful."

"Well, all she said was that she was an agent of good, and that she had heard a wish upon a shooting star and had come to help." Nellie frowned thoughtfully. "I forget what I wished, but it must have been about marrying the prince, because that's what she said she'd make happen. And she did."

"You wished you could get out of our home and away from all of us," James said quietly. "I remember."

Everyone turned to look at him, and he continued, "You said that you were better than that life, and that you were going to prove it. And then Viola wished that you would go off and marry your prince, and leave us all alone, and stop being a burden. And you did, but not for long, because you're back here."

"It sounds like it was Viola's wish that was answered more than yours," Franco said, one dark eyebrow cocked. "How ironic."

"And you marrying the prince caused us more trouble than ever having you around did," Edwina said grimly.

Suddenly I remembered the little round woman from the market, the one who I'd later seen in the carriage with Nellie in her beautiful ball gown. What had she said to me, something about…

…The ball. She'd asked if I wanted to go to the ball, and I'd laughed no. I'd said that at midnight, you had to go home and go back to normal. "I need to talk to this Gerelda," I said grimly. Even if she couldn't help me with the scales, then I'd have a few other questions to ask. Had she thought she was *helping* me? What if my answer to her question in the market had been different?

"Excellent," Nellie said. "I'll come with you. I have something to say as well. This was not what I thought I was getting myself into!"

I didn't want to spend any extended time with my stepsister, but she was more likely to be able to find Gerelda than I was.

"We may as well come," Franco said casually. "It's not the direction we had planned, but it might end up being worth it."

So it was to be the three of us, then. And while I would never choose to be the third wheel, I certainly didn't want to travel by myself. I might wake up and not even *be* myself.

"I can't believe I'm sitting on the back of a donkey cart," Nellie complained. "Why couldn't we just have bought a horse? It would have been faster."

"It would also make us a better target for thieves," Franco countered from where he walked beside the animal's head, holding its lead. "Be grateful that you're not walking the whole way. And anyway, it's not a donkey, it's a mule."

"As if that makes a difference."

I ignored their squabbling, caught up in my own thoughts as I walked just off to the side of the cart that was laden with a week of provisions. We'd all dressed as poorly as we could manage without looking like people would run us out of town, sort of at the level of a successful-ish cottager. The cooler weather meant that we all could get away with wearing our hoods up, as well as a scarf for both Nellie and I. In my case it was to hide the creeping scales; in hers to hide her distinctively beautiful face.

And here's the funny thing: Edwina had jokingly suggested Nellie travel as a boy, but everyone else had thought it a good idea. Even Nellie had reluctantly given in, although she'd put her foot down about the haircut. 'But if I have to be a boy, then

Vee does too!' she'd said.

'Not if it's a cottager and his wife travelling with their young cousin to visit family," Franco had countered. 'Go on. Let Viola be a girl.'

So here I was, travelling as a girl for once, and fake-married to Franco of all people. The thought crept into my head that with his new scarring most people wouldn't consider him as handsome, and perhaps a girl like me would have a chance. But it was a stupid thought, and I rejected it straight away. Someone who'd been stunned by Nellie's beauty would never consider someone so opposite in looks, regardless of their own impairments now.

Apparently the path to find the Wyse could take anything from three days to a week, depending on whether they wanted you to find them or not. So here was hoping they wanted us to find them, whatever that meant.

The road leading into the north east out of the capital began wide and easy, then the fields turned into forest, and the road became less tended and more rutted. Then as the day went on and we wound our way into the hills, it became steeper and more dangerous, at least in my opinion. The others agreed.

"We'll all get out and walk here," Franco said. We'd been taking turns riding in the cart versus walking, and Nellie obediently jumped out to walk close behind him. On either side of us were now steep, rocky cliffs, and the sense of being surrounded made me on edge. The scales were getting close to detaching again, even the new ones on my neck, and after a while the itching was driving me mad.

"I just need a moment," I said suddenly, moving off to the side of the road to step behind a boulder. "I'll catch you up."

I quickly stripped down just enough to scrape off a dozen gold scales from my neck, upper arms and legs, and then realised I didn't have anywhere to put them. There was a small purse of minor currency in my clothing, but there were no pockets that several ounces of gold wouldn't cause to sag or even tear. Deciding quickly, I put what I could fit into my purse, then buried the rest of it under a loose layer of gravel. Some lucky traveller would find it in years to come, perhaps, and it would make no difference to me.

By the time I came back out, the others had disappeared around the corner, and I picked up my pace to catch up. And there was the cart, rather oddly stopped in the middle of the road.

"Sorry about that," I began, but then realised what I was looking at.

$$9$$

Transformation

Franco and Nellie stood in the middle of the road, both white-faced and with their hands in the air. Franco's sword, a remnant from Delmany, was in the hands of a bearded, scruffy man with a horrible leer on his face. There was another man holding a long knife, and just off to the side I could see yet another, this one with a crossbow. "We'll see what this pretty little lad's got," the man with the sword was saying with a disgusting smirk, and I remembered in horror what I'd once heard: that a young boy travelling alone could be in just as much danger of attack as a girl. And Nellie wasn't even really a boy…

I'm not really sure what happened next. I just remember that my vision blurred, and I was so scared and angry, and I think I might have been…shouting at the bandits, perhaps? But next thing they'd all scattered, leaving the weapons lying all over the road along with a couple of strange black piles of rubbish. The mule had taken off as well, the strings holding it to the cart somehow having broken. Nellie and Franco were staring at me with their eyes wide enough to show the whites all the way around the irises, and she whispered, "Vee?"

King's crown, all the air around me seemed too hot, and I still couldn't see clearly at the edges of my vision. The light was too bright, and my back ached dreadfully. Then as a wave of nausea hit me I slumped forward to look at my feet.

My feet? There was something wrong with them, I realised in dismay. They were all strange and orange and leathery, like my shoes had changed somehow, and the old shoe leather was bursting all around my ankles. And then there was a puff of black smoke in the middle of my vision and my throat felt warm, and I began to panic.

"Don't make a sound," Franco was whispering to Nellie. "I'll try to distract her, you move slowly off to the side of the road, get behind a tree."

Nellie was whimpering, and I tried to reassure her of... what? That I wouldn't hurt her? But she was moving off now, and Franco was coming towards me, white as a sheet and with his hands raised in the air. He was clearly trying to herd me in the opposite direction from where Nellie was moving. They were *so* afraid of me, and they didn't even have weapons...

Guilt and shame overwhelmed me, and all I wanted was to calm them and let them know I meant no harm. Funny, because that was the exact same thing Franco was saying to me now. "It's alright," he was saying soothingly, even though his expression said the opposite. "You don't need to be scared."

"*Her* scared?" Nellie hissed from the side of the road. "What about *us*?"

"I'm not scared," I finally managed to say, although speaking each word was painful and difficult, like vomiting rocks. "You don't be scared."

And then I felt myself changing, felt my strange self shrinking and becoming more familiar, and my vision sharpened and the roaring sound left my ears. And then I was looking down at my own familiar body, covered in rags, and the ground around me was scattered with gold scales. But there was one more thing.

"*Ow*," I groaned. "My back *really* hurts."

"You've been shot," Nellie piped up from the side of the road where her hooded head was just visible over the top of the rock.

I tried to crane my head around to see, but a sharp pain in my shoulder blade made me stop.

"It's in your back," she added helpfully, coming out from behind the rock. To Franco she whispered, "She's not going to change again, is she?"

"No, I'm not," I said grumpily, even though I wasn't sure myself. "Did I just..."

"Turn into a dragon?" Franco finished. "Yes, you did. I think."

"What do you mean, you think?" I cried. "Did I or did I not turn into a giant, fire-breathing beast?"

"You did," Nellie piped up. "But you were the funniest-looking dragon I ever saw."

"How many dragons have you seen?" Franco sniped.

"Well, only Vee…"

"Then you're not exactly an expert, are you?"

But I wasn't listening to their argument, instead focusing on what had just happened. I'd turned into a dragon, and the strange black piles of 'rubbish' now made sense. It seemed that the bandits hadn't even had time to run away. "Nooo," I cried. "Nononononooo. This can't be happening!"

"Don't panic," Nellie said urgently. "Or you might turn back again. It seems to be when you get upset."

Suddenly I remembered how 'the candle had fallen onto my bed' more than once, on nights when I'd had bad dreams. And Nellie and Mother had both asked me if I'd been smoking…

I sat down heavily onto the road, *clink* on top of some scattered gold scales. "By God in heaven," I moaned, a heartfelt, confused prayer. "This can't be happening."

"So you already said," Franco said matter-of-factly, moving towards me. "Yet it is. And think of it this way; at least it was here, where there was no one to see you change. If it had been back in the city…"

I thought once more of the 'dragon sightings' not too far from this very area, and the breath was taken from me once more. "Too late. It's obvious that I was already sneaking out of bed at night and destroying things. King's crown, I could have killed someone!"

Our eyes all turned to the charred piles just feet away, and then Nellie said something extremely unhelpful: "Looks like you already did, Vee."

"But they were bad," she was still saying an hour later, long after I'd stopped vomiting and we'd started moving along the road once more. The wagon had been left behind; not much use when the mule was still missing. "They were bad people, Vee. It doesn't *count* if you kill them."

I groaned again, and Franco interrupted. "Stop saying that

word, Nellie. Let's pretend it never happened."

"Hard to pretend when I don't know if I'm going to wake up one night on fire," she muttered.

"Shut it," I said finally, made even more irritable by the wound in my back. It didn't seem all that deep, or so they said, but the bandage covering didn't feel like nearly enough. "Franco, what did I look like?"

I didn't need to say 'as a dragon'. "Maybe the size of a horse," he replied after a moment of thought. "Orange. Dragonish, I suppose. I didn't take in that much, not really. One moment you were yourself, and the next you were different."

"Wings," Nellie added in. "Really big ones, with feathers. But I got a better look than he did, and you weren't really orange. It was more of a pale yellow with orange shadows. And you didn't look like the dragons in stories, you only had two legs..."

Two legs, like the giant flightless dragon in my dream. And now we knew who'd been stealing sheep. Urgh. "Feathers?" I queried, changing the subject. "Really? I thought dragons were more like giant lizards."

"I didn't notice any feathers," Franco said. "You're probably adding details in your head, Nellie."

"There were too feathers," she countered, then frowned. "At least I think there were."

"Never mind the feathers," I said dryly. "But only the size of a horse? That's not that big." Not compared to the descriptions in the diary, of a dragon the size of a building.

"Seemed big enough to me," Franco said.

In between vomiting bouts I'd finally admitted the full truth. I'd had to, especially considering that they'd seen the dragon scales scattered all around the road, looking very much like diamond-shaped gold pieces. And then I'd had to tell the full truth about the diary too, and about the real source of income for the house.

Naturally Nellie had zeroed in on the second point. "You told us you didn't get anything from the Dragi!" she argued. "And the whole time you had *gold*? Damn it, Viola, I could have gone to the ball without even needing that Wyse woman if you'd just been honest!"

"I hadn't known at the time," I'd argued. "And then after

that we didn't know what to do. There weren't many, and we didn't want people to find out about it in case it all went bad."

"Did you know before the prince came?"

"Er…"

She took that as a yes. "You did! Did 'Wina know about this? Did your mother and James?"

She'd calmed down just a little upon hearing that James hadn't known either, but was clearly still fuming. Franco, on the other hand, had watched me assessingly since I'd admitted the truth. It wasn't as if we'd been friends exactly, but I had felt as if we had more in common since he'd arrived yesterday. Now it felt as if there was a barrier there, as if now he *knew* I was dishonest. I should have been used to it, but for some reason it stung.

"I was basically deformed," I said defensively. "I didn't want people to know about that! And besides, I'd be just asking for a kidnapping. I'm growing gold!"

And that seemed to be enough to silence the conversation, at least for then. But I could still tell the others weren't happy.

We eventually found the mule wandering up the road by itself. By that time there was no point going back for the cart, supplies or not, and as the others pointed out, we didn't exactly lack for money. "Not necessarily useable," I pointed out. "Do you want to leave a trail of people who've been paid in dragon's gold?"

"You're going to need new clothing," Franco replied, and his eyes slid away from me as if he was embarrassed. "You look like you've been in a fight with a pack of wolves."

Only if they'd somehow managed to shred my cottager's dress and not draw a drop of blood. I was decently covered, but only just, thanks to my cloak that hadn't been affected by the shapeshift. "It'll have to wait until we reach the Wyse folk," I said crisply, ignoring the warm flush in my cheeks. "Besides, I doubt I'd see anyone who could sell me anything of the sort. We *are* in the middle of the forest."

We'd been given wildly different ideas of how long it could take to reach the Wyse, from three days to three weeks, and the only thing the few people we'd asked had agreed on was that you had to stick to the road. Don't leave the road, they'd all said, or else you'll never find them.

The sun was setting, so we made camp near the ruins of what might have been an old castle, almost completely overgrown with hawthorns so that only the occasional stone was visible. Sleeping under the stars is rather less romantic than it sounds. For starters you can't really *see* the stars through the canopy of trees, and the cold and the night sounds stop you from ever really relaxing. Or me, anyway. And I was so aware of the others so close, of what had happened these last two days, that I was afraid that if I fell asleep then I'd change again.

But somehow I managed to fall asleep, and when we woke up we were no longer alone.

It was the sound that had woken me. At night we'd been amongst quiet, lonely ruins, but by light it was a completely different environment. The ruins weren't ruined; instead a slightly chaotic, beautiful gateway that marked the entrance to a walled town. We had slept by the open gates, and inside were dozens of small, gorgeous buildings, each beautified rather than damaged by the greenery which overran them. Amongst the houses and shops were people walking, but not ordinary people. Some were too small, some were too large, some had wings, and some were in colours that you never saw on a human being. Weird or beautiful or simply different, and I couldn't take my eyes off them.

Near me Nellie stirred and sat up, noticing the change almost immediately. But unlike mine, her gaze was more assessing. Clearly she knew what she was looking for, or who, rather.

I woke Franco a few moments later. "We're here."

He sat up, his short hair sticking up comically on one side of his head. "Where?"

"At the Wyse town. *Look.*"

"I don't see anything," he muttered. "Where are we looking?"

I stared at him. "Do you really not see anything? Here, come stand by me."

He shuffled forward, clearly still half asleep. "What? It's an old ruin."

"What? Right there? It's full of people!" I finally grabbed his head, turning it to face where I was looking. "Can you see it now?"

"What- oh!" Franco's eyes widened as he took in the scene,

and feeling awkward, I removed my hand. Then he frowned. "It's gone again. Here, give me your hand."

This time I awkwardly extended my hand, and he took it, not seeming to notice. "Oh, it's back again. I wonder why I can't see it by myself."

His hand was warm and dry in mine, and I was acutely aware of both the size of it, and our closeness. Did I have morning breath? Did he even notice? The Wyse folk, even though they were so close, didn't seem to notice us, except for the occasional glance sent our way. They knew we were here, but we just weren't that interesting, it seemed. Somehow that was comforting.

"Well this is going to be awkward," Nellie said, noticing the way we were standing. "You two aren't going to walk in like that, are you?" She looked a bit disgruntled, even though I knew she wasn't really interested in Franco. I supposed it was more of a dog in the manger thing: any eligible male around had to be giving *her* attention.

I let go of his hand, and he looked at me in surprise. "Aren't we going to go in?"

"You can walk with me," Nellie said with a sweet smile, proving exactly what I had just thought.

"We should have a wash and breakfast first," he replied casually, turning away from her. I had to hide a smile.

We washed as much as we could from our small water supplies, and the whole time I was hyperaware of the town so close by. Then finally we couldn't put it off any longer. Nellie shot on ahead, clearly raring to go, and after a few moments Franco looked back to where I was lagging behind. "Are you coming?"

I hadn't realised I'd slowed down so much. "Of course," I replied. "It's just..."

"That if they can't help you here, then nobody can?"

I looked at him in surprise. "Something like that, yes. Or that they'll choose not to help, or they'll give me some massively difficult task before I can be free."

Franco paused at the high stone pillars on either side of the entrance, waiting for me to catch up. "I can't think of any reason that they would choose not to help. And if there's a task to perform, then I'm sure you'll be up to it. You're a very capable person, Viola."

I felt myself warm with unexpected pleasure. "Thank you." *You are too,* or, *You're not as awful as I once thought you were* came to mind as possible replies, but luckily he'd already walked through the gate and I didn't get the chance to say either.

Up ahead Nellie was bending down to talk to a small, animated male Wyse, and as we approached he turned to look at us. "See, that's the one there," she said, pointing at me.

The little man looked us up and down, focusing on Franco for a moment before turning to me. He was perhaps five feet tall, with a round hunch to his back and narrow, pointed fingers. His large black eyes blinked and flickered, and overall he rather reminded me of a hummingbird, if that was possible.

"Ah, I see," he said in an unfamiliar Cristonian dialect. I could understand, but it was as if he spoke with a very strong accent. "Yes, yes, I can help you. Just follow me."

He turned and began moving quickly away towards a side street, and I realised that the hunch to his back had been a pair of small wings, closed into a rounded circle like the shell of a ladybird. Now it was open, they fizzed and hummed into a blur, carrying him just above the ground. When we hadn't followed quickly enough he turned back. "Come, come!"

"What did you tell him?" I hissed to Nellie. "Do you even know who that is?"

"Malmario or something," she said casually, following after. "He's a Wyse, Vee! And he says he knows Gerelda. What could go wrong?"

Lots of things, obviously, but we followed behind anyway, mostly ignored by the others moving around the streets. It reminded me very much of my own village, except for the difference in the appearance of the people. Everyone knew what they were doing, and we were watched with a little curiosity, but everyone seemed too busy to waste time on us.

Malmario went in through the low door of a crooked, dark little building, and after a moment's hesitation we followed after. Inside was dark, but after a moment my eyes adjusted and I saw that the inside of the small place was lined with bottles. Hundreds and hundreds of them, most smaller than my hand, all stacked on shelves in different shapes and sizes, and with labels in some mysterious, archaic-looking script.

Still moving as quickly as the hummingbird I'd compared him to, the little man zipped over to a nearby wall then hovered upwards until he reached the top shelf, grabbing first one bottle and then another, darting around until his arms were full of them. Then he moved down to a wide bench and spread the whole range out before him.

"Now we have the medicine for the pain of the heart, of the lungs, and of the liver," he rattled off, pointing at one bottle after the other. "And there for the change of face, the change of body, the change of heart-"

"Change of body?" I broke in. "For...shapeshifting?"

"Yes, yes," he agreed, nodding. "The change of shape." He raised his hands to his chest, indicating a bountifulness that I knew I didn't have. "Change like this, yes? Only ten silver, or for you, I'll give a special price, just seven."

Geez. "I don't want *that*," I said irritably, embarrassed. Quickly I pulled down the collar of my high shirt, revealing the scales that even now were turning gold. Almost my whole front was covered now, tightly packed enough to turn away an arrow if needed. If only I'd been shot in the front rather than the back, hmm? Although even the pain of the wound wasn't so bad after a night's sleep; more like a dull ache. "I keep turning into a dragon. Can you help me with that?"

Malmario's jaw dropped, and a moment later he slammed it shut. "Dragon?"

I tried to think again of the right Cristonian word. It was close to Delman, but perhaps he wasn't understanding my accent? "I was cursed by the Dragi," I explained. "Even though I was trying to help them." Kind of. "And just yesterday I turned into a dragon and killed some bandits, and I really don't want it to happen again."

"Cannot help dragons," the Wyse finally replied, his black eyes blinking rapidly. "Dragons are bad luck. I cannot help you here. Are you sure you do not need a love philtre, perhaps? Mine are very good."

"I don't need a love philtre!" I snapped. I didn't need to be told that I was bad luck; I already felt like I was terribly unlucky. "I need a way to fix this. If you can't help me, can you tell me who can?"

"Curses are not my business," he said briskly, moving back with a distinct sense of fear. "You need to go north, to the stone folk."

I fell silent. I'd heard of the stone Wyse, a type of Wyse folk who were rumoured to be even more elusive, more knowledgeable, and more powerful. They were said to be coloured the grey of the rocks they lived amongst, and even when they hid themselves in other forms, you could identify them by the touch of dusty grey to their skin.

Or so I'd heard. I thought again of the round woman in the market with her grey hair tucked into her headscarf, and wondered if she would be hidden all the way in these mountains as Malmario seemed to think.

"But what about Gerelda?" Nellie complained. "You said that you knew where she was!"

"North," Malmario said firmly. "Follow the mountain road until you have gone far enough, and then there you are."

"How will we know if we've gone far enough?"

"How did you know you had arrived here?" he countered. "You were earnestly looking for this town, and you meant no harm. Therefore you could enter." He looked thoughtful for a moment. "So if you see any old building or rock formation that seems unusual, stay there for the night."

"As long as we don't end up staying with a bunch of mountain trolls by mistake," Franco said dryly. "We had no idea that this place was even here until morning. I couldn't see it at all until I walked in through the gates." Which had been lucky, I supposed, or else we would have been holding hands all day. Awkward.

"Don't be silly," Nellie said dismissively. "The trolls all live up north in the mountains of Nordante. There aren't any within miles of here."

I turned to look at her in amazement. "How on earth did you know that?"

She shrugged. "Royce told me."

The same Royce who she'd fled from, claiming he was trying to kill her. Nice to know they had some actual conversations. "Well, if we're done here, I suppose we should be going," I announced. "Any objections?"

"No, that's fine," Nellie agreed airily, moving for the door. "Thank you, Malmario."

As we left, I heard the little man say, "Who's Malmario?"

Franco was a little longer to follow us out of that small dark door, and when he did I saw him putting something in his pocket, a furtive expression on his face.

"What have you got there?" Nellie asked curiously.

"Just a philtre to help with my burn," he replied briskly, looking away. "Nothing interesting." Then to Nellie he said, "I'm surprised you didn't buy anything. He was promising a lot, that Martin. You could have had all sorts of things."

"I've had enough of Wyse folk and their promises," she replied, sounding disillusioned. "It might bring short-term results, but they can't guarantee a happy ending, can they? And who's Martin?"

"The Wyse man, of course."

"Not Malmario?" Nellie asked in surprise. "I could have sworn he said Malmario. It sounds like a good Wyse name, doesn't it?"

More like a big gap between the Delman and Cristonian dialects, plus poor Martin's strong accent. True though, he *did* look like a Malmario.

We'd almost reached the green-covered gates again when Franco asked abruptly, "Did anyone ask anyone else besides Martin about Viola's curse, or are we just taking one man's word for what to do?"

"Good point," I agreed. "Let's-"

"I'll ask," Nellie cut in quickly. "Why don't you wait outside the gate with the donkey?"

It was a mule, and we'd left it tied to a tree surrounded by enough long grass to keep it occupied all day. But we'd already begun walking, just making it through the gates when I said, "She didn't get Martin's name right. Should we really be trusting her with this one too?"

"Hmm. I'll just go back," Franco began, turning around to face where we'd just come from. "Ahh...I forgot I can't see the town from out here without you. I wonder why."

"Probably just that Nellie and I have both been power-touched, for better or for worse. You haven't, have you?"

"Not that I know of," he agreed, stretching out his hand. "Would you mind?"

"Of course." But I still couldn't hide the lurch in my stomach at the thought of touching him. *Fool.* "Oh. I can't see the town anymore either."

"What?" He frowned at me. "Not at all?"

"It just looks like the old ruins we saw last night," I admitted, squinting and turning my head sideways to see if anything would change. It didn't. "That's strange. Why don't we try touching again, see if it helps?"

But when I put my hand in his, there was no change. Just the same sprawling stone ruins from the night before, this time lit up green and pretty by the dappled sunlight through the overarching trees. The mule continued to chew placidly at the grass around the tree where it had been tied, its meal beginning to create a circle of cut grass, but Nellie and the town was still nowhere to be seen.

We tried walking through the gates again, we tried wandering around the ruined castle, we even tried going away down the road then coming back again. "It's no good," I said finally. "We'll just have to trust Nellie on this one. I wonder why they won't let us in?"

"I wonder how foolish we looked walking through the town and seeing nobody and nothing," Franco added, letting go of my hand. It was silly, but I felt the loss of its warmth.

I moved away, pretending to occupy myself with giving the mule a scratch behind the ear. It wasn't pretty, poor thing; old and scarred, but it did its job without complaining. "Good boy," I told it.

"Actually it's a girl," Franco corrected, moving to stand beside me. "I've called her Buttercup."

I raised my eyebrows, and he shrugged, a little embarrassed. "She does a good job. She deserves a name."

It was so close to what I'd been thinking that I half smiled.

"What?" he asked defensively.

I shrugged a shoulder. "You're a kind person, aren't you? Sometimes, anyway."

He looked uncomfortable. "No one ever *thinks* they're

unkind, do they? And besides, that's a bold thing for you to say after what happened to you."

"True," I agreed slowly. "And I'm not saying that you never did anything wrong. But you didn't give me up for pushing you off the bridge, and then you helped me escape, whatever your motives were. You're helping me now too, even if it's still for Nellie. I don't care, because I'm getting the benefit."

"It's not for Nellie."

Franco said it with such finality that I turned to look at him in surprise (and a little pleasure. Yes, I'm petty). "What do you mean?"

"I did it because my options had become very limited because of my past actions," he replied after a moment of thought. "I did it for me, I suppose, more than because it was the right thing to do. I don't...I don't know what the right thing is anymore."

Ooh, this sounded interesting. Moving away from the green-covered gate, I sat in the shade and made myself comfortable. "Do you mean in this situation, or in general? Because it sounds like your white knight tendencies are fading."

"White knight?" He scoffed at that, then came to sit beside me. "Stupidity, more like. Would you pass me the ale?"

I dug around in the saddlebags then handed over the large flask we'd brought with us. Then I watched curiously as Franco pulled out a small bottle from his pocket, downed it in one go, then finished it off with a swig of ale. "What did it taste like?" 'It' being the bottle he'd bought from Martin/Malmario.

He shrugged. "A little like lemons. Not much, actually."

I craned my head to study the red burn still marking his cheek and neck, but I couldn't see any change. "I wonder how long it will take to work?"

"It's not for looks, it's for the pain," he said briefly. "That's what I care about the most, not my pretty face."

"So you admit you're pretty," I challenged. "I knew it. Boys like you always know what you look like."

Franco flushed. "What? I'm not pretty. I've never been pretty in my life!"

Maybe it was the quietness of the wood, or the strange situation, but I found myself remarkably relaxed and careless, without the usual inhibition that I'd feel around someone like him. "Handsome, then. Let's not play with words."

He reached a hand to touch the burn mark. "Maybe once. Not now."

I laughed. "Oh, come on, do you really think that makes a difference?"

"It's a bloody huge mark!"

"It's on the side of your face! It'll add character. It just needs time to heal, that's all."

He turned to look at the empty gateway and ruined castle, and then when he spoke again it was more quietly. "Nellie thinks it makes a difference."

"Nellie's a dimwit when it comes to men," I replied just as quietly. Suddenly I felt very serious, and I wanted him to understand that I meant what I said. "I know my opinion's not much compared to hers, but I think most girls aren't like Nellie, imagining handsome princes and cloth-of-gold dresses, and not being satisfied with anything less. Don't let her ideas define how you feel about yourself."

Franco looked at me with raised eyebrows for long enough that I realised what I'd just revealed. I may as well have just shouted out that I admired him. What an *idiot*. Why didn't I just put myself into the stocks? It would be less humiliating. "It's just a scar," I muttered, turning away to rummage again through the saddlebag. "Do you want lunch now?"

He looked once more at the still empty gateway. No Nellie emerged, and he shrugged. "I suppose so. We've got nothing to do but wait."

And we waited. We waited for another hour, occasionally breaking away to test the 'touch' theory (even more awkward after what I'd just said) or to take a private break, or to get some exercise. We'd moved the mule to its third tree with fresh grass when Franco suddenly stood up. "This is stupid. She can't *possibly* be taking this long! Something must have gone wrong."

He marched into the centre of the ruins again, calling out her name, and I followed behind. "What did Martin say, that we found this place because we were earnestly seeking it and meant no harm? I can't see why we can't find it now."

Franco stopped, hands on hips and clearly exasperated. A shadow of beard was beginning to mark under his jaw, and with the poor man's clothes and the burn, he looked quite dangerous. Perhaps the Wyse folk couldn't guess *motives* so well? "Maybe we can only get in once," he said grimly. "Maybe that was it, and we'll just have to wait."

"Maybe time travels differently for the Wyse," I suggested. "Alright, it's a long shot, but it could be true. Maybe Nellie thinks she's still chatting nicely with some friendly Wyse, not even realising we're waiting."

So we kept waiting, of course. In the long silence I started to think about what had happened that day and overall, and what I didn't understand, and started to guess what it might mean. But then I fixed my attention on that one thing that Franco had said, that he hadn't been doing this for Nellie. That he didn't know what was right or wrong anymore, and I was *so* curious to know what he meant.

None of my business, I scolded myself. *Leave him to his own thoughts.*

"I have a question," Franco said suddenly, breaking the silence. Even the mule turned to look at him.

"OK…"

"Why did you take the jewellery?"

I stared at him quizzically. "What jewellery?"

"You took the jewellery I offered you," he said abruptly. "Nellie's hairpiece, even though you knew I had far less than you did. Why?"

I paused, trying to work out what he meant, then realised that he was talking about when he'd helped me escape from the castle in Delmany. It seemed an eternity ago. And I had to consider my answer, because it seemed like an important question, one that impacted on his opinion of my character.

"Not because I was greedy," I replied finally. "It was because I can't go throwing around dragon's gold without people wanting to know where it came from. The smaller coins you gave me were much more useful." I paused. "Besides, I was very angry with both of you over what had happened…with the prince and the inn. I didn't want to do you any favours."

He was silent, dark eyes narrow, but he seemed thoughtful rather than disgusted. "Are you still angry?"

I thought about it. I'd been so furious with Nellie when I'd seen her, and I still felt resentful, kind of, but that was as much from the years of feeling second-rate as from anything else. The anger was fading, because quite frankly, it took energy to keep up.

"I don't know. I do know I don't *want* to be angry. We're told to forgive, that our sins won't be forgiven if we hold the wrongs of others against them; and…"

"And?"

I finished quietly, "I *really* don't want to turn into a bitter, horrible, unforgiving person, and I know that will happen if I don't let this go. So I suppose that whether this is justified or not, I don't *want* to be angry."

Franco seemed to think on that for some time. "But people would say it is justified. And you can't just let them off, let them get away with what they've done."

I looked at him curiously. "Who are we talking about here? The king, or Nellie?" *Or you?*

He turned away uncomfortably. "In general, I meant. When someone's done you wrong."

"But are they really getting away with it?" I waved my hands around as I tried to explain what I meant. "God is the ultimate justice, right? No one ever truly gets away with anything, even if it seems like they have during their lives. We'll be held to account for everything we've ever done for good or evil, and it's between God and us, not even between us and the one we wronged, or who wronged us. It's their debt to pay, not ours, and it doesn't go away."

"Fine, if that's true, then how does it help me now?" He flushed. "I mean, you. Whatever."

"Well…if *I* hold the pain of what happened, then I'm miserable, aren't I?" I replied simply. As I spoke it was making more and more sense to me. Forgiveness wasn't just an option, it was the absolute best choice. "If I let it go and decide that I won't hold it anymore, it has less power in my life. It won't affect the person I'm going to be."

"But what about when it *hurts*?" Franco persisted. "You can't just say that something is forgiven, but still be cut up about it inside. It's lying to yourself, and to them, and why would I- *we* put ourselves back in the position to be hurt again?"

"We don't have to," I replied, thinking of Nellie and the royals back in Delmany, and even our town. "Honestly, I don't think I'll ever go back to Delmany, and I'm not sorry about that. I'll never live with Nellie again either, because I don't hate myself, and I simply won't go through that again, and it would be very easy for a repeat. But at the same time, I can't and won't spend time thinking about what happened, or even when I see you or Nellie. It's not easy, but I'm trying not to think about it."

"Nellie," he muttered, looking back once more to see the empty gateway. "She's not at all what she appears to be, is she? I can't trust a single bloody word she says. Excuse my language."

Now it was all making sense. Franco had hinted at this earlier, that he was disillusioned with Nellie for whatever reason, and now he was saying it outright. "I'm guessing that something happened on the way from Delmany."

He shrugged a shoulder. "Having to spend three full weeks with her, seeing the difference between what she says and what I saw actually happen, means that I don't see her at all the same way. She's a liar, isn't she?"

It was said so bitterly that I truly felt for him. It hadn't taken long for me as a child to see the difference between how Nellie saw the world and how it truly was, but I also couldn't leave him viewing her like that. The truth was somewhere in between.

"She's not a liar," I said softly. "She's…she's just very run by her emotions, and her view of the world is warped towards herself. She says what she thinks is true at any one point, but you have to learn to take it with a grain of salt. A heaped teaspoon, rather."

Franco looked at me in disbelief. "So you're saying she's not malicious, just incredibly self-centred?"

"That's exactly what I'm saying. She can be remarkably kind, sometimes. She doesn't mean any harm." I frowned. "It seems to happen by accident, even though we can see exactly what causes it. She never seems to understand."

"Hmm. Well, that's better than thinking she's purposely tricking me," he muttered, turning back towards the gate. Luckily there was still no one to be seen, or else Nellie would be sulking all day over hearing herself described so. "I'm not saying I'll believe every word you say, but I'd like to hear your version of what happened with Nellie. If you don't mind."

"No one's believed us in years," I said frankly. "I just stopped defending myself when people said those terrible things about us, because I just looked like a liar and a fool. So if you're not going to believe me either-"

"You said that Nellie's words are warped by her emotions. How do I know that you aren't the same?" he asked reasonably.

Well, when he put it like that... "Alright, then. Nellie has been spoiled her entire life, first by her father who never denied her anything or ever made her do anything she didn't want to do, and also by every other person she met. At least that's how it seemed to me, because even when we were children and we moved to Delmany, she was the prettiest girl I'd ever seen. And she was only seven! We had a couple of servants to help out when her father was alive, but after he died we found out that he'd been in debt, and we had to give up a lot to pay the creditors off."

I frowned, remembering that awful time. "And Mother had been badly injured in the carriage accident that killed my stepfather, and she couldn't even get out of bed for three months. We had to look after her hand and foot, as well as try to keep the inn going. Everyone needed to help, even though Nellie and I were only twelve. So yes, she had to work hard, but so did we all. Except..."

"She didn't want to work," Franco said flatly.

I shrugged. "At the time we were all so shattered over what had happened, I think that we might have been hard on her. She hadn't worked before, but her whining – excuse me, I know her father had died, but that was how it felt at the time – was the only thing we could get angry about and actually change. Or we thought that we could change it, maybe, but Mother was sick for so long that it was really just me and 'Wina trying to keep things going. And James was so little...it was a very hard time.

"It's funny, now I can't really remember what happened. Maybe we *were* mean to her, but I had been forced into a parent's role, and there Nellie was, my age, and refusing to do her share of the work. Or she did do it, eventually, but she would sigh and use those big blue eyes every time she was sent out to market to buy supplies, and it wasn't for a year or so that we realised how our reputations had been damaged. And then it just spiralled out of control. Once people have an idea in their heads, it's very hard to get it out."

"Didn't you tell Nellie what was happening?"

"I think at first she was angry at us, blaming us in some way for what had happened to her father, so she didn't care. And then later when she did care, she couldn't see that her own actions had led to it as much as anything else." I shrugged, not wanting to think on it. It was a part of my old life, and now I was here…hopefully moving on. "Like I said, she's just self-centred. Oh, and beautiful. Let's not forget that."

"She's not that beautiful," Franco said grumpily, and then when I stared at him in disbelief, shrugged. "Fine, she is, but it doesn't affect me anymore."

"Quick work."

"You don't believe me, do you?" He grinned suddenly. "Well, I can prove that it doesn't. If Nellie was to jump out here and tell me that she loved me and wanted to marry me, I'd tell her to get lost."

I couldn't help turning to look once more at that gateway. There's no way she could have approached so silently, but if she *had* heard…

And that was when I realised that we had bigger problems than just Nellie's mood. The gateway, the ruins; they were all gone.

10
Stone Pathways

Franco and I stood there dumbly for a moment, staring at the forest where once the castle had been, and then looked at each other. "What the…" I whispered. "Is it because of the things we were saying? Have we been really shut out?"

"They were true," he countered harshly. "Why should we be punished for telling the truth? And now she's gone, isn't she? Lost in the land of the Wyse. Well, at least it solves the problem of how to hide her from the royals."

"Wyse-land isn't a real place," I said thoughtfully. "It's just the way that they hide their homes from everyone else, or at least that's what I've been told. And she might not be missing, you know. Why don't we sleep on it, then see if it's back in the morning?"

So we did. And in the time we waited, Franco finally told me exactly what had happened to put him off Nellie so. And I listened, not because I hated Nellie, but because I understood in a way that few people would.

It had been small things, apparently, which was so often the way. He'd found out that Nellie had been saying how he, Franco, 'would do anything for her, how close they were' and 'how they had a special friendship' and so forth. She'd pretty much created the situation with Prince Royce's jealousy, simply by her wording, whether it had been true or not. And then once they'd left, he'd found that the things she said to people they met on the way were different from the way he'd remembered it.

For example, on the second day of the trip when they'd been riding on a barge downriver to Cristonia, she'd told the bargeman that they'd been travelling for a week and were exhausted from the miles they'd walked. But when Franco corrected her – because they'd barely walked at all, and two nights was hardly a week – she'd said that it *felt* like a week, and she was mentally exhausted, and wasn't that the same thing?

He had said that it wasn't, it was misleading, and Nellie had just brushed it off, thinking it meant nothing. And that was when he realised that she must always talk like that. And what was exaggeration but a form of lie? He couldn't take her at her word, and he never should have.

For the average person, finding out that a friend was less than completely honest was a blow, but to Franco it had been heartbreaking. His golden, glowing image of Nellie's perfection had been completely shattered; with her completely thrown from her pedestal. It was a long way to fall, hence his intense feelings about it now…or no feelings at all, he claimed.

He'd asked me for more stories of things Nellie had said or done that weren't accurate, and a list of the worst were on the tip of my tongue when I stopped myself. "I don't think this is the most helpful thing for you to hear right now," I'd said instead. "I find that the more I focus on why I should justifiably be angry, the worse I feel." I considered telling him about some of Nellie's good points to try to round out his view, but he wasn't in the mood to hear them, and honestly, I wasn't in the mood to tell.

Morning came along with dew, birdsong and dappled sunlight, and absolutely no sign of ruins, Wyse villages or even Nellie. We finally agreed that we'd leave a note tacked to a tree, as cryptic as we could manage without confusing Nellie were she to find it, saying that we'd be back this way. Worst case scenario we could just ask the stone folk about what to do.

We began on our way, with just Franco, me and the mule possibly called Buttercup. It was strange just having the two of us, especially with the intimacy of last night's conversation, and it almost felt like we'd shared too much, like there was a barrier once more.

I broke the silence. "Why are you coming with me, Franco? You don't have to, you know."

"Do you not want me to?"

"It's not that I don't want company," I hedged. "I just

wonder what you get out of all this. It wasn't your fault that this happened, you know. I can see that now. You've just been a bystander."

He shrugged. "I feel partially responsible. And even if I wasn't, I've got nothing better to do."

"Oh." Fair enough. "So where will you go after all this is over? To family in Sudante, was it?"

He shrugged a shoulder. "That's what I said, didn't I?" He paused. "My mother said that her brother lives there, but I've never met the man. Never even sent him a letter. I think that he and my mother had a falling out a long time ago. Of course it's too late to mend now."

Because his mother was dead. "Perhaps he'll want to meet you anyway," I suggested. "But it's a long way to go on just a possibility."

"It's a smart thing to do for someone who's apparently run off with a princess," he countered.

"And it always comes back to that," I said lightly. "Funny to think that if you ever were found, you might have to admit that you'd lost Nellie in a Wyse village. I wonder how that would go down."

"Oh, king's crown." For the first time Franco looked downcast. "I do hope she's alright. I don't want her dead. I don't *hate* her."

"I'm sure she'll be fine," I assured him. "I'm pretty sure the Wyse don't make a habit of killing people."

"Just messing with their lives immeasurably," he muttered. "But there are a few Wyse folk that you shouldn't go within a mile of. The bad ones…"

"The ones who make gingerbread houses or who marry kings and talk to mirrors? Don't worry about them," I said with more surety than I felt. As with anyone else, some Wyse would become wicked simply because it was easy to do so. Power and knowledge came more easily to their people than to others. Too much power, too much potential to misuse it. "Surely none of those would be living in such a quaint little town, hmm?"

"Sure." But he didn't sound convinced.

I changed the subject. "How's the pain in your burn? Any better?"

He looked blank for a moment. "Oh. The burn. Ah, fine, I suppose."

"Martin's potion must have worked, then."

Franco raised a hand to his chest, looking thoughtful. "I suppose it must have." I wondered why he'd touched his chest rather than his face, but he asked me a question. "Any more gold scales?"

I reached into the neckline of my high collar, poking at a couple of the closest. They were still stuck, but only just. "Not yet, but it's getting hard to tell. I can't feel them coming off any more." They were too tightly packed together, like real dragon scales, and the grey thickness would appear immediately underneath.

"Maybe that's why dragons are famous for having hoards of gold," he suggested. "Maybe they just fall off, and so the dragons lie on them."

I scrunched up my nose. "And so these treasure hunters are trying to find what's essentially someone's toenail clippings? Yuck."

To my surprise, Franco laughed. He had a nice laugh, deep and pleasant, and I found myself smiling back. It lightened the atmosphere even though we were coming into a barren, more rocky area, with a little stone bridge arching over a shallow ravine just ahead of us. "Most toenail clippings can't buy you lunch, let alone a house," he began.

As we approached the bridge, a stocky figure clambered out from underneath it to block our path. I'd been so caught up in our conversation that this new assailant caught me completely by surprise, and I stopped still, my vision blurring. In front of us was a shaggy, dark blue humanoid figure with what might have been a loincloth, and he held a small club in one bulky hand. No, it was a large club…actually I couldn't tell, because the shape and form seemed to sway and twist before my eyes. I could feel the air in my throat growing hot.

"Toll for a troll!" the shape declared.

"Calm down, Viola," Franco soothed hurriedly. "It's just a gnome."

"Troll, I'm a troll!" the troll said. "I'm just small of stature. Not a mountain troll, you know, we don't grow that big. Er…

what's wrong with her?"

"I'm cursed to turn into a dragon when people annoy me," I said, my tone vague. "I killed three bandits yesterday."

I saw the fuzzy dark shape back away, a distinct whine coming into its voice. "I try to keep this area nice for visitors, and when I ask for a little benefit to repay my hard work, people get all angry and upset, and then there are the jokes about billy goats-"

I felt Franco's hand warm and restraining on my arm, and he said, "Here, take this. We'll just move through fast, alright? You won't ask for anything else, and we won't..."

"Burn me to death?" the troll suggested. He took something from Franco, hurriedly moving to get out of our path. "Er...have a good journey. And good luck with the stone people!"

I felt Franco lead me down the path until I felt my vision clear and my breath come back to normal, but even then I still couldn't speak. So close, so close to changing, but I hadn't.

"What did you give him?" I asked finally. "Some of your coins?"

"Something like that," he murmured. "So much for there not being any trolls around here, right?"

"How big was he?"

Franco looked at me in surprise. "You couldn't see?"

I shook my head. "My vision was blurred. He could have been tiny or huge, I have no idea. I swear, I thought I was going to kill him."

"Well, you didn't." He paused, the corner of his mouth curving. "He was only about four feet tall, Viola."

"Didn't he have a club, though?"

"A stick. We weren't in any danger, and he knew it."

I frowned as I tried to imagine a hairy little troll with a stick trying to make any kind of living out here in the wilds. "At least I didn't transform this time. It's like any time I-"

"Get a fright? Remind me not to jump out on you."

"Please don't." It sounded like a joke, but both of us were entirely serious. I didn't seem to have much control over the shapeshifting, and the idea of harming anyone I cared- I *knew* was a terrifying one. "Are you afraid of me, Franco?"

"Do you mean in general? Or with this curse?"

I smiled crookedly. "Either, I suppose."

"In general, no. You don't smile much, but you're hardly scary. With the curse..." He petered off into silence. "I'll be happier when it's broken, that's for sure."

So he was afraid of me. After what had happened with the bandits, I didn't blame him. "You don't have to come with me," I said impulsively. "You can go find Nellie, or find your family, whatever you like. You don't owe me anything, and you don't have to put yourself into danger."

Franco stiffened. "I've already said that I'm coming with you, so I'm coming with you. Besides, I don't really feel in danger."

"Oh?"

He grinned. "We walked over a bridge and you didn't even push me in. So you must like me, just a little."

"Just a little," I agreed archly, turning away to hide my blush. If he knew that it was more than just a little, I'd be mortified. I changed the subject. "How's the pain? Did the potion work at all?"

He looked startled. "My face? Fine."

"Well that's good, isn't it?" I said brightly. "Good to know that Martin isn't a complete quack."

He grunted, and I took it as an end to that conversation. The road we followed had been neglected and overgrown all the way since we'd left the Wyse village, but as it had led through rocky hills it hadn't mattered too much. There wasn't much to overgrow.

But now we'd moved back into forest, and this time it was much darker and less pleasant than before. It was only the middle of the day, but the thick trees blocked out the light, each gnarled and twisted and somehow too dark for the location and the time of day. I didn't realise how uncomfortable I'd grown until the mule suddenly jolted and snuffled, and I just about leapt out of my skin.

"Hush, Buttercup," Franco soothed, dark eyes darting around to scan our surroundings.

"She's just an animal," I muttered under my breath. "It should be me you're soothing."

He gave me a narrow look, then said in exactly the same tone, "Hush, Viola."

"I didn't realise you could hear me."

"Surprise."

There was a faint rustling through the forest surrounding, and we all jumped, even Buttercup. "Maybe she can hear something we can't," Franco muttered. "Just...don't panic, alright? It's probably just another half-sized troll."

I nodded, trying to breathe regularly and not lose control. "You're probably right."

But then the creature exploded from the undergrowth, and I didn't remember anything much after that.

"It was just a raven," Franco said grumpily some time later. We were wandering along the road, hoping that we'd catch up with Buttercup, but she'd proven that she could move very quickly when she was startled. "You didn't need to go and *change*."

"I didn't mean to," I countered. "But you were just as on edge as I was." Ironically the forest seemed far less terrifying now I'd seen it from dragon perspective: especially when I realised how easily the big scary trees could catch fire. "Lucky that stand of trees was separate from the others, yes?" The raven hadn't been quite as lucky.

"Luckier that you seem to be able to recognise me when you're a dragon. And Buttercup too, I suppose." He sighed. "At least I've still got my sword and that loaf of bread. We won't starve."

He'd been wearing the sword out of sight beneath his long cloak, as it was forbidden for lower classes to wear such a weapon – unless they were soldiers, of course.

I watched him out of the corner of my eye as we walked, my own cloak wrapped tightly around me. My dress hadn't fared well with that second shapeshift – if the change of size hadn't torn it, the accidental fire would have finished it off. "Are you scared of me *now*?"

"No."

"I don't believe you. *I'm* scared of me."

Franco stopped in his tracks, turning to look at me straight in the eye. "Do you remember what happened right before you changed back?"

"I don't know. It's kind of a blur." But I did remember

seeing his dark eyes so very close to me, the only clear thing in the whole mess. But I wasn't going to tell him that.

"After you changed and Buttercup ran off, you stopped and looked at me. Just looked at me, and I said your name, and then you changed back to human."

"Just like that?"

"Just like that," he confirmed. "So I know you won't hurt me. You seemed far less aggressive that time, more like you knew who you were."

What a relief. "There was no real danger. That probably helped."

"Mm." Franco paused thoughtfully. "You know, I got a better look at you that time, and much as I hate to say it, Nellie was right. You *did* have feathers; on your wings and on your head. You looked more like some sort of bird than a lizard creature."

I looked at him in surprise. "A giant, fire-breathing bird? Does such a thing exist?"

He shrugged. "You do, so I suppose it must. Or more likely that dragons come in all shapes and sizes. They say the one that ate King Atticus was the size of a house and had jaws like a crocodile, but it was such a long time ago."

I tried to imagine myself as a cross between a goose and a crocodile, and eventually gave up. I didn't want to change again – I didn't – but if I *did* change…then it would be nice to do so in front of a mirror. Just once.

As we walked it was growing dark for real, the end of our third day. The mule was still nowhere to be found, and neither was any sign of shelter or villages; no ruins or even strangely shaped rocks. It was just a rocky, barren area with the occasional stand of trees, the creepiest part of the forest having been left behind.

"We need to find shelter for the night," Franco said. "It's going to be too dark to walk safely soon."

"Just what I was thinking."

But we couldn't find anywhere decent to stay, and a distinct chill was coming into the air with the descent of night. It grew colder and colder and darker and darker, and I couldn't help letting out an exaggerated shiver.

"That's it," Franco said. "We need to just find somewhere to stop. We won't find anywhere better tonight."

In the end we just huddled up in a slight crevice in the side of a cliff. It was barely enough protection at all from the cold, and I once more cursed the loss of Buttercup. Yes, she smelled, but she was also big and furry and warm. I didn't have the body fat to keep me warm in weather like this. We managed to start a small fire with scraps of wood we'd found lying around, and while it was better than nothing, it was hardly comfortable.

But the cold meant that we lost our sense of boundaries, and we ended up sitting close to each other with the fire at our feet. "You know I could just change again," I joked. "I bet I wouldn't be cold then."

"I bet you'd take off into the night," Franco replied dryly. "I bet I'd never see you again. But go on, if you think you wouldn't be cold."

Perhaps not. "I wonder what Nellie's doing right now," I mused. "She'll be alright, won't she?"

"Yeah. Sure."

I turned to look at him, his face now so close to mine. "Do you really think so?"

"I think that it's not our problem," he said sharply. "And she surely can't be any worse off than us. At least she's got a town of short-sighted Wyse folk to look after her beautiful self."

So much for having got over her. I couldn't hold back a sigh.

"What's that for?"

I shrugged, looking at my arms wrapped around my knees. The whole of my plain brown cloak looked orange in the low firelight, and even though I knew the fire needing topping up, I didn't want to unfold from this warm position. "Nothing."

"It's not nothing. What was it?"

After a few moments I replied, "Nellie. I can see she's still taking up a lot of your headspace. But that's none of my business."

"You're right, it isn't your business. And you're wrong, because I don't even think about her," he said confidently. "I haven't thought about her all day. Any…any stupid infatuation is long gone, I can promise you that."

Right, and three weeks ago he'd been in love with her? I couldn't hide a disbelieving smile.

"What?" Franco said arrogantly. "It is. And I *know* it is, because-"

Pause. "Because what?"

"It's just…it's sorted, alright? I don't care about her at all now!"

A thought crept in, one that had been around the edges of my mind all day but I'd never really grasped at. "That potion you bought wasn't for your face, was it? It was something to do with Nellie."

His silence told the truth, and it saddened me. If he'd had to use a potion to change his emotions towards her, then it was certainly a deeper entanglement than he claimed. And so often that kind of power wasn't even permanent. Just look at Nellie's silver dress that had disappeared at midnight. "The change might not last, you know."

"I know," he muttered. There was a long silence, then he said very quietly, "I suppose now I've left the castle I'm neither useful *nor* handsome in her mind. A shame, but I'll get past it. That's what the potion was for."

"For heartbreak?'

He shrugged a shoulder. "Close enough."

"I told you that Nellie's mind is a ball of fluff," I replied just as quietly. "Trust me, you are both useful *and* handsome, no matter what she thinks. Try to forget her, Franco. She's no good for you."

He turned to look at me, and now his face was very close. "You said that before. Does this mean you *do* like me more than a little?"

I felt my face redden from my chin to the tips of my ears, but I didn't look away. "If you hadn't worked that out already, then you weren't paying enough attention. But don't worry, I don't have any expectations."

Franco let out a short laugh. "You never do, do you? You expect nothing from life, and you get exactly that."

"Not nothing," I murmured. "I just try to be realistic, to protect myself. Wouldn't you?"

"If I could go back in time and stop my foolish self from entertaining foolish hopes?" His face was so close now that I could feel his breath against my cheek, and all I'd have to do was turn… "I'd not fall for a silly, pretty girl, that's for certain."

He was in love with Nellie. He'd taken a potion to change his heart. The reminder jolted me, and I turned away abruptly. I was done with being second to my stepsister. When and if I ever married, once all this curse nonsense was dealt with, I'd find a simple man with simple tastes. Someone who wouldn't compare me to other, more beautiful girls, and I wouldn't compare him to tall, dark, handsome sons of kings. It was only fair. But in the meantime, I'd keep my distance.

"And I wouldn't have tried to sneak those figurines back to the Dragi temple. I'd have given them to you instead," I said. "But the past is gone, and I can't do anything now except try to make the best choices for my future. I suggest you do the same."

I wasn't looking at him anymore, but I could feel his gaze intent on my face. "What if that's what I am doing?"

Did he really mean what I thought he did? For a moment I felt another pulse of excitement, but then it hit me. Not only was he angry with Nellie, currently penniless and alone, but here I was, the girl carrying around a lifetime's supply of rare gold. Forget that I was too tall, too thin and too plain; I could have had a face like a warthog and it wouldn't have mattered. No wonder he was determined to 'help' me, even to the point of risking a fiery death.

"Then I wish you luck," I said briskly, turning away and huddling into my cloak. "Good night."

We eventually found Buttercup the next day, not even an hour into our walk when the sun was well and truly coming up. She was just outside the rocky valley we'd sheltered in, placidly munching grass near the entrance to a wide, green plain bordered on one side by a steep cliff speckled with the native white stone, and on the other by a low, neatly arranged forest.

"At least she didn't get lost in the forest where she ran off," Franco said, giving the mule a pat on the neck. "Look, her reins are caught in this crack in the rock. She's lucky we found her before something else did."

"There aren't wolves or bears round here," I said confidently. "Mother always said that Cristonia was far safer than Delmany and the east, that they didn't have any large predators. She might have starved to death, though." But when I went to scratch behind her ear, she shied away. I knew why; that she connected me with the raging beast she'd met the day previous, poor thing, but it still somehow hurt my feelings.

Franco saw my disappointment and shrugged. "Don't worry about it. She's just a mule."

With a better sense of self preservation than him or Nellie, apparently; because neither of *them* had run away. I turned away, looking out over the green plain that the road would lead us through. "Look, the forest stops so neatly there because of that stream," I pointed out. "It leads along the whole length of this plain. I wonder why it hasn't grown across."

"The livestock keep it trimmed," a small voice near my elbow came, and this time when I leapt in fright, I managed *not* to change form nor barbeque anyone.

The young boy just looked at me. He was perhaps ten or eleven, with large, solemn eyes, a dirty face, and a messy thatch of fair hair on the top of his small head. He carried a shepherd's crook in one hand.

"And you'd be the local shepherd," I said once I'd caught my breath. "Where are your sheep?"

He waved a hand out towards the open green plain, and as if my vision sharpened, I realised that what I'd thought were scattered stones were actually sheep, off in the distance. "So, what brings you here?" he asked.

Franco and I exchanged a glance. "We're looking for the stone folk," he said eventually. "Do you know if we're close?"

The little boy folded his hands over the shepherd's crook, leaning into it thoughtfully. "Depends what you want them for. Need a curse broken, do you?'

"Is that normal?" I asked, startled.

He shrugged. "We probably get one, two people a year coming this way for that reason. Seems the Wyse folk back in the forest keep sending them up this way, to get them off their hands, more like."

The disappointment overwhelmed me as I realised what he was saying. "So the stone folk can't or won't help us, is that right? Do they even *exist*?"

"He's just a child," Franco cut in. "He's probably only

repeating what he's heard his parents say. Come on, Viola. We'll find them ourselves."

And if we reached the north coast or found that we'd gone all the way into the next country, Danvia, then it would be fair to say that we'd missed them. I gave the boy a nod. "Thank you, but I agree with Franco. We're going to keep trying until we find out for ourselves."

We moved past him and began walking out into the open green area, following the almost-invisible path down through the plain. The boy skipped to catch up with us. "What's the matter? I know all about curses, you know. There are the sleeping ones, and the sadness ones, and the death ones, and the ones where you can't say certain words or else you get really angry…"

"Don't tell him," Franco told me. "Enough people know about this as it is. We'll tell the stone folk when we find them."

"Ooh, something embarrassing, is it?" The child looked up at me with knowing eyes too old for his young face. "You can tell Brax. I won't pass it on."

I raised an eyebrow, annoyed. 'Brax' clearly knew nothing, and was just looking to entertain himself during the boring job of minding sheep. I could understand that, but I wasn't his entertainment. "Alright, here it is. My curse is that I turn into a-"

"Viola!" Franco cut in.

"…a giant fang-toothed sheep, and eat children who ask too many questions," I finished.

"A giant sheep?" Brax looked unconvinced, scrambling to keep up with our longer-legged pace. "I've never heard of any sheep that'll eat flesh. What did you do, annoy some kind of witch or bad Wyse?"

"Made some bad decisions," I replied briefly. "But I figure I've more than paid for it. If you're right, and these stone Wyse aren't reachable…"

"What if they are reachable but just can't help you?" Brax countered. "I haven't ever heard of anybody being turned into a sheep for more than a day at a time. Usually Wyse curses end at midnight, but that's just the low level ones, to get someone out of your way, or to make them sorry without real harm. The other sort…"

"It's the other sort," I replied, interested in spite of myself.

Clearly he couldn't help us, but he knew a lot for a ten-year-old. "The sort that's hard to break, and gets steadily worse."

"Usually you have to do something to break those," the boy said. "Y'know, like with the story of Snow White and the kiss... oh wait, that was poison. Well, what about that nobleman a year or two ago who was turned into a beast? They say that he was freed by the love of a good woman, or something."

I paused. "I haven't heard this story."

Franco scoffed, picking up the pace. "Probably because he's making it up as he goes along." But he didn't tell the boy to go away.

We were well into the open green plain now, and the closer sheep were lifting their white heads to watch us pass. One of them ambled closer, Brax giving it a wave with his crook to keep its distance. "Nosy boggers, these sheep are. Can you give me a ride?"

"What?"

"On the mule. I'll tell you the story as we walk, but my feet are sore. I'm not very heavy, I'm sure Buttercup won't even notice I'm there."

"How did you know her name was Buttercup?" Franco asked, his tone unconcerned. Clearly he'd decided the boy was no threat, and perhaps even a little interesting. "Were you listening in on us?"

"Yup," Brax agreed unashamedly. "I caught her, you know, and left her there in case anyone came along. I was watching her, though. Wouldn't want anything to happen to a poor little mule."

Or big mule, as it turned out, because she was far larger than this small boy. Franco hefted Brax up on Buttercup's back, and after a moment he settled in, smiling at the height. "I think I'm taller than you now, Miss."

I laughed. "You don't even reach my nose either way."

"Maybe you're too tall, then."

"Maybe you need to tell your story and keep the insults out of it," Franco cut in sharply.

Brax was unbothered. "I meant no insult. But haven't you noticed that the world's made for people of a certain type? A certain size or appearance. I'm too short for anything to really fit me, and you're a bit too tall. You aren't a giant, but I bet you need to always add cloth to the bottom of any bought gowns so you don't show off your ankles."

We all looked down at the hem of my ragged gown, now in much worse condition than it had been when it started out. The bottom two inches were a slightly different fabric than the rest of it, because he was right, standard gowns certainly weren't made for someone of my build. "Well observed," I said smartly, unbothered. My height was the least of my problems at the moment, and I didn't even care that he was bringing it up. Much.

Brax gave Franco a sneaky glance. "Bet some people wouldn't care if you showed a bit too much leg, eh?"

"Just tell the story," I said quickly, flushing from the neck upwards. Franco and I might be travelling as a couple, but nothing could be further from the truth. "A man who turned into a beast, yes?"

"Ah, yes. So once upon a time…about three years ago, in a land far, far…well, not that far, actually. It was only in Brelfne-"

"So three years ago in Brelfne," Franco cut in. "There was a man who was turned into a beast. And?"

Brax gave him an arch glare as Buttercup plodded along, but continued, and to my surprise he was a good storyteller for a child. He told the story of a nobleman, handsome and charming and all of those things that people who'd never met actually the upper classes expected. But he was also cruel and careless and generally hated, to the point that a Wyse woman heard about it all the way from here in Cristonia. She went to see if he was as bad as claimed, because as we know, Wyse folk are nosy and always getting in people's business.

As it turned out, the nobleman *was* that bad. The Wyse woman had turned up at his opulent country home in disguise as a ragged old lady, asking for protection from a storm. He'd laughed at her for being ugly, then kicked her out into the wind and the rain. Naturally, she'd turned around and told him the truth, and then had put a curse on him.

"To turn him into a beast," Franco concluded. "Not that clever."

"To make him look on the outside like he was on the inside," Brax corrected. "And it just happened that it made him look like a horrible, hairy, fang-ed beast."

"Fang-ed?"

"Fang-ed," he agreed. "Just like the giant sheep you turn into. And the curse would only be broken when he came to repentance. You know, saw what kind of person he had been, and wanted to change."

"So where did the good woman come into it?" I asked.

"Some village girl who had been working at the house to pay a debt for her father. She was the last person left behind, because all the other servants fled after the nobleman changed. I do hear he was *very* ugly, but more importantly, very nasty. Anyway, she was there, and eventually he decided that he did care for her good opinion. And then he saw the difference between the way she talked and treated people and the way he did, and finally realised what he'd been like, and wanted to change. It was enough to break the spell permanently."

He'd been turned on the outside into what he looked like on the inside. The thought that my situation could be the same made me feel sour. What had the Dragi priestess said, that she wished I would get what I deserved? Did I deserve *this*?!

Untold wealth, and the ability to destroy your enemies? Not so bad.

I'm a monster! I argued with the thought. The money…it was nice, but it was nowhere near enough to counter the fact that I turned into a giant, terrifying creature and burned people to death. I didn't *want* that life. I just wanted to be normal.

"I guess the girl was flawlessly beautiful," Franco said a little sourly. "They always are in these stories."

"It's a *true* story," Brax corrected. "Besides, I believe she was rather plain. Or at least nothing to draw your eye at first, but she had the loveliest spirit. Even a plain face becomes beautiful when you love the person behind it."

He had a point, even though it was too close to home. I'd always thought that Edwina was very pretty, and it surprised me that anyone else might consider her plain or even, God forbid, ugly. Her features seemed very pleasant to me, as did Mother's. But then love will do that to you. "Well, I wasn't cursed by a Wyse woman for being badly behaved," I said. "It was someone else, and while I can see that I didn't act entirely as I should have," – I should have taken the figurines straight to the guards – "I still *certainly* have nothing in common with that nobleman…"

My words petered into silence as I realised what I'd said. The nobleman had been hated, and so had I, whether it was true or not. But the nobleman had to realise that he *was* that way before he could have a prayer of changing. "Oh king's crown," I moaned. "Am I like that, Franco? Am I really?"

"How should I know?" he replied reasonably. "All I've got to work off is your terrible reputation, and the week or so we've travelled together. I wouldn't have thought so, or if you are, then you hide it very well." He frowned. "There was that time in the castle when you made Nellie cry…but now I know what she's like, I expect she deserved it."

He would remember that. "Well, that Gerelda decided that Nellie deserved what *she* got," I pointed out. "I think the Wyse folk are full of horse manure. Power or not, they go by appearance as much as anyone else!"

Brax was watching us in fascination, his small body bobbing up and down with every plodding step Buttercup took. We were well out into the plain by now, passing dozens of sheep and coming 'round to a steep curve in the hill, and he took that moment to jump off onto the ground again. "Well, I think I've told you what I know. You take care, alright?"

"Thanks," I said dryly, unsure of whether or not I felt thankful. "You be careful too, Brax. Are your parents far from here?"

He pointed over towards the forest, where I could just see a tiny hut all alone at the edge of the trees. "Me and my gran. She does the cooking, I do the men's work."

Tough for a five-foot-tall 'man'.

"Is there a village nearby?" Franco asked.

Brax shook his head. "Not for miles. Just us."

I felt a sudden surge of pity for this little boy, living so alone and so far from any civilisation. Reaching inside my tunic, I grabbed one of my bags of gold and pushed it into his hand. "If you ever decide to leave here, this should do you well. But whatever you do, don't say where you got it from!"

He peeked into the small opening, then looked up at me with wide eyes. "This comes from being a giant sheep some of the time, does it?"

What...? Oh. I'd forgotten I'd told him that. A little shamefaced, I amended, "I don't really turn into a giant sheep. I was teasing, and didn't realise you'd believe me."

"So you don't really eat annoying children?"

I almost responded, but then saw the teasing glint in his eye. Perhaps he wasn't as clueless as he appeared. "Not usually."

Franco and I moved down the grass-covered path around the corner of the hill, and Brax called after us. "I wouldn't go that way, if I were you."

"Oh? Why's that?"

"The road's a dead end."

We turned the corner and saw that he was exactly right. The plain ended suddenly, with a narrow space where the road led out towards open air. "What the-" Franco began, striding forward to stand at the end. "Viola, it's a dead drop!"

My heart sinking, I ran forward to stand beside him. The green grass came to an abrupt end, and what seemed like a mile below, a patchwork of green fields spread out towards distant blue hills. The cliff extended far off on either side, with steep rock to our left, and the forest edging over the drop to our right.

I looked back at Brax in dismay. "Why didn't you tell us before?"

He shrugged, looking shamefaced. "You would have just gone away, and not talked to me." There was a pause. "You can have your gold back if you like."

"I don't care about the gold," I moaned. "We've wasted our time. We'll have to go back."

<h1 style="text-align:center">11</h1>

Gerelda

We stood at the edge of that high cliff, looking out over the drop where the road most definitely did *not* go any further. Brax stood behind us, watching curiously to see how we'd react, and I just wanted to slump to the ground in disappointment. "We've missed the stone folk," I said, "And that's if they even exist. This *can't* be the right road!"

Franco stared out over the drop, then turned and looked back over the plain with narrowed eyes. "There was only one road, so we can't have missed it that easily. Remember the ruins?"

"The last Wyse village was disguised," I said in growing realisation, turning to study the plain once more. But all I could see were sheep, trees and a big old cliff. If anyone knew... "Brax..."

"Yes?" He stood behind us, that bag of gold still clutched in his small fist.

"Is there a Wyse village around here? And we'd appreciate a truthful answer."

"Why should I give you truth when you've lied to me?"

I did a double take. "When did I lie to you? If you meant about the sheep thing, I told you I was joking-"

Brax shrugged. "Lie of omission. Who are you, and what do you want with the stone folk?"

Franco and I exchanged a questioning glance that said, 'Is he serious?' and then a shrug that answered, 'Probably, let's just go along with it'.

"I'll tell," I told Franco. "It's my problem, anyway." To Brax I said, "I'm Viola Cadence, and this is Franco...what's your last name, Franco?"

He looked a little embarrassed. "It's Knight."

"Knight, as in someone with shining armour?"

"Yes. It's my mother's father's name."

I tried to hide a smile – it really did fit him – and finished speaking to Brax. "There you go, Franco Knight. Although I thought we'd already told you that."

"You didn't."

"Oh. Well, we were told we could find help here. We want to speak with Gerelda, over a gift she gave a friend of ours, and also see if anyone can help us break a curse placed by…by some bad people."

"Who? Names, please."

Suddenly the small boy seemed so much more serious than his age and small size would indicate, and I only paused a moment before answering. "The Dragi of Ostraime. Priestess Theodora, to be precise."

"Did you steal something from them?"

"No! I gave back stolen goods, actually." After a moment I added, "I was supposed to give them to the- to the guards, but I purposely avoided them to see if I could get a reward."

"It was Nellie's idea," Franco pointed out. "You would have given them to us…to the guards."

I shook my head. Whether Nellie was to blame or not was irrelevant, because I knew that I had made my own choices. "I decided to take them myself," I said firmly, "And nobody made me do it. I did it out of greed, and I've been punished for it."

"Or gifted," Brax said. "This gold, it comes as part of the curse?"

I nodded. "I'm…I'm changing form."

"And what kind of creature grows gold, hmm?"

Had I said that I was growing the gold? I didn't remember. "A dragon, apparently."

"Are you sure?"

"I turn into a giant, winged, fire-breathing beast," I said, feeling as though I was repeating my earlier conversation with Nellie and Franco. "What else could it be?"

Franco nodded in agreement, and Brax gave a sudden little clap. "Come with me." He took off at a brisk pace away from us, heading over the plain towards the forest.

We picked up the pace to follow him, Buttercup being led on her rope, and then suddenly the boy stopped, right next to the small river running down the length of the valley. There was a bridge here that we hadn't previously noticed, and as Brax reached it, a stone archway appeared in front of him. It was only a little taller than he was, and anyone who went in would have to stoop.

"What are you?" Franco asked in amazement. "Some sort of gatekeeper?"

"You might say that." Brax looked at us, and suddenly he looked much, much older, his large eyes dark and knowing in a lined grey face. He looked like a roughly-built statue of a child, miraculously brought to life.

Our jaws dropped. "What are you?" Franco asked. "No, wait. You're obviously one of the stone folk. Is your name even Brax?"

"Mmhmm. My full name is a little longer," – and now the stone Wyse reached up and placed a small hand on a random place in the archway, revealing a tiny pair of feathery grey wings in the middle of his back – "But Brax is a lot easier to say, I think. So Brax it is."

Beyond the archway stone streets appeared, full of small grey people. Most of them turned to look at us as we followed Brax through, ducking to enter the archway along with our mule. "You can't come in if you're too arrogant to stoop," he called back to us. "Humility is the key to freedom!"

I didn't care at this moment about sage, mysterious sayings, only that we'd finally reached the stone folk, and they'd actually let us in. Hooray! And *that* was why Brax had a dirty face – to hide the grey tint. I hadn't even noticed until now.

He led us down a series of winding streets, the locals turning to stare at us as we went, until finally we stopped at a small water fountain in the middle of an almost abandoned cobblestoned square. In the centre, a stone cherub holding a jug poured the barest trickle of water down into a wide, empty catchment; with benches to sit on arranged around two sides.

Brax clapped his hands once more. "You wait here." And then within a blink he had vanished, leaving the three of us alone in this quiet square. Buttercup nosed forward into the catchment of the water fountain, slurping at the bare few drops of water at its base, then looked up to where the water jug had come to a complete stop.

"Poor girl," I murmured. "We should have watered her at the stream, but I was so excited about being let in that I didn't think to."

Franco let out a snort. "I should have known that no one would leave a little boy out all alone in a place like this. It was a good disguise, don't you think?'

"Mm," I agreed, trying to look into the stone jug to see if it was blocked. At the base was just the tiniest little hole, calcified to the point where only drops could get out. "Do you have a pin? Or even a sharp stick would do."

He moved over to look, and I realised that his 'suspicious narrow-eyed' expression was actually just how he looked when he was thinking. He looked like that most of the time. "No, a stick might break off and make the problem worse. We need metal."

We searched through our meagre belongings until we found a hat pin which somehow had got put away with the food, then tried widening the hole. When it was about the size of my little finger we gave up, realising that it wasn't helping at all. The water remained stubbornly absent.

"We'll wait for Brax to come back, then ask," Franco decided. "I'm sure he won't be that long."

But time ticked by and Brax was nowhere to be seen. We used the last of our own stores of water for Buttercup to drink, but enough time passed that we began to wonder if we'd been forgotten. "All we seem to do is spend our time waiting," I said with a sigh. I almost wondered aloud if Nellie was alright, then remembered what a sore spot it was for Franco.

"Mm. We just have to remember that they don't owe us anything. If they're helping us out of- what, kindness? Then we just have to take what we can get."

I sighed, thinking about Gerelda's biased version of kindness, and resolved not to accuse her of anything. "And remember that they can turn us into frogs, if they want."

"Might be a step up in your case," Franco teased. "Doesn't that curse break with a kiss? And I think frogs are probably more kissable than…than your other form."

Good point. You'd have to be absolutely insane to try to kiss a dragon of any kind. I thought once more of those vivid dreams I'd had, the ones of being chased by an enormous orange beast, and shuddered. A kiss to a creature like that would end up with you missing your head.

Tick. Tick. Tick. We looked down to see a tiny shadow flickering across the ground, almost in jumps from one cobble to another, and with every touch to the ground it would make that tiny ticking noise. "What on earth-" I began, but then it stopped next to the base of the fountain and began to change.

It grew into a cloud of dust, darkening and growing until it was taller, taller, as tall as Nellie, and then the cloud solidified into the rough form of a woman. She looked like someone had hewn a statue of a 'cuddly baker's wife' out of coarse rock, not bothering to polish it into realism. Dark eyes looked at us out of a familiar face, and I saw both hesitancy and hope in that face.

Gerelda.

"I hear you've been looking for me," she said, her voice much smoother than her appearance would indicate…and very familiar.

"You *are* the woman from the market!" I exclaimed. "You were there with a young man when I was buying pumpkins, and you asked-"

"If you wanted to go to the ball? Yes. And you said no, because the power ended at midnight." Gerelda shrugged. "It seemed like a good idea. Wyse gifts always have to have an end point, you know. We folk aren't God, we can't make permanent changes. People have to *want* to change."

I wavered between all the things I wanted to ask her about, and settled on the easiest. "You look different."

"I don't exactly wander around in this form," she replied. "It attracts too much attention, and ignorant people always think I'm a troll. They don't see the wings." She turned to display a tiny pair of grey wings, much the same as Brax had had.

"Surely you can't fly with those," Franco said. "You'd be far too heavy."

Gerelda smiled, the skin around her dark eyes creasing in a distinctly unstonelike manner. "I'm not actually made of stone, you know. I'm just grey."

"Oh."

"And as for the wings – have you ever seen a bumblebee fly? It seems improbable, yet it happens." She shrugged once more. "Although practically speaking, there are other easier ways of travel. I don't fly unless I need to." She paused. "But you're not here to talk about me. It's about Nellie, I presume?"

"Yes," Franco said, just as I said "No". We looked at each other, and Gerelda cocked her head on the side.

"Well, which is it?"

"What happened back in Delmany was ridiculous, and certainly hasn't been in our or even Nellie's best interest," I burst out. "But we would have left it. We got away, and we wouldn't have come to find you just for that reason. In fact, we don't even really need you." I suddenly felt angry, and I stood there, my arms crossed as I looked down at the shorter woman. Wyse woman or not, she'd been incredibly interfering.

"Yes we do," Franco said quickly. He turned to Gerelda. "Do you have any idea what's happened since you interfered in Nellie's life and sent her to the ball?"

Gerelda's expression closed down. "Why don't you tell me?"

So we did. Franco and I took turns telling about how after the ball the prince had arrived at the inn and taken Nellie away, and how it had ruined my family's lives, and how the king had made scapegoats of us. We told how I'd been kept at the palace before Franco helped me escape, and then how the prince's jealousy had led to Franco's scarring, and then to Nellie and Franco fleeing to Cristonia. And of course we had to tell *why* the king had seemed to target me and what Nellie had overheard, and then the whole story of my curse and change spilled out.

We stopped talking and looked at her. "And then we lost Nellie at the other Wyse village, and eventually got here."

"Hmm."

There was a long pause where she said nothing, and I exclaimed, "Don't you have anything to say?"

"It's a lot to assume," she said slowly, "that all of this came about because of my one action in getting Nellie to the ball. Many, many other people made decisions on the way, and any one of them could have changed things. Now do you want my help, or do you want someone to blame?"

"Both," Franco muttered, and then gave a little, shamefaced laugh. "Will you help us anyway?"

Gerelda turned deliberately behind us, moving to the fountain. She tapped a finger on the dry, empty jug and water began gushing out of it once more, pouring into the wide catchment. Buttercup moved forward eagerly, uncaring of any conversation or argument happening in the background. Mules had simple tastes.

"Yes, but you must understand something first."

"What?" I asked.

"It's not always about you."

My eyebrows shot up, and I looked at Franco in surprise. "What do you mean? Our lives have been ruined-"

"Let me give an example," Gerelda cut in. "What did you notice about this fountain when you first arrived?"

"It wasn't working," Franco replied. "It seemed to be blocked, but we couldn't clear it."

"So you assumed there was something wrong with the fountain," she finished. "And yet the truth is that the fountain was stopped on purpose, to allow strengthening of the pipes that feed from the river as they'd been in serious danger of breaking. Yes, your mule went without water, but now she won't even notice that it happened at all." She gave Buttercup a quick pat on the head as she slurped happily at the catchment.

"That's all very well, but we're not mules," Franco said flatly. "We don't forget pain that easily. None of Viola's family can ever go back to Delmany. Neither can I, for that matter. And my face will never be the same. I can't just *forget* that."

"You're only halfway done," Gerelda murmured. "You can't see the full picture, so how can you make judgments?"

"Can you tell us outright?" I interrupted. "It sounds like you're saying that we're not all that important, and that what happened to us is just because of something more important somewhere else. Is that what you mean?"

"It's about a king, a queen, a dragon and a missing baby, all of which affect the fate of one or possibly many nations," she answered. "Is that enough for you?"

We stared at her. "Baby...? Do you mean old King Atticus's child, the one that disappeared?" Franco asked finally.

"Mm," Gerelda said mysteriously. "I'll tell you about it, but not here."

We followed her to a small, simple house at the edge of the plain, where Buttercup was tied up with plenty of room to graze. There was no wall to this city: they didn't need one, since no one could even notice it was there.

A few sheep wandered over to keep Buttercup company, and I looked at them curiously. "Do you think they're actually Wyse folk in disguise?" I whispered to Franco.

Gerelda overheard, and laughed. "Just regular sheep, I'm afraid. We do use the wool, and Brax enjoys looking after them. He's our resident shepherd as well as our gatekeeper."

When I'd realised that the boy was in fact a grown man (of sorts) who'd clearly been testing us, I'd rewound all the conversations we'd had, trying to figure out what we'd said that had made him let us in.

Franco had clearly been thinking much on the same lines. "Was it the gold?" he asked as we stooped to move through the low doorway. "That made Brax let us in, I mean?"

"Dragon's gold has no value to Wyse folk," Gerelda replied dismissively. "It smells funny, and we can't forget the source. If anything it was your willingness to give it up that mattered more than anything else, that and the fact that you realised you haven't been blameless. Brax told me what you talked about, even though you haven't said as much to me. If people insist that they've been perfect and every bad thing that happened is entirely someone else's fault, then we can't help them much."

We were inside the room now, and a light slowly grew as if a tiny sun was rising. Then I saw that the inside was much different from the outside. It seemed a lot larger, for starters, and there were bushes covered in fragrant flowers extending around the sides of the room, along with a small, neat waterfall pouring into a small stone pool at the far end. A male Wyse stood there with a watering can, filling the vessel. He wasn't one of the stone folk, though; he had large orange and black butterfly wings sprouting from his narrow back, and when he turned to greet us

I realised I'd seen him before.

"This is my husband Gaelen," Gerelda said. "He was with me at the village market the day I met you."

Husband? He looked *so* different from her. He was prettier than Nellie.

Pretty Gaelen smiled politely, then set down the watering can. "Are you hungry?"

And we ate. Gaelen's voice was small and soft, rather like himself, but he and Gerelda seemed remarkably united in the way they talked and moved. He was a regular Wyse man, originally of the forest town we'd just been to, ironically, and he and Gerelda had made a bit of a stir by their relationship. If we thought that Nellie and the prince had been an odd couple, then this was even more unusual. I wondered what their children would look like, or even if they could have any.

We were bursting to have our questions answered, but it seemed that Gerelda wanted to talk before we did. She had something to say, and I had to admit, after coming all this way I was curious.

"So I'll tell you all of this, because you've got yourselves smack bang in the middle of the whole mess. Especially you, Viola, what with your shapeshift, and more importantly, finding that diary."

"How is finding the diary more important than the shapeshift?" I asked, self-consciously touching my collar where I knew that the scales were barely hidden. "We destroyed the diary. I told you that."

"But you read it first," Gerelda countered simply. "The shapeshift is the result of a simple curse – *not* from the Dragi priestess's words as you might think, but rather from touching the cursed metal to your skin. It spread like a virus, and that's why you're shapeshifting." She frowned. "That is rather my fault, but I'll go into that later. But the diary is a different story. As far as we can tell, it's the only definitive proof of what we've known all these years, but the rest of the world hasn't. And I can see from the look on your face that you don't understand the significance of what you read."

I shook my head. "It was about a woman who was in love with a sleeping dragon, a really big one. The diary said that it was the dragon that killed King Atticus."

Gerelda and her husband exchanged a wry glance. "In a manner of speaking. And what I tell you must not go out of the room. Not yet, anyway. The knowledge spreading could mean all manner of disaster, not just for you, but for many."

"Alright," Franco said finally. "We won't tell. We're in enough trouble as it is. Do you need us to swear on a Bible or anything?"

She shook her head. "If you're a truthful person, your word will be enough. Performing any rituals won't make me trust you more. Now, the thing you need to know is this. King Atticus wasn't killed by a dragon forty years ago... He *is* that dragon."

There was dead silence for a few moments, then Franco and I both spoke at once. "How is that even possible?!"

Another glance between the two Wyse folk, and this time Gaelen spoke, his voice soft enough to match his appearance, yet confident. "I'm afraid it was my fault. Gerelda and I were young, just setting out in life, and we'd both been determined to be Wyse godparents. You know, the type that go around helping people?" At our unimpressed expressions he looked apologetic. "Well, we try to. Some of us have a lot of power, and we know it's a gift to be used wisely. But we're only people, and we get things wrong sometimes. Sometimes we try to fix things that are really unfixable..."

Forty years ago Gerelda and Gaelen had been freshly out of training and not yet married, and they'd gone their separate ways in the world, determined to do good. Gerelda had gone north up to Gentravia, helping people in myriad small ways, while Gaelen had gone into Delmany. He'd heard that the king was a truly awful man, consumed by greed, and he'd wanted to know if it was true.

He'd found out that it was. And it was the story that I already knew, except with a few variations. Atticus had famously married a young woman with the ability to spin straw into gold (or so she'd claimed), but when the new queen couldn't reproduce the ability, he'd been furious. The girl had gained the help of a magic-using dwarf, Rumpelstiltskin, who'd taken advantage of her desperation to make her promise her firstborn child in exchange for the favour. When the dwarf had shown up, demanding the payment, and the girl had managed to get rid of him, Atticus had acted pleased at first. It *had* been a rather public drama, after all.

But he was still so angry at his wife for tricking him that he planned revenge. He got in contact with Rumpelstiltskin, offering the lives of both the queen and infant in exchange for access to any wealth Atticus chose. After all, he could always marry again, but gold – in his mind that was irreplaceable. The dwarf accepted the offer, and the queen and baby heir to the throne vanished mysteriously on a trip to the countryside. The official story was that they'd been killed by bandits, but the truth was that the dwarf had taken them. He'd killed the woman, and the baby was nowhere to be found.

"That's horrible," I interjected. "What kind of man gives up his own family for wealth?"

"A wickedly greedy one," Gaelen replied. "And that's where the trouble had started."

See, it was Wyse policy to never give up on people. Even the most awful person must be given the chance to change, and sometimes they did. And those who had been wicked but changed their paths often ended up doing great good.

So Gaelen had met Atticus in his palace where he'd been gloating over the acquisition of a set of rare gold elephant figurines, and had told him that he'd been judged, and what his punishment would be. He'd set a 'Beast' spell, much like the one Brax had told us about. It was intended that the king's outside would match the state of his heart, but it backfired terribly. The intense greed turned Atticus into the one thing that personified such traits: a dragon, a creature of huge power and strength that was obsessed with gold. Oh, and could breathe fire too, and wasn't at all sorry for his new form. There was no chance he'd even try to break the spell.

Once Gaelen realised what he'd done, he'd panicked. Having your hair set on fire would do that to you. So he immediately did a second spell, a Sleep one this time. He set Atticus to sleep until such a time as true love's kiss would awaken him, then quickly hid the massive body in a neglected building. He'd thought that even if Atticus was found, no one would ever love a dragon. So

Atticus would never wake up, and nobody would care. Besides, the kingdom would go to a young distant cousin, what with the heir being missing.

"The diary," I said in dawning realisation. "The one who wrote it – she loved the dragon."

Gerelda nodded. "It was a sick, twisted love, but still love. Fortunately only true, selfless love will break a Sleep curse, so Atticus barely stirred rather than woke entirely. But here you see the start of the Dragi cult. The temple is built directly over his body – it used to be a school."

"And the priestess must be the school teacher," I finished, reminded of all those lavish descriptions I'd read in the diary. Ugh.

"Gerelda and I met again," Gaelen continued. "And I'd largely forgotten about what had happened with Atticus. Or tried to, anyway. It's on record with both the forest village and here, but if anything else happens, it's my responsibility. Gerry's helping me, of course." He smiled, just a little. "We passed through your inn, you know. We'd gone to the temple to find evidence of what the Dragi were doing, and we took the diary along with the figurines. But we already know that you found them."

"You were the sisters from Brelfne!" I exclaimed, unsure of how to feel about that. "Your disguises must be excellent."

"They are," Gaelen said modestly.

"But then you must have intended for someone to find the objects," Franco pointed out. "Didn't you know what this could lead to?"

Gerelda and Gaelen exchanged a glance. "That's exactly the point," she said gently. "And it's where Nellie comes into it as well. We didn't realise that the shapeshift curse had leaked out onto the figurines. Atticus had been holding them when he changed, you know, so we didn't realise that you would be affected in such a way. We'd hoped-"

Gaelen suddenly touched her arm, and her eyes widened, and then she said a word I really didn't expect to hear from her mouth. "We have to go."

The two Wyse folk stood abruptly, moving quickly to gather their things.

"Wait!" I called out in panic. "What about my curse?"

"It'll get sorted," Gerelda called back. "Just-" And then the rest of her words blurred into nothingness as both she and her husband vanished. Around us the pretty little garden-house began to shimmer and disappear, and suddenly we were standing alone once more at the edge of the plain, the forest behind us. Even the sheep had vanished.

I slumped down in dismay, and beside me Franco cursed. "Are we doomed to try over and over and never actually get anything done? Where in blazes did they go?"

I didn't scold him for his strong language, instead heading back to where the bridge had been and trying to find something, anything that would let us back in, anything that would make the village reappear. "If she can't help us then I'm sure someone else can," I said with more conviction than I felt.

But there was no entry. Just like with the previous village, it was gone without a trace. I was just about ready to cry when Franco suddenly bent down to pick something up. It looked like a large pink flower, but as he lifted it, the petals fell open into what was almost a little book. "There's writing in here," he exclaimed. And so there was: the small, scrawling text was growing from petal-page to page as though it was being written even as we read it.

Apologies for leaving you so quickly – there's been an earthquake in the northern lands and we've got some people to dig out. We will come back as soon as possible, but in the meantime, be careful.

Viola, I give you the gift of self-control over your shapeshifts. No one will make you do anything you don't want to. I also recommend that you assume the best rather than the worst especially when it comes to others' motivations.

Franco, forgiveness will heal you far faster than any mix of herbs or Wyse gift. Release the grudge and the desire to hold them accountable, and you will truly be free. And don't blame yourself for falling into a pit that so many others have, it's a natural part of living. P.S. Martin is a quack. I'll give you something for the scarring when I come back if you want it, but don't worry. It's not nearly as bad as you think it is.

Then underneath that was one final page: *P.P.S. Go back quickly on the path you came by, but use the river to return to Ostraime. The Dragi are tracking you.*

As we read that, the book melted into thin air, leaving a fine film on Franco's hand where he'd held it.

We looked at each other in horror. "King's crown," I breathed. "I don't even know what to focus on first!"

"The Dragi are tracking us," Franco said. His face was white and he clenched his fists as he moved towards Buttercup, grabbing her halter and pulling her away from the bunch of grass she'd been munching on. "We need to move now."

I almost had to skip to catch up with him, as long as my legs were. "I've just realised what this means, Franco. If King Atticus is still alive-"

"If we count being a sleeping dragon as being alive, sure."

"...then that's why King Barrick wanted me," I finished in a rush. "I mean, why I was in danger. He thinks I saw the diary, and that I know that he doesn't actually have the right to be on the throne."

Franco stopped suddenly, turning to stare at me. "But you didn't even know that. You just found out from the Wyse folk, same as me."

"It's stupid anyway! I don't like Barrick at all, but I'd rather have him than Atticus, whether he's a damned dragon or not!"

We were walking again, as quickly as Buttercup could manage, and our thoughts over what we'd just read spilled out.

"And why did she tell us to take the barge back to Ostraime?" Franco mused grumpily. "There's no way I'm going back there, and *you* certainly aren't either!"

"And why did she have to leave so suddenly? And I'm *still* in danger of getting a fright and burning someone to a crisp-"

"No you're not," he cut in. "That was one of the pages. That you would have self-control, or something. I don't remember the rest."

But *I* did. She'd said that I needed to assume the best rather than the worst, and all I could think about was how I'd thought that Franco was probably staying with me so he could get rich off the dragon's gold now that he had to leave Delmany. That was thinking the worst. Thinking the best would be that he was helping me because he *cared* so much about me, 'the ugly stepsister'. As much as I'd like to think that was true, I wouldn't fool myself, not about something that could cause so much heartache.

I sneaked him a glance as we walked, his still-handsome face creased in a scowl. No, he was helping me because he felt guilty, and because he was a kind person. *And* because he had nothing else to do at the moment.

"Well, I hope that it's true," I said finally. "My worst fear is that I'll harm someone in a way that can't be fixed."

"You won't."

"How do you know?"

"I won't let you," Franco replied simply.

There was a moment of awkward silence as I considered all the things I could say – that he couldn't do anything about it short of killing me in dragon form or getting burned himself – but then decided that I would assume the best, not the worst. He meant well. "Thank you."

He shrugged self-consciously. "Nothing to thank me for."

The road back down through the forest and past the rocky cliffs where we'd slept seemed short and easy now we were travelling it once more, and at such high speed. We didn't stop to sleep, reaching the beginning of the original forest near where we'd found the old castle ruins early the next morning. I was exhausted and figured Franco must be too, but panic kept me moving.

Then up ahead I saw a small figure off to the side of the road, standing stiff with their back pressed into a mass of green undergrowth. I blinked, then recognised them. "Nellie!"

"What's wrong with her?" Franco muttered.

We'd drawn closer, and I saw the expression on her face. She was hollow-eyed and pale with fear, like I'd never seen her before. Tingles of apprehension began to run up my spine.

"Vee?" she whimpered.

And then the others stepped into sight.

12
Return

There were too many of them; those big, green-cloaked men that I'd seen around the palace, and they moved out to stand behind Nellie, with spears or swords at the ready. Their leader was unfamiliar to me, lean with a short, greying beard, and a completely merciless expression. "Hands in the air or see your friend die," the Dragi ordered.

"He's got a knife to my back," Nellie squeaked.

"You don't want to hurt the princess," Franco said soothingly, raising both hands as ordered. I followed suit, feeling that buzzing heat begin to close in on me that meant a change was coming.

No, not now! I told myself urgently. *Not when we're surrounded by armed men!* I wasn't *that* big as a dragon, and the Dragi's knife would move faster than I could change. It wasn't worth risking our lives. I pushed at that buzz, pushed it as hard as I could, and it began to recede. But it didn't go away, instead feeling like it was just within arm's reach.

"But the princess was already murdered by her scorned lover, a disgraced guardsman," the leader said flatly. "We've been sent here to avenge her on behalf of the prince and the king. Good of us, don't you think?"

It took a moment for what he was saying to sink in. So that was how they'd managed to cover her disappearance – they'd claimed that Franco had killed her. It was so awful on so many levels, because it meant that our lives were worth nothing. Not now.

I spoke up, my voice hoarse. "What do you want from us?"

"The diary," the leader said coldly. "Where is it?" I didn't answer at first and he added, "We've already visited your family in Cristonia, but we will be most happy to revisit, and less gently this time. Unless you want to give the information? Miss…Viola, is it?"

If I told them it was destroyed, they'd have no reason not to kill us. If I was able to tell them it was back at Bluebell inn, they'd kill us the moment they found it. But either way, Nellie and Franco's lives would be forfeit before we even walked away. I had to get Nellie away from that knife. Then we'd finally have a chance.

I lifted my chin, aware of my ragged clothing and my lack of natural charm, but determined not to show any fear. "That would be me," I said coldly. "Unhand my stepsister, and I'll tell you whatever you want to know."

"Uh uh," the leader taunted. "We have the girl and the knife, so we have the power. You do what I tell you, or she dies." He must have pushed the knife in, because Nellie cried out in pain, and my resolve strengthened.

I forced myself to laugh, and it actually sounded natural. "Haven't you heard? I despise that useless fribble. She ruined my life, mine and my family's. So if you want to kill her, then go ahead. But know that if you do, I won't tell you a single word. I'm that spiteful." I paused only briefly, ignoring Nellie's stricken expression, and added, "But if you let her go, I'll tell. I will expect to be paid well for my efforts, of course."

There were a few seconds of tense silence where Nellie whimpered, pasty with fear, and then the Dragi suddenly shoved her forward. "Alright, off she goes. And you, Ugly Stepsister-"

She was past me, just a step past me, and I reached for that warm, solid power I could feel at the end of my fingertips, the power to *change*. I grabbed it and pulled it into myself and then I *exploded* into dragon form, but this time I knew who I was, I knew where I was, and I knew what I was doing.

I launched a massive ball of flame at the dumbstruck group, then turned and looked at Franco and Nellie intently, trying to urge them to *flee.* But there was no time, and the Dragi were ducking off the side of the road and grabbing for their weapons, and I went crazy. I let every ounce of terror and humiliation empower me, refusing to think of them as people, but instead as targets.

They were small as children to me now, these big, dangerous men, and I wasn't afraid. A swing of my tail, and one went flying into the trees. Then another was coming up behind me and I turned and breathed fire on him even as I struck him aside. A weapon might have glanced off my side, but I didn't feel it. All I felt was fury as I went for one target, then another.

But after the initial few moments, they began to regroup. They weren't like the bandits who'd just fled, scattered into chaos by the emergence of a dragon. No, they knew what they were doing. They surrounded me on every side, more of them than there ought to be considering what I'd just done, and then there was a net over me, pulling me to the ground. I reared up, trying to throw it off one side, but there was a sharp pain from the other, and as I turned in furious pain, I felt the net pulled down tight, so tight I couldn't even open my mouth, as they staked each point deep into the ground.

Sharp pain after sharp pain hit my neck and undersides, under my arms, and I collapsed. The last thing I saw when I looked up was the leader, cradling one blackened arm as he stared down at me; and just beyond him was a familiar, grinning fair-haired man. It was Jonley the Horrible, and he strode forward with a spear and then there was an intense pressure in my neck, and that was the last thing I remembered.

Viola! Wake up! VIOLA!

I stirred, vaguely aware of the chill air on my back and the hard ground under me. Someone was shaking me, and I was so *tired*… "This better be important," I muttered as I dragged my eyes open. "Did I set fire to the bed again?"

The attractive, blonde-topped face stared at me in bafflement, or was it upset? And now it was crying…

King's crown, Nellie. What was *she* doing here?

But reality slowly sank in as I remembered what had happened, and I pushed myself to upright position, looking around slowly. We were alone, just Nellie and I: alone on this quiet forest road. The net was nowhere to be seen, although the stake holes were still apparent, and both the Dragi and

Franco were gone. I recognised a few scattered rags as being my clothing, which had *not* survived the latest changes. I was next to nude, underneath a small cloak that surely must have been Nellie's fake-boy one. As she saw that I had woken, she rushed over and wrapped me in a tight hug, complete with tears and incoherent babbling.

How *embarrassing*, but at least the others weren't around to see me like this. "What happened?" I asked Nellie in shock. "The last I remembered I was fighting the Dragi, and they had a net…"

She finally sat back enough to answer, tears streaming down her face. "I ran away when you changed, and they didn't come after me because I was invisible, but I saw that they took Franco, and Viola, I thought you were dead! There was so much blood, and you weren't even moving, but then you just set on fire! And then when I thought you were going to burn up, you changed back to human and you were lying there like you were dead-"

"Did you say invisible?!"

"The Wyse folk at the village gave me a philtre," she babbled, "but never mind about that. Are you hurt, Vee?"

I checked my neck to find it whole, and then looked under the cloak. I couldn't see one wound or even a drop of blood, and my own chest looked unfamiliar to me for a moment. There were a few faint grey patches that disappeared even as I studied it, and then I was just pale and smooth-skinned, without a hint of anything unusual.

A miracle.

"I'm healed," I breathed in amazement. "The scales are gone."

"Do you think it's because they killed you?"

'Killed me'. Or nearly did, anyway. "I suppose it's possible." But it wasn't surprising that I hadn't tried that before – almost dying in order to break the curse. I stumbled to my feet, wrapping the cloak tightly around myself, and looked around narrow-eyed. There was something missing… "Nellie, there are no scales. None at all."

"They took them all," she said, wide-eyed. "When they took Franco back to Ostraime."

"How do you know-"

"He told them that he knew where the diary was!" she

wailed suddenly. "And he said he wanted to be pardoned, and he'd tell them everything he knew! Viola, I think he doesn't care about us at all!"

My first inclination was to agree with her, but then I remembered what Gerelda had said. I should assume the best, not the worst. "Nellie, when I told the Dragi that I didn't care if they killed you, did you believe me?"

"Of course not," she replied in outrage. "You would never do that. You were just trying to get me away so you could change."

"Then I'm sure Franco was doing the same thing."

She shook her head. "You don't know how angry he is with me, Viola. He hates me now." Her fine blonde brows furrowed. "He used to be so kind to me, you know. I don't know what changed."

I knew. He'd imagined her to be perfect, an angel, and had been horribly surprised to find otherwise. The higher the pedestal, the harder the fall. "I suppose he's just hurt," I said instead. "Did they say exactly where they were going?"

"To the palace. Well, they didn't *say* that, but I know that's what Franco would do."

"We have to go after them," I said. "We have to save him. They'll kill him, you know."

"But Viola, you've got no clothes on!"

Good point. I awkwardly tucked Nellie's too-small cloak around me like a simple tunic, looking around as if I'd spot a convenient gown or robe hanging on a tree. Unsurprisingly there was nothing except a great big scorched patch where apparently I'd died and been reborn…and a single, pale feather in the centre of that darkness.

I picked it up curiously. "Nellie, is this mine?"

"Of course it was," she replied dismissively. "I told you that you looked like a big bird, didn't I?" She frowned. "I think you ought to have flown us all away to escape, but you just attacked those Dragi instead, and that didn't work very well. It's a shame your curse is broken, because otherwise you could fly us both to Ostraime right now, and save Franco." She sighed deeply. "I suppose I'll need to beg the Wyse for another favour."

She hadn't even considered getting ourselves there by foot or vehicle, but I ignored that. I was too caught up in what she'd said about me looking like a big bird. A big, yellow bird with big orange feet, apparently. And then that made me think of what Brax had said when I'd told him I turned into a dragon – *are you sure?* And he'd taken the gold, even though Gerelda had said that dragon gold smelled funny to stone Wyse.

Then I thought about the curse being broken, and realised that I could still feel something there, something tingly and powerful and within arm's reach. I stretched for it cautiously, and in my mind's eye I saw a fiery, feathered head turn towards me, with the curved beak and bright eye of a predatory bird...

Phloomf. That was how it felt: one moment I was me, the next I was a giant, bird *thing.* I looked down at myself, at my massive, almost-white feathered chest with hints of gold underneath, and big wrinkly orange bird feet under *that,* and I flailed my arms in shock before realising they were actually wings. I'd actually lifted off the ground a bit before panic overcame me and I managed to change back. I landed with a thud on the hard ground, belly-first. *Ouch.*

Nellie clapped and cheered. "You did it again, Vee! And this time you didn't even catch fire!"

I awkwardly got up, feeling like wearing clothing was a lost cause, and decided not to be embarrassed. "Catch fire?! I thought I was supposed to *breathe* fire."

"Oh, you do," she told me earnestly. "It came out of your beak. It was only the once that you caught fire, after I thought the Dragi killed you. But you really must get control of that, or how else will we get out of here?"

"This is mad," I muttered to myself. "Who ever heard of a giant, fire-breathing bird?"

"We shall ask the Wyse just as soon as we've saved Franco," Nellie announced. "Now come on. We've no time to lose!"

Well, I couldn't let Nellie be braver than I was, could I? So I made myself change back, and I made myself get used to being something other than human. After all, I was still the same on the inside, no matter what I was on the outside (and what was I, again?). I took a few minutes to strut around on awkward bird feet, spreading my wings and giving them an experimental flap, the breeze from which sent Nellie's hair blasting back from her face.

"Whoa, be careful," she scolded. But then her eyes brightened. "Is that gold under your wing?" She poked at me – luckily I wasn't ticklish in this form – and a couple of bright pieces fell into her palm. "Wow!"

'It might be gold, but it came from my armpit,' I tried to say, but my voice only came out in a husky, almost unintelligible squawk. Oh. I couldn't talk well in this form.

Nellie surmised as much, giving me a pat on the shoulder like I was some kind of pet. "Never you mind, Vee. I'll do the talking for both of us. Now let's go!"

Nellie showed her bravery then, and she was definitely able to talk for both of us. Always had been. But it turned out that she wasn't so good with heights. After the initial shaky take off where I almost veered into a stand of trees, she put her arms around my feathery neck and screamed the entire way. And then when she wasn't screaming, she was humming something in a slightly panicked voice, and I knew her eyes were tightly shut, because she told me so. I'd managed to get out a few words by using my tongue and not my beak (you try talking without lips! It's not easy) but she kept her word to carry the conversation for both of us. Oh, how she talked.

She told me about how she'd come out of the Wyse village after trying to talk to Martin again and had stood at the gates, listening to Franco and I speak, and that we'd sounded like we hated her. I was dismayed by this, because it was exactly what I'd feared had happened.

"We don't hate you," I tried to say, and I think she must have understood. "I was angry for a long time, but I don't hate you."

"Well, you made it sound like I was a terrible person, and I was so mad that I just didn't want to go any further with either of you." She paused. "But then I thought that you might have been right, just a tiny little bit. I have been spoiled, as hard as it is to think that of myself. I never mean to hurt anyone, you know that, but I do think of myself, and then things happen…"

Her voice drifted off for a moment. "I wanted to change. I wanted to help for once, to make a difference, and that's why I got the Wyse folk to give me this." She tapped something against my neck. "But you can't see it, can you? It's a little bottle, and you just have to open the lid and breathe it in, and it will break your shapeshifting curse. It will put you back to your real form."

"What the-" I let out an angry squawk/roar. "Martin said that he couldn't help me!"

"Who's Martin?"

"Malmario!" (Or, *al-ah-ee-oh!*)

"Oh." I felt Nellie shrug, and as a gust of wind buffeted us, she squeaked in fright, holding tighter until we finally stabilised. We weren't flying as high as most birds would, but enough that the trees and cottages below looked like toys. Humans were *not* meant to have this view, but it was wonderful in its own way. Once I'd got over the fear of changing, I found I rather enjoyed it.

"Looks like Malmario wasn't the best in the village," Nellie continued. "After I heard you two, I went back and asked for a way that I could sneak past you without you hearing me, and he gave me a philtre. But I tested it, and it didn't even work! It turned me into a pigeon, and that was *not* what I asked for."

"A *pigeon?*"

"Mm. So you're not the only one to experience shapeshifting, hmm? And I suppose that would have got me past you, but I was so flustered and confused over what had happened that it took ages to find someone who could help me change back. They gave me one of those little bottles that I just showed you, and it worked like a charm. Oh, and they gave me a proper invisibility cloak too, except it only works when the hood's up, I'm afraid. That was how the Dragi caught me, because I had *finally* managed to get out of that darned village, and then I'd changed my mind about wanting to leave you and Franco, and I came to find you, and then the Dragi just grabbed me."

She sounded quite miffed. "They were so rude and rough, Vee. I daresay I've got quite a nasty cut on my back from that big hairy one. He wasn't nice at all, no matter how I spoke to him! And I thought it must be because I was dressed as a boy, but they knew I was the princess, didn't they?"

I thought about the leering face of Jonley the Horrible, and little Nellie all alone in the woods. "It could have been a lot worse," I managed to say.

There was a pause, and I heard her sniffing. "You don't think that Royce would have sent them after me, do you? He said he loves me. He can't want me dead."

"But you left him, Nellie. You said that you were afraid for your life."

"I am. I was." Her voice softened. "But- perhaps he wasn't quite as bad as I remembered. He did grab my arms once when we were arguing, and it bruised, but I don't think he really meant to hurt me. It was really his father who frightened me, and I was upset that Royce didn't believe me, and…perhaps I- I might have exaggerated just a little bit." There was another pause. "I don't suppose he'll want me back now, though. I think I've made a mistake."

And when Franco heard about it… "Perhaps don't tell Franco. Not yet."

"Mm."

We came into the outskirts of Criston, to those small villages that had carried the rumours of dragons not long before. And even though we were high up, I could hear the screams and shouts of the people below. Flying might be fast – it got us here in only an hour – but it sure wasn't subtle, and all they would have seen from below was a massive winged shape. I wondered again about how Atticus had managed to get all the way out here from the Dragi temple, if he had, and it seemed the only answer was that he had changed, like me. Had no one noticed the long-dead king wandering around…?

We touched down in a forest just outside of one of those small towns, and I sent Nellie to get a change of clothes for me while I waited in hiding. All that I'd learned, all that had happened swished around in my head, and I came to a few conclusions.

Firstly, that I completely understood why King Barrick had reacted the way he had towards me. Not that I thought it was acceptable, just that I understood it. If the truth about Atticus came out then Barrick would have no right to rule. *The king is dead, long live- oh wait, he's still alive. Give us the crown back, please.* And that was ignoring the thorny question of whether or not Atticus's child was still alive too. I didn't have those answers, obviously, but that question of right to rule meant my life and my family's were in danger. And the Dragi had something to do with it…

Speaking of the Dragi, I was trying to figure out how they'd tracked us so easily, and it wasn't hard. It was well known that my family was Cristonian, and we'd publicly said that we were going to visit Mother's family. I supposed it wouldn't be difficult to find out exactly where Aunt Melicia lived, and then to find us. I could only pray that they hadn't found my family, but if they had, surely they would have just got the truth of the diary's destruction from Mother and Edwina?

Ah, but they'd found us on the road to the Wyse folk, and how would they have known *that* without asking?

You stink of gold, and there is only one group of people who can break curses, and only one place where they live. Well, two; but near enough.

I didn't know where that thought had come from, but it was a good point. I remembered the way that Dragi had sniffed me at the palace, as disturbing as it had been; as though like me, they'd been partially changed in their senses alone rather than in body. Again, if they were fairly bright then they could have worked out our location without needing to harm my family. *Oh please, please may they not have harmed my family....*

They'd harmed *me* easily enough, I thought grimly, and they'd even stabbed poor Nellie in the back, not that she seemed too damaged by it. Clearly compassion wasn't their strong point.

I shuddered, remembering the odd pressure of being stabbed, like an immense blow followed by numbness for a moment before the pain hit. And then through my *neck*...but it all felt far away, almost like a distant dream, and that was a good thing. I might wake up screaming in the night as it was, afraid that I'd be stuck in this form forever.

I shifted impatiently from one leathery foot to the other. Nellie was taking *forever*, and the wrongness of being in this form was making me itch to change back. I might be so much more powerful like this, and I might be able to fly (pretty awesome, it was true) but the whole sensation of being *different* felt like being forced into a new pair of shoes, a pair that wasn't too small, exactly, but was all the wrong shape for your feet. Like those curly-toed ones that were fashionable in some parts of society – not only did you look ridiculous, but they squashed your toes.

As I thought that, a gold scale worked its way through my

feathers to land softly in the undergrowth. I would miss the steady supply of gold once I'd used Nellie's little curse-breaking bottle, but at least I wouldn't have to worry about hiding those scales, or setting people on fire by accident.

I suddenly realised that there was a far better use of the bottle than for myself – namely for one giant, vicious, greedy dragon-king…

Just then I heard footsteps and whispers; people crashing through the brush. They might have thought they were being quiet, but my hearing was so good that they sounded like they were just next door. From their hushed conversation I gathered they'd come to kill the dragon. Not so good.

I quietly changed back, incredibly self-conscious of my unclothed state, and then climbed into the nearest tree to hide. Not a moment too soon. Half a dozen men burst out into the space where I'd been standing, armed with swords and spears and bow-and-arrows and in one notable case, a pitchfork. "I saw it come down around here, I swear it!" one of them whispered to the others. "Big as an ox, it was!"

"We all did," another whispered back. "And we won't give up 'til we find it! We're not losing any more sheep to that beast. Milford doesn't have any more sheep to spare."

Milford was a village just outside the Cristonian capital, the one that my mother and Aunt Melicia had grown up in before moving to the city. It was good to know where we'd ended up, but I hadn't touched their sheep! I was annoyed for the barest moment before realising that they weren't talking about me. There *had* been another dragon after all (perhaps the only true dragon), although stealing sheep seemed to be a very poor use of all that strength. Perhaps the Dragi weren't feeding Atticus well enough at that temple.

Just then one of the men stood on the gold scale – *crunch.* "Hey, what's this?"

They all inspected it for a moment. "It's a bloody dragon's scale, is what it is," one of the others exclaimed excitedly. "It's around here somewhere!"

They all went dead still, eyes darting about much like a bunch of mice looking for a cat, and I froze in my place up in the tree. It was thickly branched, but they might still see me if they just looked in the right direction…

The sound of screams and sudden shouts came from the village, and I strained to make sense of the noise. But it didn't take long to figure out what they were saying.

"DRAGON! DRAGON!"

We had company.

Ten seconds later the men had all gone charging back in the direction they'd come from, the scale-finder having quickly pocketed his booty, and a bare moment after that, Nellie just appeared. That was the only way I could describe it, like she melted into view, standing at the base of my tree with a cloak pulled down over her shoulders. "I've got your clothes."

"Wow, your invisibility really does work," I found myself saying, genuinely impressed. "Er…is there really a dragon?"

She shrugged. "How would I know? I've just been stealing clothes- oh, don't look at me like that! I did leave money, you know, more than they were worth. Here, do you want to be a man or a woman?"

I grabbed for the dress, slipping it over my head and quickly tying it into place. As expected it was too short, and also a little too loose, but not as much as I might have thought. By some miracle, I'd actually put on weight since leaving Delmany. Must have been the easy lifestyle. "We've got to see that dragon."

Coming out of the forest, I could hear the screams before I could see anything. And then there it was, green-black and enormous and sinuous, with broad leathery wings that dragged behind it as it stalked around the village, sticking its long snout into one building and then another as if it was searching for something.

Oh, king's crown. What was the bet that 'something' was me?

I froze in place and beside me Nellie gasped. In spite of the chaos, in spite of the screaming men charging at it and the screaming people running away from it, the dragon heard. It turned and stared right at us with one golden, slit-pupilled eye, and then began lurching in our direction. Perhaps dragons were graceful in the air, but on land they moved like drunken toddlers, clumsy but oh-so-fast.

And then Nellie was pulling me down and a cloak was being pulled around my shoulders, and then while I didn't *feel* any different, I saw our invisibility in the dragon's reaction. It jolted, sniffing at the air, and then half a dozen men were launching weapons at it from every side. The spears stuck a little, fell out, glanced off; and the dragon shook itself and turned to face the new threat. I could see it wasn't scared of them, but they were an irritant. Then finally it shook them off and lurched away, one clumsy flap and then another as it struggled to get in the air.

At the last moment it almost casually grabbed for a small sheep in a nearby pen, and I heard the cursing of some of the villagers as it took off with what was no doubt someone's livelihood.

"Noooo!" There was a child's scream, and a small boy came sprinting out from his hiding place to launch himself at the sheep, which was still hanging in midair. He grabbed it around the belly, and the startled dragon kept trying to climb, ignoring the weapons flying in its direction. And then to our horror the dragon was taking off with not one but two unwilling passengers, and the boy didn't have nearly as much grip as he needed. His arms slipped, and then suddenly he was falling *splash!* into a nearby millpond, and I let out a breath I hadn't known I'd been holding. He'd be stinky, but at least he hadn't hit hard enough to break bones. A mere moment later the dragon fumbled and the sheep went tumbling after, right into the pond.

Baaaa - splash.

The dragon gone, the villagers focused on retrieving both the boy and the sheep from the pond. I could easily spot the mother by her tears and scolding hugs (only mothers could be so contradictory) and the boy just stubbornly hugged the sheep. It seemed that it was his pet, and it didn't look any worse for its ordeal.

In the sky above us the dragon was climbing higher with each flap of those broad green wings, too high for any weapons to reach, and exposing its pure gold underbelly. Or perhaps not quite pure gold – there was the sound like rain, and then a faint scattering of scales fell to land all over the village. One landed near where Nellie and I hid, and I moved out from the shelter of the cloak to pick it up. It was harder than my gold scales, more like stone, and as I touched it, it changed from a shining pale yellow into a rough pumice-like texture, shrivelling a little in my hand. I sniffed it and got a hint of sulfur.

Yuck. And Brax had been right; dragon gold *did* smell funny.

Nellie didn't seem to notice. "It almost got us, Vee! Do you think it was going to eat us?" She didn't wait for me to answer before adding, "It must be the one that killed horrible old King Atticus, because surely there can't be more than one dragon flapping about – not counting you, because you're not a dragon, you can't be, because you didn't look a thing like that beast. It must be been twice your size when you're changed, don't you think?"

I'd forgotten she didn't know the truth of King Atticus. "I've no idea, Nellie. I can't really tell how big I get except from what you tell me." I looked after the dragon with narrowed eyes, noting that it was heading back in the direction of Delmany. That tiny dark speck got lower and lower and disappeared into the horizon – or perhaps had hidden in the inter-kingdom mountains to change back.

It hadn't been as big as the description in the diary. The priestess – I was assuming she had written it – had described the dragon as colossal, building-sized, but then what did I know? She'd also written a lot of disturbing things, including some contradictory ones. I frowned, wondering if my dreams had got mixed up with my memories, and if the diary was even reliable at all. At least I knew one thing for sure – there *was* a dragon.

"Do you think it was looking for us? The dragon, I mean. Maybe the Dragi sent it out here after us," Nellie suggested.

"Well, that would be quick work considering it's only been a single day since we met them, and we only got this far because we flew," I replied. "Besides, if they had horses somewhere and went straight up river, I'm sure they wouldn't make it back to Ostraime before tomorrow night at the very soonest, and that would be a miracle. So how would they have sent a message to Atticus-"

"To who?"

"Long story," I said distractedly. "But the point is that we must have beaten the Dragi here, and we can find them somehow, get Franco back. Who can we talk to...?"

"But Vee," Nellie said meekly, "you know that it wasn't this morning that we met the Dragi, right? It was yesterday morning. I- I ran for a long time, and when I finally came back it was the next day. The Dragi might have Franco in Ostraime already, or very soon."

"Damn." I thought of Franco's life being at risk, of him being in the hands of people who cared rather less for him than for their power or reputation, and the knot in my stomach tightened. "Then we've got to go right away. Do you know how much the king cares for him? Do you think he'll save him, if he can?"

"Oh, I'm sure Barrick wouldn't kill his own son," she replied confidently. "He's not *that* awful. I just wonder why he's working with these Dragi. I can't see that he'd gain anything from it except perhaps wealth, although I suppose that might seem worth it."

"Actually…" I quickly recounted what Gerelda had told us about Atticus, about how Barrick' position on the throne was actually very precarious, and the Dragi knew it.

"That absolute beast!" Nellie exclaimed. "He's not even really the king, is he?" She paused, looking reflective. "So I'm not really a princess either."

I sighed. "Who knows."

She sighed as if in sympathy. "Who cares, right? We need to do something about this."

We were so out of our depth with this whole thing, and all I could think was that we needed help. Gerelda or anyone, anyone at all: but we didn't have time to go begging. Franco might already be dead.

"So we've got my changed form, your invisibility cloak, and that curse-breaking bottle," I said briskly. "It might just be enough to help, unless you've got something else in your pockets?"

Nellie looked sheepish. "Well, actually…"

"I can't believe I flew with you on my back when you had thousand-league boots," I muttered as we walked up through the gates of Ostraime, just as the sun was dipping low in the sky. We'd made it here in barely two minutes once Nellie had pulled those two paper-thin shoes out of her pocket. They were all power, and once slipped on the feet they'd whisk the wearer within steps to wherever in the world they wanted to go.

It seemed that she'd been given quite a supply of various supernatural aids from the friendly Wyse folk (far friendlier than they'd been to Franco and I, that was for sure) and it hadn't occurred to her that more than one person could use them. In a weird repeat of this morning, I'd put her on my back and taken one, two, three steps – and then we realised eventually that we'd gone too far, since Delmany was *not* this warm – and then took another step back. Boom, we were outside the gates of Ostraime.

"All's well that ends well," she said staunchly. "Now we just need to make sure it ends well. You find Franco, and I'll go deal with the dragon."

I gave her a narrow look. She might have the boots and cloak and bottle, along with a series of supernatural housekeeping shortcuts that were completely useless in our current situation (a self-sweeping broom, really?) but I was *not* leaving her to such a dangerous task. "I'm the one who can make myself fireproof, so I'll deal with the dragon. Actually…" I took a deep breath. "Will you let me go in, Nellie? With your cloak?"

She put her hands on her hips, still looking absurdly pretty even in her odd, mixed clothing. She was already getting curious glances from passers-by. Just wait 'til they found out who she was… "And what exactly am I supposed to do?"

And here was the only thing we could do, the only power we had. It was in our voices, because once the secret was out, it would lose its strength. It would be a whole new game then. "Will you cause a distraction? A big one, I mean. I can't just set fire to the front of the building, they'll know it's me. I need something that won't look like it was us."

Nellie paused, and then a gleam came into her eye. "Just leave it to me."

13
The Temple

Ileft Nellie just down the road from the Dragi temple while I took the cloak and the bottle. I didn't know what she was planning, but by the expression on her face, somebody would be sorry.

I eventually located the temple's back door. It was well hidden down a narrow lane behind a sheet of what looked like ivy, and I knew that I wouldn't have seen it at all if I hadn't been looking carefully. There was a Dragi guard outside, slumped against the wall with a lit pipe and a bored expression. He wasn't as tall as the ones I'd seen earlier, perhaps only my height, but he made up for it with broad muscle. I would *not* be trying to fight him to get past.

Just then the door opened and another guard leaned out of it. "Hey, Alby," he called to the first guard. "There's some crazy folk screaming out the front of the temple, it's the funniest thing I ever saw. Something about ducks and lip rouge? You've got to see this."

And that must be Nellie's 'distraction'. It was surprising to see that she'd given up her dignity in such a way – but it was for a good cause.

"Oh yeah?" the broad-shouldered Alby retorted. "Worth giving up my smoke for?"

But I didn't hear whether it was worth it, because I'd ducked in underneath the second guard's arm, right inside. He didn't seem to notice, and I quickly moved away until I was in a narrow hall. It was dark from lack of windows, with the skirtings and walls unsurprisingly decorated with serpentine forms all trimmed in gilt. Except for the dragon deco, it rather reminded me of the nicer parts of the palace that I'd occasionally visited.

I followed the hall around a corner into another, wider one lined with closed doors, leading off in both directions. I paused, debating where to go next, and just then a dark-haired woman came into view. She wore a modest, high-necked gown in dark green, and was walking briskly with an open book in her hands. I recognised her immediately as Theodora, the priestess who'd 'blessed' me.

My heart pounding, I ducked back into the narrow hall, but realised a moment later that thanks to the Wyse cloak, she couldn't possibly have seen me. I was *invisible*. But still she paused too as she passed, her perfectly coiffed head cocked to one side as if she'd somehow heard me, and her dark eyes narrowed.

I froze, waiting for her to move on, but she didn't. Instead she leaned forward, sniffing at the air, and I remembered in dismay that I had a bag of gold scales in my pocket...and that the Dragi seemed to have freakishly good noses for gold.

Uh oh.

Several tense seconds passed where it seemed I'd be caught before I'd even found Franco, but then finally, miraculously, she turned away and continued down the hall, that open book still in her hands.

I slowly let out the breath I'd been holding, feeling my heartbeat slow a little. But I was scolding myself as an idiot. After everything I'd gone through, how could I forget that I was carrying gold in the Dragi temple?

Well, that was probably because in spite of what the Wyse folk had said, I couldn't give up the gold that easily. It might smell funny to them, but they could just use their power to whip up a new house or a trip to some foreign land. We had to *pay*, and so money was control and power over our own lives.

But the promise of wealth wasn't worth our lives, no matter what so many people seemed to think. I'd planned to come in here with the cloak, find Franco and cover him as well, and then toss the curse-breaking vial at the dragon. And if I had to get rid of the last of my own gold, then so be it.

I slipped the bag into the nearest vase, then quietly followed the priestess through the otherwise empty hall. I checked every door we passed, trying to find any indication of where Franco might be hidden, but had no luck. What had I expected, a sign saying 'Prisoners through here'?

The hall began to slope downwards, and we walked until I was certain we must be beneath ground level. Then finally, *finally* she stopped before a set of plain double doors. I paused some distance away, watching as she opened the door and stepped inside, then closed it after her far too quickly for me to follow.

Damn.

It was quiet down here; quiet and dimly lit, but the hairs still stood up on my arms. There was something here, I knew it. Something serious, and that was why I crept up to the door, pressing my ear against the dark wood.

Thump. Thump. Thump.

The faint, rhythmic sound was just audible through the door, and I furrowed my brow in confusion. What on earth was that, and how was I going to get in without anyone noticing me?

I was debating just turning the handle myself when the door swung open abruptly and a big, bearded man stepped out, almost knocking me over. It was the leader of the group who'd attacked us in the forest, and he cradled one arm stiffly to his chest – the arm I'd burned.

Serve him right.

He called to someone inside, "Tell Jonley to leave him unharmed for now. We've got better things to do than play games."

There was a muffled reply that I couldn't quite make out, and then the bearded man grunted in agreement before walking away. I just managed to duck through the door before it slammed shut, but then found I couldn't move. The cloak had been caught in the door.

Uh oh. I began to panic, pulling at the unseen cloth in a desperate attempt to free myself, but then I looked up and saw what was in the room, and other thoughts fled my mind.

The dragon. This was the dragon, and it certainly was not the one I had seen back at the village. That one had been slender and dark green, with a head about twice the size of a horse's, but this one matched the first in species only.

It was huge, simply enormous, and it dwarfed the first dragon I'd seen. It slept with its massive orange-red head cradled onto curving claws, the colossal vibrant wings as big as a ring top circus tent – and that was folded. Outspread, they'd be large enough to cover this entire building. The head alone was the size of my dining room, and I knew the dragon could easily swallow a man whole. But at the moment its eyes were shut, and the occasional puff of smoke issued from those dinner plate-sized nostrils.

It was clear that the temple was so big for one reason only – to house this beast. I didn't see any doors it could escape from if, God forbid, it was to wake.

I'd been so caught by the sight of the dragon-that-was-Atticus that I hadn't noticed the activity going on around it. Now here were all the Dragi: dozens and dozens of them moving around the dragon, doing things with tubes and what looked horribly like huge needles: collecting the hundreds of gold scales (no wonder the Dragi were rich!), a tube inserted in the massive mouth to power the furnace and the lighting of the huge room… working with a faint thump, thump, thump that I'd heard through the door earlier.

The red glow of the place reminded me of some sort of industrial hell, and the dragon its king. A sleeping king, it seemed. Gerelda had been wrong – the dragon was deeply asleep, and I thanked God for it. Surely it wouldn't allow itself to be used so if it were awake, and if it were to try to stretch its wings…

Ah, but not quite. Here, just off to the side of the room, was a throne. It was only large enough for a human, and the priestess sat on it, surrounded by familiar guards in their dark green armour. Before her was a kneeling figure in plain brown, his face battered and weary, but with a distinctly stubborn expression.

"So you don't know where the diary is," the priestess said in a slow, almost surprised tone, as if she was getting him to repeat a startling fact. "And yet you had us bring you here."

"I was leading you away from the others," Franco replied. His voice was lower than usual as though something was wrong with his throat. "Not that it did Viola any good. Do what you want with me."

Oh, silly Franco! Did he *want* to die? I tugged again at the trapped cloak, my mind spinning with different scenarios of how this could go, how he could die. Any moment now someone would pull out a sword, or feed him to the dragon, or strangle him-

Riiip.

The cloak came free with an audible tearing noise, and I froze for a moment, terrified. But no one even looked around. And I never found out what the priestess would have said to Franco, because suddenly the huge orange dragon began to stir, and there was panic.

"AWAKENING!" someone bellowed, and then the priestess was off her throne and running down towards the dragon's head, straightening her clothes as she went. It blinked long, yellow eyes and tried to turn its head, but the myriad tubes held it in place, and then as she stood in front of it and began muttering some *spell* it opened its mouth and a tongue of flame roared out to consume her head.

I stood, frozen in fear, but the woman just shook it off, patting it out with her hands. Her clothes were in tatters around her neck but her pale skin was unharmed, and she barely scowled, watching as the huge dragon lowered its head once more into slumber. "That was too close," she said tersely. "What brought that on? You weren't picking half-ready scales again, were you Phillip?"

One of the Dragi shook his head sincerely. "I swear that I wasn't, my lady. He's just been…restless lately."

The priestess tapped one foot on the tiled floor, staring off into space as she pondered, then suddenly she snapped. "Has that damned Barrick got here yet? I sent for him hours ago!"

"Thirty minutes," someone said, and I realised it was Jonley the Horrible, who was also clearly not smart enough to know when to keep his mouth shut. The priestess stared at him for long enough that his stupid grin began to fade. "Sorry…?"

I kept waiting for her to say 'off with his head,' or something equally brutal, but she just stared at him like he was a fly in her ale, then turned away. "You, king's son," she ordered Franco. "This man was once your subordinate, yes?"

Franco took a moment to answer, seeming startled that he was even being asked such a question. "He was once, yes."

Before he'd been demoted and scarred, that was.

"Hmm." And that was all she said. *Hmm.* But it was a sound that held a world of meaning, and I suspected that the priestess didn't forget any grudge she held.

Just then there were footsteps approaching through the thick door, and it slammed open. In stalked Prince Royce, followed hastily by King Barrick, who was looking so much smaller and more ineffectual than I'd remembered him. Perhaps the change of surroundings helped with that.

"He insisted on coming," the older man said huffily. "I told him it was nothing to do with him, but he wouldn't listen."

But Royce had stalked right up to where Franco still knelt on the tiled ground, his face a picture of fury. "What have you done with my wife?"

Franco blinked. "I haven't done anything-"

"I know you ran off with her, you little bastard! Don't lie to me! I-"

"Enough," the priestess said, and her voice was like a silencer. Everyone listened. "Your silly little wife left of her own free will, and this boy was fool enough to aid her. You will not interfere with my judgements any longer. If you must be here, you will be silent."

Royce opened his mouth to argue, but nothing came out, and after a few moments he stepped back, white-faced. A man like him wouldn't be used to being made to do *anything*.

"He's just a boy," the king said quietly, looking scared. "He doesn't know about any of this." It seemed he was referring to the prince rather than Franco, although Royce was well into his twenties.

The priestess gave him an arch glare over one elegant shoulder. "And yet if you were to die now, the rule of our whole land would rest on his shoulders. That is not a job for a boy."

"Why did you call me here?" the king asked finally. "Is it about…this one?"

'This one' being Franco, apparently.

"And other, more important matters," she replied. "The diary is yet to be found, and your *son* refuses to reveal its whereabouts. I *know* that he knows where it is. And don't say he's not your son," she added quickly when it seemed that Barrick would speak. "Your blood is clear to see."

After a delay, King Barrick turned to look at Franco. "Well? It's for your own good that you answer."

"Are you going to stop them from killing me?" Franco asked frankly. "Because I don't think that you can, not when King Atticus is lying over there with a tube up his nose."

It was clear that Royce was the only one who hadn't known, and he did an exaggerated double take, then choked as the word-binding spell seemed to fade. "Father, what is he talking about?"

"Something that affects both of us," the king muttered. "Boy, I need you to just listen for now, and I'll tell you what you need to know later. But no more about that girl-"

"But Father-"

"No!" Barrick shouted. "You listen to me this time, is that clear? You'd have been better off to avoid that peasant like the plague instead of marrying her. Marrying beneath yourself only causes trouble, and we *need* to sort this out now. Franco, you must tell us what you know of the diary, no matter what happens. I order you to tell me, as your king and…and as your father."

There was a long, cold moment where it seemed like Franco wouldn't respond, but then he lifted his head, his dark eyes almost closed. I'd never seen him look so depressed.

"They had a knife to Nellie's back, and when Viola tried to save her, they killed her. Viola, not Nellie. They killed a teenage girl. Do you think they'll have mercy on you, *Father*?"

"Don't call him Father," Royce muttered, sounding rather like a petulant little boy. He looked confused and scared. "You're not to call him that."

Franco snapped. "Why, I should stay the king's dirty little secret for the last few hours of my life? I know who I am, not that it's done me any good at all, and not that I'd want to claim *you* as a brother after what you've done to my face and to Nellie-"

"I never hurt *Ella!*" Royce burst out. "And your face – some people just got a bit carried away, alright? I didn't mean for it to be so bad, I just wanted her to stop looking at you like she did!"

'Her' being Nellie, no doubt. But just when it seemed the argument would go on forever, the king cut in again. "Well, thank God that one problem's dealt with. We couldn't trust that girl not to talk, and the rest of the family will be found soon enough. But you must tell us what you know, Franco. I'll- I'll promote you to Captain again, give you a full pardon. Gold, anything you want." He sounded desperate now. "Tell us where the diary is!"

"I don't care about your bloody gold or titles," Franco said furiously. "You killed my- my dear friend, even if not by your own hand, you did it, and you don't even care!" (Me? Did he mean *me?*) "I want nothing from you. As for the diary, I can tell you for certain that only Viola had seen it. She'd hidden it from her family, and she didn't even understand what she was seeing. But the book's been burned, alright? There's nothing left of it." He swallowed, and his eyes gleamed wetly in the dim light. "Nothing left of her, either. You've no fear of the truth getting out."

King Barrick seemed to sag with relief, but the priestess stepped forward. "And you, king's bastard? What of your promise to keep your mouth shut?"

"What of it? I'll keep my promises just as you keep yours."

"Not a promise then," she said crisply. "Jonley..."

The guard stepped forward, clearly eager to make up for his earlier lapse. "Yes, my lady?"

"I want you to take this one out into the hall and kill him."

The king and prince's faces paled, and Jonley's smile faltered. It seemed that he wasn't *quite* as terrible as I'd expected. "Mm-my lady?"

"Are you questioning me, Jonley?"

"N-no, my lady, but-"

"No buts," she said firmly. "Go."

"See here," King Barrick interjected. "You can't just kill him, he told you that the diary was destroyed. He's just one boy..."

The priestess glared at the king, and he seemed to shrink back. "Yet he would not make such a promise, and I wouldn't trust him even if he did. So what do you suggest that we do with him, if we cannot kill him?"

King Barrick licked his dry lips, swallowing awkwardly. "He- we can just give him some money to leave Delmany, to leave this whole region. He's just a bastard anyway, no one will believe that his words come from anything except spite. You don't need to hurt him."

Geez, and I'd thought that *my* family could be bad. This took it to a whole new level, even though I knew that the king was trying to save Franco's life.

There was a long, tense silence that reaffirmed what I already knew: the king had no power, not over this woman, not over these people. He was as helpless as I'd been, as Franco was.

Then the priestess smiled. "Very well. We shall not hurt him, but we certainly shall not send him away. We can always do with more workers in the metal pits under this building."

As if on cue, two guards came forward and grabbed Franco under the arms, lifting him to his feet and beginning to pull him away. He called back to his family: "You've got a tiger by the tail with these Dragi. They'll turn on you too, no matter what you've given up to appease them."

After he was gone, the king ran one hand over his sweating brow. "Come, Royce," he ordered his legitimate son, with a bare glance at the woman as if to ask for permission before moving towards the door. She didn't stop him, and the prince began to follow after, looking very young and uncertain. For the first time I almost felt sorry for him. Almost, but not quite.

Then it was just me, the priestess and the scattered workers around the dragon, and it seemed that now would be my chance to break the spell. I tensed, gripping the Wyse vial tightly and resolving that the moment she left, I would do it. But now the other Dragi were leaving too, as though they'd coordinated themselves, and it was just the two of us.

But then she spoke. "You can come out now."

I froze, but she wasn't looking at me. She couldn't know I was here, surely?

"You, girl. Invisibility only blocks the eyes, not the other senses. I know you're there."

One, two, three seconds of indecision, and then I pulled the hood back off my head, no longer unseen. And then it was just me standing there with a few very valuable objects in my pockets, but otherwise helpless. She didn't have any weapons either – that I could see – but I was beginning to suspect something about this woman. Those high-necked green gowns... Why green rather than orange-red like the dragon she adored? Green like the other, smaller dragon…

The priestess stared at me for a moment, then to my surprise she smiled. "I thought you'd stay hidden. I didn't realise you had the courage – or were so foolhardy."

"What are you going to do with Franco?" I asked instead. "What are the metal pits?"

She shrugged a shoulder, moving to pick up a goblet that had been set nearby, and swirling the liquid around with a smooth motion of her hand. "Under the temple. We need to process those goods provided by His Majesty, and Barrick provides the labour from his dungeons. It's a hard job, so we find that the workers need constant replacing."

Not because they'd been given a holiday, I suspected. At least Franco wouldn't be killed right away.

"Did you come here just for him?" she asked, arching an eyebrow. When I nodded, she smiled. "How sweet, and what a shame you couldn't have dramatically appeared to show him you were still alive. You planned to sneak out with him under the cloak, I assume?"

My silence answered that clearly enough. Was I so transparent?

"And you did destroy the diary?"

I nodded. "No one else read it. Just me, and it gave me horrible dreams."

"Dreams of dragons?" She screwed up her nose. "You might call those horrible, but I don't. I think they're lovely." She turned towards the enormous beast so close by, almost caressing it with her gaze. "Do you not think him beautiful?"

"Not precisely."

Her gaze narrowed on me. "And did you think yourself beautiful, in your shifted form? A giant golden bird, alight with flame?"

I jolted in surprise, and she sneered. "Yes, of course I knew about that, although I don't yet know how you are standing here when my Dragi said they left you dead on the road in Cristonia. You tricked them with illusion, of course."

I didn't answer. It hadn't been illusion, but if she didn't know what had happened, then I wasn't going to enlighten her. I wasn't even certain myself. "Did everyone who touched the figurines change, or was it the curse you gave me?"

"Curse? Oh, you mean the blessing." The priestess laughed. "Just words, my dear. No, it was most certainly the figurines, although as far as we know they only heighten the senses, particularly the ability to find both gold and power. Very useful in my guards. But most do not gain the ability to change form."

Most. Not all. And I was beginning to think that I wasn't the only one who could change. There *was* another dragon, wasn't there? "Except you did," I said. "That was you looking for me on the outskirts of Criston, wasn't it?" The high necklines on her dresses had finally made sense to me. Few people wore those by choice, and the priestess had to hide her own scales. So similar to my own, but yet so different.

Another slight smile, and she cocked her head on the side. "Not entirely stupid, then. Although I never found your family. The address was outdated."

Because Mother and Aunt Melicia had lived there as children, but had long moved, thank heaven. But it explained why the dragon had been haunting the edges of the city – taking off with the sheep would have only been a cover for why she was really there. "And you wrote the diary, didn't you? You found the dragon when you were young, and you wrote about it." Like an obsessed crazy person.

She took a step closer, still swirling that damned goblet, and I watched the movement almost like a mouse unable to move before a cat. "Yes, I wrote about him, because I loved him, although not in the way you might imagine. I was just twenty when I found this place. It was deserted, and nobody came near it even though it was in the centre of the city. Almost like it was guarded by a spell to keep people away."

It had been, of course. That's what Gaelen had said.

"And then I came in with my stepbrother Declan, who I believe you met on the road here. You did him some injury, and he seemed to think he had killed you – I'll need to speak to him about that. But I saw the dragon and I was *different*, because I understood what he was. I realised that he wasn't a beast, not like everyone else believed. I was raised by a dwarf, did you know that?"

"Ah- no, I hadn't known that." She was changing subject so

quickly, still focused on me and swirling that goblet, and it was making me seriously uneasy. My hand tightened on the vial in my pocket.

"I was raised by a deranged, depressed, sorcerous dwarf who bought me from my father as an infant," the priestess said. "He taught me how to use power, and he told me all about what had really happened, because he wasn't as easily fooled as a human. Can you guess his name? I'll give you three attempts."

Three attempts to guess the name, but I didn't even need one. "Rumpelstiltskin," I said in sudden realisation. "You're the king's child. Atticus's child."

She turned and looked once more at that huge, deep-orange dragon lying asleep under that low roof, and her smile was a little sad. "Yes. And even though Atticus sent my mother to her death, and even though he abandoned me, and even though he was the most gold-hungry person I'd ever known, I couldn't hate him completely. Do you understand that, girl? That sometimes you can love as much as you can hate?"

Yes, I could understand that, because I'd felt a hint of it with Nellie. And this woman had been abandoned and hurt in every way, but was still desperate for the love of her undeserving father. But this twisted love/hate of the dragon had made him stir, but not awake. Only pure love would break a spell. Ironically, the way she used him now seemed the furthest thing from love.

She saw me looking at the tubes and the weights holding the dragon down, and her eyes narrowed. "He owes me, girl. He owes me for the life I missed out on. I should have been a princess, yet I lived like a peasant for many years before Declan and I finally killed Rumpelstiltskin and came here almost two decades ago. So now we live like the rulers we should be."

"You don't look forty."

"One of the benefits of being around so much power. I don't have one single wrinkle, and I never will. And one day soon, when I decide the time is right, I'll drop this pretence of having any obligation to Barrick, and show who I really am. The law states that if the king has only daughters, and there are no first cousins to take the throne, then the throne reverts to the females. Me. And dear Barrick is only a second cousin, don't you know."

She was making perfect sense, but at the same time I was

increasingly uncomfortable. She wouldn't be telling me all of this if she'd been meaning to let me go.

Theodora seemed to be thinking the exact same thing. "I told Barrick that unless he dealt with you in a way that couldn't be traced back to the Dragi, then I would reveal the truth, and he would lose his throne. He tried, but he didn't have the guts to dispose of you fast. Hence our meeting here."

She was still swirling that goblet, and now she was barely three feet from me. "A bit of a mishap on part of those thieves, to allow you to find the figurines. And the paint they'd put on them – it took hours to get them clean."

"I'm sorry…?"

"Yes dear," she said almost gently. "You will be."

Then she moved so fast that I could barely even lift my arm to defend myself, and she tossed the contents of the goblet right over me. I felt the liquid seep into my clothing and my skin and settle there, leaving a heavy numbness, and next I was on my knees, and she was changing before me.

"It's been nice to talk to someone who understands," the dragon-woman was saying, her features growing ever more reptilian under that loose robe she wore, the outer layer being shed to allow for the growth of enormous, spreading wings. "But I can't just leave you here. Another shapeshifter wandering around, and one who has the help of interfering Wyse folk? You're too dangerous, and I don't give up my power for anyone."

By now her voice had changed along with her form to that deep rumble I recognised, and the long, almost black muzzle opened, and bright red glowed at the base of her throat. She was going to burn me, I knew, and as if in slow motion I reached for that little vial inside my cloak. I barely managed to knock the cap off and lifted it towards her…

The dragon-priestess inhaled once, briefly, and then her eyes widened; a strange thing to see in a dragon. Then her wings convulsed, and then very suddenly and quickly she was shrinking back down, as fast as she'd grown in the first place, except this time she was shaking and weak and her clothes were torn, and her eyes wide. There were distinct lines around her eyes – forty years' worth of them.

"What did you do to me?" she gasped hoarsely.

Wasted the curse-breaker, apparently, if you could call saving my own life 'wasting' it. But whatever had been in the goblet still held me bound, and I saw the realisation of what had happened dawn in her eyes.

"I'll just use the figurines again," she spat at me, striding over to grab something from the arm of the throne. It was a short sword disguised as part of the decoration, but it was most definitely usable. "You'll be dead either way."

Just then the doors slammed open behind me, and I heard a familiar, pompous voice. "Put the sword down, witch!" Prince Royce announced. "You won't take another life today!"

What on earth – how had *he* got back here so quickly? I craned my head to look around, and there he was with guards at his back (*not* green-garbed ones) and a familiar, dark-haired figure, almost hunched over as if he was in pain. But then Franco saw me, and his jaw dropped, and his whole posture lightened. "Viola?"

"Watch out for the woman," I managed to say. "She's crazy." Not quite true, but enough to make them pay attention. She'd kill if she could.

Franco rushed over to where I still knelt, our positions reversed from just minutes earlier, and put his arms around my shoulders to help me up. "I thought you were dead! I saw them kill you! What happened?"

His touch seemed to reduce the numbing of the goblet's contents, and I felt myself strengthen. All I wanted to do was hug him. I was alive, he was alive, *one* dragon at least had lost its power. "It broke the curse. I'm free now." Sort of.

And then he did hug me, and he was big and warm and maybe smelled a little of the stressful journey, but it wasn't a bad thing. I hugged him right back, thinking that at that precise moment I hadn't cared so much for anybody in my entire life.

"Royce suddenly gained courage and came back," Franco murmured in my ear. "Something had distracted the Dragi, I'm not sure what, and he got me out. He said he wouldn't be controlled the way his father was."

I froze in indecision. If Royce meant to kill Theodora, then he'd essentially be usurping the throne that belonged to her. But perhaps there were special circumstances… "Don't kill her," I told the prince urgently. "Do the right thing."

He gave me a baffled, uncaring look (had he even noticed that I was supposed to be dead?) and then nodded. "Arrest the priestess!" he ordered his guards. "But be careful. She's a witch."

Seeing that she had only one small sword against four- no, six- oh wait, a whole hall full of palace guards, the priestess suddenly turned and ran over to the sleeping dragon. She set her hands against its huge muzzle, ripping out the tubes that had been set in its mouth and nose and screaming, "Wake up, Atticus! They're going to kill you!"

"Atticus?" one of the guards said. "A bloody dragon?" I saw the horror on all their faces as they realised what was in this room with them. The Dragi didn't worship *imaginary* dragons.

Not at all.

14
Atticus

"**S**top her!" Royce ordered. "Unless you want that thing awake!"

Theodora shook him, screaming it again: "WAKE UP! I NEED YOU TO WAKE UP!"

The dragon's yellow eyes opened just a crack, and then snapped wide. Then it all seemed to happen in slow motion, although in truth it must have taken mere seconds: he pushed himself to his forelegs and then he was filling the room, right to the ceiling. There was just enough room when he slept, but awake his orange horns hit the tiled roof, sending plaster raining down over all of us. And then the vast wings spread, far too many times bigger than this building could manage, and the dragon king began to thrash about, trying to get free.

His long tail whipped around, hitting a couple of the guards and sending them flying, and then even the priestess was backing away, trying to get out of harm's reach. There was a sort of gleeful horror on her face – she knew that she might die, but at least the rest of us would as well. The guards with their swords didn't have a chance, and even though the prince seemed suicidally brave (he was still dancing around with that sword of his, trying to get a stab at the non-fire-breathing end) he'd be turned to ash before he could get near a soft spot. And this was why humans hated dragons – hated and feared them, because we knew that they were armour and weapon all built into one oversized body with a mind as smart as a human's. Too much for us to handle on our own, too much indeed.

"We need to get out of here," Franco told me urgently. "If

the curse is broken, we don't have a chance. The others will have to fend for themselves."

Like a series of puzzle pieces clicking into place, the answer suddenly came to me. "But it's not entirely broken," I said almost apologetically. "I can still shapeshift. The gold just doesn't grow anymore." And then I took off the cloak, shoving it at him along with the vial. "I'll distract him while you get close enough to get the rest of that liquid in his mouth."

Franco looked panicked. "But Vee, I can't lose you again-"

He'd picked up my family's nickname for me, and I almost melted. "You won't," I told him briskly. "I can handle this, and I'm really hard to kill. Now go!"

"But the cloak-"

"Is for invisibility. I was in the room through that whole conversation with the prince. Go on!"

I didn't wait to see what he'd do, instead bursting out into my bird form and flying at Atticus. I felt the flame come from my mouth as I did so, rushing over my head and my back until I was alight. But Atticus didn't speak, he didn't act like a thinking being even though I knew him to be one. Instead he turned on me, watching me with curiosity and then anger when I ducked and dashed for his eyes, then skimmed away quickly along his back.

Being so much smaller felt like being a wasp at a picnic, trying to avoid being swatted away. But being so much smaller also meant I could move more easily in the tight space, trying to keep the big dragon's attention while somewhere the invisible Franco tried to get close enough to use the vial. I didn't know if it was good for more than one use, but I couldn't take the risk that it wasn't. If it worked, then we would be very lucky. If it didn't...

But while Franco was nowhere to be seen, Prince Royce and a couple of the braver guards still kept at the dragon, trying to find a weak spot in its belly even as it divided its attention between me and them. I didn't even consider whether what we were doing was right or wrong: whatever Atticus had been, this is what he was now, and I saw him clearly. He was an evil creature, something that must be stopped.

The walls of the temple began to shake and more plaster rained down on us as the building was rocked by the thrashing tail, and then it caught me in a blast of flame. But rather than being hurt, I was knocked back against the wall. It crumbled behind me and I felt cool air as the inner building was exposed to the world, but it wasn't what drew my attention. And then Atticus was turning back on Royce, who was standing right in front of him like an idiot with his sword looking like a tiny sharp toothpick. I launched myself at the back of the beast's head to try to draw him away, but too slow. Atticus lurched forward, the massive body falling on Royce...

And then like a balloon being deflated, the dragon began to collapse in on itself. It shrivelled smaller and smaller until it was the size of a horse, then its shape began to change into something more humanoid, with the wings vanishing and the muzzle melting away into a man's features. I sucked in a breath, and just as it seemed that everyone would see what the dragon had truly been, there was a sound like a glass breaking in the dead silence.

Poof. The whole thing turned into a pile of ash, blown about in the breeze from the open wall.

There was a stunned silence, and the prince – who had almost been crushed by the falling beast, but had been wise enough to put his sword out first – looked down at the weapon in shock. Was there a little blood on it? But then the guards were all cheering, and Theodora the priestess was weeping on the floor, and I couldn't help but feel for her. It *was* her father, after all. And I didn't even know how he'd died. It was only certain that he *was* dead, and everyone had seen it. There was a crowd of cityfolk gathered at the break in the temple wall, staring down at us, and it was clear that they'd seen everything.

Uh oh. No one was looking at me, so I quickly hid behind the pillars at the side of the room and changed back to human, doing my best to look innocent and *not* as if I'd just been a giant fiery bird. It seemed to work.

And now Royce, hailed as the conquering hero, was ordering the arrest of the priestess for harbouring a dragon and for blackmail. She was screaming that she was the true heir, that she was the daughter of Atticus, and the prince, showing some wisdom for the first time, said, "If that's true, then why did you hide all this time? Why didn't you come forward? And if it's true, then will anyone even *want* you as their ruler?"

Delmany wasn't democratic – it didn't matter what anyone *wanted* – but he did have a good point. And in all the chaos and excitement, I couldn't see Franco. He could have been crushed in that cloak, and we wouldn't know until someone stepped on him. Had I sent him to his death?

Of course I hadn't. Like stepping through an open door, Franco stepped back out into sight right beside me, and I jumped. He looked amused. "You really couldn't see me, could you?"

"No! That's the point of it being invisible," I retorted. I wanted to hug him again, but didn't want to be inappropriate, so I just settled for smiling. "Did you manage to use the vial at all? Did it work?"

"Of course it worked," he replied in surprise. "I used all of it, too. Didn't you see the dragon disappear?"

The whole vial was gone. But that wasn't what made me stare at him. "It was a curse-breaker. It was supposed to turn him back to human. That's what it did for the priestess – she was the dragon that had been trashing Cristonia."

"Oh." And it was an 'oh' laden with meaning. "You didn't know it would die. *He* would die."

I shook my head, unsure of how to feel about this. Did it make me a murderer, because I'd given Franco the vial? "Everyone thinks the prince killed the dragon anyway. That's what it looked like."

"And you haven't had your curse broken after all," he commented. But he didn't look as upset as he might have. "And you're not a dragon when you change. You do know that, right?"

I pulled the cloak around me self-consciously. "Yes, I do know that. I don't know what I am, though."

"I know. I finally worked it out after I saw you this last time. You didn't just breathe fire, it consumed you, and you basically came back from the dead. Do you know what that means, Viola?"

"No, I do not," I said, half amused, half irritated. "Just tell me, will you?"

"You're a phoenix," he announced. "A firebird. Myth says there's only ever one in the world, and that they hate evil…or something like that. And that if they ever die, they're reborn from flame."

"Oh." I let that idea sit for a while, and realised I rather liked it, if it was true. It *sounded* true. "Except everyone saw me, and I bet they don't know that."

"No, they saw *something*," Franco corrected. "They don't know it was you, I'd swear it. Is anyone even looking at you funny?"

No one was looking at me at all. They were all looking at the prince, and at the screaming priestess, and at the destroyed remnants of the temple.

I let out a deep sigh of relief. Strangely enough, they weren't, and my own little part in this drama seemed overlooked in what came next.

There was hushed chatter as the crowd parted, and then Nellie was standing there, just inside the wrecked building. Her clothing was plain and her hair was in messy, frizzled curls around her face, and her eyes were wide and pleading. She looked stunning. "Royce?" she whispered.

I saw the moment when the prince's heart changed, or perhaps he'd never been that mad anyway. He strode over to her, then pulled her into a tight embrace. "Ella. My Ella."

"Oh, Royce!"

"Just like a fairytale," Franco said sarcastically as the two exchanged hushed, intent words. "And look, he's even killed the beast. How good of him. I bet we'll just be overlooked, the bastard and the stepsister, and-"

But then Prince Royce was looking over at us. "Captain Franco!" he called suddenly. "A word."

I saw Franco's jaw drop a little at being called 'Captain', but he looked at me, confused pleasure clear on his face, then walked over to the prince and bowed slightly before him.

As for me, I stepped back as far as I could into the shadows, pulling the cloak tighter around me. No, that wasn't good enough. I pulled it over my head, seeing my feet and whole self vanish as I did so.

"This man," Prince Royce began. Then he paused, and his expression twisted as if fighting some internal battle. "My *brother*," he said finally, and I heard the crowd gasp. Franco's eyes were wide. "My brother has been working undercover this entire time," he said loudly enough for everyone to hear. "He infiltrated the wicked Dragi who'd kept this terrible beast hidden for so many years, and who even kidnapped my dear bride. But now he's played a true part in saving our city, even enduring the loss of his own looks as a result."

Wow. Oh, wow. Was Royce actually *praising* his brother? In front of everyone? Sure, there was an insult thrown in there too, but…compliments?

I saw Nellie stand on tiptoe, whispering something into Royce's ear, and he nodded. "And that is why I am proud to call him the new Count of Novantine, and pardon him for all crimes that he was falsely accused of… in the process of working for the Crown, of course."

My own jaw dropped even as I saw pleasure wash over Franco's face. He bowed lower as his brother tapped him on each shoulder with that same sword, and then I felt tears pricking my own eyes. It was ending so very, very well for Franco, even though it seemed Royce had as clear a grip on truth as Nellie did at times.

But what about me? Did I want to be praised too, and by the very person who'd so humiliated me?

Definitely not while in the nude, I decided very quickly. And the idea that Royce would blame the Dragi for my own misery too – well, that was too much.

I watched a moment longer as Franco took in the excited congratulations of people around him who were apparently discovering his 'true heroism'. Then as he was surrounded, I quietly slipped away.

In the hours and days to come, life changed very quickly for us, and the story presented to the public was quite different from what had really happened.

Prince Royce was a hero who'd slain the dragon kept hidden by the wicked, scheming, blackmailing Dragi. The Dragi had long been disliked by the people of Ostraime for their power and their mystery and that slightly inhuman element given by the figurines, and now with this proof that they truly had been keeping secrets, it was an excuse to hate them properly. The damaged temple was opened to the public, and hundreds of fascinated people tromped down those stylish halls, now empty of anything except memories. The Dragi guards had vanished, the few that were found having been sent to the dungeons along with Theodora. A date for the trial was set two weeks hence.

I heard all the stories secondhand. Still wearing the cloak, I used the thousand-league boots to get quickly back to Criston city. My family was ecstatic to see me, especially when I told them of everything that had happened. I did admit in private to Edwina and Mother that I could still shapeshift, but as Mother said, 'As long as you're not going to burn someone to ashes by mistake, we don't care'.

Fair enough.

And they didn't even care that the gold supply had largely stopped. Maybe every time I shifted in future I might get a little more gold, but at the moment we didn't need it. We were rolling in gold, more than enough for living costs and even dowries, although we were definitely thinking about starting another business. Living idly was fun for a while, but it was no way to live in the long run.

I tried to go back to normal life, to *make* a new normal. Even though my family had been concerned for me, they'd settled in well in the months since leaving Delmany. Those horrible stories hadn't followed us here, and Edwina had even found a beau in the son of Aunt Melicia's neighbour. Even better, James had made good friends with both his young cousins and some of the other local boys, and looked to be forgetting what had passed with the inn.

Maybe.

The letter that arrived three weeks later was a surprise. It was in beautiful cream coloured stationery and bore the red seal of the Delman royalty – from Nellie. It also had an official pardon attached for me and for the whole family, although what we were being pardoned of, I didn't know.

Nellie was a little clearer in her letter.

Dear Vee (and 'Wina and Stepmother Hazel and James)
I have good news! The Bluebell is yours again, even though it really always was. Royce (he's such a dear, even though he can be too stern when he gets carried away) had thought he was being helpful when he had it stewarded like that, but I was very firm with him and explained that you had always done a very good job, all of you, and that he

*shouldn't listen to gossip. Oh, and also that the inn is only half mine –
the other half is James's inheritance, of course.*

*So you're welcome to come home any time, and you mustn't think
that the neighbours will think less of you. We've spread the story that
Viola and the whole family were also undercover as well as the Count of
Novantine (isn't it funny to think of Franco as that?) and now everyone
thinks you are all heroes rather than villains, as it should be.*

Nellie hadn't taken any personal responsibility for any of
our problems, of course, but I didn't care anymore. Her next
words showed some sensitivity, though:

*I miss you all, but I understand if you aren't planning to come
back to Delmany. It must be lovely living so close to Stepmother
Hazel's family. If that is the case, then we will buy the inn from you
for* (and here she listed a sum that was equivalent to about two
years' income) *and I do think that considering it barely scraped by,
that's quite generous. Either way I plan to update the inn, to make it as
beautiful as it ought to be. Naturally I won't be working in it again, but
those gifts from the Wyse folk will go a long way to making life easier.*

Lots of love, Nellie.

And then, almost overlooked in the excitement of the
letter, was a large, awkwardly-shaped parcel. Inside were the
aforementioned gifts: a broom that swept for itself, a dish rack
that washed dishes, and a polishing rag that polished glass and
mirror all by itself.

When I explained to the others what the objects were, Mother
unexpectedly laughed. "Even though Nellie won't be cleaning
again – unless she gets upset with Royce again and runs off to
be a maid, and I can't see that happening – she still thinks that
we would suffer for having to work. It's her way of being kind,
I suppose."

"Well, *I* won't be sorry to use them," Edwina said staunchly.
"I never liked washing dishes."

"Nobody likes washing dishes," Mother replied crisply. "But
we'll have help this time. We won't be doing it all ourselves."

It had been decided, then, that whatever we did next, we
would hire servants. Except that didn't sound right, because
they wouldn't be serving *us*, they'd be serving alongside us.

"I still can't get over the way Nellie went and told all of those
beggars that the one who made the most noise was going to get a

packet of gold scales from the Dragi," I mused, thinking back to that day in Delmany where so much had changed.

"You ought to have known that she wouldn't embarrass *herself* creating a distraction," Edwina said dryly. "She always gets other people to do her dirty work." 'Wina still hadn't quite forgiven Nellie for what had happened. I hoped that she could let it go one day, even though I doubted it would truly be forgotten.

"So what do you think, girls?" Mother asked. "Shall we accept that price for the Bluebell? It will be more than enough to start up again here, and this time it will divide between all three of you. I never liked that I had no inheritance for you girls, although of course the gold scales more than cover the lack."

Edwina agreed readily, but I found myself more hesitant. Even though we'd left Fortrente so quickly and with such bad blood, it seemed like my whole life had been there, and I felt an ache, like I'd been displaced. But then I hadn't had as long to settle in here as the others had, and I'd had rather more to worry about.

In a perfect world, Criston and Fortrente would be an awful lot closer, and we'd have friends in both. I would go back and run the Bluebell with enough money to make it beautiful and profitable *and* to rest (because yes, I could see now that I'd been working too hard) and everyone would treat us if not with love then at least with respect, and life would be good. And I'd...

Marry Franco, had been the evil thought to sneak into my head, but I tossed it away. Maybe one day I'd visit him, or perhaps write to him, but it wouldn't be today. Not until my emotions were a little less invested: because it still hurt to think of him. In the end it seemed we'd been friends, but I wanted more, and I couldn't have him just as a friend. It was too painful, too much a reminder of what I wasn't. Maybe he'd write to me, because surely he must know where I'd gone...

But of course he didn't write, and I tried unsuccessfully to stop thinking about him. But his face kept popping back into my mind, the way he'd laughed, the way he'd been so happy when he saw I was still alive, the way he'd spoken when he'd thought I was dead...and the original discord between us was long forgotten.

A week later I found the letter again, almost buried under a pile of clothes. Edwina had outdone herself shopping, and the results were everywhere. But when I picked the letter up again, I noticed that there was writing on the other side that we'd earlier missed. It was a brief message in a different script, and it was addressed to me. My eyes skimmed to the signature, and my heart leapt. Franco *had* written to me?

Dear Viola,

I'm sorry you left so quickly, although I understand why you did. I didn't expect that you'd leave without saying goodbye, though. I don't know if you'll ever come back or even if you'll write to me again, so I'll be honest now about how I feel. Don't laugh.

As if I would ever laugh at his honesty.

You are a wonderful, fascinating, strong girl, and I've never met anyone like you. The longer I knew you, the more your looks appealed to me, and I- and here something was scribbled out and then written rather more messily, *I just wish you hadn't left so fast. Maybe you could write to me. Or don't, I'll understand if you don't want to. Maybe just send your regrets?*

Then there was another dark smudge where something had been scribbled out, and it just said, *Franco.*

Oh. *Ohh.* I sat there next to the pile of newly bought clothing with that letter in my hand for I don't know how long. What did that even mean, the contrast between him saying that he'd never met anyone like me – which I supposed meant that he *liked* me, right? – and then asking me to maybe write, or if I didn't want to, to send my regrets.

Franco, I'm writing to inform you that I must regretfully decline to write to you…

Even if I'd ever be so contrary, I certainly wouldn't be so rude. But did he even care what I did?

I glanced across at the nearby wooden desk that held our small supply of paper, as well as ink and quills. What if I did write to him, if I hinted again at my true feelings, and it turned out that I'd misunderstood? I'd be humiliated all over again, and this time in a way I'd never been before. My hand clenched into a fist at the thought. I'd rather 'send my regrets' than experience that kind of pain.

In that moment I realised that I'd been sending my regrets my whole life. Not just romantically, but in so many areas. I'd assumed that people would reject me, so I kept my head down, never put myself at risk. I felt competent in many areas like with running the inn, but personally? Making friends, or even reaching out for more than friendship? Never. Not ever. If I didn't take a chance, then I couldn't be rejected.

Just then a quiet thought crept in. *But what if Franco does mean it, and he's the one who's hurt by your rejection?*

That was assuming a lot, I told the thought. *I'm hardly that important.*

Did you even look at the letter? my inner self persisted.

The memory of Gerelda's written words echoed in my mind: *Don't assume the worst of people, assume the best.*

I huffed out a sigh. This went against all habit, but assuming the best, Franco *did* care what I did. He *did* want me to write.

I could write to him, I mused. It wouldn't be that hard. I didn't know what I'd say – something unimportant, probably, but I could do it. Ha, I still had the thousand-league boots and the invisibility cloak. I could just show up on the new Count of Novantine's doorstep: 'Hi, you said I could write, but I decided to come in person. Aren't you happy to see me?'

And he might be…but he'd only asked for a letter.

Ugh. Enough deep thinking, I decided. I was going to have lunch.

The thing about having a big question hanging over your head is that you never really relax, it's always at the edge of your mind. So when James came up to me in the drawing room and said that I had a visitor, my first thought was that it was someone tall and dark, whose handsomeness was made more *interesting* (in my opinion) by a scar on the side of his face.

Nope. Instead it was someone small and round and rather plain even in her human form, and without her customary accessory/husband. Gerelda.

She smiled at me when she was shown in, although there was some hesitance in it. "Hello dear. Do you mind talking for a minute?"

She wasn't a used carriage salesman – of course I didn't mind talking. "Not at all. Can I get you a drink, something to eat?" I had a plate of cooling biscuits in front of me, leftovers from Edwina's morning cooking jag. I'd never be voluptuous, but even I had to admit that I wasn't bone thin anymore.

"Just a cup of tea, thank you."

Niceties over, the Wyse woman sat down on the couch and looked at me. There was a long silence, and then I blurted out, "You left us very suddenly at the village. Do you know what happened afterwards?"

She nodded sympathetically. "You found your stepsister, fought the Dragi, and lost. Your spell was broken. They took Franco, then you and Nellie followed them back to Ostraime. As far as I can tell, you won in the end. Well done."

That was a brief, uncompassionate summary from a woman who was supposed to help us, but who'd abandoned us at the last minute. It seemed just good luck that things turned out so well. "Whose side are you even on?" I burst out. "I would have thought it was ours, but where did you go? Why didn't you come back? Wasn't this whole dragon thing your husband's fault in the first place?"

Gerelda tilted her head patiently, unfazed by my outburst. "So many mistakes, but so many different ways things could have gone, too. We don't control the world, we just do our best to make a difference just at the right time, as much as is within our abilities. I believe that's what happened in your case, if you will allow me to explain."

"Go ahead."

She paused briefly, taking a breath, then: "Forty years ago Atticus chose to give up his family for revenge and for the promise of more money. My husband's attempt to intervene and show him the error of his ways backfired. See, some people will change once they realise what they're like, others won't, but they all deserve the chance to choose. That's what we believe, what we live by. It's not our place to decide who lives or dies. Atticus needed to change his life for the sake of his people and for himself, but the means was flawed. You understand this?"

I nodded. It made sense.

"Whether he'd died or not, his daughter would have been gone, his wife dead. This wasn't something we did, it was his choice. His daughter went to a sad, lonely dwarf who raised her as a sort of child/servant. If we'd known about her fate back then, we would have done our best to change it, but we didn't know. So that would have remained the same, with the heir missing presumed dead, and with Barrick on the throne instead. Yes?"

I nodded again.

"Now Barrick, as you well know, is a flawed man, although not a bad king. But once Theodora decided to pursue her birthright and he realised who she truly was and also that Atticus was still alive, he asked her to stay silent in exchange for a position of power and respect. A cowardly choice, of course, because if he'd had her brought before the courts to test who had the right to rule, he may well have been allowed to remain as regent, or even king, especially because of the situation with Atticus. A dragon cannot sit on the throne of Delmany, and neither can someone who also holds a position as head of any religion. While she was attached to the Dragi, she wouldn't have been able to rule."

I tried to remember back to what the priestess had said to me, something about enjoying pulling Barrick' strings for a while, but that she was losing interest. "I think she would have tried to just take control, if she could have. That's what she said."

"But by the time you spoke to her – and you were very brave, I know that – things had changed a lot. Prince Royce knew what was going on, and for all of *his* flaws, at heart he wants justice. Even his mistreatment of you came about because he believed he was being just. That doesn't mean that it hurt you any less, but he didn't act out of malice. But the moment Royce understood what was going on, he was inspired to take his best guards and try to sort the matter out."

I raised my eyebrows. "I wouldn't have thought it would be that easy."

Gerelda gave a curious little smile. "Eh, well. He did have a little help, of course. I've been keeping an eye on Royce, since he's so tied into the fate of Delmany – as are you, now."

"I didn't choose to be." I paused, studying her. She seemed so ordinary to have so much power and influence, and while I wasn't exactly angry with her anymore, I didn't understand the way she thought. "You put me into the middle of it all when you left those figurines in my inn, and when you sent Nellie to the ball. Why?"

Gerelda sighed. "Because I try to make big decisions based

on what I feel is right or wrong in my gut, and that felt like the right thing to do at the time. I couldn't have foreseen where it led, but has it really been such a terrible fate? I thought it turned out rather well, in the end."

"But you left me," I cried plaintively. "You could have helped, but you just left us to muddle our way through. Why?"

"Would you rather I swept in and solved everything for you, taking all the praise and all the condemnation? Or that I gave you just enough to do it for yourself, with all that comes with it on the way? You aren't the same person you were before Nellie went to the ball, before you took the risk to go through that forest by yourself. For better or for worse, you're far braver and stronger and more resilient; not brittle at all. I gave Nellie the opportunity to go to the ball for herself, Royce and for this kingdom. But I gave the figurines for the country, for your family, and for *you*.

"You're being hailed as a hero back home in your village, don't you know. Most people seem to think that you were in on the whole plan from the start. They're asking when you'll be coming back."

That last piece of information made my jaw drop, and I lost my irritation over her 'is it really so bad?' "They are?!"

The Wyse woman cocked her head to the side, watching me solemnly. "There'll be a place for you if you choose to go back, you know. In more than one way."

She might have been referring to Franco, but I didn't dare ask. I didn't want to hear 'no' or even worse, the uncertainty of 'maybe'. "My family won't go back."

"You've still got the thousand-league boots. The only question is whether you don't mind sleeping overnight in a different house from your family."

Maybe if that question had been asked a year ago, I would have said no way, I wasn't ready to be away from my family. But now things had changed a lot. *I* had changed a lot.

"I'll think about it."

"Very well. But in the end, it's your life, your choices to make. Be glad that you *have* those choices."

I felt strangely settled after that conversation. Maybe it was hearing that the opinion of the (stupid, stupid) Fortrente villagers had changed, or maybe it was having my own thoughts confirmed, but it was like a weight had lifted. I *could* go back if I wanted, and the only reason I knew was because Gerelda had taken the trouble to come and talk to me. I certainly hadn't planned to go back and ask her.

"Thank you for coming here to talk to me about this. I know you didn't have to."

She looked surprised. "But it's what I do. Of course I don't mind."

"Was it the wish upon a star? Was that the reason why you did all this?"

"All those months ago? The wish didn't hurt, but the truth was that my husband and I were already looking for a way to weaken absolute monarchy in Delmany. Barring recent events, Barrick isn't too bad, and Royce probably won't make a dreadful hash of ruling when it's his turn, but Atticus showed that birth certainly isn't an indicator of ability to rule. Having a commoner as queen may not seem significant to you, but it changes things in the eyes of the population, in the eyes of the rulers. Even though Nellie is imperfect, she is kind hearted, and that is what truly matters. For Delmany, it's a good start."

I should have known there was *some* reason why she'd helped Nellie go to the ball beyond just being swayed by a pretty face. "Don't you ever get tired of helping other people? Of messing about with other people's lives?"

"We aren't judged in comparison to what other people have done, but in comparison to what we *could* have done, had we used our talents and our opportunities to the fullest. When I get to the end of my long life – which I will, because death is a certainty no matter what you are – then I want to have no regrets." She smiled again, a small curve of her round cheeks. "And besides, I find that I enjoy it most of the time."

"Except perhaps when angry people hunt you down and tell you you've done it wrong."

Gerelda shrugged. "I'm not so easy to find if I don't want to be found. Now, my dear, I have one final question for you."

"The shapeshift curse," I burst out. "Do I want it broken?"

She looked startled. "I was going to ask if you minded if I used your bathroom. It's a long way back home for me. But the curse is already broken, Viola. Haven't you noticed you can't change anymore?"

Quite frankly, no. "I hadn't tried," I admitted guiltily. "But when I was, er, killed back on that road, that broke the curse, didn't it?"

"Mostly," she agreed. "You weren't controlled by its power anymore, but it hadn't left you. You could go back if you wanted, but now you can't, not since Atticus died and the power left the figurines too. Do you mind?"

I shook my head without hesitation. "Not at all. I'm happy to be human, thank you very much." Then realising that might be offensive to a non-human, amended, "In my normal form, I mean."

She nodded firmly. "And so you should be."

In time I came to realise that for all of the things it seemed Nellie or others had that I didn't, I was blessed with things they didn't have. I was remarkably resilient, and I got things done. I had the strongest sense that no matter what had come before, what was ahead would be good. Whatever I set myself to do would prosper.

I did move back to Delmany, and by 'move' I meant put on those special boots and walk back to the palace in five minutes, then ask to see Nellie. I was in my best dress this time, but I had to force myself not to cringe when I was there. Whatever *had* happened before wasn't happening now, and while I wouldn't say I was welcomed with open arms, there was a definite respect that hadn't been there earlier.

Nellie, on the other hand, did welcome me with open arms, reminding me of why I loved her even as I had disliked her. The past didn't matter, I decided, and I wasn't going to let my hurt define me. It was a new day, and I had so much in front of me, the least of which was the Bluebell Inn. Nellie deeded it to me as a thank you gift, paying out her portion straight to James as his inheritance. She didn't need it, you see, even though I joked that she was welcome back any time she liked. You should have seen the look on her face.

Prince Royce came in just as Nellie and I finished talking, and I saw the genuine affection on his face when he looked at my stepsister. I still don't know everything that happened to send her running, since her explanation was convoluted and a bit pointless as was her manner, but it seemed both of them had laid the blame on King Barrick, who'd laid it on the Dragi. That could make family dinners a little awkward, but I didn't think it would happen again. As for Prince Blockhead, he still was reserved around me, but I decided to be magnanimous and not hold his dreadful behaviour against him. After all, he was my stepbrother-in-law now.

Oh – and here's something I almost couldn't believe at first – they gave me a title. It came with the inn and the land around it, but it was an honorific without any power: if I chose, I could now be known as Lady Viola of Bluebell Inn.

As if I ever would. I'd be far too embarrassed to even try that one, but I didn't need it. Gerelda had been right about the people of Fortrente having revised their opinions of me. I got so many friendly nods and interested conversations when I got back that I didn't know what to do with myself at first. It seemed so foolish: they'd hated me because of false rumours, and now they loved me because of false rumours?

Well, kind of true, because I had been instrumental in bringing down the Dragi (even if it wasn't on purpose). But they didn't know that. No, most of them just based their judgements on gossip or on the way others acted. So silly, so unfair, but it was the same as with Nellie. I could decide whether I'd hold their stupidity against them – and give up the chance on ever being happy here in Fortrente – or I could decide to let it go and move forward with my life.

I did the second, of course, and it wasn't long before everything felt back to normal. But money had been pumped into the business while we'd been 'away', and everything was newer, fancier. Even the servants were newer and fancier. I got rid of the steward and his wife as they'd been instituted by the king and were less than friendly, but I kept the footman and the ostler and the cook and the two chambermaids… The inn was doing far better than normal, just because I'd become infamous, and because of Nellie, of course. At least I knew that I could keep paying them.

I also wrote to Franco, telling him that I'd moved back, and what my new address was. I also congratulated him on his title, and then- proving I really had no practise writing to men or possibly even to anyone – I commented on the weather.

The weather. *It's been a rather cold spring don't you think, what with the recent snow fall…*

Unsurprisingly Franco wasn't driven to write back immediately. In fact, three days went by and I didn't hear from him, even though I knew the messenger I'd paid to take the letter would have brought it by the first night, and then should have brought any reply back on the same day. Unless they'd been held up by the snow, or something. Oh, well, I hardly knew him anyway, and then we had that uncomfortable background where he'd insulted me and I'd pushed him off a bridge…at least I still had my family, just five minutes away with my new boots.

I wasn't *lonely.*

The following day was fine, the first in quite a while, and the blue sky shone brightly over the rapidly melting snow. It sounded pretty, but really meant that all the people who'd previously been held up from leaving/arriving either left or arrived – absolute chaos for an inn, especially one that was as busy as the Bluebell had been lately. Oh great, and now Nellie had dropped in for a visit. There was her fancy royal coach, because no one except her would come from that location, and the timing was really bad. Hadn't I told her not to come in the middle of the day anymore?

But still I was smiling as I wrote in the log book for the day – all the guests had paid in full, which was a good reason to smile. I heard the mixed *ding-creak* of the doorbell and the front door opening, then the clomp of boots on the new tiles. Hmm, must be the footman, because Nellie sure didn't walk like that. For a moment there was a twist in my gut as I remembered the time the prince had showed up and everything it had led to, but it didn't last. That time was over.

"Viola."

My heart skipped a beat, and I carefully put down the ink-dipped quill back in its holder. Now *that* voice was one I hadn't expected to hear, but also one that I recognised in an instant. Yes, it was Franco, wearing a slightly better version of his usual uniform, and just as I'd remembered him, right down to the mostly-healed scars on the side of his face.

He was smiling hesitantly at me. "You wrote," he said.

I felt myself flushing pink. Here I was in my nicest work clothes, but still work clothes. I might look better than I ever had before, but I was still no Nellie. "I did. I thought perhaps you would write back."

Franco was still watching me intently with those dark eyes, and I thought that he had to be the handsomest man I'd ever seen in my whole life, scars and all. "I didn't want to write."

"*Oh.*" A pang of disappointment shot through me, quickly chased by confusion. Why would he come all the way here just to say such a thing?

"I wanted to see you in person. You left without saying goodbye, and I'd thought we were closer than that. Was I wrong?"

"No. I mean, yes, we were closer than that." I looked down. Now my blush was one of pleasure, but I couldn't meet his eyes. For all of my usual strength, I was shy around this one person. "I wasn't sure if it was just because of the Wyse folk and all that. I thought- I thought the philtre you took for Nellie might have worn off. I didn't want to take the chance."

He let out a short laugh. "You didn't want to take the chance of what, that I'd fallen in love with her again? Philtre or not, Vee, that ship has sailed. Nellie will always be attractive on the outside, but she doesn't appeal to me anymore. I've found my tastes have changed." He smiled crookedly, the scars making his grin oddly appealing. "Like deciding you prefer whisky to lemonade."

There was a long pause, then he added, "I'm comparing you to whisky, Vee. It's supposed to be a compliment."

I finally found my tongue. "What, appreciated only by grizzled old men?"

"Valuable and intoxicating," he said. "In a good way."

Intoxicating, *me*? "Am I right in thinking," I asked slowly, "that you want more than just friendship?" *Yes, yes, please...*

"Heavens yes!" Franco said in frustration. "Do I have to spell it out for you? I love you, Viola of Bluebell Inn, whether you're a lady or a firebird or a penniless, soot-covered fugitive, and whether you're rich or poor. And if you *dare* to suggest it's anything to do with the gold, I'll-"

"You'll what?" I asked softly, a smile appearing on my face. He *loved* me? *Me?*

"I don't know," he replied with a shrug, suddenly looking solemn. "How can I convince you that I love you unless you believe you're fit to be loved?"

"Saying it was a good start," I offered. "As was coming here."

I think he could see my answer in my tone, because his expression lightened. "Has anyone told you you're difficult, Viola?"

"Sorry."

"You should be," he said grumpily. "Now are you going to marry me or what?"

My jaw dropped, and he suddenly looked anxious. "Nellie said that you loved me, that she was sure of it, but was she wrong? Not that I'm going to take it back if you don't- like me like that. I meant it."

"She wasn't wrong," I finally managed to get in. "I just wasn't expecting…*this*. But I do love you," I added hastily when I saw his face fall. "And if you ask me that same question in a much more romantic way – and not right now, please – I'll give you an answer you'll like."

Franco smiled finally, a big, beautiful smile that lit up his whole face. And then because there were no guests to be seen, we took advantage of a minute or two of time alone, and I had my first real kiss. Let me tell you, it was worth waiting for.

"Does this mean we're engaged to be engaged?" he asked me a few minutes later.

I thought about it. "Kiss me again, and I'll tell you."

And when he finally did ask that question again a week later in an impressively romantic (and embarrassingly public) proposal, I did have an answer for him that he liked.

It was yes.

The End

Dear Reader

(Contains spoilers)

The idea for *Viola sends her regrets* came from watching a certain children's movie, wherein the stepsisters/villains were just… the worst. Ugly, rude, piggish; and I thought, 'good grief, no real person is like that!' In that moment I wanted to tell another side of the repeatedly-told Cinderella story, one that went far beyond the glass slipper.

But that was only part of the inspiration. Another part was noticing that whenever a normal person stands next to a very good-looking one, they actually look plain in contrast, even if they're not. Their flaws all seem to stand out. (Don't ask me exactly how I know that.) It got me thinking that someone might be called 'ugly' in such a situation – and that was the situation I created for Viola and her family.

And as always, there were the dreams. I don't know what variety of cheese I'd been eating before bed, but it must have been something potent. I had a series of dreams about dragons: being chased by a dragon that wanted me to worship it; a woman finding a huge dragon hidden under an old building; *being* a dragon…and then even a dream that ended with me going 'aha! There are *two* dragons!' I can't remember any other details from that last one, except that it built into the Theodora/Atticus twist. Viola was also originally going to turn into a dragon, but my editor and I decided it had too many negative connotations. I was quite happy with the phoenix angle instead.

The whole storyline about the cursed figurines was also from a dream, right from the guards (Franco looks like a young Ben Affleck, and his name was also from the dream) through to finding them in a closet with a diary, through to trying to smuggle them through the woods. What a wonderful thing the sleeping mind is.

The *Fairytale Memoirs* series is one of my favourite worlds to write in. At the moment there are four stories in existence, with another half-dozen plotted out. If you enjoyed this novel, don't forget to leave a review. It would be much appreciated. Also keep an eye on my website for upcoming novels: **mmarinanbooks.com.**

Read on for an excerpt from *Breaking the Glass Slipper* – a weird, wonderful, futuristic fairytale. (Not a part of this series.)

Life's
no
fairytale.

Breaking
the
Glass Slipper

M. Marinan

Breaking the Glass Slipper

EXCERPT

Real News 2 March 2097 AD
Six-star resort set to reopen amid high expectations

In the shallow waters of picturesque Silver Bay, a six-star resort has undergone a Cinderella-like transformation after fire damage last year.

"Sweetheart Island will be more than just a luxury retreat," the project's co-owner John Carver tells us. "It'll be a one-of-a-kind opportunity to experience your fantasy in the most beautifully designed environment that this hemisphere has to offer."

Now while the reclusive billionaire might be excused for being biased – this project has been underway for the last fifteen years in some shape or form – one can't argue with the cost. It's estimated that twenty billion credits went into the transformation of this sparsely populated island: rebuilding the hotel that closely resembles a castle, and with an entire village of boutique shops and charming cottages to round out the fantasy. But then when one considers the locals...

"A full half of them are AI," Mr Carver tells us proudly, "created just for the set, and programmed to act out various characters as needs require. This is revolutionary technology, and I dare any customers to tell the difference between the AI and the human staff."

But with a week's accommodation costing six months of this journalist's wages, it's safe to say that only the ultra-rich and fanciful will ever face that particular-

...and the text cut off. I tapped at the bottom of the touchscreen inset in the coffee table in front of me, trying to pull more of the article into view, but the screen flickered then changed back to the same drinks menu all the other touchscreens showed.

"Chestnuts," I muttered. "I was enjoying that."

But I'd learned something new, and I studied the gleaming hotel foyer with fresh eyes. A fantasy-themed resort, hmm? Kingsley hadn't mentioned that, and I couldn't see it myself. Everything was…white. White, shining, and beautiful. Not a hint of destruction from the fire that the article had mentioned. I'd have to ask him about it…if he ever got here.

Forgetting the article, I looked up again towards the huge panes of weather-sensitive glass that made up the entryway of the White Hotel. It was late afternoon, the low sun dimming the glass to a soft pink. I could still see all the way from my secluded alcove off the side of the large foyer, right out to where the hotel guests came and went: bright patches of colour in the pristine white surroundings. Staff moved about too, unobtrusive and emotionless in matching white uniforms. No Kingsley.

I reached for my cinnamon latte, found it was cold, then set it back on the table with a grimace. I ordered another through the touchscreen menu, then leaned back into the comfortable couch, tapping my fingers impatiently on my knee. The large ruby on my ring finger perfectly matched the scarlet of my sundress, and at the sight of it a little burst of happiness fluttered through my belly. Engaged – again – but this time would be better than the last. Kingsley was better than the others. *I'd* be better, I vowed. I'd be selfless and charming and flawlessly beautiful as long as age allowed me to be, and he'd not regret a thing.

Just then a message flashed on my silver wristpiece. *Hello, Fairest. I'm sorry I'm late. I can't wait to see you again, but I was held up a little. I have a surprise for you…*

I smiled to myself and reread the message. Didn't he know that all I wanted was his undying affection? But gold – or chocolate – wouldn't hurt either.

Just then, there was the sound of female laughter from the alcove next to mine. It was separated from me by an ornate white screen that blocked the view, but didn't do a thing for noise. I smiled in response to their happiness: I was happy too, so the whole world should be.

The hushed whispers came through the screen, and then a woman said more loudly, "I know, right? Her dress is *so* trashy! I know this is going to be a themed hotel, but what does she think she's trying to be? An escort droid?"

Ouch. My smile faltered at the thought of whichever poor girl these women were verbally tearing apart. Being compared to a robotic streetwalker was never flattering. I tried to distract myself by checking my lipstick in a small, handheld mirror, but I couldn't block out their conversation.

"She's clearly had work done," a different female voice continued. "No one has a figure like that naturally. And her colouring – hasn't she heard of tanner? Fish belly-white skin went out of fashion centuries ago!"

My own pale reflection frowned back at me from the mirror. Surely they didn't mean me? Sure, I had a nice figure. Nature had been kind to me, and I'd done what I could to keep in shape. Not that it was hard when I was only twenty-one… And not everyone had to be tanned, right?

"Aren't natural blondes supposed to be pale?" a new, male voice cut in, sounding a little defensive. "I don't know what you ladies are talking about. I thought she looked very nice."

"You would!" the first woman retorted, and there was another burst of feminine laughter. This time it sounded distinctly mocking.

"But what I don't get," the second woman said in a low voice, "is why she hasn't had that mole removed. Lord, it must be the size of a pea! Can you imagine seeing that thing staring back at you all day? It makes me shudder!"

This time they were definitely talking about me. I snapped the mirror shut on my horrified reflection, complete with blonde hair, careful makeup, and a small, dark spot beside my nose.

"Beauty mark," I said under my breath, feeling my face heat with embarrassment. "Not mole." And it was flat, too; not at all pea-like. Kingsley had called it distinctive. *He* clearly didn't mind it. "Your cinnamon latte, Miss Redwell?"

I jumped a little, feeling as though I'd been caught eavesdropping. A blandly handsome server stood before me, dressed in the hotel's compulsory white, and holding a tray with a tall, steaming silver glass. He smiled at me pleasantly.

Oh, it was only an android server, and it wouldn't judge me for eavesdropping, or for having a mole. AI didn't do anything that it wasn't programmed to. I sighed, scrubbing a hand over my flushed cheeks. "On the table, thanks."

BOOM.

Just as the server set the drink in front of me, a loud, sudden noise sounded from outside the hotel. It reminded me of an explosion from a movie, or perhaps a gunshot, and I gasped, throwing a hand to my chest then rising to my feet. I could hear a burst of startled chatter from the next alcove too, and I looked around anxiously. I couldn't *see* anything wrong, not even through those big glass walls.

But the server continued as though nothing had happened, removing my old, cold drink and then moving as if to leave, and I set my arm on its sleeve. It looked back at me with polite curiosity – all programmed, of course. Being entirely robotic, androids were never curious about anything. Apparently not even suspicious explosions.

"What was that?" I asked it quietly, hearing the urgency in my tone. "That noise."

"What noise, Miss Redwell?"

"That loud booming noise," I snapped, a little agitated. "Don't tell me I imagined it. Check your communications. Is there any kind of danger?"

The server just stared at me; its perfectly-shaped blue eyes unblinking.

The silence stretched on long enough that I was tempted to panic. Then I realised the issue. Privacy breach – perhaps it thought it couldn't tell me, since I was a guest. "You know I'm Valentina Redwell," I told it impatiently. "I'm going to marry the hotel's owner, Kingsley White, in two days. You should know that already too. Soon enough I'll co-own everything, so you *can* answer my question."

There was a brief silence where the server must have been checking back with the main intelligence hub, then it replied, "There is no danger, Miss Redwell. The sound was just a car backfiring."

I frowned. "What's that?"

There was another silence, and I sighed. It didn't matter what 'backfiring' was, because clearly there was no danger or the server would have said. That was the thing about AI – it couldn't lie. It couldn't pass for human either, I thought with some humour, even if it could be more flawlessly gorgeous than even the most beautiful human (and without moles, too). The android servers that kept the White Hotel running were a perfect example. They'd smile and say the right things (as long as the question wasn't too hard), but they didn't eat, and they didn't drink. They also had no sense of humour, nor of subtlety.

"Never mind," I said finally. "But it's actually Mrs Redwell. I'm a widow."

"Yes, Mrs Redwell."

I sighed. Even coming from an android's mouth, completely with unmoving tongue, that name sounded wrong. "Strike that. Call me Ms, will you? Mrs makes me feel like someone's mother, and I'm way too young for that. Besides, I hate people asking about my first marriage, it's embarrassing. Not that it's any of their business…"

I petered into silence, realising I was babbling to what was essentially a toaster. It was those stupid people in the next alcove, I decided, who had shaken my confidence. "You're not even alive," I told the android with some humour. "You may as well call me 'Your Supreme Highness'. It won't make a difference to you either way."

"Yes, Your Supreme Highness."

I snickered to myself, now feeling a little better. I was so easily amused. "Thank you. You can go."

"Yes, Your Supreme Highness."

The server left, and I sipped slowly at my latte, trying to regain my sense of composure. The volume had dropped in the next alcove; perhaps the guests had overheard my conversation and realised that if they could hear me, then vice versa. And Kingsley was still late…

I looked up again towards the front of the hotel, and saw through its glass panels a familiar vehicle pulling up at the entrance. It was a white limousine, and that could only belong to one person.

My heart skipped in joy and anxiety, and I quickly pulled out the hand mirror again from my small purse. Teeth check: all clear. Hair: good enough. Mole…still there.

"Chestnuts to that," I muttered under my breath, replacing the mirror in the purse. "It's a beauty mark." But in my excitement

I fumbled and dropped the thing on the floor. I bent down to pick it up, and spotted something odd stuck underneath the table top. It was the size of an old coin, round and metallic grey, but it was otherwise completely plain. I tapped at it curiously, and it came off into my palm, like it had been waiting there for someone to collect.

I scolded myself for being fanciful and tried to stick the thing back under the table top. But whatever had held it there was gone, and it just fell back into my hand. Finally I stuffed it into my purse along with the mirror, then promptly forgot about it. I had more important things to think about – Kingsley was here!

Deep breath. Here we go…

I rose to my feet and strolled towards the entryway, ignoring what felt like burning stares from the neighbouring alcove. I returned the possibly-android doorman's polite nod, then stepped out into the sunlight.

Well, tried to step. I stumbled on my high heels, falling forward and almost smacking my face on the marble bannister leading from the doorway. But I caught myself at the last moment, my hand on the pillar, and my nose an inch away from being bloodied on the white rock. Awkward, but at least the blood would have matched my dress.

I took a moment to check if anyone had noticed, but didn't see anyone pointing and laughing. "We'll call that a win," I told myself, straightening my shoulders. "Be graceful, Valentina." Or if I couldn't manage that, at least I could be careful.

Up ahead the limousine had parked outside the carved marble steps at the front of the hotel. White-clad servers were moving to empty it of its baggage, and the vehicle's occupant stood on the tiled footpath. He was tall and strong and handsome, the sun gilding his greying dark hair as he bent down in conversation with some brightly-dressed shrimp of a village girl. But with the harshness of the late afternoon light, he looked nearly old enough to be her father…and mine.

Had he looked that old the last time I'd seen him? I found myself wrinkling my nose, and carefully made my face relax back into a welcoming smile as I moved down the long flight of polished steps. He *was* thirty-six, I reminded myself. Or was it thirty-eight? But then even Prince Charming had to age sometime.

Aside from the sizeable age gap, he was perfect. Kind, generous, adoring, rich...very rich. Best of all, he had no baggage. One long-dead wife, no children. I crossed my fingers. Third time lucky.

I paused at the bottom of the stairs, trying to look both genuinely happy and flawless (no easy task, even having practised it in the mirror!) and waited for him to notice me. But five seconds ticked by, then ten. My eye started to twitch from the strain of holding the expression...and he still hadn't looked up from his conversation with that same girl.

I dropped the smile, studying her with irritation. Her conversation must be scintillating, because she wasn't much to look at. Small and thin, with skin powdered chalky white, ink black hair, and heavy eye makeup that made her light blue eyes look washed out. I would have mistaken her for one of those retro goth girls if not for the cheerful yellow sundress and fire engine-red lipstick.

Damn. Except for the fact that my dress was red rather than yellow, we were dressed almost identically.

I took a step closer, a mere arm's length away from the two, and coughed gently, now feeling a little foolish.

Kingsley didn't budge, but the not-goth girl saw me. "Oh Daddy," she said in a breathy, high voice. "I think someone's trying to get your attention."

Daddy. I instinctively recoiled at both her tone and her use of the word. I hadn't known my own father, but I hated it when girls called a man 'Daddy' unless he was actually their parent. The strongly negative emotion startled me. I really wasn't myself today, I mused, since I was usually a calm, difficult-to-upset sort of person. Being upset was...upsetting. I'd have to try harder to control myself. Besides, in a minute the girl would be gone. Problem solved.

My fiancé finally turned to face me, his handsome face creasing into an expression of delight. "Fairest!" he exclaimed. "Look at you all in red, like a rose in snow. How beautiful you are." He leaned in to kiss me and I let him, feeling much more cheerful than I had a second earlier. This affection, this adoration, was why I was trying again. How could things go wrong with a sweetheart like this?

"Of course I'm beautiful," I told him dryly, pleased he'd noticed the contrast of my red gown against the white surroundings of the hotel. I'd chosen the dress carefully, wanting to make the best impression possible after our three week separation. "That's why you're marrying me."

Kingsley laughed as though it was a joke. "Silly Fairest. I'm marrying you because I love you, and I can't live without you."

Love, infatuation; did it really matter? Either way, we'd make it work. He linked his arm through mine, although made no move towards the hotel.

"Fairest?" the girl chirped in her too-high voice, looking from me to Kingsley, then back again. A lock of her ink-black hair fell into her eye, and she tucked it behind one ear with a thin white hand. "That's an interesting name. Why are *you* marrying Kingsley White, Fairest?"

I felt my eye twitch again. I decided in that moment that if the girl was working at the hotel, she'd have to stay far, far away from me. "I'm sorry, we haven't been introduced," I told her politely, "and that's a rather personal question for a stranger to ask."

The girl's mouth curved into a slight smile. "A stranger, is it?"

"Yes," I dragged out. "That's when you don't know someone, so you act more carefully around them. You don't ask intrusive questions, for a start."

Tired of the conversation, I turned back to Kingsley, only to see him break into a rumble of laughter. The girl joined in; hers chiming and as high-pitched as her voice.

"That's funny," she said, moving to rest her hand on Kingsley's other arm. "Daddy, you didn't tell me how funny she was."

He just stood there, smiling in his usual, good-natured way, and didn't say a word. I tightened my hand where it rested on his arm, my knuckles showing white through my already pale skin. A spiral of dread was moving through me. He hadn't corrected her... He hadn't told her to use his real name. "Who is this person, Kingsley?"

He stepped away from the two of us, holding both our arms

and turning us so the girl and I faced each other. She looked up at me and her small mouth curved into a smile that didn't reach those pale eyes. It was like she knew the punchline to a joke that I hadn't realised was being told.

But on Kingsley's face I saw what looked like genuine affection as he looked first at me, then fixed his gaze on the girl's smug little face. "Fairest, I'm so happy to finally introduce you to my daughter Snow."

My daughter Snow. I froze, those three words echoing over and over in my head but still not making sense. My hand fell loose in Kingsley's grip.

He didn't seem to notice, continuing, "I said I had a surprise, and here it is! I know that once you spend some time together, you'll love each other just as I love both of you." He beamed. "Snow, say hello to your new stepmother Valentina."

No. *No!* I couldn't move, and I could only stare in shock and horror at this person who should never have existed. This was *not* a good surprise. It felt like opening a jewellery box to find it full of spiders instead.

But the horrible, unwanted, slightly-gothic little parasite clearly didn't feel the same way. Her painted face broke into a wide smile, revealing the smudged lipstick on her small white teeth. "Val!" she crowed, throwing her arms around my waist in a tight hug. "We're going to be best friends!"

Blurgh.

I threw up my cinnamon latte all over the back of her cheerful yellow sundress.

Breaking the Glass Slipper is available in ebook and print.
See **mmarinanbooks.com** for all retail options.